Rock King

Dear Angel,

Rock King

Nothing but Trouble,
Book One

TARA LEIGH

Hope Rock King is a pretty addition to your bookshelves!

xoxo

Tara Leigh

FOREVER
YOURS

New York   Boston

Copyright © 2018 by Tara Thompson
Excerpt from *Rock Legend* copyright © 2018 by Tara Thompson

Cover photography © Henrik Sorensen/GettyImages. Cover design by Elizabeth Turner Stokes. Cover copyright © 2018 by Hachette Book Group, Inc.

Forever Yours
Hachette Book Group
1290 Avenue of the Americas, New York, NY 10104
forever-romance.com
twitter.com/foreverromance

First published as an ebook and as a print on demand: February 2018

Forever Yours is an imprint of Grand Central Publishing. The Forever Yours name and logo are trademarks of Hachette Book Group, Inc.

The publisher is not responsible for websites (or their content) that are not owned by the publisher.

The Hachette Speakers Bureau provides a wide range of authors for speaking events. To find out more, go to www.hachettespeakersbureau.com or call (866) 376-6591.

ISBNs: 978-1-5387-1278-8 (ebook), 978-1-5387-1277-1 (POD edition)

To the awkward thirteen-year-old girl that forever lives inside the women we become—may you always harbor a secret rock star crush.

Acknowledgments

A huge thank-you to my agent extraordinaire, Jessica Alvarez of BookEnds Literary Agency. Your critiques and career guidance are invaluable!

Lexi Smail—within a half hour of meeting you, I was dying to work with you. *Rock King* is so much stronger because of your efforts. Thank you for seeing the potential in this series and inviting me to join the Forever family of authors. Many thanks also to the rest of the Forever team: the talented cover designers, the publicity team, Kallie Shimek, and everyone else who has played a role in bringing the Nothing but Trouble boys (and the women who love them) to life.

I owe a huge debt to Jeannie Moon, of the Long Island Romance Writers of America chapter. Not only did you encourage me to attend your annual luncheon, but you pointed me toward Lexi's table. Three weeks later, I had a three-book deal with Forever.

Sue Bee, from my very first book, you have been a valuable sounding board. Thank you for all of your advice and encouragement, and especially for your unfiltered honesty. (I hope you approve of Shane's hair. ;))

Moments by Andrea, thank you for the fabulous headshot. And Heather Herve (and her lovely interns), thank you for the lovely profile in *Good Morning Wilton*.

There are several authors who have been beyond generous with their time and expertise. Alessandra Torre, your invaluable website www.alessandratorreink.com is a must for every new author, and you have built a virtual cheering section via Facebook. The writing team of Riley Mackenzie, you guys are amazing and I'm so glad we're friends. Rochelle Weinstein, I'm so glad we met and I can't believe we haven't known each other forever! Shelly Bell, you write sizzle like no other, and you are the sweetest. And many thanks to my fellow authors of CTRWA!!

When Jessica Alvarez was submitting my first book, *Penthouse Player*, to publishers, she told me to write *anything* while we waited to hear back—except the next book in our proposed series. I had recently read Heidi McLaughlin's *Forever My Girl* and the first two books of A .L. Jackson's Bleeding Stars series. Heidi and Amy, I loved your stories so much that I decided to try my hand at writing a rock star myself. Shane Hawthorne takes some of his DNA from Sebastian Stone and Liam Westbury.

Thank you to Jill Saracino and Joan Gibbons for being such great cheerleaders through Facebook—I love seeing all your posts of support!!

I am lucky to have a great group of girlfriends surrounding me. My CSHHS ladies—and in particular, Robin, who forgives me for ignoring her calls when I'm writing.

My neighbor Cindy, you are a wonderful friend to me and an absolute blessing to my kids. Moving next door to you was one of the smartest decisions Stephen and I ever made!

My favorite blondes: Devon, Jessica, Sarah M, and Sarah T. I adore you all!

Lisa D, Andrea B, Maggie B, Taryn R, Josephine J, Melissa P, Josee T, Melissa S, Jennifer J—thank you for your support and encouragement.

Anne Flanders, thank you for pointing out how egregiously I was breaking rule number one in writing—no head hopping.

My brave brother, a NYC police detective, helped me with the legal consequences of Delaney's accident. Any mistakes I made in this book are entirely my own.

Grandma, you left me nearly twenty years ago, and not a day goes by that I don't miss you. For any smokers reading this—put the cigarette down. Think of the people in your life who will one day watch you struggle to breathe and, when you lose that battle, will miss you desperately.

Thank you to my parents for your continued encouragement and for being great grandparents.

Stephen, thank you for being a wonderful husband and supporting my dreams. I love you. Logan, Chloe, and Pierce, thank you for being so considerate of my writing time. I am blessed to be your mother.

Our lives are enriched by our sweet rescue puppy, Pixie. The wonderful organization that brought Pixie into our lives is Goofy Foot Dog Rescue, and if you would like to welcome a dog into your family or donate to their organization, please visit their website: http://www.goofyfootrescue.org. And if you would like to see more pictures of Pixie (and who wouldn't?) please sign up for my newsletter at https://goo.gl/394ppn—she's my writing buddy!

And a huge, huge thank-you to my readers, bloggers, and reviewers. Without you and your love for sexy stories well told, writing them wouldn't be nearly as fulfilling.

Rock King

Chapter One

Shane

Fucking Malibu.

The last traces of sleep evaporated as I stared out at the sea from the terrace off my bedroom, my right hand running through the hair on my head as my left idly plowed a destination farther south. I was naked, but the waist-high plants along the perimeter would block the view of any intrepid paparazzo. Inhaling air thick with salt and fog, I closed my eyes and listened to the rush of the waves crash along the beach.

Normally the rhythm of the tides soothed me.

But not today.

My eyes snapped open, scowling at the relentless surf. The sun was just cresting the horizon, the ocean a quivering mass of gray and blue, littered with bruised shards of purple and orange. It wasn't the view that was pissing me off. I'd been on edge before I got out of bed. Before I went to sleep. Hell, I'd been a bundle of nerves since we finished the album.

One more week until the latest Nothing but Trouble tour kicked off.

One more week and, for two hours out of every twenty-four, my view would be stadiums packed with thousands of fans screaming my name.

The rest would be filled with impersonal hotel rooms, private planes, tour buses, and way too many people I didn't want to look at—let alone talk to—fighting for my attention. Autographs. Selfies. Groupies with glossy lips whispering invitations for everything from blow jobs to backdoor action. Easy sex with an STD chaser.

No thanks.

My last counterfeit companion walked out a month ago, when I'd been spending every available second in the studio tweaking the last couple of songs, which had taken forever to get right. She'd already found someone else to sink her claws into, an up-and-coming actor who made sure he was photographed in public, the more compromising the situation the better, to cover up the fact that, behind closed doors, he was about as interested in tits as a kid with a milk allergy.

Not that I missed her. It was time, and we both knew it. She had gotten what she'd wanted out of being Shane Hawthorne's "girlfriend": name recognition, a place on the Best Dressed lists, even a small part in a big-budget movie. It was time for someone new. Past time, actually. Someone who engendered more than apathy.

Except I hadn't met her yet. Maybe she didn't exist.

Of course, if she did, I sure as hell didn't deserve her.

My gut twisted, forming a gnarled, ugly clump leaching anxiety and tension into my bloodstream. The truth was, no one deserved me. I was a jagged knife, the tip of my blade edged with poison. Brutal. Messy. Lethal.

The wind was strong this morning, stronger than usual, and each salty gust chafed at my skin. I welcomed the abrasion, wishing I could be swept up. Swept away. Days like these were too long, littered with too many opportunities to get lost in my own mind. That was a dangerous place for me. Dangerous for everyone around me.

Being on the road sucked. But staying in one place, trapped with my memories, with my guilt...well, not even a beach house in Malibu could make that bearable.

From the half-open door, I heard my phone. Recognizing the ringtone, I headed back inside to take my agent's call. "Hey, Travis." He slept even less than I did, and that was saying something.

"I'm just confirming. You're coming tonight, right?" Travis only had one setting: steamroll.

My disgruntled sigh fogged up the screen. "Let me guess. There's someone you want me to meet."

"Of course. Several actually. You'll have your pick."

Agent. Lawyer. Matchmaker. Travis was a one-stop shop for me. He'd been on the hunt for my next girlfriend for a while now, and I was still single. Neither of us was happy about it. Left to my own devices, trouble was always too close for comfort. "Fine. I'll be there."

Disconnecting the call, I took my first deep breath all day. Travis and I had a deal. He found candidates worthy of being "Shane Hawthorne's girlfriend," but I had ultimate approval. I don't mean prostitutes, either. Hell, I practically had to beat chicks back with a stick. Everywhere I went, there were girls beg-

ging me to fuck them against the nearest wall, or dropping to
their knees on the dirty floor of a public restroom. Three hundred and sixty-five days a year was my only constraint when it
came to sex.

But life on the road was different, and the first few weeks of
a tour were especially nerve-racking. So many new people, so
many moving parts. It wasn't easy to get back into the groove of
things. Waking up in a new city every day, surrounded by a sea
of new faces—I needed the people in my inner circle to stay the
same. My agent, bandmates, tour manager…and my girlfriend.

I know how it sounds. Sleazy with a capital *S*. But sex isn't
part of the deal.

Not that it didn't happen, of course, just that it wasn't what I
was paying them for.

Being the girlfriend of a rock star shouldn't be a hard position
to fill, but it was. Sexy, beautiful, reasonably intelligent—those
were basic requirements for someone I'd be spending months
in close quarters with. And she needed to be drama-free, someone who liked my music but wasn't a super-fan, stalker chick.
My "girlfriends" were a thin veil of armor against the hordes of
groupies that clawed their way toward me, offering anything I
could ever want. And too much I didn't need.

Truthfully, I didn't mind the groupies. At my core I'm a hustler, too. Been hauling around a five-pound sack filled with ten
pounds of problems since the day I was born. But I've made
it, busted my way to the top of the fucking heap. Lead singer
of Nothing but Trouble. A list of hit songs so long a tattooist
couldn't fit it on my arm if he tried. More money than I knew
what to do with. A dozen Grammys at last count, and even an
Oscar for best original song last year, the only golden statue
awarded to an otherwise unremarkable movie.

I hired Travis years ago to build up my career, and now we were in protection mode, just trying not to crash and burn. *Shane Hawthorne* was a brand now, one worth millions. And yet, losing everything we had worked for would be so easy. Just one offer of things I couldn't resist: an asshole named Jack Daniel and that gorgeous white powder that made my brain feel like a shaken snow globe, cloudy with glitter.

So, maybe tonight I would meet my next girlfriend. Someone contractually obligated to be by my side at every show and party, every press junket and photo op. Someone with me day and night, pretty enough I wouldn't mind the view. Someone with a fun-loving personality, who knew better than to actually fall in love with me.

I've done a lot of stupid things in my life, but that was a line I had yet to cross. A line so far in the distance it wasn't even a smudge on the horizon. And I wasn't heading in its direction anytime soon. Preferably never.

Love was the one luxury I couldn't afford.

Assuming I felt a spark of connection with one of the women at Travis's house tonight, he would lock her into a nondisclosure so tight the press would never find out that she was just an employee, a prop. That our relationship was fake.

What she wouldn't know, what no one except Travis knew, was that we would have something in common.

Because *everything* about me is fake.

Shane Hawthorne, resident King of Rock n' Roll and the cause of dripping panties everywhere, from shrieking tweens to bored housewives, is a sham. More myth than man.

Shane Hawthorne doesn't exist. He's the stage name I used for the first time at sixteen, expecting to be hauled off by a pair of cops if I so much as breathed my real name.

Sometimes I've wondered what my fans would think if they knew the truth. Would I still be hailed as *People* magazine's Sexiest Man Alive if anyone knew who I really was?

Who am I? I don't even know anymore.

Fraud.

Runaway.

Addict.

Murderer.

Not so sexy now, am I?

Delaney

"Delaney? Delaney Fraser, is that you?"

I froze as the familiar notes of a voice I hadn't heard in years practically stomped up my spine, leaving angry hives in its wake. The voice, and the person belonging to it, were from a life I'd left behind several years ago.

Bronxville, the insulated Manhattan suburb where I'd been raised, was not merely three thousand miles from Los Angeles; it was in an entirely different galaxy. And yet, this particular meteor had dropped into the upscale steakhouse where I worked without disturbing anything but my peace of mind.

My pivot was purposefully slow, needing a minute to firmly affix a smile onto my face and every ounce of concentration I could muster to remain standing. "Piper. Wow, small world. I didn't recognize you."

"Me?" Piper Hastings, former queen bee of the Bronxville School, took a step back and looked me up and down as if I were a mannequin wearing an outfit she was considering. "I almost didn't recognize *you*."

I managed a small shrug. "We've all changed since gradua-
tion, I guess." Although, I've probably changed more than most.
The last time I saw Piper, I'd been solidly on the chubby side
of average, sporting braces and barely tamed hair. The excess
weight was gone now, along with the braces, and I kept my
hair under control via daily altercations with a salon-strength
straightener, a life-changing invention I'd only recently discovered.

Piper wasn't buying my brush-off. "You've more than
changed—you're practically a new person. Or at least half of the
one you used to be, anyway. What did you do?" She'd always
been irritatingly tenacious, a dog with a bone.

How exactly to answer Piper's invasive questions? Heat rose
up my neck, probably depositing telltale patches on my cheeks,
too. Gee, Piper, after the Accident, food just didn't hold much
appeal anymore. "Nothing really, just a hormone imbalance."
These days, lies came easy.

But Piper only nodded enthusiastically, her perfect blond
hair swinging. "I'm so jealous. I have to practically live at the
yoga studio just to fit into my jeans!" Her face was expectant, as
if waiting for a round of applause. I gave none, and she continued her rapid-fire questions. "So, what are you doing in California? Did you transfer?"

My eyes narrowed. Could she really not know? After my father was held responsible for my mother's death, life as I knew
it came to a screeching halt. "Something like that." I proffered a
question to stem the tide coming from Piper. "How about you?"

Piper flaunted a Colgate-bright smile. "I graduated from
UCLA two years ago and now I'm working in public relations
for a Hollywood agent. Super-agent, really. Wild horses couldn't
drag me back to Bronxville."

I returned the grin, although mine was only half-hearted. "Same here." Because no one, wild horse or otherwise, would be doing the dragging. My father was in jail, my mother was buried six feet under, and keeping in touch with friends from my former life hurt too much.

I wanted what they still had. Family. Security. A belief that life would magically work out for the best.

I knew better now.

Piper made a sweeping arc with her hands. "So, you work here?"

Eager to extricate myself from Piper's well-manicured claws, I slipped back into waitress mode, pen hovering above my order pad. "Yep. What can I get for you?"

"A glass of sauvignon blanc, if you have it."

"Sure. Be right back." I had to force myself not to run to the bar. Despite knowing Piper Hastings for most of my life, that was probably the longest conversation we'd ever shared.

By the time I returned with her drink, an older man had seated himself opposite her. Medium height with a build that was solid without being stocky, he had an attractively shaved head. A starched white button-down shirt set off his tan, and gold cuff links flashed at his wrists. Setting down Piper's wineglass with only the slightest wobble, I turned to him. "What can I get for you, sir?"

Piper spoke up before he could answer. "Delaney, this is my boss, Travis Taggert. Travis, Delaney's an old friend from back home."

Old friend? Talk about an exaggeration. I would have laughed, but Travis's dark, appraising eyes didn't inspire levity. "Nice to meet you, Delaney." His voice was gruff but polite.

"Likewise. So…" I cleared my throat, itching to get away again, "something from the bar?"

Another nod. "Grey Goose, rocks, three olives."

Travis's hooded gaze followed me as I crossed the restaurant to fetch his cocktail. "Delaney," he said on my return, "I'm having a party tonight. You should come. I'll bet Piper would love to spend more time with one of her friends from back home."

The glare Piper gave Travis from across the table belied his assessment. "I don't get off until late tonight," I said, not exactly jumping at the chance to hang out with her either.

Travis responded with a short shake of his head, the restaurant's recessed spotlights glinting off his bald scalp. "Not a problem. My parties don't get good until late, anyway."

I flicked a tongue over suddenly dry lips. "Well, I'm not exactly dressed appropriately, and I don't have a change of clothes here," I said, looking down at my standard waitress attire of white shirt and black pants.

"Oh, Delaney, that's too bad. I guess we'll just have to do it another time," Piper chirped, the obvious snub bringing back memories that filled my mind like a swarm of angry bees, buzzing and stinging at will.

Oh, Delaney, you don't really want to try out for cheerleading, do you? I mean, being out in front of the stands, representing our school, it's just such a huge responsibility. And, of course, the uniforms aren't exactly forgiving.

Oh, Delaney, this party's not really for the whole school. Just a few friends, and friends of friends. You understand, right?

Oh, Delaney, I'm jealous you have so much free time to study. Between cheer practice, football games, hanging out with my squad and all the players, and of course, chairing the prom committee, I barely have time to crack a book.

How many "Oh, Delaney's" had I heard from Piper and her

friends over the years? Too many. And her caustic tone was just as abrasive now as it was then.

Travis rolled his shoulders, eyes narrowing as he looked back and forth between us. "You two are just about the same size, and I've never seen you in the same thing twice, Piper. I'm sure you have something for Delaney to wear."

My breath caught in my throat. Was I really the same size as Piper Hastings? I cast a discreet glance her way. Not quite, but not too far off either. Grief was a pretty effective diet. "That's really generous, but I just don't think—"

Piper let loose a high-pitched chortle. "After being on her feet all day, you can't blame Delaney for not wanting to put on a dress and heels." I gnashed my teeth at the latest comment from the peanut gallery. Piper didn't want me at Travis's party; I got the hint, loud and clear.

Travis, not so much. He flicked an exasperated glance at Piper. "Last time I checked, I had plenty of seating. Besides, no one turns down an invitation to one of my parties, Delaney."

A tingle of curiosity pricked at my skin. I wasn't in high school anymore. Why was I letting Piper exclude me from all the fun?

Fun. Did I even know what fun was anymore?

Maybe it was because I hadn't been to a party in three years. Maybe it was because I was enjoying the irritation smeared across Piper's face a little too much. Maybe it was because Travis didn't seem like he was going to take no for an answer. Maybe it was all three, because when I opened my mouth, not a single one of the dozen excuses I had at the tip of my tongue emerged. "Well, I guess I wouldn't want to spoil your perfect track record."

"Great." Travis slapped the table with a resounding *thwack*. "What time does your shift end? Piper will pick you up here."

"Around eleven, sometimes a little after," I answered, my brief flare of rebellion already fading. Partying with Hollywood A-listers? Not exactly my crowd, any more than Piper's cheerleading squad and the jocks they hung out with had been in high school. "But there's no need for that. If you give me your address, I'll call an Uber." *Yeah, right.* Another lie. Without a doubt, I'd be in my pajamas by midnight. As usual.

My hesitation must have been obvious, and Travis was clearly no fool. "Absolutely not. Piper will be happy to pick you up after your shift ends, with something suitable to wear. Isn't that right, Piper?"

I winced at the little daggers of outrage glinting from her wide-set eyes. "Sure thing, boss."

"Good. It's settled, then," Travis pronounced.

Settled? Crap. *What have I done?* "Are you sure, Piper? I don't want to put you out of your way," I sputtered, silently begging her to get me out of the mess I'd created.

An overly bright smile twisting her perfectly lined and glossed lips, Piper's voice was honey with a saccharine chaser. Nauseatingly sweet with an artificial aftertaste. "Don't mention it. Coming back to pick you up, bringing an outfit, it's no trouble at all. I'm just thrilled you don't already have plans."

I hadn't made *plans* in three years. Why bother when life stole your lemonade and pelted you with rotten lemons instead? If I wasn't working, I was usually home with my nose buried in a book or binge-watching shows from my Netflix queue. Living through fictional characters whose lives were so much better than mine. "Well, okay then." I pushed the words out of my mouth, wishing I could swallow them whole instead. "I guess I'll see you later."

Travis set down his cocktail. "Going to be a good crowd tonight. Trust me, you won't regret it."

Too late. I already did.

But what the hell, just add it to the list. I'd accumulated a lot of regrets in my twenty-four years. What was one more?

Chapter Two

Delaney

Hulking at the top of a steep driveway, Travis's house was a contemporary behemoth. Beyond a pair of dark, oversized doors, the all-white decor served as a stark backdrop to the ridiculously beautiful people casually clumped in small groups everywhere I turned. My borrowed heels clicked on the marble floor as I tagged behind Piper, who entered the house like she owned it and was now making a beeline for the open doors leading to a back terrace and infinity pool.

More people were outside, including Travis, who was holding court from an oversized sectional. I hung back, feeling a lock of hair become ensnared in the lip gloss I'd applied using the overhead mirror in Piper's car. Prying it loose, I nervously tucked the wayward strand behind my ear and watched as Piper edged around the back of the couch, resting a manicured hand lightly on Travis's shoulder until he acknowledged her presence by leaning back, his head cocked expectantly to the side.

She whispered something in his ear and discreetly pointed in my direction. Travis looked up, his eyes locking onto mine immediately. He smiled and I reluctantly smiled back.

Maybe tonight wouldn't be so bad.

Piper reappeared at my elbow. "Come on, let's get a drink." She had been significantly nicer to me on the drive here, as if she'd resigned herself to her fate and decided to make the best of the situation. Or maybe Travis had picked up on the mean girl sarcasm after all and told her to quit it.

A bar had been set up at the far end of the pool, staffed by a bartender in a tight black T-shirt and dark jeans. Piper flashed an aloof half smile at him, his lowly worker-bee status apparently deserving only a brief glimpse of her shiny teeth. "Two mojitos please," she ordered, not bothering to ask if I liked the minty Cuban cocktail. As he mixed the drinks, she turned to me, her voice hushed. "Listen, be nice to Travis. If he likes you, he's definitely a good guy to know."

I frowned. "What if I don't like him?"

Piper blanched, as if the idea were so outlandish she'd never considered it. Then she took our drinks from the bartender's outstretched hand and walked toward a tree glittering from the soft white lights wrapped around its trunk and branches. I followed. "Don't be silly. Everyone likes Travis."

"I pay her to sing my praises at every opportunity, you know." A silvery voice appeared inches from my ear.

I turned, instinctively knowing there was a grain of truth to the deceptively casual comment. "I guess Piper deserves a raise, then," I said.

Travis offered a small nod to Piper, who quickly handed me

my drink. "So, you and Piper were friends in school?" he asked, turning his attention back to me.

I spied my *friend* quietly slinking away. "Not really," I answered honestly. "But Bronxville is a small town. I guess you could say we were all friends."

He was wearing jeans, but Travis's compact, muscular frame begged for a suit. "I'm from back East, too. Yonkers though. Not quite the same as Bronxville."

No. If Bronxville were an honor student, Yonkers was its troubled, dropout cousin. The invisible border that separated the neighboring towns may as well have been a gaping divide the size of the Grand Canyon. "What brought you out here?"

"UCLA has great weather and, at the time anyway, the cheapest tuition." He shrugged dismissively. "One thing led to another and I never left."

I lifted my chin. "Looks like you made a good choice."

Another shrug. "When you do what I do, L.A. is the place to be."

The lights suspended in the tree overhead trembled as a breeze gusted, their dancing glow sinister on Travis's face. "Piper said you were an agent. A super agent, actually."

He crooked a smile. "Said like someone from my PR team."

I took the last sip of my mojito, the mint sharp on my tongue. "So, what's your super power?"

He waited for the ice to settle back in my drink. "I fix problems."

Gesturing at his huge house and stunning view, I trilled out a high-pitched laugh, expecting Travis to elaborate. When he didn't, I said, "So do exterminators, but I doubt they can afford a place like this."

Travis looked out over the Hollywood Hills, offering a self-assured chuckle. "We both deal with pests, but I charge a hell of a lot more than Terminix."

I looked around for Piper. Where was she and why had she left me alone with her boss? "Do you represent anyone I know?"

His chuckle graduated to a belly laugh, flashing teeth so white they couldn't have been real. "Probably."

"Oh, um, cool." Jesus. What was I doing here? I hated small talk and big parties.

Travis eyed me with open interest. "So, what brought you out West?"

"I guess I just needed a change," I answered, sounding slightly strangled. After my father's conviction, I'd packed up and kept moving west, working at bars and restaurants just long enough to afford another bus ticket. The Pacific Ocean had put a halt to my travels. Any farther and I'd need a plane ticket. Of course, I could have changed direction, gone north or south. But I couldn't decide between the two, so rather than make any decision at all, I had stayed in L.A.

"Did you get it?"

Travis's question interrupted my thoughts. "What?"

"Change," he said, his eyes narrowing at the edges, focusing on me to the exclusion of everything around us.

Change. From Ivy League coed to an L.A. waitress just trying to get by? Yeah, you could say that. "I did," I said.

"I've never met a waitress who wasn't just biding her time, figuring out their next step. Tell me, Delaney, what's yours?"

I didn't have a *next* anything. I was trapped in the past, unsure I deserved a future at all. My lips tightened, and I took a half step back, suddenly suspicious of Travis's perfectly shaved pate and dark, piercing eyes. "Why do you want to know?"

Travis gave a small sigh. "Maybe I don't." Turning on his heel, he walked back toward the group he'd been talking with earlier, smoothly reclaiming his seat as if he'd never left.

Shane

I pulled up to Travis's house late, after midnight. Not because I had anything better to do. Just that I didn't want to arrive before *my* girl. For the next few months, anyway. I didn't know her name yet, or what she looked like, although Travis knew what I liked. Dark hair, light eyes, and curves that made me believe, for at least a few minutes at a time, that life wasn't all sharp corners and jagged edges.

Travis's parties were always a scene, and although I loved the stage, I hated crowds. Hours passed like minutes in a cramped recording studio, but even the thought of being trapped in conversations with people I didn't know—or want to know—sent a shiver of revulsion sprinting across nerves already stretched to the point of breaking.

I'd been to Travis's house so many times it should have felt like a second home to me. Then again, I didn't know what home felt like. Never had, really. Was it a place, a concept? I had a house of my own now, but to me the Malibu bungalow was nothing more than a five-million-dollar assemblage of windows, steel beams, doors, and drywall. And a view I'm told is priceless, whatever that means. But *home*? I'd ruined any chance of that long ago.

Parking on the street, I kept my head down and hugged the shadows. I didn't bother heading for the front door. Instead, my feet crunched on mulch as I walked along the perimeter of Travis's backyard, just beyond reach of the spotlights popping up from the ground at odd intervals between trees, meticulously arranged to create intermittent patches of darkness for anyone seeking privacy without actually leaving the party.

Not surprisingly, there were people everywhere. In the front, in the back, inside the house. Unless you were one of the lucky few on his star-studded client list, scoring an invite to a Travis Taggert party was a coveted prize, and he always assembled an interesting mix of people. Plenty of celebrities and their associated hangers-on, the moneymen who made their careers possible and the press and bloggers who stroked their egos with one breath and ripped them to shreds in the next. Travis also included people who were still green, still intrigued by the money and fame, by the beauty and allure of it all. People who hadn't been sidetracked by bad press or good drugs. Yet.

The throng was easily three-quarters female, Travis's way of stacking the deck in my favor. Would I be tempted to leave the comfort of the shadows tonight? Travis said so, but I wasn't feeling it. Sighing, I scanned the crowd for my agent, debating whether to say a quick hello before I slipped out the same way I had come. I spotted him standing beside a tree that looked as if it had been caught in an electrified fishnet. He wasn't alone.

My chest squeezed as I caught sight of the girl he was talking to. She stood out like a tropical fish in a sea of dense algae, and although I didn't know her name yet, I knew exactly who she was. *My girl.*

From afar she was strikingly pretty, her skin luminous. I wanted to get closer, determine whether her features were as delicate and finely drawn as instinct told me they would be. The kind of beautiful that pulled you in and held on tight, quelling any desire to escape.

I was good at escaping. Better than good, actually. Maybe the best.

No one had ever been able to hang on to me. Not my father, who'd tried to hold me down and beat the insolence out of me. Or my mother, who'd been so lost inside herself, she could barely make eye contact with me. Not my brother, who wasn't there when I needed him the most. Not the parents of my best friend, Caleb, who'd let me live with them after my parents died, while I was still in high school. Not the cops who were probably still itching to charge me with Caleb's murder.

Escape. I knew it well. I was a fucking expert.

Travis pulled away from the girl, and I watched as she took a quick sip from her nearly empty glass, those big eyes sweeping over the crowd like a bewildered Dorothy dropped into Oz. I stepped onto the lawn, soles sinking into soft grass before my mind caught up with my body's decision to move in. She was wearing a dress I wanted to rip off her with my teeth. Not much bigger than a Band-Aid, it still covered way too much of her creamy skin.

Her back was to me when I found my voice, usually the one constant in my life. As soon as I did, I could feel Shane Hawthorne descending, the persona I'd created, the barrier I needed between me and…everything. Life.

I wore Shane like a geeky teen slipping into the personality of his buff, heroic alter ego in his favorite video game. Shane Hawthorne was my avatar, and everyone thought he was real.

Every girl wanted to fuck Shane Hawthorne.

Every guy wanted to be Shane Hawthorne.

No one more than me.

Delaney

"Not looking to become Travis Taggert's next client, huh?"

"I think the feeling's mutual," I answered, turning around to introduce myself. Except, I had no words. None. Shane Hawthorne, lead singer of Nothing but Trouble, the hottest band on the charts, was standing in front of me. I sucked in a deep breath, my eyes widening in surprise. Holy shit, *Shane Hawthorne.*

Seriously, I could get lost in his face and enjoy every minute of my journey. Glide across the high plane of his forehead, cartwheel down the sharp angles of his cheekbones, slide along his jaw to land at his mouth. Full lips, slightly crooked at one corner, smiled down at me.

"You're in the minority, in this town at least. What are you doing here, at Casa Taggert?"

Somehow I managed to pick my jaw up off the flagstone patio and glance around at the people illuminated by the floating lights scattered on the surface of the pool. "To be honest, I have no idea. I'm a friend of a friend. Sort of."

Up close, Shane's longish hair was a river of brown, from dusky caramel to burnished mahogany, threaded through with shades of henna, chocolate, and deepest umber. He wore a snug black button-down shirt, setting off his tall, buff physique perfectly, the sleeves rolled up just enough to catch traces of ink on his tanned forearms, leaving me fighting an urge to push aside the fabric and expose everything that remained hidden. I longed for a pocket to stuff my hands into, settling instead for awkwardly wrapping both around my sweating glass.

Shane eyed me curiously, as if he knew I didn't belong. As if he knew the direction of my wholly inappropriate thoughts. "I guess you're here for me, then." A grin spread across his face, punctuated by a sexy-as-hell dimple in his left cheek.

"Me?" I choked. What on earth would Shane Hawthorne want with me? I swallowed thickly, my eyes darting around for Piper. *I am so out of my league.*

With a hand in the back pocket of his ragged jeans, Shane followed the path of my anxious stare. "Expecting someone?"

My focus snapped back to Shane's face. "No." I shook my head. "Sorry. This is just so not me. I don't wind up at Beverly Hills parties talking to rock stars. I mean, this is crazy." My fingers twitched. There was no part of him I could look at without wanting to touch—especially the two-day growth of scruff covering his strong jaw, which practically guaranteed goose bumps if it brushed along any part of my anatomy.

"Imagine how I feel."

I tilted my head. "You?"

"Yeah. I'm usually stuck in a tour bus or chartered plane flying to some city I won't actually see. But tonight I'm at a Beverly Hills party where I don't really know anyone, besides my agent and a few industry suits, talking to the most gorgeous girl in the place. Pretty lucky, huh?"

Feeling like a complete idiot, I looked around again. And then I pointed at my collarbone with my index finger. "Me?" I repeated.

Shane threw back his head and laughed. Instantly I wished I could record the sound on my phone so I could play it on repeat. Forever. It was the most delicious noise I'd ever heard. "Yeah, you. Where did you come from, anyway?"

"Bronxville," I squeaked.

Shane laughed even harder. When he finally got control of himself, he brushed at his eyes. "And do you have a name, or should I just call you Bronx all night?"

All night. "Delaney. Delaney Fraser." I extended my hand.

"I'm Shane." Offering his last name would have been redundant. Shane's fingers closed around mine, the pad of his thumb pressing into the center of my palm.

I nearly groaned. *Please don't let go, ever.* "Would I sound like a groupie if I said I already knew that?"

He quirked a rich, sable brow. "Are you a groupie?"

I shook my head. "No. But I'd be lying if I said I wasn't a fan." Since high school, when lusting after rock stars I'd never meet was safer than talking to boys I encountered in my real life, who eyed my chubby body and frizzy hair with barely disguised revulsion.

"I do love my fans." Shane's throaty growl pulsed in my ears, and for a moment I let myself believe he might be flirting with me. But then I looked down, a blush staining my cheeks as a sea of uncomfortable memories rushed in. *Get a grip, Delaney. Why would Shane Hawthorne ever be interested you?* All those years of awkwardness, of feeling so uncomfortable I almost couldn't bear it, were still trapped inside me even though my reflection in the mirror had changed.

Shane lifted his other hand to my jaw, pulling my gaze back to him. "Don't do that."

His fingertips were hot, controlling my blood flow like some kind of stylus. I could feel it rushing to the surface of my skin, surging to meet Shane's touch. "Do what?" I asked, my voice a ragged whisper.

"Look away from me. I like feeling your eyes on my face." He balled his hand into a fist against my cheek, stroking my flesh with his knuckles, each touch erasing a tiny piece of the self-conscious teen living inside me.

Knowing this was probably the last time I would be so close, I studied Shane. Memorized his face. His lips, I decided, were almost too full to belong on a man's face. Tried to imagine how they would feel on mine.

"If you keep looking at my mouth like that, I won't be held responsible for what happens next." Shane's comment interrupted my perusal.

Color me gullible, but I couldn't help myself. "What would happen?" I breathed. There was a moment before Shane answered, a moment when I lost myself in his eyes. His pupils were black flies caught within a whorl of amber. My heart thudded inside my chest, trapped by the darkness I saw within the depths of his gaze. Shane Hawthorne wasn't just some vapid one-dimensional celebrity. He bristled with intensity. And even in the center of a Beverly Hills party, punctuated by popping corks and trying-too-hard laughs, waves of danger rolled off Shane's broad shoulders, swirling around me like the chilly waters of the Pacific.

I should have been scared. I was, actually. But not scared off. I wanted to meld my body against Shane's taut length, potential groupie status be damned. Desire filled my lungs, every breath a heady cocktail, and I swayed toward him, catching myself just before crashing into the perfectly carved statue wrapped in tight jeans and a shirt that did nothing to hide his rippling abs.

Shane stood still, watching the flicker of emotions on my face with interest. "Maybe we should go somewhere else. Somewhere with a lot less people. Somewhere we could both be wearing a lot less clothes."

Pulling my eyes away from Shane's blistering gaze, I looked

down at the trail of feverish skin exposed by the plunging neck-line of my borrowed dress. "I don't think I could wear anything less and still be considered dressed." I didn't even recognize myself right now. Was I flirting?

His laugh was a caress, the rich timbre soothing nerves rubbed raw by his overwhelming presence. "That's my point. Exactly."

Breath punched from my lungs and I staggered back a step. Shane didn't mince words, did he? I raised my face back to his, just as he reclaimed the distance I'd put between us.

"Let's go," he added, one of his hands reaching out to cup my elbow.

A shiver tore through me at Shane's blunt command, reality hitting hard from the shock of his palm sliding against my skin. Instinct made me step back, out of reach. I didn't have room in my life for Shane Hawthorne. He was a distraction I couldn't afford. There was only one man I should be focused on right now, and he was sitting in a jail cell. Because of me. I was the only one who knew he was innocent, except he'd made me promise not to say anything. I was free because of him, but feeling alive—smiling and laughing and having *fun*. It had been three years since any of those things felt appropriate, or even possible.

Tonight, I did feel alive. And I was smiling and laughing and having fun. God, it felt so good. And so *wrong*.

There was a woman lying in a cold grave tonight whose laugh I would never hear again.

What Shane was offering—more of this, of him, of feeling this way—terrified me. Spending the night with Shane Hawthorne, or even just a few hours, would either be knock-my-socks-off amazing, or a bitter disappointment. Either way, when he walked away from me without a second glance, I'd be crushed.

I had reached my quota of broken dreams already. One more might break me.

"Sorry. That's not who I am." I forced the words out through gritted teeth, the quivering kaleidoscope of butterflies in my stomach launching a winged protest. I'd already started to walk away when Shane grabbed my arm, pulling me so close I could feel the washboard of muscles ridging his abdomen. His touch seared my skin, melting my willpower.

"Who are you?" he whispered in my ear. Shane's breath was hot along my neck, sending ripples of need racing in all directions before making their way to one spot in particular. Throbbing en masse.

My resolve wavered, desperate to claim the promise shining from Shane's eyes. The promise that he'd outshine everything in my world for just a few minutes. That he'd make me forget about the wrecking ball that had slammed into my life and shattered everything I'd ever believed in. But this kind of reaction, just from a touch…No. Any more and I'd go into toxic shock.

I glanced around, not wanting to make a scene, wrenching my arm from Shane's grasp with a small grunt and forcing words past my lips that left a bitter taste in my mouth. "No one you want to know."

Piper was talking to someone on the other side of the pool, but she broke away when she saw me striding toward her. "If you don't get me out of here right now, I'm going to walk home," I hissed, passing her.

"What? Why?" Piper responded immediately, but it was too late. I blew right by, heading for the front door, but not before catching her quick backward glance at Travis, an anxious, apologetic pull to her lips.

"Delaney, wait!"

Halfway down the driveway, I spun around. "Are you going to take me home or not?"

"Jesus Christ, slow down. You're not a prisoner, for God's sake." Piper moved as fast as her stilettos would allow. "I'm not exactly dressed for a sprint, in case you hadn't noticed."

I released an angry breath. "Sorry, I just…That party wasn't exactly my speed."

Fishing a set of keys from her Prada clutch, Piper unlocked the car and opened her door. "I saw you talking to Shane Hawthorne. Most girls I know wouldn't let themselves be unglued from his side, let alone run away from him. What happened between you two?"

I slid into the passenger seat and slammed the door, her deliberately casual tone scratching at my last nerve. "Nothing." *Nothing except he mentioned getting naked…and it might have been the best idea I've ever heard.*

Piper glanced over, arching one perfectly waxed eyebrow. Waiting for a straight answer.

"What?" How could I possibly explain the effect Shane Hawthorne had just had on me? I was having an allergy attack, my skin itching with need for a man whose interest in me didn't go beyond what was between my legs. Or maybe it was because I was certain he was already hitting on any one of the gorgeous girls back at the party. Girls who probably wouldn't be dumb enough to turn down a night with Shane Hawthorne.

Chapter Three

Shane

"Making friends, I see." Travis appeared at my side, both of us watching Delaney's tight ass wriggling in her dress as she stalked off.

The list of things I wanted to do to Delaney was a mile long, but being parked in the friend zone? Not on it. "I don't need any more friends, Travis."

"Of course not. You have me." He lightly *clink*ed his glass against mine in a mock cheers. "Speaking of which…I did good, right?"

Ignoring his question, I asked one of my own. "How did you find her anyway?" The girl was a unicorn in a field of mules.

"I have my ways."

I arched an eyebrow, looking pointedly at my longtime agent. "That's your answer?"

"What? I can't leave anything to the imagination?"

Frustration spiraled inside my stomach, dead-ending into a tight knot. "I want to know. Seriously, Trav. I wouldn't put it past you to send out a casting call for this."

Travis raised his hands, palms facing outward. "I swear. I just met her this afternoon and knew she was perfect." He gestured at the crowded patio. "But hey, there's got to be twenty, thirty chicks here who are just your type. You're not into Delaney, go find someone else."

"You didn't coach her? Tell her what to say, how to act?"

Travis snorted. "I've yet to meet a female that knows how to take direction well, Oscar-winning actresses included. Believe me, meeting Delaney today was just a coincidence."

"You don't believe in coincidences, and neither do I." I didn't know what I believed in anymore.

He huffed out an exasperated sigh. "I might have to reevaluate my opinion. Turns out that Delaney's an old friend of Piper, a girl who works for me. Listen, if you two didn't hit it off—" Travis slapped his hands together "—no harm, no foul."

I stared him down, trying to gauge the extent of his honesty. With Travis Taggert, it was a sliding scale.

"So, are we good?" he prodded, always looking to close a deal.

I shook my head, crossing my arms as adrenaline spiked inside my blood. *Yes, so fucking good.* "No. Let her go. I'll make do with someone else."

"What?" Travis reared back as if my words were bullets. So much for "no harm, no foul." "What are you talking about? Delaney's perfect."

He was right. She was. *Perfect.*

Too fucking perfect.

Because, offstage at least, I was completely, abysmally imperfect. I knew it. Travis knew it. There were cracks in my soul that couldn't be filled no matter how hard I tried. And I had tried, over and over. In bed. Beds, actually. And on buses and planes and in countless bars. I'd tried everything, although I had my favorites. Whiskey, women, and a white powder that made me believe, for a just few hours, that I was whole. One was good. All three were better. Overindulging in the dangerous trifecta was so tempting, it had nearly killed me. More than once.

It was Travis who had come up with a solution to my problem. My addiction. Not Alcoholics Anonymous, or Narcotics Anonymous, or Sex Addicts Anonymous.

I was Shane Hawthorne—I wasn't Anonymous.

At first I'd laughed him off. Hire a girlfriend? They had a name for that, and it was illegal. But in Hollywood, nothing was off-limits. Closeted sex symbols hired boyfriends and girlfriends all the time, sometimes even married them. Addicts hired sober coaches and passed them off as romantic relationships. There wasn't much that was real in this town, and as Travis bluntly pointed out, the relationships I entered into on my own had been nothing but disasters.

Women were my gateway drug. Left to my own devices, I gravitated toward party girls, chicks with invisible wounds as deep as mine. They alone saw the blackness in my soul, would hang around as long as the party raged. Meanwhile, I just raged.

So, I'd agreed to let Travis trim my options, weed out the bad choices. He looked at L.A.'s pool of stunning starlets and found the ones with half a brain, who viewed the experience as an opportunity, not a romance. By now, launching a new girlfriend was almost like rolling out a PR campaign, garnering as much press as a new album. And for the most part, it had been a successful solution for me. Aside from the occasional setback, I hadn't touched cocaine or whiskey in years. I stuck to wine or beer, not too much, and the high I got from performing in front of a live audience. My short-term, faux relationships might be superficial, but they were monogamous, and most importantly—disease- and drama-free.

I'd had more than enough drama in my life already, the kind that belonged on the *Jerry Springer Show*. My rock-star veneer might be thin, but it was my only protection against getting dragged back into…I stopped myself. There were places my mind didn't need to go. Dark, desperate memories I'd been hiding from for well over a decade now. If the truth ever caught up with me, the fact that Shane Hawthorne was rock 'n' roll royalty might be the only thing to save me. I needed to maintain my place at the top of the food chain. Predator, not prey.

And if I needed a goddamn "girlfriend" to keep my ruse going, so be it.

With the newest Nothing but Trouble tour just days away, Travis was nervous. I was, too. So far, the only thing that kept me from getting sucked in by the excesses so abundant behind the velvet ropes of rock and roll was to be preoccupied by a woman who was just as tempting. A woman who wasn't an addict. A woman who softened my image, just enough, so that when I fucked up, the millions of women who bought my music, believed in my brand, didn't write me off. Sometimes it was a starlet looking for the career boost being Shane Hawthorne's girlfriend would give them. Sometimes it was a model looking for more exposure. Travis insisted that the woman in question be hampered by an ironclad confidentiality agreement and locked into a contract that ran the length of the tour. After that, she could leave, and usually did.

My girlfriends were temporary companions. Interesting enough to be worth my time, attractive enough to get my attention. They were good while they lasted, and when they were over we parted amicably and moved on.

There were a whole bunch of words I could use to describe Delaney Fraser. Beautiful, sexy, lean with curves in all the right places. But what I'd discovered during our all too brief conversation couldn't be captured in words. She called herself a fan, and maybe she was. But not the crazy kind who would attach herself to me and declare that we were "meant to be," or the saccharine-sweet kind with no backbone, giving me everything I wanted without batting an eye.

I should insist that Travis find a sweet little thing to bring on tour, like he'd done in the past. Someone happy to smile pretty for the paparazzi and eager to spread her legs whenever I wanted.

But damn, I was so sick of sweet. I wanted someone to make me work for it.

Delaney was no easy lay, I could tell. She had mounds of smooth, dark hair I wanted to plunge my hands into, framing a round face with delicate features that gave her a dreamy, angelic look. But her aquamarine eyes had blazed with caution, as if one glance at me and she'd known immediately I was toxic.

Delaney made me feel off-balance, like the control I'd worked so hard for was tenuous at best. And if that happened, no one was safe. Especially her.

A flicker of lust had fought its way into her gaze, teaming up with the sensual curve of her lips to tempt me. Intrigue me. And yet—she'd stood up to me without a second thought. Shrugged off my touch as if it was unwanted, stalked off without a backward glance. Delaney had a temper inside her centerfold-worthy package. And I liked it. I liked that she hadn't fawned all over me while I made one obscene suggestion after the other, responding with incessant giggles that made me want to shove something in her mouth just to shut her up.

I'd done just that with other girls before, and there were more than a few selfies floating around cyberspace, a grinning girl with my dick stuffed in her mouth. Easily found if you typed "Shane Hawthorn, dick pic" into Google.

Welcome to my life.

Travis was having none of my reluctance, listing Delaney's attributes as if she were a prize hog at the town fair. I cut him off. "There has to be someone else. Someone not like all the others, but not like—" I raked a hand through my hair and then gestured at the women preening like pink flamingos all over his patio, before finishing lamely "—them."

"Who? If you don't want Delaney, fine. Go mingle, find someone else. But I've introduced you to a dozen girls in the past month. You've turned them all down. Too dumb. Too tall. Too short. Too quiet. Too loud. The last one was too bat-shit crazy, if I remember right. You want Delaney, I can tell. So, what's the problem?"

Nothing. Except that she made me feel things. Want things I didn't have a right to want. Not anymore. Maybe not ever.

Travis pounced on my non-answer. "See. You can't come up with a reason to reject her." He had that look in his eyes, the one I'd seen in meetings with studio executives and moneymen. The look of a hunter who'd spotted weakness in his quarry. "Okay, Shane. This is what I'm going to do. Since you've shown more interest in Delaney than you have anyone else I've introduced you to lately, or anyone here tonight, I'm going to ask her if she wants the job. Who knows? Maybe she'll be one of the one percent to turn down a tour with Nothing but Trouble. Maybe she has commitments here."

He rocked back on his heels, hoisting his shoulders up and then dropping them. "Maybe she has a boyfriend."

That last comment hit my eardrum like a sonic boom. Boyfriend? Some other guy running his fingers through her hair, kissing her perfectly pouty lips, sliding his hand between her thighs. *Oh, hell no.*

I stalked off, heading back the way I came in. "Get me her address. Don't do anything until you hear from me."

My phone vibrated with a text before I'd even started the engine. Travis was nothing if not efficient. I sat inside the locked doors for a moment, blood rushing through my veins so loudly I may as well have been clinging to a damn raft. No oar in sight, just an inky black night and no fucking clue where the current was taking me.

A frown was doing its damnedest to dig a ditch across my forehead, and I let go of the steering wheel in an attempt to rub it away. What the fuck just happened?

Delaney. Delaney Fraser.

Even her name sounded like a lyric. Soft and hard. Sweetly sinful. That whispered *shhh* toward the end, as if she were a secret I wasn't meant to discover.

The girl who walked away from me without a second glance.

Delaney Fucking Fraser.

Beautiful name. Beautiful face. Beautiful body.

Beautiful packages were a dime a dozen, though. Especially in Tinseltown. And backstage, too. Everywhere I looked, really. Gorgeous girls were within reach wherever I went. Inviting me to take what I wanted, when I wanted, wherever I wanted.

But they were easily discarded, easily forgotten.

I'd reached for Delaney, and the damn girl had slapped my hand away. My frown eased as a begrudging grin pulled at the corners of my lips. With a low chuckle, I started the Italian engine and shifted into gear, the quilted leather seat throbbing beneath my ass. *Delaney Fraser, I'm coming for you.*

Delaney

I couldn't wrestle the too-tight, too-tiny dress off fast enough. What the hell was I thinking—trying to run with Piper Hastings's crowd? I hadn't been able to pull it off in high school, and despite leaving my baby fat and bad hair back in Bronxville, I wasn't cut out for it now.

Breathing a sigh of relief once the dress was just a black puddle at my feet, I swept my hair into a ponytail and pulled on Lycra capris and a T-shirt. So. Much. Better.

The buzzer sounded just as I was taking out my lingering aggression on my teeth. Thinking Piper had turned around and decided to retrieve her dress tonight, I hastily spit peppermint foam into the sink and grabbed the dress from the floor. "Be right down," I called into an intercom system that had a fifty-fifty chance of dispensing only static, before quickly sliding into a pair of flip-flops and grabbing my keys. I lived on the fourth floor of a four-floor walk-up that was more than I could afford but the cheapest place I could find. Jogging down the stairs, I pushed open my front door, eager to shed any connection to Piper and a night I'd rather forget. "I would have dry-cleaned it—" My head jerked back, lungs rattling inside my chest as I shuddered to a stop.

Shane Hawthorne was at my front door, looking every inch the sex symbol that had captivated me from the moment I saw him, his presence no less overwhelming now than it had been an hour ago. Maybe more. My breath caught in the back of my throat, my heart tripping over itself in an effort to run away. Telling *me* to run away. But I couldn't run. Couldn't even breathe.

"Hey, Delaney." He spoke my name like he'd said it a million times before. Like we were old friends.

Without my heels, Shane seemed taller, his chest wider. And his shirt did absolutely nothing to hide the well-defined muscles beneath. Heat broke over my skin. "H-hi." The word was a hiccup, at best.

His eyes swept over me, from the top of my messy ponytail to my bright pink toes, lingering slightly over the bubble letters stretching across my braless breasts. "A Hello Kitty fan, huh?"

My nipples puckered beneath his gaze, a flush traveling from my exposed collarbone to settle on my cheeks and the tips of my ears. I swallowed. "Isn't everyone?"

The air between us crackled with sexual tension, electric energy rushing straight to my head. "Absolutely." Shane's husky answer raised the voltage another notch.

Fighting the temptation to swoon like the awkward teenage fan that still lived inside me, I crossed my arms over my chest, straightened my spine, and dragged my muddled mind back to reality. "What are you doing here?"

The cockiest smirk I'd ever seen blazed from Shane's gorgeous face, streetlights shining on the deep dimple in his left cheek that hinted at easy smiles and quick comebacks. "I was in the neighborhood."

Ignoring the lurch of my stomach, I jerked my chin at his gleaming sports car blocking the fire hydrant at the curb. "Bad call. Too much time down here and you might need a new ride."

His full lips twitched, telling me that's exactly what he'd come for.

Indignation pricked at my temples, and I stepped back inside the small vestibule of my apartment building. "I'm not your next *ride*."

Shane grabbed the door, his booted foot blocking it from closing. "Did I say you were?"

"You didn't have to."

He sighed. "Look, can we start over? I drove here because I didn't like the way we left things, okay? I didn't mean to offend you, to send you running off in the other direction."

I eyed him skeptically, not buying that the hottest heartthrob on the planet had followed me home solely to issue some sort of mea culpa. But regardless of his reasons, I just wanted to go back upstairs. This night was way more than I could handle, and it needed to end. "Fine. All is forgiven. You can go home with a clear conscience."

The bitter laugh gurgling from Shane's throat scraped at my nerves, tapping a well of empathy I didn't realize I still had.

"Don't know that I have one of those anymore, and even if I did, *clear* is about the last way I'd describe it." There was a rawness to his voice that had nothing to do with Shane's singing abilities, a serrated edge that hinted of past hurts to rival even my own, that touched me somewhere deep. Somewhere familiar. I let go of the door, trying to get a read on the man beneath the grit and gloss that was Shane Hawthorne, rock star.

His burning eyes locked onto mine, flaring briefly. For a second I caught a glimpse of vulnerability in him, an openness. But then they went dark, his chiseled bone structure settling into an impenetrable wall once more.

Shane raked a hand through the famously rugged hair that framed his face like a lion's mane. Paired with his luminous topaz eyes, he bore a vague resemblance to Mufasa, surveying his domain with a wary kind of confidence. When *Rolling Stone* proclaimed Shane Hawthorne the new King of Rock, they had definitely gotten it right.

He crossed his arms over his chest, shirtsleeves riding up his forearms to offer another glimpse of the ink marking his skin. "Maybe I just wanted to see if you taste as good as you look." This time Shane's voice wasn't raw, and the words coming from his mouth felt practiced, like he'd used them before. Often.

Shane hadn't asked a question, but I answered it anyway. By slamming the door in his face.

Except that his foot was still in the way, so it bounced off his boot and I had to stagger back to avoid being clipped by the rebound.

Flustered, my gaze landed on the man planted in front of me.

The grin started at the corners of Shane's lips, pulling them into a crooked smile before his full-bellied laugh wrapped itself around me. I covered my own mouth, not wanting to laugh with him. But it was no use. His mirth was contagious.

As quick as it came, the lighthearted moment disappeared, leaving us silently staring at each other. The invisible current between our bodies sparked, electricity burning off the oxygen and leaving me light-headed. I had the strange sense that he was just as surprised to be here as I had been to find him at my door.

Finally I found my voice. "Why are you really here, Shane?"

He gave a long blink, then shrugged. "No place else I wanted to be."

The blunt sincerity of Shane's answer was enough to make me swoon, but the way he was looking at me, like I held the key to a mystery he'd been trying to solve his whole life, was the knock-out punch. "That's…sweet."

His soft chuckle floated on the charged air between us. "Never been called that before."

"Maybe you should try deserving it now and then."

"Nah. Not good for my image." He glanced up and down the block, then turned back to me. "Can I come in?"

Fighting the urge to nod, I gave a slow shake of my head. "No. I don't think that would be smart."

"No?"

"Yes. I mean—no. Definitely no."

"A hard no?"

Very hard. This time I didn't trust myself to speak, instead drawing my lips inward and biting them as I blinked at Shane. "Mmm-hmm." I was already shattered. I didn't need anyone—especially not the man in front of me—shaking up the pieces I was barely holding together.

"How about a walk? Would you at least go for a walk with me?"

"A walk?"

"Yeah."

"Now?"

"Now."

In my Intro to Psych class I'd learned that one of the surest ways to get a yes from someone was to simply keep asking questions. Everyone relented eventually—more often than not, after only two tries. Apparently I was no different, caving like a cheap tent at the second gust of wind. "Um, okay." Stuffing Piper's dress into the wall-mounted mailbox assigned to my apartment, I eased out from behind the door. "Just a walk, right?"

Shane pulled a baseball cap from the back pocket of his jeans and pulled it over his head, lowering the brim so I could barely see his eyes. "Scout's honor."

I rebuffed the pledge. "Don't even pretend to be a Boy Scout." It came out more harshly than I intended.

For a moment, his smile dropped, lips turning down at the corners. "We're all just pretending, Delaney."

Chapter Four

Shane

Delaney was right. I'd never been in the Scouts. That would have required money, and at least a shred of parental interest. I'd struck out on both counts.

But my shitty childhood was the last thing on my mind as Delany tucked her keys inside the waistband of a pair of pants that clung to every one of her delicate curves. She joined me on the sidewalk, regarding my baseball cap skeptically. "Does that thing usually work?"

"Sometimes." Rolling my shoulders in a half-hearted shrug, I started walking. "We'll see."

Every guy we passed eyed Delaney, my right hand curling into a fist as they lingered over her full breasts bouncing beneath the thin fabric of her shirt, fingers twitching with the need to knock their hungry stares right off their faces.

By the time we reached the end of the block, we'd passed a tiny bodega, a hookah bar, a strip club, and a fortune-teller. "Interesting neighborhood. Do you like it here?"

"Sometimes."

The slight quiver in Delaney's voice made me hesitant to press for more. Instead I stepped closer, enfolding her hand within my own. I might as well have been holding napalm. Energy from the contact raced up my arms, singing through my veins. Girls like Delaney shouldn't be walking down dark, dank L.A. streets with guys like me. I was just as decrepit as any of the buildings rising above us. And yet here she was, her tiny fingers interlaced with mine, flip-flops echoing off the dirty pavement.

After a few blocks, a trio of drunk girls stumbled through a door, surrounded by a verbal cloud of off-key voices. I made a face, rubbing at my ears. "What the hell is that?"

Delaney stopped, an impish grin stretched across her full lips, aquamarine eyes gleaming. "It's a karaoke bar."

"People really go to those places?"

"We're in Koreatown. There's at least a dozen of them around here."

The door swung open again, more awful music polluting the air. "I think my ears are bleeding."

Delaney looked thrilled. "We should totally go inside."

I shook my head. "No way. The second I open my mouth, everyone will livestream it and the place will be mobbed."

She deflated, pink toes kicking at a discarded cigarette butt. "Oh. I hadn't thought about that."

Why would she? Delaney still had her privacy, a luxury I'd traded away a long time ago. I didn't regret it. The perks of celebrity were pretty damn hard to beat, but there were occasional moments like these when it would have been nice not to be recognized.

The dejected slump of Delaney's shoulders was killing me though. I barely knew this girl, but when her smile disappeared it was as if someone had stolen the sun. "*I* can't sing. But that doesn't mean *you* can't."

"Me? I can't sing."

"Says who?"

"No one. Because I know well enough to leave it to the professionals."

I tipped my chin at the blackened window with neon lettering. "Those are definitely not professionals."

"But—"

"How about we make a deal? You sing a song for me, and later I'll sing one for you."

A confused frown pulled at her delicately arched brows. "I thought you said—"

"I can't sing here. But I'll let you pick any song, songs even, and I'll serenade you with a private, a cappella concert. What do you say?"

Delaney nibbled at her lower lip, each gentle bite of the sensitive flesh sending waves of lust ricocheting inside my jeans. Her shallow nod was all I needed to tug on the door handle and give her a slight push.

Once inside, the music was even worse than I'd expected. But the place was dark as a cave, except for a small stage with a couple singing a duet, "Crazy in Love," the music video playing on a screen behind them. I would have given the contents of my bank account for a pair of earplugs. Beyoncé and Jay-Z they were not.

There were several free tables, and I led Delaney to one in

the back corner, pointing to a booth near the stage, with a huge binder open on the counter. "I think you sign up over there."

Her eyes were huge pools in her face. "You really expect me to go up there?"

I nodded. "Yep. I really do."

"I think I need a drink first."

It wasn't long ago that I needed a drink just to get out of bed in the morning. I flagged down a waitress, keeping my head low. After we placed our order, Delaney begrudgingly gave her name to the guy in the booth. "You didn't look through the book," I said when she returned.

"I already knew which song I wanted."

The couple was replaced by a thin older man sporting glasses and a sweater-vest who launched into a halfway decent imitation of Eminem. "Yeah? What are you going to sing?"

Our drinks arrived, some fruity concoction for Delaney and a beer for me. She took a nervous gulp. "You'll find out when I get up there, if I don't wimp out."

"You won't."

She gave a sad, disparaging smile. "And you got that impression when I ran away from you at Travis's house?"

"Actually, I did. Anyone else would have been perfectly willing to duck behind the nearest tree with me." I lifted the bottle to my mouth, not because I wanted a sip of beer, but to keep myself from reaching across the table and devouring *her*. "But not you."

Delaney Fucking Fraser.

There was something different about her. I couldn't put my finger on it. Maybe it was just that I'd been living in a bubble for the past decade or so, and Delaney only seemed different because she wasn't a Nothing but Trouble groupie or an L.A. wannabe starlet. But I didn't think so.

We watched the next two acts. Or rather, Delaney watched them, and I watched Delaney. She was at the edge of her seat, holding her drink, taking quick pulls of her straw as she rocked her head from side to side in time to the beat. So when she said something to me, I had to ask her to repeat her question.

"I said, do you do anything else besides sing?"

And what a loaded question it was, especially with her lips wrapped around the straw giving me all kinds of ideas. I quirked an eyebrow, feeling the slow churn of lust grabbing me by the balls. "Anything you want."

Following the obvious, and clearly X-rated, direction of my thoughts, Delaney released her straw, cheeks nearly as pink as her toes. "I mean, musically."

She may as well have stuck a pin in my balloon. I looked down, swiping at the condensation that had accumulated on my beer bottle. "Started out playing guitar," I mumbled.

Delaney must have been a lip-reader, because she acted like I'd announced it over the speakers. "Guitar? Do you still play?"

I did, but only when I was writing songs. Being reminded of the reason I'd taken the mic in the first place was just too damn hard. I managed a stiff nod. "How 'bout you?"

"Does the recorder count?" Her impish smile managed to drag my mind back to the present. "I tried playing violin and then the flute. But truthfully, I was horrendous. I think the only one happier about me quitting was my mom, who had to listen to me practice every day. After a couple of years, I gave up and stuck with chorus."

"Chorus, huh?"

She glanced at the stage. "Don't get your hopes up. No one ever gave me a solo."

But my hopes were already up, along with another part of my anatomy. I leaned forward in my chair, elbows propped up on the sticky table. Needing to be closer to her. Pulled by something I didn't understand.

She leaned in, too, anticipation quickening her breath.

"Delilah!" came through the speakers, followed by a, "Sorry, Delaney?"

We both fell back, spines making contact with the wooden spindles of our chairs, the moment broken.

"Get up there and break a leg, Delilah," I teased, remembering a time when I'd been called the wrong name, too. In my case, it had worked out just fine.

The color drained from her face. "I can't believe I'm doing this," she said, dropping her depleted drink on the table and standing up.

Fuck. No way was I letting her get up there in a top that left little to the imagination. "Wait." I jumped to my feet, quickly shrugging out of the black shirt I'd worn over a white tee. The back of my knuckles grazed her breasts as I draped it over her shoulders, pulling the ends together.

A shock of awareness lit into me, gripping me by the throat.

Delaney felt it, too, her eyes flaring, the pulse at the base of her throat fluttering wildly. Unable to stop myself, I wrapped my arms around her, pulling her sweet, sweet body into mine. Had anything ever felt so good, so right? Like the entire universe had conspired to bring us together. But what I really wanted to know was—why the hell it had it taken so long?

The asshole in the booth called her name again, and she stumbled back, giving me one last confused look before weaving through the tables and making her way to the stage.

I sat back down, feeling like I'd just run a mile in wet sand.

Exhausted and energized at the same time. Body buzzing, mind whirring, breaths coming heavy.

Delaney took her place in the center of the small stage, her hair glinting chestnut beneath the lights. She reached out for the mic, adjusting it before giving a quick nod toward the booth. And then she stared straight at me, looking all kinds of composed. Not exactly confident, but steady and sure.

I was impressed. It had taken me years to get up the courage to sing in front of an audience. Thousands of hours of practice and friends up onstage with me, too. Beneath Delaney's tight pants, she had quite a set of balls.

Reverence was shoved aside by recognition as the first chords came through the speakers.

No.

Of all the songs in the universe, Delaney had picked the only one with the power to crush me.

Of course she did.

"Shoulda Been Me" had put Nothing but Trouble on the map. Took me from relative obscurity to the top of the charts. A song I wrote from the depths of a drunken, drugged-up stupor, when the pain in my head, in my heart, couldn't be contained any longer. I hadn't sung it in years.

Now my lyrics, those tainted shards of emotion, were skating through Delaney's trembling lips in a voice that was untrained, but even and pure. They wrapped around me, pulling tight. Each line another coil, encircling my abdomen, my chest, my throat. Squeezing. Suffocating.

Panic rose, surging through my veins. The sound of my racing heartbeat not nearly loud enough to drown out Delaney's voice singing my words.

I must have been looking away
On that senseless day
They say actions have consequences
I committed the baddest blunder of them all
Why did you have to take the fall
Shoulda been me
Shoulda been
Shoulda been me.

Coulda woulda shoulda—held on harder, stronger
Drivin' crashin' dyin'—heaven got another martyr
Shoulda been me.

The lyrics were dark, but I'd set them against a melody that was quick and upbeat, almost buoyant. One of the reasons I'd stopped performing it was because the audience would sing it back, smiles on their faces, looking so damn happy. Not Delaney. Maybe she was just nervous, or unused to the lights, but I could swear she was blinking back tears. There was no hesitation as she sang, no forgotten words or missed beats. She didn't even spare a glance at the monitor in front of her, which had a bouncing ball lighting up each syllable in tune with the music.

As I listened to Delaney sing my song, it became hers, too. Like she knew exactly what the lyrics meant, the place they had come from. Almost as if she'd written them herself.

As the last notes faded away, Delaney set the clunky microphone on its stand and made her way back to our table.

"Hey." She appeared in front of me, a little breathless but radiant. The stage did that to a person, gave them a buzz in all the right places. "How did I do?"

You were fucking breathtaking. What came out instead was a brusque, "You ready to get out of here?"

A flash of hurt streaked across her expression. "Yeah, sure."

Dropping cash on the table, I cinched an arm around the curve of Delaney's waist and propelled her toward the exit. The air outside smelled of exhaust and weed, but I took a deep breath and ran a hand over my face.

Delaney sidestepped my embrace, looking worried. "Are you okay?"

I dropped my hand, opened my eyes. Shook off the effect she'd had on me. Enough to function, at least. "Yeah. I'm fine."

"You don't look fine to me."

I scanned the street, trying to orient myself. Right or left? I had no clue. Listening to Delaney had pulled me out of my shell, and now I was just a quivering, spineless mollusk standing on a dirty L.A. street. In a goddamn baseball cap. "Which way back to your place?"

Delaney turned away and began walking. I followed, using the time to pull myself together. We walked in silence, not exchanging another word until we were standing in front of her apartment building again. I eyed it cautiously. I'd lived in worse places than this. Hell, I'd lived on the streets. Crashed on floors and couches, or with anyone who would have me. But still, I didn't like leaving Delaney here. "How about I take you back to my place?"

"For my private concert?"

"For whatever you want." I wiggled an eyebrow, adding a liberal dose of wickedness to cover up my unease. Like a magician hiding his tricks with a sleight of hand, flirting was my fallback whenever I felt someone getting too close.

Delaney backed up against the door, her knowing eyes staring right through me. Burrowing beneath my Shane Hawthorne veneer. Getting a good hard look at all the shadows and sins I kept under lock and key.

"I think I'll pass." Shying away from them.

I shifted from one foot to the other. Any other girl and I'd already be back in my car. Zero fucks. That's how I lived. Not caring about anything but my music, my career. Myself. Delaney had walked away from me not two hours ago. Why couldn't I walk away from her now?

There was something about this girl that made me feel better just knowing we were breathing the same air. I edged forward, needing to be closer. "How about you let me come upstairs, then?" Was I seriously begging? Yes. Yes, I was.

With barely an inch between us, her shuddering breath rippled across my skin. I dipped my head, planting a light kiss on her forehead, lingering as a nearly inaudible whimper escaped her throat. "You want to. I can tell." I pulled the elastic from her hair, took a whiff as a shower of dark chocolate strands tumbled to her shoulders. So sweet—better than a box of Godiva. I wanted to swallow her whole.

Pulling back, I expected to see an easy, wanton smile tripping from those lush lips of hers. Instead, Delaney's lower lip was tucked between her teeth. Curiosity and compassion radiated from her expression, as obvious as her high cheekbones and thick lashes.

She didn't belong at Travis's party earlier tonight, and she sure as shit didn't belong with me now. Didn't stop me from wanting her though. Didn't stop me from edging even closer, pushing denim against cotton, proving just how badly I wanted her. "Delaney." I groaned her name. Running my nose along the elegant sweep of her cheekbone, I breathed in the desire rising from her skin like fog off the morning tide. My palms skimmed over her rib cage, fingers dipping beneath the waistband of her pants. Finding a satiny sliver of skin. And a set of keys.

Leaning back, I dangled them between us. "Let's go upstairs."

Eyes that had been as soft and smooth as sea glass blinked into focus, narrowing at their corners. "You really have a one-track mind." Disappointment trekked across her features.

I slapped away the impulse to explain why—that if I didn't stay focused on the easy, the attainable, I'd be dragged down by my inner demons so fast, running away would be like trying to sprint in quicksand, each panicked step making me sink deeper. "Doesn't have to be a bad thing."

"Maybe not for you." Delaney reclaimed her keys, ducking away from me. Grabbing for the door handle, she gave it a firm twist. It squeaked open, sounding mournful and sad. Sounding like an ending. "But the track I'm on doesn't leave room for middle-of-the-night booty calls with a guy who can't even be bothered to tell me what he thought of the three minutes I spent onstage—for him. Good night, Shane. Save your voice for some-one still willing to listen."

And then she was gone. Leaving me with only the memory of her bewitching smile and pure voice. And a knot of remorse sitting heavily in my chest, leaching toxins into my bloodstream with each dull, disappointed thud of my heart.

Delaney

I wasn't planning to look out my window when I went back to my apartment, but I couldn't help myself. There was no way Shane would ever show up at my door again, not after I'd given him the brush-off twice in one night. And I certainly wouldn't be invited to another Travis Taggert party. But I couldn't resist the urge to catch one more glimpse of my teenage crush—even if it was just to watch him walk away.

Except that he wasn't walking away.

Shane was sitting on the back bumper of his car, his body tense as he stared at something just beyond my view. I raised the window slowly, holding my breath and hoping it wouldn't squeak. Once there was enough room, I stuck my neck through the opening like a nosy turtle. A couple was stumbling toward Shane, their arms intertwined as they zigzagged from one end of the sidewalk to the other, their manic laughter and broken bits of slurred words audible even from my fourth-floor window.

Suddenly, they broke apart, the guy scrounging in his pocket and pointing something I assumed to be his key fob at the car behind Shane's. It flashed its lights and chirped, and the guy tripped off the curb and rounded the bumper to the driver's side. My breath hitched in the back of my throat. Neither one of those two should be driving. Before I could even think to call 911 from my phone—not that it would do any good; by the time the police responded to a call from this neighborhood, they may have killed someone already—Shane's deep baritone echoed off the street. "Hey, I just saw something crawl into your engine."

Oh, no. What did Shane think he was doing? He wasn't in Beverly Hills anymore.

No one would ever accuse Shane Hawthorne of not being able to take care of himself in a fair fight. Hadn't I just read about him training in Krav Maga, the Israeli martial art that looked like a crazy mash-up of karate, Zumba, and tai chi, with some acrobatic tumbling thrown in for good measure? But in this neighborhood, fighting fair wasn't a given. Here, thugs carried knives and guns. Shane's rock-star veneer might impress his fans, but it was far from Kevlar.

Drunk guy was clearly not a fan. "You shittin' me?" he shot back, punctuating his retort with a loud belch. He was wearing faded jeans and a grungy tee, not quite as tall as Shane, but heavier by at least fifty pounds. And maybe not as drunk as I'd thought. Confronting Shane, his words had lost most of their slur.

"Pop the hood; check it out for yourself."

Drunk girl leaned against the car, her shirt rising to expose a wide tattoo covering her lower back. "Don't do it." She snarled the warning. "How do we know this guy's on the level?"

Keeping the brim of his hat low, Shane moved aside to expose the Ferrari crest, holding up his key. "This is my ride. Not lookin' to trade."

Christ. Was he trying to taunt them into a carjacking? What if they had a gun? I ran to my bedroom, rooting around in my nightstand drawer until I found what I was looking for, and sprinted back downstairs on bare feet. By the time I poked my head through the door, cell phone in one hand and a can of Mace in the other, the hood of the Toyota was open, Shane's boots just barely visible underneath.

A second later, the hood slammed down with a *bang*, and I saw Shane toss whatever he'd pulled from the engine through the sewer grate.

"What the fuck do you think you're doing?" the guy bellowed.

I was about to race out of my doorway and attempt to save Shane and the streets of L.A. with my can of Mace when Shane reached into his back pocket and pulled out his wallet, handing a wad of cash to the guy, whose expression quickly transformed from furious to dumbfounded. "You don't want to get behind the wheel right now. Take a cab home tonight, and use the rest of this to buy a new spark plug tomorrow." Without a second glance, Shane turned on his heel, got into his own car, and drove away.

As I eased back inside the stairwell, I saw the guy counting the bills in his hand, his *whoop* of excitement chasing me up the stairs.

Once I was back in my apartment, I yanked my window closed, not caring if anyone heard, and crawled between my sheets, trying to make sense of what I'd just seen.

The only way it made any sense at all was if Shane wasn't the arrogant, self-centered jerk I thought he was.

* * *

Looking over my assigned table the next night, I recognized a newly familiar face. My shoulders tensed, inching toward my ears. "What are you doing here, Travis?"

He toyed with his knife, casually running his thumb up and down the serrated blade. "Shane Hawthorne took quite a liking to you."

I fidgeted with my order pad and pen. *Maybe he did, but after I basically slammed the door in his face last night...* "I doubt that." Which was too bad, because the Shane Hawthorne I'd caught a glimpse of when he thought no one was looking was a hell of a lot more intriguing than the guy whose face had graced my bedroom wall.

"It's true. As a matter of fact, he'd like you to join his team."

"His team?" After one night of karaoke, had I earned a spot as a backup singer?

"Yes. He's going on tour next week and he needs an assistant. Someone to make sure his dressing room is organized, keep him on schedule, that sort of thing."

Oh. He didn't *like* me. He just wanted to hire me. Definitely not the same. I gestured at the dining room of the sumptuous restaurant. "I have a job."

Travis chuckled. It was early, and so far he was the only person at any of my tables. "Don't look a gift horse in the mouth, Delaney. I did a little digging after we met yesterday." Leaning his elbow on the table, Travis stroked his left eyebrow, dark eyes holding mine captive. "Looks to me like you ran as far away from home as you could get. Never got to finish school. Going on the road with Shane Hawthorne…it's a pretty well-paying gig." He mentioned a sum that would more than cover the three semesters of tuition and expenses it would take to earn my degree. I almost choked. "You're a bright girl, Delaney. I'm offering an opportunity you shouldn't turn down."

I'd been saving as much as I could from my various jobs over the past three years and it wasn't even close to covering textbooks, let alone tuition. Travis was dangling a carrot in front of an emaciated horse. Unfortunately for me—it was a carrot in the form of Shane Hawthorne. But Travis was right. I didn't want to be a waitress for the rest of my life. I wanted to go back to school, get my degree. But I couldn't, and not just because I didn't have enough money.

How could I move forward with my life while my father was sitting behind bars, charged with my mother's death?

"What do you have to lose? You're a young girl; it's a six-month tour. All your expenses will be covered, so you can bank everything you earn. And when the tour's over, you can catch your breath and figure out what you really want to do with the rest of your life." He smirked. "Because we both know it's not waitressing."

Bitterness rose, coating the back of my throat. It was the truth. I had nothing to lose.

Because I'd already lost everything.

What I *wanted* was to have my old life back. I wanted to call home. I wanted to hear my mother chiding me for spending too much time with my books and not enough time making friends. I wanted her to pass the phone to my father, who would question me about my coursework.

I wanted a lot of things that were never going to happen again. Ever.

Out of the corner of my eye, I spotted the hostess seating an older couple at one of my tables and decided to be blunt. "What's the catch?"

Travis smiled. "No catch, unless you find the prospect of spending six months with Shane Hawthorne unappealing."

Yesterday I would have said that I'd rather spend the next six months sunbathing in hell. But today the problem was that I found the idea too appealing. Because the guy I'd caught a glimpse of, the one who looked more like a Good Samaritan than a bad boy, had the power to make me forget about what brought us together in the first place. Make me forget the reason I was an L.A. waitress instead of an Ivy League student. And that was not good at all.

Pressing my lips together, I held back the outright refusal banging against my teeth and turned away to take care of the older couple. A boisterous foursome came in next, followed by a group of girlfriends looking to catch up over drinks and dinner. By the time I got back to check on Travis, he had finished his cocktail and was halfway through his steak. A thin stack of paper sat at the empty place setting across from him, with NONDISCLOSURE AGREEMENT centered at the top in boldface type. "I was going to ask if I could get you anything else, but it looks like you've brought something for me instead."

Travis crossed his knife and fork on his plate and steepled his fingers. "It's just a standard agreement. I'll need your signature before we can move forward."

I reached for the document. "I'd like to read it first."

"Of course." Travis wiped his mouth with the linen napkin and pushed back his chair. "My steak was excellent. I'll be back tomorrow, and I expect you will have had ample time to review the contract by then."

Shane

I fucked around most of the day, keeping busy doing a whole lot of nothing much. Busy enough to convince myself that I didn't have time to call and cancel this afternoon's meeting with Delaney. Despite my reservations, I wanted her to sign Travis's gag order, wanted her to come on tour with me.

Which was exactly what I'd told Travis on my way back to Malibu last night, still amped up from my confrontation with the drunken fool who'd been about to get behind the wheel of his car. I'd made some fucked-up decisions in my life, but only one of them had led to a funeral.

If I'd been drunk that long-ago night, if I'd had any alcohol at all, I would have stuck around, let the lynch mob have their way. But I'd know how it looked, so I took off, selfishly saving myself.

And now I was here. Living in the shadow of a mountain made of regrets.

I couldn't let that jerkoff ruin his life, or anyone else's. Tragedy was a greedy motherfucker—it never contained itself to those who deserved it.

Then there was the matter of the door Delaney had slammed in my face. I would have given anything to be on the other side of it right now, working through the jumble of emotions last night had stirred up in me. Preferably in her bed, although anywhere would have been fine. Couch, kitchen counter, wall, floor, tub. So long as her smooth legs were wrapped around me, pulling me close, letting me breathe in all her delicious sweetness. Creamy skin and glossy hair. Pink lips and lush curves.

I should have slept on it. Given my brain a chance to tell my dick to shut the fuck up. Because that's the head that talked to Travis.

It was wrong. So wrong to even consider taking Delaney on the road. But I'd spent every minute since she stormed away from me longing for another glimpse of those eyes of hers—a roiling jumble of blue and green that could make the Caribbean sea jealous. I wanted to wrap myself in the guileless innocence she wore so well. I wanted to know why she hadn't thrown herself at me like everyone else in this superficial, celebrity-obsessed town did.

I wanted to know why she'd run away from me, looking almost panicked.

Walking into Travis's office, it was my turn to be scared. Scared that she would turn me down. More scared that she wouldn't.

Travis was right. I wanted Delaney to be my girl. But while I watched her on that shitty stage, singing *my* song, an overwhelming urge had risen from the depths of my soul. A hunger too loud to be ignored. I wanted...something more. Something real.

I wanted *Delaney* to be real. Not a publicity stunt. Not a placeholder. And I wanted her to be mine.

It was ridiculous, I knew. A pipe dream. As Shane Hawthorne, nothing about my life was genuine. But Delaney, she was *real*.

Now I felt like I was sixteen, about to ask the cutest girl in class to be my date for prom. Not that I ever had the chance. I'd been long gone by the time my high school prom rolled around.

Pulling up short, I nearly walked right back out the door, biting the inside of my cheek so hard I tasted blood. What the fuck was wrong with me? Did I have some sort of internal sonar that drew me toward the sweetest, most genuine souls out there, unable to resist corrupting them?

"Mr. Hawthorne." Travis's assistant was making a beeline for me, and I groped for my rock-star smile, finding it just in time. "Ms. Fraser is already here. If you'll follow me, I'll take you to the conference room now."

With a brusque nod, I pushed off the wall that had been holding me up and followed her sure-footed steps toward a woman, if I had any mercy at all, I should leave the fuck alone.

But then the door opened and I saw that shiny mess of dark hair, wayward tendrils sliding against pale, sculpted cheekbones. Curiosity shone from Delaney's eyes, as if she'd come for answers and expected me to have them.

Answers? Beneath the weight of her stare, I didn't even know my own name.

I turned back, pretending to close the door Travis's assistant was pulling at from the other side, needing a minute to get my shit together. It felt like it had been scattered to every corner of the earth, but I found my center right as the door *click*ed closed. *You don't have to be yourself; just be Shane.*

And suddenly, he was back. Self-assured, cocky. Full of my-shit-doesn't-stink bravado, Shane Hawthorne pushed his shoulders back and grinned. "Hello, Delaney."

Chapter Five

Delaney

Although I looked for any excuse not to sign, I couldn't find one. As Travis explained, the nondisclosure agreement was basically identical to several I found online, and he was right about something else, too. I was tired of hiding, tired of wallowing in the past and pretending I didn't have a future. I wanted to *do* something with my life. And I was tired of trying to convince myself that Shane Hawthorne was the devil. I'd seen him do more good in three minutes than I'd done in three years.

So now I was in Beverly Hills, sitting in an elegantly appointed conference room with sweeping city views.

Waiting for my future to begin.

Waiting for Shane Hawthorne.

Ten minutes later, he swept into the room. Shane's rich

brown hair was tousled, his jeans perfectly snug. His lips just as kissable as they'd been the other night. Damn him.

"Hello, Delaney." Even a simple greeting coming from the rock god could be the sexy start to a swoon-worthy ballad.

A tingle raced up the length of my spine, my stomach executing a flip worthy of an Olympic gold medal. "Hello," I croaked, unable to look away from Shane's confident swagger as he came toward me. His feet stopped just inches from mine, my head tilting backward until it touched the edge of the chair, heart thudding against my rib cage as if trying to escape.

Rather than take a seat on the other side of the table, Shane pulled out the chair to my right, his left thigh nudging mine as he sat down. "I'm glad you came." Dimple flashing, Shane leaned forward and reached out to lightly stroke the narrowest part of my arm, just before it tapered to my wrist. "I wasn't sure you would."

Time stood still as I watched his thumb leave a trail of goose bumps in its wake. My skin thrilled at his touch, a shiver of desire sending every nerve into overdrive. *My employer shouldn't be touching me like this…*

I wrenched my gaze away from the sight of Shane's long, elegant fingers and met his eyes. They had smoldered from album covers, music videos, and countless TV appearances, but his amber stare was infinitely more intense in person. Now they were turned on me. And I was melting. "Me neither," I answered honestly, a knot of pure lust heating the blood racing through my veins. Did Shane Hawthorne have this kind of effect on everyone? It didn't help that he was looking at me as if he wanted to make a meal out of me, devour me whole until I was just another part of the Shane Hawthorne mystique.

And in that moment, I was tempted. By his face, by his body, by his voice. But most of all, by the part of Shane he didn't even know I'd seen.

Not just tempted. Terrified. Because I'd never gone for guys like Shane. With or without a microphone, Shane Hawthorne was a walking advertisement for heartbreak on two legs. But those legs. His jeans did nothing to hide the muscles corded beneath midnight-blue denim. Hard and powerful, they made all sorts of promises about what a ride it would be.

At least until I was dumped at the side of the road, gutted.

I licked my lips, the taste of my peach lip gloss oddly jarring. What would Shane Hawthorne taste like?

Shane's mouth moved, and I struggled to focus on his words. "I already have an assistant."

My heart plummeted. Did he call me in here just to tell me he didn't want me, after all? I had walked away from Shane twice. Was this his way of having the last word? Could he be that cruel? I studied the hard line of his jaw, a scar marking the indent where it met his neck. Yes. Yes, he could. I should have been relieved. Grateful, even. But I wasn't. Disappointment lanced through my lungs. "Oh."

But instead of getting up, walking out of the room, out of my life, Shane kept talking. I leaned forward in my chair, embarrassingly eager for every word. "But I need you on my team. Compensation will be as Travis explained, although our relationship will be a bit more…personal. I'd like to hire you. As my girlfriend."

My breath hitched in the back of my throat as I glanced nervously toward the door. Shane Hawthorne wanted me, Delaney Fraser, to be his *girlfriend*? Something told me I should make a break for it, leave now before he reduced my world to rubble. But I didn't. I stayed put, waiting for him to supply more details.

Waiting for Shane to redefine my world, because as far as I knew, relationships didn't require conference rooms and contracts.

"I'm sure you've seen the gossip rags. I'm no choir boy. But I'm not looking for drama, Delaney. When I'm on the road, fans and groupies are constantly trying to sneak their way into my dressing rooms, hotel rooms, even onto the tour bus and private planes. The best way to discourage them is by having a beautiful woman by my side. I want that woman to be you."

I tilted my head to the side, something telling me I should read between the lines, but I didn't even understand where the lines were. "Me?"

A rumble erupted from deep in Shane's chest. Dear God, his laugh was even sexier than his voice. "Yes, you." He widened his thighs, pulling my chair closer and drawing my knees between his legs.

As if in slow motion, I watched his hand coming toward me, a shiver of pleasure rolling down my spine as it curved around the back of my neck, his fingers blazing a path into my hair as he leaned forward. Then all I felt was Shane's full lips descending on my own, his mouth brushing against mine in a whisper-soft caress. But he pulled back too quickly, leaving me wanting more. My eyes fluttered open, absorbing the impact of his provocative grin like a kick to the solar plexus.

This *wasn't* happening. This couldn't *be* happening.

And then it happened again. Shane pressed harder this time, swallowing my breath as his tongue pushed into my mouth.

Shane Hawthorne tasted like spearmint and something headier, muskier…liquid testosterone maybe.

When he broke away, he took my soft groan of protest with him. One taste of heaven wasn't nearly enough. "So, what do you think, Delaney—will you be my girlfriend?" Shane looked at me as if asking me to share his life was the most natural thing in the world.

Swallowing the want surging up my chest, filling my lungs, clawing at my throat, I managed a quiet whisper. "I think it's a bad idea."

Shane hooked a thumb beneath my chin, holding me still as his needy gaze scanned every inch of my face. "But it feels so good bein' bad."

He clearly didn't know the first thing about me. All my life I'd been a good girl. Coloring between the lines, following the rules. Until one night, I slipped up. Put my own needs and wants ahead of anyone else's, without considering the consequences. I learned a painful lesson. Being bad came at too high of a cost.

"Be bad with me, Delaney." His words ghosted across my lips, and I opened my mouth, breathing them in. I felt myself yielding to Shane's persistence, succumbing to the strength of my own desires.

The pull I felt toward Shane was a stronger lure than the money Travis had offered. But I was entirely wrong for the job. If they only knew what a mess I'd made of my life, they would never hire me to maintain order in Shane's.

Shane said he wasn't looking for drama. Of course—because he didn't need to. Drama found him. And now he wanted to bring me into the center of the storm. His storm.

Electricity buzzed between us, the air still and sharp. Every glimpse of Shane, every taste of him, sent my body and soul plunging into chaos. And with him so close, every breath sent a shower of sparks racing along my skin.

The connection between us…it was volatile. Hazardous.

I was powerless to resist it.

As his lips twitched, I found my voice. "I saw you." It was only a whisper, but it was enough.

"'Course you see me," Shane said, his voice light and teasing. "I'm right here."

"No. I mean the other night, outside my apartment. After I went upstairs." His eyes narrowed, the easygoing expression in them disappearing like sunlight behind blackout curtains.

"I don't know what you're talking about." But he did. I knew he did.

Liars recognize each other, in the same way a magician is rarely fooled by another's tricks. And we were liars. Shane knew exactly what I was talking about. He just didn't want to admit it. I felt a nervous flutter in my stomach, realizing I'd invaded his privacy by spying on him. I wasn't going to press him on it, but even if I wanted to, I didn't have the chance because the door behind Shane's chair suddenly flew open.

Travis strutted into the room, the door *hiss*ing shut. "Just a few more details." He dropped a sheaf of papers on the table in front of me. "There's more to being Shane Hawthorne's girlfriend than just smiling pretty for the paparazzi."

I tore my eyes from Shane's and reached for the document. I began to read, Travis and Shane becoming almost invisible as the words whispered, then shouted at me. Each line tearing at the superhero cape I'd foolishly believed Shane was hiding.

Shane Hawthorne was no hero.

When I finally looked up, Shane had vanished, along with any possibility he was worth falling for. "Is this a joke?"

Shane

Had Delaney really seen what I'd done? *Shit.* Like a gambler's tell, my actions gave away a part of me that I wanted to keep hidden. *Needed* to keep hidden.

Shane Hawthorne lived life with zero fucks, damn it. He was every inch the cocky, confident rock star. He wasn't some bleeding-heart do-gooder.

For fuck's sake—you are *Shane. Pull your shit together and act like it.*

Other than charity concerts, all my philanthropic efforts were done through a dummy corporation I'd had Travis set up. No one needed to know what issues mattered to me, using them to see inside my head. Or worse, into my past.

Despite my internal pep talk, the frown twisting Delaney's brow pulled at my conscience. Angry lines slashed across her forehead as she turned the page, raven strands quivering against her shoulders as she scanned each sentence. I wanted to wrap my hands around her tiny waist and pull her into my embrace.

More than that, I wanted to soothe away her inner storm and put all that enraged passion to good use.

Just moments ago, Delaney's lips had softened beneath mine, and I'd swallowed her sigh as if it were a lifesaving drug. For me, maybe it was. Maybe there was someone on this earth who could save me. Then again, maybe there was a Santa Claus, too.

I needed to get out of here.

Rather than face more questions, or Delaney's turbulent reaction, I unfolded myself from the chair and quietly left the room. Because if I stayed, I might just let her walk away from me again, from everything I wanted from her. And I wasn't willing to do that. Not anymore. The thought of Delaney being with anyone else was ripping me to shreds.

No, I would leave, let Travis do what he did best. He would smooth things over, like he always did. That's why I kept him on my payroll. When we first met years ago, he'd been a lawyer who was just starting to represent a few bands and B-level actors. He'd promised to make my life easier, to take all the time-sucking minutiae off my plate so I could concentrate on making music and performing in front of increasingly larger audiences.

Most agents didn't hire fake girlfriends for their clients, but Travis did, and so much more. His client list was more exclusive now—A-list only—and he was insanely expensive. But I could easily afford his rates, and Travis was worth every penny. He'd work his magic, and Delaney Fraser would become Shane Hawthorne's newest girlfriend.

Recalling the flush that crept up her collarbone whenever we touched, I was looking forward to exploring all the parts of her I hadn't yet seen.

That wasn't part of the contract, of course. But damn, how long could Delaney resist the inevitable?

Every cell in my body wanted to collide with hers, and I knew she felt the same.

It was chemistry.

I sauntered down the hall, politely smiling at every head that swiveled my way. Confidence and cockiness were fine, but the days of the rude rock star were over. To have a long career, it was important to be professional and courteous to everyone, all the time. An idol of mine once told me that the most important lesson he'd learned after fifty years in the business was that "killing 'em with kindness never did no harm." Everyone remembers an asshole—and not in a good way.

After getting in my car, I headed to Blue Cocoon, my go-to option for stocking my closet. Tours were crazy and chaotic, and everyone wanted a piece of me. No matter how many jeans and tees, sunglasses and—don't even get me started on underwear—I took on tour, by the last show, the remains of my wardrobe could fit into a small carry-on, with room to spare.

Jude, the man responsible for getting me on more Best Dressed lists than I'd ever known existed, was waiting for me just inside the door of the shop I forced myself into every few months, escorting me quickly into a back room that felt like an enormous closet. Gnashing my teeth, I tried on everything Jude handed me, standing still while a tailor pinned and tucked and chalked with grim precision. I'd come a long way since bounding onstage in dirty, ill-fitting jeans and loose T-shirts emblazoned with other bands' logos.

After two hours, Jude finally walked me to the front door. "Everything will be ready in a few days. Should I bring them over?"

I nodded. "Yeah, like always." Jude would let himself in, arrange the clothes in my closet, and an assistant would pack them based on climate requirements. I could be in Michigan one week and Florida the next. "And I'm sending someone over, a girl named Delaney Fraser. She'll be coming on tour with me. Make sure she's taken care of." All my girlfriends came to Jude, too.

He nodded. Never once had Jude so much as batted an eye at the revolving door of women that entered and exited my life. "Of course."

An elegant mannequin stood by the door, wearing a red dress. I had avoided looking at it on my way in, but my eyes were drawn to it now. The deep rich color sent my pulse racing.

Repelling me.

Tempting me.

"Mr. Hawthorne, are you all right?"

I unlocked my jaw. "Make sure to include that dress."

Jude's head swiveled. "Which one, sir?"

"That one." I pointed.

Knowing my aversion to the shade, he hesitated. "I'm sorry, but it only comes in the red. I can find something similar in another color—"

Squashing memories of another red fabric, one that hid bloodstains so well I hadn't realized the extent of the injuries until it was too late, I overrode Jude's commentary. Maybe it was because of the couple in the street the other night. Maybe it was because Delaney admitted that she'd seen our interaction. Maybe it was because of Delaney, period. "That one. In red." It had been more than a decade. It was time.

Delaney

Travis regarded me soberly, his thick brows drawing together in a fierce line. "I don't joke about business."

"Business… This isn't business!" I threw the offensive document across the lacquered mahogany conference table. "What you're asking me to sign can't be legal. It's—it's…" I sputtered. "It's practically prostitution."

He reared back, clearly offended. "Absolutely not. It says so right here in Clause Seven. 'Any sexual contact between Delaney Fraser and the Client is beyond the scope of this contract and entirely at their discretion.'"

A humorless chuckle bubbled up from my throat. "Are these

the kinds of problems you solve? Ironing out the details of your clients' sex lives?"

Ignoring my questions, Travis calmly picked up the contract, flipped a page, and began reading. "'Delaney Fraser will act as the Client's girlfriend, responding agreeably to public displays of affection such as hugging, kissing, necking, and using commonly accepted terms of endearments to convey her intimate relationship with the Client.'" He looked up. "This is unacceptable to you?"

"That one's fine," Delaney snapped. "It's all the—"

"'Delaney Fraser will consent to being interviewed and photographed in her role as the Client's girlfriend. Her comments and actions will reflect a loving, contented, and monogamous relationship with the Client.'" He stopped. "This is problematic?"

I rolled my eyes and sighed. "No."

"'Delaney Fraser will carefully monitor any attempt by the Client to engage in excessive alcohol consumption or illegal substances, up to and including limiting opportunities for such behavior. She will immediately report any such incidents, and all parties involved, to a member of the Client's management team.'" Travis looked up. "You may use your best judgment, but I expect you will reach out to me first. However, should the situation warrant it, you may speak with anyone on our security team."

"You expect me to spy on Shane?"

His scowl deepened. "I'm asking you to help keep my client alive. If that's not a worthy aim, then I guess we really are done here."

I sighed, feeling petty and spiteful. "That's not what I meant."

Travis ran his palm over his shaved head and looked back

down. "'Delaney Fraser will be styled by a member of the Client's team for all public events, details of such to be specified by a public relations contact person.'"

Okay, being *styled* sounded intriguing. Travis glanced up at me and I waved him on.

"Let me skip ahead, then. 'Delaney Fraser and the Client will undergo thorough STD medical testing, the results of which will be made available to both parties.'"

That one. "Why do I need to take a blood test if I don't have to do much more than smile for the cameras?" I snapped, daring him to provide an acceptable answer.

Travis dropped the contract on the table and leaned back in his chair, steepling his fingers and peering over them as if I were a remedial algebra student in an advanced calculus class. "Shane's a musician, not an actor. Neither are you. And I'm not blind. I saw the chemistry between you two; hopefully everyone will. You're going to be together for the next six months. In case you do want to engage in some extracurricular activities, at least both of you will be clean."

I swallowed. The word "clean" had never sounded so dirty. "If I'm not expected to have sex with him, then why am I required to be on birth control?"

His voice dripped with condescension. "Delaney, you're going to spend almost every night watching Shane Hawthorne put on a show that makes every woman in the audience, and more than a few of the men, wish for just five minutes alone with him, preferably naked. Maybe you're the outlier, the one woman on the planet who doesn't harbor a secret hope of seducing him and having his baby. But Shane's hired me to look out for his best interests. Birth control is nonnegotiable."

I had a sudden vision of a pint-sized Shane, all long limbs, shaggy hair, and amber eyes shining with curiosity. I'd never babysat much in high school, never felt particularly drawn to kids. But Shane Hawthorne's mini-me…Even I couldn't deny the twinge in my ovaries. I dragged my attention back to Travis. There was a caustic, albeit resigned, edge to my voice when I said, "So, you're paying me to be Shane's fawning, STD-free, in-fertile girlfriend?"

Travis bristled. "You're being paid to *act* like his girlfriend. In public. What you do in private is entirely up to you and Shane."

"And he's read this? He knows I'm an employee, not some long-term, well-paid escort?"

"Of course," he enthused. "Although, I'm not going to lie. In order for the press to buy Shane being in a committed relation-ship, a certain amount of intimacy is essential. In the past, this has led to…more," he finished lamely.

My cheeks burning, I crossed my arms in front of my chest. "And after the tour is over, what happens then?"

Travis hesitated before answering, telling me everything I needed to know. Shane Hawthorne didn't need *me*. He needed a life-sized Barbie doll. One he could throw away as soon as it outlived its usefulness.

Ten minutes ago, I'd practically crawled into Shane's lap. The connection between us was powerful, and too potent to ignore. Now Travis was putting an expiration date on it. "No."

"No, what?"

"No, I'm not signing this ridiculous contract. No, I'm not go-ing on tour with Shane Hawthorne. No, I won't be his fake girl-friend. I've heard enough." I catapulted out of my chair, heading for the door.

Travis beat me to it, blocking my escape. "You didn't read the last page."

"I don't need to."

He ripped it off anyway, handing it to me with a flourish. I looked down. "What the—" It was a prisoner transfer request form.

"Your father's incarcerated in upstate New York, right? Maximum security. Hard time." He pointed to the top of the sheet. "You spend the next six months on tour with Shane and I'll have him moved to a minimum-security facility in Westchester. Still prison, but it's a country club compared to where he is now."

I felt like I'd been sucker punched. I hadn't managed to do a single thing for my father in three years. All the air left my lungs in a rush, and I grabbed for the edge of the table to steady myself. "You can do that?" I wheezed. "You can have my father transferred?"

Travis tipped his smooth head forward in a confident nod. "I manage some of the biggest acts in the business. I'm the difference between throwing a fundraiser at the local VFW and a private concert demanding thousands per ticket. Politicians fucking love me."

The page in my hand trembled. "I don't understand. What do politics have to do—" My mouth snapped shut as the dots finally came together.

But Travis took pleasure in spelling it out anyway. "Exactly. Wardens are appointed by governors, who always seem to have another campaign to fund."

"And you're paying me, too?" I couldn't afford to be shy. I had to be sure.

"Of course." Travis sniffed, straightening his tie. "This is a job, Delaney. I expect you to conduct yourself professionally, and to earn it."

"What if we break up before the tour is over?"

"Break up? That's why you're signing this contact—so that your relationship won't be subject to the unpredictable whims of emotion."

"I get that. But what if—"

He interrupted. "What if you walk away early anyway?"

I gave a shaky nod.

Travis picked up the sheaf of papers from the table. "That unfortunate circumstance is detailed in Clause Nineteen. And you'll notice that those funds will be deposited into your bank account weekly."

I read the paragraph giving a detailed formula to calculate my earnings if I quit, then looked back up at Travis. "I would make less than I do now, waitressing."

"Exactly. Therefore you have every incentive to stay. However, should *we* choose to terminate your contract, your compensation will be as described in Clause Twenty."

Turning the page, I saw that he was telling the truth. Double what I currently earned, but nowhere near what I had been promised if I made it through the entire tour.

"And if you read through Clause Twenty-Seven, you will note that rebuffing physical contact of any kind, when you are in private, is not an acceptable reason for termination."

Black-and-white proof that I wasn't selling my body along with my soul.

With that, the last of my excuses were swept aside. Finally, something I could *do* for my father. Swallowing the golf-ball-sized lump in my throat, I slumped back down into the nearest chair. "Where do I sign?"

Chapter Six

Shane

Two days after walking out on Delaney, I again claimed the empty stretch of curb in front of the water hydrant outside her apartment. The sight of her waiting for me on the sidewalk sent a wave of relief crashing into me, so hard I could feel my lungs rattling around in my chest. The entire way here I'd almost expected to discover she'd disappeared without a trace.

The vise that had compressed my chest for the past forty-eight hours finally eased as I unfolded myself from the low seat of my Ferrari, rounded the car, and tossed her suitcase into the minuscule trunk.

It felt suspiciously like the calm before the storm, the moment tinged with guilt. *What was I about to drag this sweet girl into?*

Delaney backed up against the passenger-side door, shoving

her hands into her pockets and leaning that cute ass of hers against the window. "I just want to know one thing."

Closing the trunk, I studied her warily from behind mirrored aviators. I'd never met a woman willing to settle for just one *anything*. "Okay."

"Why me?"

It wasn't the question I'd been bracing for—a repeat of the one she'd asked me in Travis's office about my interaction with the couple from the other night—but it was hardly a softball. I quirked an eyebrow. "Why not you?"

"I asked the question first."

I shrugged. "I asked second." Could play this game all damn day.

Delaney tilted her face to the sun, eyelids fluttering shut, lips moving as if she was counting to ten, or praying for patience. By the time her eyes snapped back on me, I was barely an inch away. "You can have anyone you want. I just don't understand, why do you want me?"

"Do you like ice cream?"

"What?" Her flash of exasperation was palpable.

Rocking back on my heels, I tamped down the grin threatening to swallow my face. "I said, do you like ice cream?"

Delaney's sigh was weighted with irritation. "Of course."

"Me too. It's cold, but it melts in my mouth. It's creamy and sweet." I dipped my head, murmuring low, unhurried words against Delaney's ear, my hands gently slipping up her arms. "I love ice cream. It's delicious." Wrapping my fingers around her shoulders, I pulled her off the car and into the well of my chest. Delaney's curves pressed into me, her scent—vanilla and honey—giving me a buzz. "Just like you."

Delaney shivered, taking her hands out of her pockets and

laying them flat on my chest. Needing to kiss her more than anything else in the world, I swallowed Delaney's small whimper of resistance and licked at her lower lip, her tongue slipping out to tangle with mine. She tasted minty and sweet, almost exactly like mint chocolate chip ice cream. My favorite.

Her hands balled my shirt within her tiny fists, nipples sharpening into firm peaks and pushing against my chest. With a pained groan, I dragged my mouth away from hers and pulled Delaney toward the building's door. "Let's go up to your place."

Delaney resisted. "No," she whispered, the mournful tone to her voice licking at my core.

I pulled away, needing a glimpse of the story behind that single syllable. Delaney's eyes were bright jewels caged behind inky black lashes, swirling with want. But her jaw was set, those pretty pink lips pressed into a firm line. I raked a hand through my hair, scanning the sidewalk. If we stayed out here much longer, we'd be surrounded by fans clamoring for autographs and selfies. And all I wanted was Delaney. Reaching behind her, I grabbed the door handle and jerked my chin toward the open door, cursing the hour drive to my house. *Fucking Malibu.* "Get in."

She nibbled at her lip, making no move to follow my direction. "I read the contract before I signed it."

I swallowed an impatient sigh. "Good."

"Sex is not one of my job requirements."

It took a minute for her words to make it all the way to my brain, but when they did, they sent a husky chuckle rumbling from my throat. I bent low, my lips less than an inch from the delicate shell of Delaney's ear. "No. But it could be one of the perks."

Delaney

Sliding into Shane's sleek sports car, one that probably cost more than all four years of college tuition, I tried to make sense of my body's knee-jerk reaction to Shane. He started the ignition, his mouth a taut slash below his designer shades. The vibrations from the powerful engine amplified the effect, and in the confined space, the scent of expensive leather and Shane's overwhelming maleness permeated every breath.

It was an unsettling start to my new job.

Technically, I'd begun working for Shane a couple days ago, although I hadn't seen or heard from him since the afternoon in Travis's office, not that I'd had a free moment. After signing the contract, Travis announced that Piper would be the "public relations contact person" specified within its loathsome pages. We spent six hours at an upscale boutique together, with me trying on shoes and clothes and accessories while Piper stood by my side, taking pictures with her iPhone as she ticked off various events and anticipated appearances. By the end of the day, I almost felt sorry for the girls that had been in her high school clique. Piper Hastings was relentless.

The following morning she dragged me to several Beverly Hills salons. The hair on my head had been cut and highlighted, the hair everywhere else either waxed into submission or removed entirely. That afternoon, I had a manicure, pedicure, and deep cleansing facial. And that night, Piper spent hours teaching me how to pose for the paparazzi without actually looking posed, how to deal with the fans that followed Shane's every move, and reviewing a binder of pictures of everyone that had been hired for the tour, so I would know who belonged backstage and who to keep an eye on. What I really needed was a massage, but apparently Piper couldn't squeeze that into the schedule.

Although the Nothing but Trouble tour wasn't opening for a few days, Travis insisted I move in with Shane early to give us time to work on our facade. He assured me I would have my own bedroom though.

What I hadn't tossed into the dumpster in the alley behind my building, I stowed in a small rental storage unit. I was walking into Shane's life with just one suitcase, although I probably didn't even need that much, given the full wardrobe Piper had bought for me on Rodeo Drive.

Music came through the car's speakers, but there were no words, just haunting melodies and dramatic guitar and drum solos. "Do you not like listening to other people sing?" I asked, trying to pretend I wasn't hanging out with a guy I'd crushed on since sporting braces on my teeth and a hairstyle that had made me look like a poodle.

If Shane noticed my nervousness, he didn't show it. "No. I do, actually. We were just laying down tracks for something new and I was listening to it on the way over. You don't like it?"

I shook my head. "It's beautiful." And it was. Haunting and lyrical, and a little bit sad. I wish there had been lyrics to go along with it, because somehow I knew they would tell a story I wanted to hear. Maybe even help answer why Shane had lied straight to my face in Travis's office, when he'd denied what I'd seen with my very own eyes. "Do you write all of Nothing but Trouble's songs?"

"Most of them." Shane took his eyes off the road to glance at me, and his dimple flashed. "Sometimes the words come first; sometimes the music does. It's the only thing in my life I don't try to control."

The comment touched a nerve. A few years ago I'd been slapped with the reality that everything I'd thought was under control—wasn't. And I didn't know how to fix it. There was nothing I could do to bring my mother back to life, and my father was still behind bars. Where was *my* control?

When the song ended, an indignant question shot past my lips. "So that's why you needed to hire me? Because a real girlfriend couldn't be controlled…or because you can't control yourself?"

"Believe me, Delaney. I've got all the control you'll ever need." His answer was flippant, a brush-off disguised as a sexy tease, but with one glance, I took in Shane's tight jaw, his white-knuckled grip on the car's steering wheel, the tension coiled through his muscles.

"I thought rock stars were supposed to be wild and untamed." The rebuke slipped out before I could pull it back. Shane seemed to have that effect on me.

He ran the tips of his fingers along my thigh, his touch burning through my jeans. "Is that what you were hoping for, Delaney? A wild ride, a man to tame?"

Unbidden, a stab of lust prodded my belly. From the husky timbre of his voice to the snug cut of his jeans, Shane Hawthorne was every inch a rock star. And he wanted me, Delaney Fraser. Goose bumps broke out on my forearms.

Clinging to the door handle as Shane hurtled along the Pacific Coast Highway, thoughts of what he might do to me in bed flickered as vibrantly as the ocean. I imagined his lips closing over my breasts, his fingers exploring my body. Imagined what it would feel like to have Shane Hawthorne inside of me, filling my body with his own. I turned my face to the window as my cheeks warmed, veins flooding with desire.

Shane's voice shredded the last of my nerves. "You know, I think I like your suggestion. I'll provide the wild ride, if you promise you'll try to tame me."

My head whipped back around, the twitch of Shane's lips telling me he was enjoying my discomfort.

That made one of us.

Shane

Delaney's Hello Kitty shirt may have been prophetic. She was acting like a frightened kitten, hissing and clawing. Even so, I had absolutely no doubt she'd be crawling into my lap soon, purring in pleasure from my touch.

For once, L.A.'s normally jammed roads were clear and the needle on my car's speedometer edged toward one hundred miles an hour. I made the drive often enough to do it in my sleep, and even after slowing down in the spots I knew cops often hid—not that I was worried about a ticket, I just knew better than to attract unnecessary attention from the police—we arrived at my bungalow in less than an hour.

A welcoming party of paparazzi was clustered along my street. John Legend and Chrissy Teigen lived next door, Adele was renting a house up the block, taking over the lease from the latest Real Housewife castoff, whose fortune had been about as real as her breasts, and one of my bandmates lived somewhere in between. The close proximity of other TMZ-worthy targets, as well as the stunning coastline, made this a particularly appealing spot for the photogs. "Home sweet home, baby," I murmured as the electrified gates swung inward and cameramen swarmed the car, shouting questions before I could hit the gas and flee into the sanctuary of my garage.

My sarcasm was lost on Delaney. Wide-eyed, she waited for the garage door to close before getting out of the car. "Is it always like that?"

I chuckled, retrieving her suitcase from the trunk. "No. It's usually worse." I opened the door to the house and held it for her, expecting her to be right behind me. She wasn't. Turning, I found Delaney standing halfway between me and the car, worry practically seeping from her pores. An emotion I hadn't felt in a long time, sympathy, pricked at my conscience. "I don't bite, Delaney. At least, not unless you want me to."

Her flicker of a smile warmed me, and I inclined my head toward the open door. "Come on in. We both have our own motives for being together, but it doesn't have to be a prison sentence."

The second I saw her flinch, I wanted to chase after my thoughtless words and swallow them down. "Shit. I'm sorry. Travis told me about your father. Bad choice of words."

Delaney straightened, forcing a smile onto her face. A bright, phony one I wanted to wipe off. "It's fine, really. And you're right. I'm in an oceanfront beach house, on a perfect Californian day. With the Sexiest Man Alive. What more could a girl want?"

I blinked as Delaney breezed past me, hating her flippant tone, her fake smile. Hating myself for forcing this on her. If the thought of leaving for the next six months and losing the only girl I'd felt an ounce of emotion for in—Jesus, forever—wasn't worse, I would have driven her right back to L.A. with whatever money Travis had promised. But I didn't want anyone else. I wanted Delaney, precisely because she *wasn't* like anyone else.

Jumping at the chance to make amends, or at least lighten the mood, I reached for the Harry Winston jewelry box on the console table. "Jewelry, maybe?"

This time a trickle of laughter floated my way as she walked farther into my house. "Yeah, jewelry works, too."

"Then consider today a good day," I said.

She turned, her eyes taking their time moving from my face to the box in my hands before snapping back to mine. Except that now a frown pulled at her brows, her stare overflowing with questions. Before she could ask any of them, I preempted her. "It's a prop, Delaney. The press eats shit like this up. No strings attached, I promise."

Relief lowered her shoulders, and she extended her hand. "Oh, right."

What I said was true, but it didn't take away any of my joy at watching Delaney's face light up as she tore at the ribbon, lifted the lid. Her gasp was magic, that pouty mouth I couldn't get enough of opening on an appreciative sigh. "It's beautiful, Shane," she breathed, her voice soft and dreamy.

The necklace had set me back a hundred grand, but it didn't hold a candle to the look on Delaney's face. "I'm glad you like it."

Her gaze skidded over me, a cautious kind of optimism radiating from the jumble of blue and green. "Would you put it on me?"

Adrenaline spiked as I took the box from her, the brief brush of her fingers sending nervous anticipation racing through me. How did this girl make me feel so out of my element in my own damn house? "Sure." I was off-balance. Not myself. Or at least, not like *Shane Hawthorne*. Every word, every look, every minute spent in Delaney's presence was battering the defenses I'd spent years building.

I set the box down, unclasping the thin platinum chain as Delaney turned away, lifting her hair up and presenting her naked neck to me. My knuckles brushed against her smooth skin as I lowered the necklace, my cock twitching with need. The loop caught and I stepped back, fisting my hands to keep from skimming my palms along every one of her curves.

Delaney spun around, her expression as radiant as a child who had found a puppy under the Christmas tree, delicate fingers petting the sapphire now sitting just above her breasts. "How does it look?"

Fucking amazing. "Looks great," I choked out, before reaching for her suitcase and jogging up the stairs. I was not going to tackle Delaney after giving her an expensive gift. I wanted to, badly. But I also wanted more than a thank-you fuck.

How much more?

No idea.

Just…*more.*

Delaney

I probably should have followed Shane up the stairs to wherever he was taking my suitcase, but I couldn't resist peeking at the mirror in the hall. Around my throat was the most beautiful piece of jewelry I'd ever seen, let alone received. A square sapphire glinted against my flushed skin, surrounded by a halo of tiny luminous green stones—topaz or maybe emeralds—and then encircled by a row of pavé diamonds. The chain was thin, with small floating diamonds every inch or so. Impressive enough to be a statement. But so delicate and finely wrought, it could be worn every day. It was perfect.

My eyes traveled upward, to the happy smile splitting my face in two. I barely recognized the bright-eyed girl in the mirror.

What exactly do you have to be so happy about?

She didn't answer. The grin slid off my face, guilt a powerful avalanche.

The necklace was gorgeous, but it was just another layer of paint on the facade my life had become. Another way to fool everyone into believing that I was the latest in Shane Hawthorne's long string of girlfriends. I dropped my hand, sighing as I turned away just in time to catch Shane bounding back down the stairs, a pair of loose-fitting swim trunks hanging low on his hips.

Shane's broad shoulders blocked the sun streaming through the windows that lined the back wall of his house, energy radiating from his inked skin. My pulse picked up, tongue flicking out to sweep across my lower lip. He stopped a foot away from me, distance that felt both too close and too far. "There's a red dress hanging in your closet. We have reservations at seven thirty. That okay with you?"

My mouth opened, but he turned away before I could do more than nod. A tumult of emotions swirled through my body as I watched Shane walk out the sliding glass door, winking as he closed it behind him.

That wink, that smile. *Jesus.*

Apparently I was going to have to get used to wearing damp panties.

I sucked in a deep breath, so much easier to do when he wasn't around. Breathing should be easy, automatic. But around Shane, even involuntary bodily functions required effort.

How was I not going to fall down the rabbit hole Travis and Shane had so efficiently dug for me? If I was feeling like this already, how would I feel in a week? A month? The Nothing but Trouble tour was slated to go for at least six months, longer if they added more dates.

The rational part of my brain knew I should stay as far away from Shane as I could, given that I was being paid to be, or at least appear to be, his girlfriend. That I should wall off my heart behind a high fence, topped with electrified, barbed wire. Keep my emotions under lock and key. Remain unattached.

A feat that was damn near impossible given that my heart practically leapt out of my chest every time he came close.

By the end of the tour, I'd either love him or hate him. Because right now I knew only one thing for sure. Expecting to be indifferent to Shane Hawthorne was downright foolish, if not completely stupid.

Shane Hawthorne was a means to an end for me. A way to help my father and earn enough money to pay for my degree. Relationships were messy, and I only had to look at the latest tabloid to know that celebrity relationships were downright explosive.

Maybe Shane's former *girlfriends* could handle mixing business with pleasure, but I wasn't one of them.

I couldn't afford to blow this opportunity over a ridiculous romantic squabble.

Before heading upstairs to unpack, I decided to wander around the main floor, impressed by the clean, modern aesthetic of Shane's home. The floors were a rich onyx, the walls slate gray. All the furniture was a shade of black or white. No patterns or bright colors distracted from the stunning water views, which were the highlight of every room. Walking toward the windows, I spied Shane trotting out from the flight of stairs connecting his deck to the beach. He dove into the surf using strong, measured strokes to swim beyond the waves, then changed direction, swimming in a straight line perpendicular to the beach.

I would have loved to join him, tearing through the water until my limbs burned from exhaustion, eating away at all this sexual tension I didn't know what to do with. A ragged sigh trembled through my lungs, and I ran agitated fingers through my hair, ruffling it as I climbed the flight of teak stairs. Beyond an open door, my suitcase was propped against a neatly made bed in what I assumed was my bedroom. High ceilings, light walls, beachy furniture. Nice.

The closet was already filled with clothes I had tried on the other day. Dozens of dresses in every hue of the rainbow, not to mention shirts, pants, shorts, shoes, and a vast array of lingerie. More stilettos and boots than I'd ever seen outside of a shoe store.

But there was only one red dress.

A quick glance in the bathroom told me I didn't need to bother emptying my toiletry bag. The shower and vanity were stocked better than Sephora. Soaps, moisturizers, body butters, shampoos and conditioners, gel, hair spray, self-tanner, sunscreen, and more makeup than I knew what to do with.

Not that I actually had to do much yet. Two hours before Shane picked me up, Piper had shown up at my apartment with a team of hair and makeup people and a casual outfit to wear in case anyone spotted us before our first official public outing tonight. All I really needed to do was brush my teeth and change.

After unpacking my single suitcase, I changed into the red dress. It fit, but despite multiple tugs of the zipper, I couldn't get it more than halfway up my back. Frustrated, I almost didn't notice the prickle of awareness that told me I was no longer alone.

Almost.

Shane was standing in the doorway, as devastatingly handsome as when he'd stared at me from the cover of *Rolling Stone*, looking like a young Jim Morrison, all untamed hair and probing eyes. Those same eyes were narrowed at me now, glittering with an emotion I would have given anything to understand. Anger. Excitement. Irritation. A combination of the three or something else altogether. I couldn't tell. "Is this the dress you meant?" I asked, the slight wobble in my voice betraying my nervousness.

Shane gave a curt nod, his jaw clenching. A beat passed. Then two.

I hurried to ease the tension between us by filling the silence. "Thank you, by the way. The clothes, the shoes, the room. Everything is gorgeous."

Shane's stoic veneer cracked, his voice a roughened husk. "Including you." Another pregnant pause, this one longer.

A gust of air rushed in through the open window, heavy and damp. It sent my hair swishing over my back and shoulders, the strands licking at sensitive skin. A tremor of desire swept through my bones, and I resisted an impulse to sprint across the space between us, climbing Shane's hard body until he made me forget about my best intentions.

My reckless fantasy was mirrored within Shane's eyes. I watched it play out as we stood, caught in the moment, afraid to move, afraid to speak. Barely breathing.

"You ready?" he finally said, the question a whispered growl, roughened by lust.

I bit down on my lip, not trusting myself to hold back all the things my body wanted to beg for. Instead I turned, sweeping my hair over my shoulders, the half-undone zipper obvious. My heart was pounding out of my chest, but not loudly enough to cover Shane's muffled curse as he pushed off the doorframe, his long stride swallowing the distance between us.

His breath ghosted along the back of my neck, sending tingles racing across my skin, awareness vibrating within my spine. I felt hollow and hot, my body blistered by his proximity. Kindling mere seconds from bursting into flame.

My breath caught in my throat as Shane gripped the zipper, and I desperately yearned for his touch to accompany the mournful metallic whimper of its ascent.

But no, not even the glancing caress of his fingertip.

Blinking back tears, I spun around before he stepped back.

Big mistake. Huge.

Shane reached around my waist, pulling me forward until I collided with the ridged muscles lining his abdomen. For a moment I simply stared at the wide expanse of his shoulders, at the tanned skin framed by his open collar. And then his hand moved up to my face, lifting my chin with the roughened pad of his thumb.

I swallowed thickly, tilting my head back.

My God. The beauty of Shane was almost severe, cutting into my vision as I struggled to keep my eyes open and take it all in. How was I supposed to resist him?

"Don't," I whimpered, as breathless as if I'd swum for miles.

"Don't what?" All kinds of temptation burst from those two words.

And I was so, so tempted.

But more than that—I was terrified.

Because this wasn't a wild fantasy come true. This was business. And when Shane looked at me like he wanted to eat me with a spoon, I could almost forget all about the women whose footsteps I was following. All the women who would replace me after I'd fulfilled my usefulness.

Six months, and I'd be barely a memory.

Don't make me think this is real. "Don't treat me like your whore," I said, forcing a strength to my voice I didn't know I had.

It worked though. Shane immediately dropped his hands and took a step back, a flash of hurt streaking across his face before disappearing behind a veil of disdain.

Maybe I wasn't the only one who found the truth painful.

Chapter Seven

Shane

The sight of Delaney in that dress…Jesus Fucking Christ. Not merely the color. *Her*. Delaney Fucking Fraser. So much beauty wrapped up in one lush package. The girl stole my breath, made my head spin with all kinds of wants—starting with sliding the zipper down instead of up. There had been a moment in her room when the connection between us had sparked into a live wire. A moment I'd known she was *mine*.

But she wasn't. A fact she'd proved with just one sentence.

That earlier jab about sex not being a requirement, and now calling herself my whore. There had been plenty of girls before Delaney, although she was the first to make me feel like a pimp.

Or was I a john?

Stifling a groan of frustration, I jogged downstairs and into the garage, dropping heavily behind the wheel and slamming the door. Damn Delaney. She was mistaking lust for lechery.

Once she was seated beside me. I gunned the engine, streaking out of the garage and sending paparazzi scattering like seagulls. Gnashing my teeth, I silently brooded over Delaney's indictment for the length of the ride, working my jaw as vigorously as the clutch. The nondisclosure agreement, the employment contract—those were just to minimize the amount of bullshit that landed on my plate while on tour. The physical stuff that happened between me and my *girlfriends*, that had always been voluntary.

Until my success in the music industry, I'd been a burden my whole life. Unwanted. Unneeded. I never wanted to feel that way again. Ever. If Delaney wasn't interested, my balls might be blue for the entire tour, but I sure as hell wasn't going to force anything on her.

We pulled up to the restaurant, our entrance captured dozens of times over by clicking cameras. I knew it was important that my picture appear in as many tabloids as possible before kicking off another Nothing but Trouble tour, but sometimes it was a grind.

After we were seated by the same fawning hostess who managed to slip me her number at each visit, Delaney leaned across the table, offering me a tantalizing peek at her breasts. I still wasn't quite used to the red, and the overall effect was more disconcerting than I wanted to admit. "So, am I allowed to drink on the job?" she whispered, her conspiratorial tone taking a small swipe at my temper.

Exhaling, I pushed a breath heavy with irritation from my lungs. The whole night didn't have to be ruined because of one comment. Meeting Delaney's guileless eyes, I forced a smile onto my face. "As long as I don't have to carry you out of here," I said, my pulse tripping over itself as I watched her teeth sink into the puffy sweetness of her lower lip, nibbling anxiously. On second thought, carrying Delaney in my arms, holding her close, didn't sound like a bad idea.

A grin tugged at the corners of Delaney's mouth and her lip slipped through her teeth, even pinker and puffier than before. "That wasn't my plan," she said, head tilting to the side, dark hair pooling at her shoulder. "Has that happened before, with other, umm…?"

I glanced around as her voice trailed off, spotting several people paying far too much attention to us. "Let's not talk about anyone else tonight, Delaney. Just us." My voice was a low rumble, almost indecipherable from the steady hum of the busy restaurant.

Sufficiently admonished, Delaney nodded. "Sorry."

I waved her apology away. "No worries." I'd been through awkward first dates too many times, with too many women. Real relationships, fake relationships—they both came with their share of ups and downs. But the one thing they had in common was that they always ended. For all my so-called fame and fortune, I had yet to find a woman who wanted to stay.

The waitress returned, and we placed our respective drink and dinner orders. Wine and kale salad with grilled salmon for Delaney, beer and a burger for me.

We made small talk until the food came. "Tell me about yourself," I finally prodded.

After spearing a piece of kale slathered in dressing and pecorino cheese, Delaney put it in her mouth and chewed thoughtfully. When she was done, she put her fork down and licked at her lips, blotting them with a napkin. "What do you want to know?"

"Hi. Sorry to bother you, but could we get a picture with you?" Two tweens were standing at the edge of the table, hopeful looks on their faces.

"Sure." I wrestled into a bright smile as the girl handed her phone to Delaney, practically vibrating with excitement.

"Oh my God, thank you so much. You're my favorite," she squealed, not a single breath between words.

Delaney took our picture and handed back the phone, staring at me with a mixture of awe and pity as the two kids scurried back to their parents. "That must get old."

You have no idea. In today's market, album sales were few and far between. Now it was downloads, Facebook likes, Instagram followers, and Twitter retweets. Unless you were a Kardashian and spent every day trying to "break the Internet," being a famewhore didn't necessarily translate into dollars. I built my fan base the old-fashioned way, with good music, frequent albums, and near constant touring. And treating every single fan as if they alone were personally responsible for my successful career. Throw in a few suggestive smiles and risqué comments—Shane Hawthorne was every girl's fantasy come to life. And guys wanted to be Shane Hawthorne too much to hate him, so they downloaded my songs and bought tickets to my concerts, too. Something for everyone.

"Just part of the game. And, getting back to our conversation, I want to know everything."

A confused look crossed Delaney's face before her memory kicked in. "Oh. Well, you already know the outline, right? Isn't that what Travis did, pry into my background to see if I would be suitable, then use it against me—" She stopped at my sharp look.

I took a sip of my beer. I wanted to enjoy our first full evening together. "Travis isn't here tonight. It's just you and me. And I'd really like to get to know you, Delaney."

"That's not how it seemed the other night. All you wanted was to get in my pants."

A lewd smirk took over my face as I recalled the way those body-hugging pants had shown every curve of her delectable ass. "Not gonna lie. I still do. But the rest of you is pretty appealing, too."

She stared at me for a moment, as if she was trying to read me. "What if you don't like what you find?"

"Try me," I prodded. I could feel myself growing hard again under the table. There was something about Delaney that drew me in. Something that felt familiar in a way that was almost eerie, but good, too.

Delaney leaned back in her chair and hoisted one shoulder up in a half-hearted shrug, a pause settling between us as she weighed how much she was willing to share with me. "I grew up in a small town, was raised by a typical suburban soccer mom and a dad who worked on Wall Street. He wasn't home much, but when he was, my mother had a hot meal and a cold martini waiting. Very Stepford."

I quirked a brow at the difference in our upbringing. "Sounds like the set of *Father Knows Best*."

She groaned. "That could have been our family's motto."

"I take it you didn't agree?"

"No. Things were great. No complaints." Her smile faltered. "Do you know that poem from *The Outsiders*. Nothing gold—"

"Can stay," I finished.

"Exactly." Her eyes were glassy when they broke away from mine to fidget with the silverware.

I had read *The Outsiders* in junior high, and those eight lines from Robert Frost stayed with me. Mostly because they were so true. Gold would eventually tarnish. Every bubble would burst, or at least deflate. Perfection, if it existed at all, was only fleeting. "I loved that book, and the movie, too."

"Ditto." Delaney lifted her glass to her lips, and I thought I saw the glass shaking.

"So, what happened? With your parents, I mean." I was genuinely interested in her backstory.

Delaney's shoulders tensed. "Travis didn't tell you all the grisly details?"

I shook my head. "Only a brief sketch."

Delaney met my gaze, her blue eyes as dark and deep as the ocean on a windswept, rainy day. "I was a junior in college, home for winter break. I went out to dinner with my parents. By the end of the night, my dad was in jail and my mom was in the morgue."

"Car accident?" I managed to choke out over the buzzing in my ears.

Delaney nodded, reaching for her wineglass again. Grief rolled off her in waves—an emotion I was all too familiar with. I wanted to comfort her. But I didn't know how.

Her admission felt like a kick in the gut. Could this be a coincidence, too? "I'm sorry." Travis had mentioned Delaney's father was in jail, but I hadn't asked why. I'd wanted to hear the details from Delaney herself. Now I wished I had let him tell me. I hated surprises, and this was a big one.

"Yeah, me too." She twirled her fork, looking at her salad as if she wasn't sure how it had gotten there. "So, not to change the subject or anything—" she flashed a smile that told me she was doing exactly that "—did you always want to be a musician when you grew up?"

I sucked in a breath and nodded, eager to talk about something else. Anything else. Well, almost anything. "Yes, always. How about you?"

"All I ever wanted to be was a finance geek, just like my father. That's what I've earmarked my paycheck for. I'd like to go back to school, finish what I started."

"But in the meantime, you're about to become the newest member of the Nothing but Trouble tour."

"Yes." She took the last sip of her wine. "Quite the career shift."

I took in Delaney's trembling hand, her heavy swallow. I was a means to an end for her. "Don't worry. I promise it's only temporary. You'll have your life back before you know it."

Delaney

Temporary. Fleeting. Here today, gone tomorrow. Why should Shane be any different?

Although his promise was almost laughable. The life I'd once known was gone forever. Locked up. Buried.

There was so much more to my story. So much I couldn't say that I was shaking. Talking about that night was never easy, and sticking to my script was getting tougher.

He can't know. He won't understand. No one will.

Not even someone who had stuck his neck out to prevent a drunk driving accident.

I'd tried to save someone once. It hadn't ended well.

Luckily, we were interrupted by another fan. Fans, actually. This time a group of four women, probably in their thirties, squealing over Shane more loudly than the tweens earlier. I took their picture, grateful for the interruption so I could pull myself together.

Eventually, they wobbled off in too-high heels, no doubt to update their Facebook status and profile pictures. Shane turned back to me, unfazed. "So, what kind of men do you usually date, Delaney?"

I looked down at my half-empty plate, then at the crowded restaurant. It seemed like too many heads were turned our way, although I'd never been out with anyone worth being stared at before. It was going to take some getting used to. "Are you asking me lots of questions so I won't be able to ask you any?"

Shane laughed. "Maybe."

"Well, I haven't dated any guys like you."

"Do you mean famous, or is there something unusually aggravating about me?"

"Both." A light laugh escaped my mouth, the tension in my shoulders easing. Staying mad at Shane wasn't easy. "By your standards, they've all been pretty tame."

"Any of them last long?"

I shook my head. "No, not really."

He cocked his head to the side, studying me as if I were the next course. "You're very different from Piper. You were friends in school?"

Our plates were cleared, another glass of wine set in front of me. Shane was still nursing his one beer. I took a small sip, then placed it back on the table. "Friends, no. Piper ran with a different crowd. I've known her forever—we even went to the same nursery school—but we've never been friends."

Shane nodded, looking unsurprised. "I've only met her a few times."

"She's growing on me now, I guess. But to be honest, I've spoken more to Piper in the past week than all the years we've known each other. She didn't want me at Travis's party, either. He pushed her to bring me."

A slight smirk lifted his lips. "And you couldn't wait to leave."

The sapphire at my neck sat heavily on my clavicle, despite weighing next to nothing. I stared at him, curiosity getting the better of me. "There had to be fifty women there... Why did you talk to me?"

"Why did I talk to you?" His voice dropped an octave, and he leaned forward, resting his thick forearms on the table and pinning me beneath his stare.

I crossed my arms in front of me, straightening my spine even though all I wanted to do was crawl beneath the table. "Yes. Was it some kind of setup?"

"Travis isn't my pimp." Shane's jaw clenched as he bit out the words, his eyes twin pools of molten fire.

I longed for his light, teasing tone, but I couldn't keep from digging into the strange twist my life had taken. The answers I needed were bottled up inside Shane's seductive, rock-star swagger. I pushed again. "Okay. So... Why did you talk to me, then?"

Shane

My eyes skidded over Delaney, taking in her flushed face and now naked lips, their gloss left behind on her wineglass. I continued my downward trajectory, sweeping over every inch she'd poured into the red dress still scratching at my corneas. "I don't know what kind of guys you've been with before—but I'm with you right now because I think you're fucking gorgeous. I look at your face and all I see is your perfect mouth, practically begging for me to kiss you."

Finishing the last of my beer, I set the glass on the table. "That night, I could barely tear my eyes away from your ass, like half the guys there. And as for the rest of you, no one needs to tell me that you were made for my touch, Delaney."

I kept my comments focused on Delaney's physical attributes because everything else—especially this strange connection we seemed to share—made me feel like I was unraveling from the deepest part of me. It was too big, too unruly, to cage in with mere words. But whatever it was, it had kept me from walking away.

My heart thudding, I tried to stem the tide of words leaking from my mouth, but they wouldn't stop. "I don't want you because Travis told me I should. I want you because…Goddamn it, I'd have to be dead not to." I cast impatient eyes for the waitress. "Let's get out of here."

Even though my shallow explanation barely went halfway toward answering Delaney's question, it appeared to satisfy her. She placed her balled-up napkin on her plate and waited for me to handle the bill.

Minutes later, our short walk to the car was lit by an explosion of blinding, flashing lights from the horde of paparazzi clustered outside. I opened the door for Delaney and waited for her to slide in before rounding the hood to my side, giving a casual smile and a brief wave then slamming my own door shut. Once the car was quietly purring, I shifted into gear and streaked down the road, heading for home with smooth precision.

Delaney's bare leg was an invitation I couldn't resist. Taking my hand off the gearshift, I rested my palm on the top of her thigh, running my fingertips along her silken skin. Knowing her face would be more of a distraction than was safe, I kept my eyes trained on the road, but my ears caught the quickening of her breath, the tapping of her nails on the armrests as she latched on to them, squeezing tightly.

It was delicious torture to keep from exploring farther beneath Delaney's dress, sliding beyond whatever thin barrier stood between my touch and her heat. I wanted to stroke her inner folds, sliding deeper with each pass, her desire coating my fingertips. I wanted to hear Delaney's throaty moans over the purring of the car's engine, feel her squirm in her seat, thighs inching apart to allow me better access.

I wanted a lot of things.

Hell, I wanted to know why I *wanted* her so badly.

The photographers had apparently gotten their quota of Shane Hawthorne shots for the night, and we slipped inside the iron gate, unaccompanied by the glare of flashing lights. I cut the engine and turned to face Delaney. "Got you back, safe and sound."

"Thanks for a lovely evening," she said softly.

I traced the hem of her dress, my fingertips slipping just beneath the edge. So fucking soft. "Do you want it to end?"

Delaney lifted her gaze to mine, the sapphire at her throat glinting, its color the same mysterious shade of blue as her eyes. She took her time answering, every second that passed scraping at a part of my soul she'd somehow exposed. "No."

Thank Fucking God.

I lifted my arm, threading my fingers into the hair at the base of her scalp, pulling her toward me. "Good answer." My mouth closed over hers just in time to capture her trembling sigh, tasting more than Delaney's natural sweetness and the tart remnants of wine.

If anyone could understand the crushing power a fatal accident had on the survivors, it was me. And yet innocence flavored Delaney's mouth, as if the harshness of the world we inhabited hadn't permeated her skin, like it had done to mine so many years ago. As I nibbled on her lower lip, enticing her tongue to tangle with mine, I hoped it never would. I'd been surrounded by sycophants and stalkers, jaded industry professionals and reporters pandering sleaze for so long, I'd forgotten what it was like to be around someone without feeling their ulterior motives weighing on me like a lead vest.

You'll ruin her.

The thought floated into my mind, as slippery and undeniable as Delaney's tongue in my mouth. I tried to bat it away, threading my fingers into her hair, groaning at the way she eased into my embrace and opened to my kiss.

You'll ruin her.

Why did she have to be different? What was it about Delaney that made me think she could fill the cracks in my soul, that maybe I could fill the ones in hers? She was a little bit broken too, I could tell. But her chips and cracks were drawing me in. So damn beautiful.

You'll ruin her.

Until now, Delaney had clung to the terms of the contract. If I did this, would she ever believe I hadn't hired her for sex? That I had made her my whore?

Most of the girls I'd met in L.A. wouldn't have a single objection. But Delaney… There was a fragility I'd seen in her eyes, the faintest whiff of optimism that hadn't quite been extinguished yet.

I couldn't bear to make her feel like she was just a commodity to be bought and paid for. I wouldn't.

She was gold, definitely. And I sure as hell wasn't going to be the one to tarnish her.

Pulling away, I scrubbed a hand over my face, three days' worth of whiskers abrading my palm. "I think you should go inside. Now." I actually *liked* this girl. Had spent the past few hours enjoying her company without wishing she were someone else.

Inside my brain, hope and guilt were engaged in a death match, setting my nerves on edge. I didn't know what to do with myself, and I sure as hell didn't know what to do with Delaney. Well, I knew what I *wanted* to do. I wanted to fuck her in every room, in every way. Until all the need and lust and hunger had burned off and I felt normal again.

Delaney's eyes flew open, her dilated pupils rimmed by just a crescent of fathomless blue. "But…I thought…" Her voice trailed off, confusion lingering between us.

"If you don't get out of the car this second, I'm going to yank you out of your seat and wrap your legs around me. And then I'm going to fuck you until your throat is hoarse from screaming my name." I was deliberately crude, needing to shock her into running away from me. Her dark brows lifted, but to my surprise, her expression was more intrigued than offended.

Fuck, this girl was killing me.

"Delaney, I mean it. If you don't want me to screw you in the front seat of this car like you're just another groupie…" I swallowed thickly. Damn that idea sounded good. Sucking in a breath, I forced oxygen and words out of my mouth. "Get. Out. Now."

Chapter Eight

Delaney

Blinking away the haze of lust clouding my vision, I opened the door and headed upstairs, more conflicted with each step.

A few minutes ago we'd been flying along the Pacific Coast Highway. Although Shane's eyes had remained on the road, a vein pulsed at his temple and his jaw was tight. The air between us was thick with sexual tension, palm trees just a linear blur outside my window. My world had been reduced to the throbbing between my legs, the buzzing in my veins. The man seated beside me.

When Shane put his hand on my skin, a shiver of excitement had raced up my spine, my nerves jangling loudly in my ears as he downshifted gears and navigated the exit ramp at double the posted speed limit. I'd been wondering…What would happen once we got back to his house?

Shane asked if I wanted the night to end, and my brain shouted: *Hell no!*

I tried to say yes. I really did. But my tongue refused to curl around the word. I'd become an accomplished liar over the past three years—but I couldn't bring myself to deny this one thing. The only part of my new life that felt real, so obvious it was undeniable.

I hadn't denied it, but Shane had pulled away anyway. Told me to get out.

I answered his question, and he answered mine.

Nothing was going to happen.

I wanted to scream, to yell, to pitch myself on the floor and throw a temper tantrum like an overtired two-year-old, hyped up on ice cream and cotton candy.

But I wasn't a toddler, and launching into a fit was hardly going to make me more desirable. Shane Hawthorne could have any woman he wanted, and probably already had. Despite what he'd said in the restaurant, he clearly wasn't all that interested in me.

Once upstairs, it was a relief to shed my clothes. Everything felt too tight, too restrictive. I glanced at the haphazard jumble of my clothes in the drawer, but the Hello Kitty T-shirt and faded terry pajama bottoms held no appeal. With shaking hands, I rifled through the other drawers, two of them nearly bursting with lingerie, and settled on a lavender silk negligee, the hem reaching the tops of my thighs. The material was cool, and slippery to the touch. It felt like I was wearing nothing at all.

I opened the window, hoping the crash of the waves would drown out the words still echoing in my ears. *And then I'm going to fuck you until your throat is hoarse from screaming my name.*

Do it. That's what I had wanted to say, but I couldn't manage to choke the words out. In the few seconds between twisting the handle and opening the car door, the dome light came on, catching the golden streaks in Shane's hair and turning his perfect bone structure into a work of art, an intriguing juxtaposition of clean lines and mysterious shadows. And suddenly it was as if a cord I'd never known existed had been plugged into an outlet. Sensory overload. So instead of saying what I wanted to say (two words, Delaney, was it really so hard?), I'd remained silent, scurrying upstairs like a virginal teenager. Actually, that was giving myself too much credit. Tween.

And I wasn't. A virgin, that is. Well, not technically. After my father was convicted, just before moving to California, I had too much to drink with a guy I barely liked and decided—What the hell? I was hurting so much already that I welcomed the brief stab of pain at his entry. It was over before I felt much else, and I packed my bags the next day.

I learned a lesson though. Casual sex was not my thing.

Except that there was nothing casual about Shane. And I wanted to have sex with him. Badly. At least, my body did. Even his lightest touch sent a thrill racing through my veins, tingles of pleasure prickling my skin. After three years of feeling nothing much at all, I felt alive around Shane. Every one of my senses lighting up in a frenzy, rioting for…*more.*

Shane Hawthorne was like an exotic plant in the wasteland that was my life, covered in thorns but topped by the most gorgeous flower I'd ever seen. The thorns would hurt, no doubt, but I was too distracted by the flower to care.

Somewhere in the recesses of my mind, an old-school ancestor of mine was holding up the contract I'd signed and yelling that I needed to keep my legs crossed. That a man didn't buy milk if he could get it for free. I'd always hated that expression, and I hated it even more now.

Six months. I could keep my legs crossed for six months, right?

Long enough to ensure my father was transferred to a better place. Long enough to afford tuition.

Long enough to make peace with the person I'd become. Long enough to forget about the pieces of my conscience I'd left behind.

Going back to school might not put me on an even playing field with Shane, but at least it wouldn't leave me feeling like a cliché. I'd give him all the milk he could drink... in six months.

If it turned out that one night was all Shane wanted from me, at least I wouldn't have to spend the next one hundred and seventy-nine pretending like he hadn't just stolen the only thing I still had left. My pride.

A flash of movement outside the window caught my eye—Shane. A nearly naked Shane, jogging toward the churning surf, wearing nothing but a pair of boxer briefs. Butterflies took flight inside my stomach as he dove into the dark water, treating me to one last glimpse of his perfect ass before he disappeared.

Seriously, disappeared.

The seconds ticked by, my heartbeat picking up with each one. Where was he? Panic constricted my lungs as I searched for Shane's head to break the waterline. Were there sharks out there? What if he got a leg cramp and couldn't kick? Or was caught in a riptide? Suddenly the sea didn't look so innocuous. It looked lethal.

But then... there! Shane's leonine head burst upward, much farther out than I would have liked. Did he have some kind of death wish? Or maybe I did, because I was going to give myself a heart attack just watching him. But knowing I wouldn't be able to sleep until Shane was safe, I merely wrapped a blanket around my shoulders and settled into the window seat.

Was I safe? My heart wedged inside my throat as I followed Shane's every move, watching over him like a helicopter mom at a busy playground. Which was ridiculous, of course. Logically, I knew Shane would be fine. But me, in his house, on his tour? *Fine?* Even I wasn't that naive.

Shane was doing laps now. Streaking across the ocean in a parallel line to the shore. Going just far enough to make my heart skip a beat when I lost sight of him for a few moments on either side. Then I would see the flash of an arm, glinting in the moonlight as it broke though the water before cutting into it again.

Hugging my thighs into my chest, I rested my chin on my knees. Watching. Waiting. Wishing those arms were wrapped around me.

After what felt like forever, Shane stopped swimming, his body slowly floating back toward the shore on the incoming tide. My nervousness had abated somewhat, at least while his stroke remained strong and sure, but now? Why wasn't he moving? I squinted. Shane's rock-hard abs glistened beneath the moonlight, his eyes closed. Was he breathing? From the second floor of his house, fifty feet of sand between us, I couldn't tell. My breath stuck at the back of my throat, and I pressed my forehead against the mesh window screen as Shane washed up onshore, his length half in, half out of the water. Waves crested and broke over his long legs, swirling around his head before receding. I counted the number of times. One, two, ten, eighteen. What the hell? Was he sleeping? Twenty-seven. Or hurt? Thirty-six.

Or dead?

I couldn't wait anymore.

Flinging aside the blanket, I darted downstairs and onto the deck, then down to the beach. Sand flew as I sprinted toward Shane, skinning my knees as I dove beside him, screeching his name. "Are you okay?"

Shane turned his head, eyes fluttering open, his voice husky and thick. Sleepy. "Sure. Why?"

Sure. Those four letters scratched at my already raw nerves. So blasé, like there was nothing unusual about lying in the sand immobile. "Why?" I shoved Shane's irritatingly well-defined pectoral muscles, my palm sliding along his wet skin and sending me crashing into his chest. I tried to get back up, but his arms wrapped around my back, holding me close. There was a shift in my emotions, anger and arousal sloshing inside my head, my heart, my veins. I fought for composure. "Who goes swimming in the ocean in the middle of the night? It's ridiculous."

He grinned. "Were you worried about me, Delaney?"

Hell yes, I was worried. I was scared of what Shane was doing to me, to my life. And downright terrified by my reaction to him.

"Of course not. But what if Jaws was out there, looking for a midnight snack? I don't think he'd be satisfied by a bedtime lullaby, even from you." I forced a teasing note into my tone, even though the slimmest specter of death had me panic-stricken.

"How about you? Would you be satisfied by a lullaby?" His expression was a wicked mix of levity and lewdness. "Or were you hoping for something else?"

My stomach flipped. "Like what?" I sounded breathless, needy. Must have been the light breeze carrying my words away.

Shane slid a gossamer-thin strap off my shoulder, licked at my skin. "I've been told singing is my second-best talent."

His mouth. His eyes. His words. Lust exploded in my stomach, scattering fiery debris throughout every pore, my body blazing with desire. "I'm a sucker for a good talent show."

Maybe I was a sucker, period.

A laugh rumbled out of Shane's throat, escaping into the air just moments before he pulled my head down, nipping at my lips, slipping his tongue inside my mouth. And I was lost, drowning in a churning surf of pleasure.

Shane

Something about the ocean pulled at me. It was reason I bought this house. The endlessness of its reach. The power of its currents. The briny scent of its tides. And tonight I needed the bite of its cold, bracing water.

With my hunger for Delaney surging through my veins like jet fuel, I hadn't dared follow her upstairs. Instead, I'd shucked off my clothes on the deck and headed straight for the beach, my feet sinking into sand that became more compressed the closer I got to the ocean.

The cold water stung my skin, a welcome distraction from my tumultuous thoughts. I paddled out past the waves, pushing myself to stroke harder, move faster. I found a rhythm and clung to it, focusing only on my form and power and breaths. Not until my arms and legs were quivering with exhaustion did I stop, flipping onto my back. The current carried me to shore, water lapping at my legs as a light breeze cooled my skin. For the first time all day, maybe all week, I let myself relax, get out of my own head. Lingering there, I felt at peace. Finally.

It was shattered in an instant.

The sight of Delaney flying across the sand, breasts bouncing beneath a wisp of silk and lace, nipples poking at the nearly translucent material, sent the sharp knife of desire plunging right back into my gut, slashing at my self-control.

I shouldn't want Delaney this much. Hell, I shouldn't want anyone this much. Especially not someone who didn't want me back.

Hadn't I learned the hard way that caring too deeply—about anyone—was the surest path to heartbreak? I swatted at my conscience before I could take a trip down memory lane I wasn't ready for. Not that I hadn't taken it hundreds, no—thousands—of times. But only buffered by a haze of drugs and alcohol to smooth the journey.

What was it about Delaney that got under my skin? And clearly I'd gotten under hers, too, if the worried look on her face was anything to go by. I wanted to fill her up with everything I had. Sing her a lullaby, too. Cuddle Delaney in my arms and croon a verse into her ear, tease her with kisses until she was writhing within my arms.

My mouth was good for more than just singing, although it had been ages since I'd been with someone who made me want to put in the effort. But right now, with Delaney, I wanted to pull out every stop I knew. Learn a few new ones, too, just for her.

My name scraped from her throat, raw need pulsing from the single syllable, chipping away at the restraint I bound myself in.

And then she was beside me, crashing into me, full breasts pushing against my chest, the ends of her hair swishing against my skin. Tempting as a goddamn siren.

A knot of desire wrapped around my lungs, squeezing tight. I slid my palms along the curve of Delaney's back, following the ridged track of her spine to her neck, pressing my thumb along the frantic pulse heaving beneath her skin. Lust spiked, seeping into my pores, filling my lungs.

I should let her go.

Instead, my hold tightened.

I *had* let her go, told her exactly what would happen if she stayed beside me for even a second longer. She'd listened to me, gone upstairs, hopefully locked her door.

But now she was back. So close my heart lurched, thundering against my rib cage in an attempt to race with hers. More beauty heaped on her than any one person deserved. Want shimmering from her eyes like gasoline on the surface of a puddle.

Waiting for a flame.

Or was the emotion I saw just a reflection of mine? God knows I wanted her enough for the both of us.

I rolled, taking Delaney with me. Pressing my elbows into the sand, I cradled her head in my hands as I traced a path down her neck, her pulse fluttering beneath my tongue. She whimpered, her head rocking back as she arched her spine, pressing into me. With a groan, I pulled the tiny excuse for pajamas from Delaney's torso, holding her wrists over her head as I feasted on her breasts, flicking pale-pink nipples with my tongue, giving each needy peak the attention it deserved. Perfect handfuls, they vibrated with longing.

"Wait, Shane." Her voice was a quivering plea. "Should we...here?"

"No," I growled. "But I don't care." Delaney's skin was slick from the humid air, and deliciously salty against my tongue. I wedged a knee between her legs, rubbing my shaft against her thigh. Still a few inches from where I really wanted to be.

Eliminating the sliver of lace between Delaney's thighs with a quick flick of my wrist, I nudged her legs farther apart, moving between them as I kissed my way down her rib cage, the delicate slope of her belly, my tongue slipping into the shallow well of her belly button. Delaney squealed, laughter hiccupping from her throat. Ticklish. I filed the bit of knowledge away for another time, too intent on a different destination.

Releasing Delaney's wrists, I rubbed my chin against the smooth perfection of her inner thigh, intent on capturing the sweetness waiting for me. Barely a breath away, Delaney's fingers plowed into my scalp, tugging at my hair. "Shane," she called out, my name laced with a skittish urgency I couldn't ignore.

I lifted my face to hers, my dick so fucking hard it was almost unbearable. Forcing a calm I didn't feel, I sucked her earlobe into my mouth, murmuring in a low growl, "Yes, Delaney."

"I don't mean to, ummm, oh God." Her fingers gripped my shoulders as a tremble shook her lithe frame. "That thing you're about to do…"

"Mmmm-hmmm." Her heat tempted me, my shaft pointing like an arrow to its desired destination.

She sucked on her lower lip. "Can you ummm…not."

A trickle of unease frayed the edges of my hunger. I tensed, pulling back to take in her face. "No?"

Delaney blinked, her eyes huge pools of ink in her heart-shaped face. She wrapped her legs around my hips, hooking her ankles together and pulling me toward her heat. "I want you inside of me."

That was my plan, too, although I'd intended to make her come first. I swore softly. Delaney was blowing my best intentions to bits. "You know, there's no rush. We can do both," I said, staring down at her, trying to gauge her hesitation. She trembled again, the curve of her fingernails pricking my skin as a fat tear slid down her cheekbone. *What the hell?* "Delaney, are you crying?"

Chapter Nine

Delaney

*Y*es. "No." I wiped at my cheek. *What is wrong with me?* I wanted this. Wanted *him*.

That fucking contract—what did words matter when the man above me was so real, our attraction to each other so undeniable? What would it be like to give myself over to his kisses, let his touch take me to a place I'd never known? A place that was ours alone, at least for a little while. Heaven, surely.

Maybe our relationship wouldn't be marked by volatility and the six months would pass smoothly.

Yeah, right. Because my life had been smooth sailing so far.

Shane lifted a hand to my face, his thumb tracing the wet smear. "Why are you crying?"

I sniffed. "I'm not. Really," I said, denying the obvious.

This wasn't some drunken hookup, I chided myself. This was

a scene out of a romance novel. Midnight in Malibu, two nearly naked bodies in the sand, pounded by a restless surf. With *Shane Hawthorne*. It didn't get better than this.

I wrapped my fingers around Shane's shoulders, intensity thrumming beneath his warm skin, pulling him toward me.

And yet...wasn't this what I'd done once before—slip beneath a man I barely knew? Who barely knew me?

No love, just lust.

I'd run away from him the very next morning.

If I ran from Shane, I stood to lose everything that was finally within reach.

The circumstances might be different tonight, but the basic truth of it was still the same. I regretted my casual decision back then, and some instinct was telling me not to do it again. That I wouldn't be able to handle the consequences.

Not that Shane was cooperating. His muscles were corded tightly beneath my hands, rigid and unmoving. Embarrassed, I let go, turning my face to the side to evade his searching gaze. The dark dome above us was littered with stars, my eyes bouncing from one to the other as I wondered how to extricate myself from the mess I'd created.

To my surprise, escape came easily. Shane rolled off me, scrubbing a palm over his face, his gruff curse carried away on the breeze as he reached for my discarded negligee and slipped it over my head. His hands came up to my face, palms resting gently on my cheeks. "I'm sorry, Delaney," he whispered, the moonlight lending his eyes an almost magical gleam. But then they shuttered closed, and he dropped a kiss on my forehead, so lightly it was barely a breath, before getting to his feet and extending his hand to me.

Quickly smoothing down the silk, I let Shane pull me up and

we turned back toward the house, our footsteps flinging loose sand behind us. It took everything I had not to drop to my knees and howl at the moon. I wanted the magic back. Even though I'd been the one to destroy it.

A moment later I really was on my knees, howling not at the moon but at the lancing pain in my left foot.

Shane was beside me in an instant, inspecting my throbbing sole. "It hurts," I gritted out.

Gentle fingers wrapped around my ankle, lifting my foot toward the light and turning narrowed eyes to inspect the wound. "Glass," he pronounced, sweeping me into his arms as if I weighed next to nothing and carrying me toward the house. I dropped my head into the nook between his neck and shoulder, my foot suddenly much more bearable.

"Assholes," Shane muttered, his voice abrading my skin like gravel, the vehemence in his tone rumbling through his chest.

"Hmmm?" I picked my head up, studying the interplay of shadow and light on his face. Chiseled and yet still rugged. Darkly handsome but with a little pretty boy thrown in. A pang of desire shivered through me.

Shane jerked the sliding glass door open, stepping inside and shoving it closed so hard it bounced off the doorjamb and receded to the other side. "The jerkoffs who drink out of glass bottles on the beach—and then leave their brokens or empties for anyone to step on."

Depositing me on the kitchen counter, Shane disappeared into the mudroom, returning with a first aid box in his hand. Brandishing a set of tweezers, he extracted the innocuous-looking shard of brown glass, not much bigger than a fingertip. After cleaning the wound, he smeared a dab of antiseptic ointment on a Band-Aid and gently smoothed the sticky tabs across my sole.

"Good as new," he said, a tight smile barely stretching his lips.

"Thanks." I leaned into Shane's extended arms, sliding against his torso until my good foot hit the ground, managing to hobble a few yards before Shane's groan had the hair at the back of my neck standing on end.

In the next instant, I was swept back into his arms, nervous hope threading through my veins with each step as Shane ascended the stairs. He kicked open the door to my bedroom and deposited me softly in the center of the mattress.

Did he hesitate as he was pulling away from me, or was I just imagining it?

"Good night, Delaney." There was a flicker in Shane's eyes, a brief flash of an emotion I knew all too well. Regret.

A dozen different "sorry's" clogged my throat as Shane backed out of the room, a stiff mask settling onto his features.

The soft *click* of the door rebounded inside my chest like a sonic boom.

I glared longingly at the white rectangular plane, willing it to open. But it remained stubbornly closed, the modern chrome handle perfectly still.

Because Shane had closed it. And even though it was my fault, I ached for the feel of his arms around me, the heat of his shoulder warming my cheek.

I should be grateful. After all, I was the one who froze up. Shane was just reacting to my tears. A rueful laugh gurgled from my throat. Barely a few hours ago I had accused him of treating me like a whore. Meanwhile, I was the one who had begged him to fuck me, out in the open, where anyone could see us. But when he realized I wasn't ready, he'd apologized to *me*.

I'd been running hot and cold since we met, sending mixed signals at every turn. The only one of us due an apology was Shane.

I was worse than a groupie. I was an idiot. A tease. A prude. After tonight, he'd be crazy to still want me.

A salty breeze blew in from the open window, and my nipples puckered beneath the thin negligee. Remembering the feel of Shane's mouth on my breast, a stab of longing twisted in my stomach.

My head knew I wasn't ready to sleep with Shane yet, that it was a terrible idea, but unfortunately my body hadn't gotten the memo. With a mortified groan, I fell back on the mattress, wondering if Shane was already on the phone with Travis, telling him to fire me.

Shane

I'm such an asshole.

Of course Delaney had been crying. All she'd done was come out to check on me, and I'd mistaken her consideration for consent. She probably felt like she was being assaulted.

Had I listened to her at all? Delaney had been perfectly clear: she intended to abide by the terms of the contract, but nothing more. And hell, I'd been pushing for *more*.

Even though those terms in no way required her to do much beyond smile pretty for the cameras, act like an adoring girlfriend if anyone was watching, and keep me from slipping back into bad habits, Delaney obviously believed they were just an excuse to lure her into a relationship where I held all the cards and she held none.

After the way I'd acted on the beach, who could blame her?

I shook my head, disgusted with myself. If tonight's goal had been to prove our contract was just a trick to get her naked…I'd done one hell of a job.

I leaned back against her door, so shaken by the last few hours I was practically vibrating. It had been a decade since I'd felt this raw. Down on the beach, when I thought we'd been diving into something real, Delaney had felt baited. Maybe even blackmailed. By me. Her tears were because of me.

Because I was an inconsiderate, self-centered asshole.

And she was right. I was every one of those things, and a hell of a lot more. But I knew, deep down, it was a good thing, too, because a weaker man would have stayed down in the gutter I came up from. If I'd been better at considering other people's feelings, I might even be in jail. But I had put myself first and escaped from the hellhole I was raised in, came to California, and threw myself into music. Into the crazy, chaotic, completely superficial lifestyle that went along with it. So yeah—I was an asshole.

And I'd never felt ashamed of it. Until now. Until Delaney.

Fuck.

Pushing off her door, I headed into my room to shower off the salt and sand. And the shame.

Not long ago I'd have brought a bottle into the glass enclosure. Hell, I had carried a bottle, or if I was trying to be discreet, a flask, everywhere I went. The accident had sent me tumbling so far down a vortex of anger and depression it was a miracle I'd managed to climb out alive. But with Travis's help, and support from the guys in my band, I did. These days I had to face everything—good, bad, hideous—head-on. And it sucked.

On the beach, kissing Delaney, breathing in her soft sighs,

tasting her salt-slick skin…I'd felt whole. Happy, even. I'd held her as if she was worth living for, and in my life, there was precious little that was. Fame? Money? If I died, would anyone miss me?

Travis?

Maybe.

The guys of Nothing but Trouble?

Okay, yeah. They would, for a little while. But not one of us had had an easy start in life. We were fighters. It was what made us such a strong band. We were just as willing to fight for each other as against any outside threat. My absence would be noticed, but Landon, Jett, and Dax—they would move on. I would be replaced.

I barely knew Delaney. She barely knew me. It was crazy. But crazy good. For a little while, it had been just me and her. Just us, and a deserted, dark beach. And the thready, seductive connection linking us together. Both of our lives had been shattered by a fatal accident. Both of us forced to pick up the pieces and move on, even though we were still reeling.

That was why I had ripped the spark plug out of that jerkoff's car. Because if I'd let him kill someone that night, it would have left another black mark on a soul—my soul—that was already so dark, it might not matter. And that freaked me the fuck out.

Delaney didn't realize how much we had in common. It was a secret I couldn't tell her, couldn't tell anyone. A secret I'd woven into the lyrics of a song I couldn't bear to sing anymore. The song Delaney belted out as if it were her own. But there was a huge difference between Delaney and me.

She hadn't been responsible for her accident.

She hadn't sent anyone to an early, undeserved grave.

She wasn't a killer.

Until tonight, I hadn't known what it was like to feel caught up in someone else's eyes, to be more buzzed from a smile than from a drink. I wasn't a fool. I didn't love Delaney. But with her, I could see a flickering thread of possibility.

I just didn't know whether to cut it with the nearest knife, or unravel it slowly, following wherever it led.

It had been the single best hour of my life. Even though it didn't end the way I had wanted it to, buried in Delaney's sweet center, her legs wrapped around me, the taste of her on my tongue, as we galloped toward nirvana together.

If I thought Delaney was just playing hard to get, I'd call Travis and have her removed from my house, my tour, my life.

But I knew better. Delaney's trembling chin, that single tear she thought I wouldn't notice, the way she'd asked me to fuck her, like she was offering herself up as some kind of sacrificial lamb…I shuddered, pressing my palms against my face. *What was I thinking?*

I wasn't. At least, not with the right head. While Delaney's luscious body had been beneath mine, I didn't give a shit about contracts or concerts, promises or prisons.

That innocence that flavored her lips, I was bleeding it dry with every kiss.

An angry shout wrenched free of my throat as I scrubbed at my hair, lathering the shampoo into a frenzy. Delaney's words drilled holes through my eardrums, piercing skin and skull to bounce around my brain. She wasn't playing hard to get. She wasn't playing at all.

Maybe that was the problem. I was a player. In life, onstage, everywhere. And Delaney wasn't. Delaney was a sweet little thing who'd gotten a bad deal.

We were going to be inseparable for the next hundred and

eighty days, give or take, and I'd already stolen all her cards. Would she like me any better by the end?

Probably not.

Some copy editor looking to boost magazine sales had proclaimed me the King of Rock.

Hardly.

I was a criminal. A clown. A pretender to the throne.

And maybe the reason for Delaney's tears was that she'd seen right through me, instinctively known the chaos and ruin I'd caused. Wanted no part of it. No part of *me*.

The words to a song I hadn't written yet coiled themselves around my chest, the rhythm of my pulse a low, ominous beat I could already see expressed as notes on a chord chart. I slammed the chrome knob back into the tiled wall, shutting off the water with more violence than was necessary. Wrapping a towel around my waist, I held my breath as I passed Delaney's door like it was a cemetery, padding lightly downstairs and heading for the small sound room I'd built into the lower level of my house. Music was the one thing that kept me steady, the one place I could unload every crazy, shitty, wonderful, awful thought cluttering my mind. Thoughts became words, words became lyrics. And in the right combination, lyrics became entire songs.

I needed a notebook and a guitar. Fast, before the melody in my head faded and the words slid just beyond reach. It wasn't often that a song ripped through my mind anymore, needing to be written down, to be heard. Years ago they had come easily, usually with the first few drinks of the night. Or morning. Gritty reflections of my reality echoed from every syllable, and the rawness of those early songs is what had propelled Nothing but Trouble to stardom.

Whatever had passed between me and Delaney would still be there in the morning. Or maybe it wouldn't. Tonight I would write about it and tomorrow I would face it.

I wish I knew what I should do about it.

But I didn't. I didn't have a fucking clue.

Chapter Ten

Delaney

Pulling the covers over my head, I stubbornly ignored the sound of a restless surf beating against the Pacific coastline. And the knocking on my door.

Instead I clung to the remnants of sleep, desperate to escape back into my unconscious, where I'd been wrapped in Shane's arms, his breaths filling my ears, his mouth blazing a trail of fire across my skin.

At some point during my mostly sleepless night, I'd finally realized the flickering thread of possibility I felt with Shane meant more to me than blindly following a set of rules I'd had no part in making. The next six months were going to pass regardless of whether I spent my nights with Shane or not. I could take a chance and make the most of our time together. Or not, and guarantee that I would be miserable.

It was a gamble, but if Shane Hawthorne wasn't worth the risk, no one was.

My epiphany may have come too late though. Outside of this cozy cocoon, my reality was filled with grief and guilt. And so many regrets. What if Shane became one of them?

"Delaney." The door swung forward on silent hinges, Shane's head appearing within the opening. "You awake?" he asked in an exaggerated whisper.

I grudgingly opened one eye, squinting against the brightness of the California morning sun. I'd forgotten to close the shades last night. *No.* "Yes."

I might be awake, but even my reality felt like a dream.

"Good morning." Shane's cheerful tone caught me by surprise, given the way last night had ended. Swim trunks were riding low on Shane's lean hips, droplets of salt water still clinging to his well-defined abs.

I dragged my gaze back to his face, noticing his thick tangle of hair was slicked back and still dripping. No man should be so good-looking. "You've been for a swim already?"

"It's almost ten."

Working in a restaurant, I'd become accustomed to keeping late hours, usually sleeping until eleven unless I was working the lunch shift. Since he hadn't fired me yet, Shane was technically still my boss. A boss with amber eyes and lashes most girls would kill for. And, of course, those abs.

I fought for something to say, some way to be useful. "Can I get you something?" *Me, maybe?* His presence changed the energy in the room, added a boost of intensity to the ocean breeze coming through the open window. Every part of me wished he would come closer, following that strangely undeniable thread between us, until he crawled into bed with me.

Butterflies dipped and swirled inside my stomach, their eager wings making me tingle in places I didn't know I had. I would have given anything to capture every last one of them in a net and release them from the balcony, watch them fly far, far away. Because I didn't want to feel this way. Off-balance and excited. Nervous and insecure. Invigorated by a man whose presence in my life was only temporary.

"What were you thinking of?" On its face, the question was perfectly innocuous. Shane's full lips, one corner lifted by a lop-sided smile, eyes shining with mischief, added another layer of meaning. I wanted to raise the covers in invitation, but I hadn't even brushed my teeth yet, and there was the little matter of crying in his arms just last night.

"Breakfast?" I squeaked, my stomach surprising me with a quiet rumble.

Shane's grin dropped, and he pushed off the doorjamb. "Actually, I'm already late for a meeting. How's your foot?"

My foot? "Oh." I'd forgotten all about it. Sitting up, I swung my legs over the edge of the mattress and stood up gingerly. I felt a little twinge, but that was all. "Actually, not bad." I pivoted, facing toward Shane. "I must have had a pretty great nurse."

Shane's eyes traveled from my foot, up my leg, landing on my skimpy excuse for pajamas. "Great," he bit out, the possibility of dialogue held in check by a clenched jaw. "I'll be back in a few hours. You should check your e-mail. Piper sent us details for a few appearances tonight."

"Oh, okay. Thanks." Shane left, and I sat back down, deflated. I should have been celebrating—I hadn't been fired. But I wasn't.

I didn't need to hear his car roar out of the driveway to know he was gone. As I crawled back beneath the covers, Shane's absence gaped as widely as a black hole. I wasn't hungry anymore. Instead I craved another chance, or maybe a do-over.

If my mother were still alive, I'd be on the phone with her already. Growing up, I'd always been more of a daddy's girl, but when I left home, I finally realized how much I'd relied on her as a sounding board for all my decisions. Rather than tell me what I *should* do, she'd helped me drill down to the core of what I really wanted all along. My mother had a way of making answers seem simple, even obvious.

I would have given anything for just one conversation with her right now.

I missed her so much. And I had no one to blame but myself.

A seagull landed on the railing outside my window, its gray beak tapping against the mesh screen.

"Go away," I mumbled.

It squawked, fluttering its wings. Another bird flew down, and I watched as they preened at each other, making enough noise to have an entire conversation. After a few minutes, they flew off together, soaring and dipping. Free.

Unlike my father.

I couldn't destroy my only chance of helping the one parent I had left.

With a groan, I flung off the covers. Whatever Shane's motives, I had a job to do. Wallowing in regrets was a luxury I couldn't afford.

I picked up my phone from the nightstand. It was dead, but once I plugged it into the charger, it came to life, beeping and buzzing like an epileptic with Tourette's. I didn't even have a chance to see what had it so agitated before it started ringing. "Hey, Piper."

"Oh. My. God. You are fucking brilliant. I can't believe I ever doubted you!"

I flinched, holding the phone away from my ear. "The pictures turned out okay?" I asked, assuming she was talking about my first experience with the paparazzi in front of the restaurant. Piper had spent nearly an hour teaching me how to stand, how to smile, the angle to tilt my head, what to do with my hands. Getting a good shot was not nearly as effortless as it looked.

"Okay? They are amazing. You in that little, barely there nightie and Shane, bare-chested, with you in his arms. Wow. Ah-may-zing!"

I clutched the phone to my ear, feeling light-headed. "Wait, what? I meant from the restaurant. What photos are you—"

"The ones from the beach. Shane's publicist must have had someone out there. Fucking brilliant, if you ask me."

A chill swept over my shoulders, and I gathered the sheet to my chest. I didn't want to continue this conversation. Truthfully, I never wanted to speak to her or Travis or Shane ever again.

Just another photo op.

We'd been a hair's breadth away from making love. Was it all just a ploy, a PR stunt? Had Shane let me run to him, roll naked in the sand with him, knowing someone was capturing every passionate moment on film? Had it all been staged to give the tabloids a few steamy photos?

With a sickening lurch, I wondered if Shane had been hoping for a sex tape.

What have I gotten myself into?

Shane

"Nice job, Shane." Travis's voice boomed through my car's Bose speakers. "You two are killing it."

I winced, grunting out a mangled, "Thanks."

"No, really. I mean, those shots on the beach. Fucking price-less."

The blood drained from my head, my vision going gray at the edges. "What shots? We didn't take any photographs on the beach."

But I knew.

I knew.

"Ha," Travis scoffed, thinking I was kidding.

I wasn't.

"Just when I think you're getting too comfortable, resting on your laurels, you prove me wrong and remind me that you're still a hustler at heart." The pride seeping from his voice slipped into my bloodstream, becoming a curdled mass in the pit of my stomach. Bitterness rose, coating my throat, burning my tongue.

Fuck. How could I have been so stupid? Just because we didn't see the camera didn't mean our every move wasn't being captured on film and sold to the highest bidder. I gripped the steering wheel, knuckles going white as I remembered exactly what we'd been doing on the beach. And how little we'd been wearing.

I swiped at my mouth with the back of my hand, as if I could erase the sour taste. It didn't help.

I was used to the circus my life had become, but Delaney wasn't. Should I call her? Warn her? I swore again, out loud this time, but Travis was too busy prattling on about hits and views to notice. I wasn't listening to him. Eventually he segued to a few new offers that had come in, and plans for a charity concert. I did my best to tune back in, but all I could think about was Delaney.

Maybe I was taking the easy way out, but the memory of her all sleepy and sweet...I wanted to believe she'd slipped back under the covers and was temporarily unaware of the bullshit being thrown her way because of me.

Eventually, I pulled into the parking lot of my label's downtown office and cut off Travis midsentence—the only satisfying moment of our entire conversation. I spent the next few hours going through the motions, agreeing to things I normally would have fought, flicking a dismissive glance over the final list of roadies that had signed on with the tour when I normally lingered over every name. Greenlighting changes to the set list without any consideration. Not that I didn't care. I just couldn't focus.

Because my head was back at the beach house. With Delaney.

"Shane!"

I jerked, swiveling my head toward whoever had pelted my name from across the room. Zeroing in on my target. "Landon, what the fuck?"

My bandmate tossed a rueful laugh. "What's up with you, man? I called your name three times."

I glanced around at the other guys in the room, their nods confirming Landon's charge. "Sorry." We were in a lounge just outside one of our label's in-house recording studios, going over a few last-minute details for the tour and deciding which single to drop next. I had yet to say a word.

Several couches were scattered around the room, and I'd claimed one of them an hour ago, sprawling across it with my

boots hanging off the side, my muddled head flopped on a cush-
ion. Landon was leaning against a wall as if he alone were holding it up, a scowl on his face and what looked like a blond rat's
nest on his head. "What the fuck's going on? You checked out,
or what?"

I heaved myself upright. "No, I'm good."

He shook his head, looking at everyone but me. "Boy look
good to you?" A chorus of *no*'s echoed from my bandmates, our
tour coordinator, and a pair of industry execs. Travis had arrived a few minutes ago, but he was too busy thumb-fucking his
phone to pay any attention.

Landon and I went way back, to when I first showed up in
L.A., signing up for open-mic nights and looking for anyone
with a guitar or a set of drums to jam with. We were the two
original members of Nothing but Trouble, had spent more than
ten years making ourselves worthy of the name.

"I'm fine," I insisted. "Just want to get on the road already."

He knew better than to take me at my word. "This have
anything to do with those pics popping up on my phone all
morning? The ones of you and the new girl?"

"Yeah, how's the new girl?" Jett piped up. If he weren't such
a damn good bass player I would have kicked him out a dozen
times over. The newest member of Nothing but Trouble, Jett
knew just enough about my past to make me a little uncomfortable. Things I'd told him when we'd partied together and I was
half out of my mind. Reason number three hundred sixty-eight
why I could never go back to my boozing, snorting, whoring
ways. I had too damn much to lose to go spilling secrets that
needed to stay buried.

But not a single detail had emerged in the press, and I knew
they wouldn't. Jett might be a wiseass with no filter, but he'd never

be some gossip hound's unnamed source. And Dax barely said a word to anyone, even the chicks pawing him at every opportunity. Especially the chicks pawing him at every opportunity.

Nothing but Trouble was a dysfunctional family, but I was damn grateful for every one of them.

"She has a name." One I didn't offer. "And she's fine. Are we done here?"

No one looked in any hurry to leave. Landon jerked his head to the recording studio on the other side of the clear glass. "Wanna dick around for a little bit?"

I sure as hell needed something to do with my dick. "Yeah."

The four of us strutted out into the next room, one of the execs calling in a producer in case we came up with something worth recording. I reached into my pocket, where I'd stuffed a piece of paper before leaving my house.

Landon eyed the crumpled page, covered in my chicken scratch. "New?"

"Yeah."

He reached out a hand from behind his drum kit, and I handed it over reluctantly, knowing the mess of emotions I'd laid bare, an alphabetic riot of love and hate and need and want. Of guilt and pain and hope and fear. My heart and head in black ink on a yellow legal pad, buzzing as loudly as any honeybee. Because that was what I was after. Honey. Sweetness. Delaney.

Except Delaney wasn't a dainty sprinkle of pollen. No. She was an iceberg lurking beneath a smooth sea, her long legs and lush curves and guileless face hiding a danger that would gouge the most vulnerable parts of me. Especially the parts I'd long considered invulnerable.

Landon's eyes, as black as pitch, took everything in, eyebrows lifting as he deciphered the words I'd bled onto each line.

I shouldn't have looked in on her this morning. Should have left a note or sent a text and headed out to deal with whatever shit I needed to deal with. Because everything I'd written last night, everything Landon was skimming, his head nodding to a beat only he could hear right now but that soon would emerge fully formed from his drums, was about me. And Delaney. And how Delaney affected me.

This morning, just once glance at her still sleepy eyes, mounds of dark hair glinting against pale wrists as she batted wayward strands off her face, and I realized it wasn't only about *me* anymore. Delaney was real. And no matter how strong my armor, there was a weak spot just her size. A hole she'd already found, slipping inside with her wide-eyed, fish-out-of-water eyes. I scared her, obviously, but there was a pulse of desire that hummed beneath her skin whenever she came near me, the same pulse that hammered in my ears at the sound of her voice.

Desire she was determined to not give in to. Knowing her reasons, I couldn't blame her.

Landon handed back the single sheet. "This is deep, man."

"Worth putting down on tracks?" There was a thread of insecurity woven through my words, and I wanted to rip it out. Music was my constant, the one thing I could count on. And somehow Delaney was making me doubt even that.

But Landon was already distracted by the thrill of a new song. "Fuck, yeah. You haven't written lyrics like these since—"

Shoulda been me.

I interrupted, not needing the confirmation. "Yeah, I know."

He held my gaze a beat longer than was necessary, then picked up his custom-made, white oak drumsticks. "Let's do it."

Last night was in the past. Exactly where it belonged.

But my song would bring it to life, keep it in the present.

Maybe not today, but eventually we would record it. Release it. Anyone would be able to listen to it anytime they wanted. Sure, the details were obscured behind soulful lyrics, melodic verses. But if they listened closely enough, they would know. I was an asshole. Damaged as hell and a danger to anyone crazy enough to get too close to me. Delaney was already close, and bound by a contemptible contract. I might ruin her, climb high with her in my arms, not even realizing we were on a pyre until it was raging all around us.

I would destroy her.

But maybe, just maybe…she could *save* me.

It had been done before, right? I mean, billions of people believed they were *saved*.

I'd sat right beside my father in church for more Sundays than I could count, reading the prayer book he would hold open for me with one hand while his other curled paternally around my small shoulder. And then we'd go home and those hands would do other things. Punching, slapping. He'd happily beat the shit out of me, my brother, and especially my mother, invoking the Lord with each bone-crushing blow.

I wasn't looking for some invisible force to save my soul.

But Delaney…I'd be damned if I didn't feel salvation every time I looked in her eyes.

Chapter Eleven

Delaney

Stay close to me," Shane ordered as the door to the limousine was pulled open from the outside. It was one of the few sentences that had passed his lips since he'd left me alone in his beach house two days ago. We'd barely spent any time together, at least not alone, since then. During press events I merely had to smile and look adoringly at Shane as he fielded questions. And apparently my presence wasn't needed when Shane was in the recording studio, which was where he'd spent most of the past forty-eight hours, working on a new song. Or at least that's what he'd told me. I'd even called Travis to be sure, worried that I wasn't holding up my end of the deal by reading romance novels on Shane's deck. He'd said Shane was well taken care of and that I could go back to my books.

Truthfully, I'd been glad. My feelings about him, about what

we'd almost done, and those intimate pictures were so conflicted. But my brief break was over. The Nothing but Trouble
world tour was kicking off tonight, and getting from the limo
into the arena had been an eye-opening experience. By the time
we pulled into the underground parking garage, the venue was
already overflowing with reporters, paparazzi, overzealous fans,
and not enough security to effectively control them all.

I followed Shane out of the car, blinded by camera flashes and
hemmed in on all sides. People were touching me, shouting at
me. "Shane!" I yelled, as someone came between us. His grip was
tight on my hand, not letting go as he pushed the interloper out
of our way. A panicked, claustrophobic feeling compressed my
chest, and I could barely breathe until we were safely out of the
public corridor and ensconced in a private suite.

Shane's arm wrapped around me as Lynne, the Nothing but
Trouble tour coordinator, shut the door behind her and immediately began spewing details of the meet-and-greet Shane was
expected at in a few minutes. She'd been waiting in the limo
when it arrived to pick us up from Shane's house and had barely
glanced at me since being introduced. No doubt Lynne knew I
was just one in a long line of many.

"Delaney?" Shane's voice cut through the noise cluttering my
mind.

"Hmm?" I looked up, surprised to see we were actually alone.

His eyes searched mine, a worried frown twisting his brow.
"Sorry about almost losing you back there."

Every pore in my body was clogged with anxiety. "That was
scary, Shane. I didn't like it."

Shane's shoulders lifted in an unrepentant shrug. "Unfortunately, it comes with the territory. You'll get used to it eventually."

I shook my head, thinking of everything that came with being thrust into Shane Hawthorne's world. Sleazy lawyers bearing ridiculous contracts, chasing photo ops yet running from the paparazzi. Private moments exposed for all the world to see. "No," I snapped. "I don't want to."

He curled a hand around my neck, strong fingers kneading the tense sinews connecting my shoulder blades. "Later, I'll give you a few lessons on dealing with the crowds, teach you some self-defense moves."

Despite the massage, I pressed my lips together, skepticism rising inside me like an overfilled pot on high heat. "I'm beginning to think you're the one I need to defend myself against."

One look at Shane's face and I wanted to race after my thoughtless words and stuff them back into my mouth, swallow them down like the toxic pills they were. Hurt trekked across his perfect features before he could rearrange his expression into the nonchalant, too-cool rock-star facade he wore too well. "Crap. I'm sorry. I didn't mean that."

I was being honest. I'd known what I was getting into when I signed on the dotted line. The basics, at least. And I was being well compensated for any inconveniences. My discomfort wasn't Shane's fault.

His mouth was a hard line. "You should."

"I…What?" Was Shane talking about the photos from the beach? We had yet to discuss them. I considered it, but telling Shane how I felt—used, embarrassed, disillusioned—seemed pointless. That's what I was here for, after all. Public displays of affection.

Those mysterious eyes of his were a roiling sea of turmoil, but the expression on his face was guarded, like he was trying to distance himself but couldn't quite manage it. "Defend yourself. From me." Shane's words were gruff, forced. A warning.

I stepped to the side, frowning up at him. Did he mean physically?

Why would I need to defend myself from a man who hadn't had sex with me even when I'd begged him to? A man who'd offered to sing me a lullaby, who had tended my cut with the same care my mother had when I was in kindergarten, who had barely touched me since he'd carried me into my own room and walked out the door. What nonexistent attack did I have to guard myself against?

But I knew. The very real danger emanating from Shane wasn't physical. He had my mind so scattered I risked forgetting why I was here, with him. Forgetting about what I'd done, and the restitution I still owed. I had to keep my wits about me, and not just for my own sake.

I didn't want to talk about the photos right now, didn't even want to think about them.

I met Shane's stare, my lungs tripping over a breath as I sucked in air. There was nothing normal about my life since the accident three years ago, and being with Shane had only compounded my strange reality. He rolled his neck, swallowed hard. That fierce self-confidence of his slipping just a bit. Maybe just for me.

On a sigh, I poked my hand between Shane's rib cage and the crook of his elbow, sliding against him like it was where I belonged. Breathing him in and remembering the way he'd inserted himself into a situation that could have ended so badly. Feeling safe. "I think I'll take my chances."

The tension coiling in his muscles didn't ease up in the slightest. "Don't say I didn't warn you."

"You did, Shane. You warned me." I rested my head against his biceps. It may as well have been a rock. "I signed on for this. All of it, not just the new wardrobe and free concerts."

He grunted. "Bet you didn't plan on the candids from the other night."

"Ah, no," I admitted, glad he'd brought them up since I hadn't had the nerve. "They could have been worse, though." At least what we'd been doing a few minutes before hadn't been splashed across every gossip site.

I was trying to ease into asking if they'd been planned, like Piper had suggested, but Shane pulled away, running a hand through his unruly mane. "I've got to go. Check in with the guys, do sound check, you know."

The part of me that had been pressed against Shane's side stung, like he'd taken the top layer of my skin with him. "I thought you had sound check this morning," I protested. He wavered, and I knew it was just a ruse. I pressed my small advantage. "Stay, please. What happened that night, not the pictures, what happened with us…" I paused for a moment to gather my pride, then forced myself to go further. "What *I* wanted to happen with us—"

But I didn't have a chance to finish my thought before the dressing room door was flung open, *thwack*ing against the wall. "Dude, why have you been hiding? The guys are all—"

Noticing Shane wasn't alone, the intruder's eyes flicked over me. "Hey there."

Face-to-face with Landon Cox, I should have been struggling to pick my jaw up off the floor. I'd only recently grown accustomed to sharing the same air as Shane Hawthorne, and his bandmates were hardly slouches in the sex-appeal department. As drummer for Nothing but Trouble, Landon wasn't quite as visible as Shane, but he made up for it by going shirtless behind his drum kit, showing off a lecherous smile and inflated biceps that girls drooled over. He was wearing a shirt now, but not a single button had been fastened and little was left to the imagination.

But all I wanted him to do was turn around and leave. I'd finally worked up the courage to be honest with Shane about the crazy feelings that had invaded my body since we'd met, and not even Landon Cox was worth the interruption.

Landon turned back to Shane, not noticing my lack of enthusiasm. "This the new one?"

My spine went rigid. *The new one.* Heat rose up my chest, racing toward my scalp, burning the tops of my ears.

Shane sighed. "Delaney, this is Landon."

Landon gave me a more leisurely once-over, a telling smirk lifting the edge of his lips. "I might like her even better than the last one, Shane. More curvy, less attitude, I think."

I would have given anything to have a snappy retort at the ready, expel a torrent of words that would put Landon firmly in his place. But my throat was dry, my brain too busy trying to process the looks passing between the two men.

"Lay off." Shane's voice was a low rumble, possessively marking his territory. The human equivalent of lifting his leg.

I glared at Shane as Landon backed away, stretching a hand toward the door handle. "No worries. Plenty of chicks just down the hall." And then Landon turned to me. "Be sure to give me a call when you get sick of this brooding ass, yeah? I promise you won't have to sign a thing."

Despite his flirtatious tone, a wave of shame crashed into me, and I collapsed onto the nearest piece of furniture, a chesterfield sofa, covered in saddle-brown leather, that had definitely seen better days, feeling like I'd just been sucker punched. All my intentions of opening up to Shane crushed. "Just so we're clear here, can you please tell me who does and doesn't know about *us*?"

Shane flashed a warning look at Landon as he left, but his voice was calm. "Just Travis, my PR people, the members of my band."

"And Piper," I added, counting silently. At a minimum, seven people knew the role I was playing in Shane's life. "And they know…everything?"

A curt nod. "Yes."

I closed my eyes for a moment, then turned them on the source of my angst. "Why?" I demanded.

Shane's brows drew together in an irritated frown. "Why what?"

The necklace at my throat was choking me. "Why am I here, pretending to be your adoring girlfriend, if everyone in your inner circle knows I'm just a prop?"

Shane

The hurt bleeding from Delaney's voice struck a chord. I knew the timbre of disillusionment all too well, and I hated hearing it from her. "You're more than a prop. If you weren't here right now, I'd be with Landon and the guys, downing shots of tequila and snorting lines of coke while some chick whose name I don't know sucks me off."

I sat down heavily beside Delaney, sliding my arm around her slim shoulders and pulling her in to me. "I don't want to be that out-of-control asshole musician anymore. I'm lucky to still be here, doing what I'm doing. I need your help to not fuck it up."

Glancing down at Delaney's face, I was nearly split in two by a jolt of longing as I watched her nibble at her lower lip. "In a few minutes I have to be at the meet-and-greet and then onstage.

I love my fans, but I definitely prefer them at a safe distance. I know my life is crazy and this is all new to you, but I need you by my side, Delaney. Can you do that for me?"

She tilted her face toward mine, her eyes cobalt whorls of doubt. If I had a better answer to her question, I would have given it. But I had my own set of "why's" crowding my mind. Probably sensing that further prodding was futile, she dropped her cheek to my chest and released a soft sigh, murmuring, "Okay."

Somehow we managed to get through the backstage bullshit that was a part of touring. Delaney kept me steady when all I wanted to do was leap onstage and wrestle the microphone away from our opening act. It had been nearly a year since I'd rocked out in front of an audience of thousands, and preparing for the sold-out crowd at the Staples Center in Los Angeles reminded me exactly why I had the best fucking job in the world.

I loved everything about music, always had. Playing, singing, recording—no matter how excruciating it was to get things exactly right, every minute was filled with joy for me. But being onstage, in front of a crowd…it was pure magic. Everything came alive. Melodies, harmonies, lyrics—they became living, breathing elements of a whirlwind.

Nothing but Trouble shows were complete chaos, yet in the center of it all, I felt only peace.

The eye of the storm.

Holding Delaney's hand, I walked from my dressing room to the back of the stage, absorbing an urgency from the crowd that made the ground beneath my feet shake from their energy. My heart tapped a staccato beat against my rib cage. *I'm coming. I'm coming.*

The guys ran out ahead of me, and the crowd erupted, their

noise coming at me like a riptide, sweeping me toward the spot-lights. I steered Delaney to a spot at the corner of the stage where I'd be able to see her. "Stay in this exact spot, you hear me?" I said, squeezing her hands. She nodded, and I dropped a kiss on her lips before striding out into the middle of the storm.

"How's my hometown crowd doin' tonight?" I yelled into the mic, their answering roar deafening.

When there's no place you call home, you can call any place home. L.A. was where I came after leaving behind who I'd been and what I'd done. The place I became Shane Hawthorne. It was as good a home as any. But being onstage, any stage, was home for me now, and I practically choked on a wave of gratitude as I shouted a greeting and let myself get swept up in the love and adoration of thousands of screaming strangers. Absorbing every molecule of energy, I swallowed it whole and gave it back in spades. The air was humid and heavy, and I sucked it in, letting it fill me up better than any drug. This was where I belonged. Cen-ter stage. Adored, appreciated.

Untouched.

Except that tonight Delaney was here. I felt her presence like the pull of a leash, could only get so far before looking back, seeking her out. And she was always there, the look on her face proving that she felt my songs. That their sweet notes and gritty underbelly were touching her in the same places I'd writ-ten them from.

Having Delaney nearby centered me somehow. Knowing that if I wanted to, I could have her in my arms in seconds, gave me a comfort I couldn't explain. My breaths came more easily, each syllable bleeding smoothly into the mic, cleansing my veins, clearing my head.

Maybe she would stay.

Delaney

The meet-and-greet had been tedious, my tight smile little more than a mask while Shane used my presence as a buffer between him and his overly adoring public. Still smarting from his admission in the dressing room, that Lynne and his bandmates all knew I was just a hired hand, I'd felt like a fraud. Then again, I was a fraud.

But from the moment Nothing but Trouble took the stage, all that fell away.

The four of them sauntered onto the stage one by one, the roar of the crowd going from a summer squall with intermittent low thunder to a roiling, restless storm rising from the floor of the stadium, shaking the foundation and electrifying the air.

Spotlights and pyrotechnics amplified the effect, flashes streaking through the air like lightning, highlighting excited faces and outstretched arms. A savage energy rippled through the thousands of fans, all clamoring for the show to begin.

Nothing but Trouble didn't disappoint.

Standing at the forefront, in a blaze of light, Shane led their fierce charge. Launching into one of their best-known songs, he commanded the audience's attention, covering every square inch of the stage and then stomping out onto a platform jutting into the churning sea of people like a boat dock. With the mic in his hands, he wasn't merely rock 'n' roll royalty. Shane Hawthorne was a god out there, immortal and larger than life. Mesmerizing.

As my heart beat to a rhythm set by Landon on the drums, my spirit was commanded by Shane's words and his beautiful, lyrical voice. Passion and emotion swirled and flitted around me, interspersed with sorrow and pain. For a moment I shut my eyes and let everything wash over me as the lights danced against my closed lids. I felt everything. I felt *Shane*.

Girls were crying, pushing toward the stage, throwing underwear and balled-up scraps of paper bearing phone numbers and erotic invitations at the band like confetti. Shane ignored the occasional fan that made it onto the stage, screaming as they tried to throw themselves at him, only to be caught and hauled off by security.

Shane and his band were on fire, feeding off the energy of the crowd and delivering an explosive set. So many people, so much energy. Every single one of them falling beneath Shane's spell.

No one more than me.

Nearly two hours later, Shane and his bandmates strutted off the stage, glistening with sweat and enthusiastically nudging each other as their fans erupted, screaming, "Encore, Encore, Encore!"

A roadie handed out bottles of ice-cold water as the collective need of thousands of chanting people pressed against my ribs. The air was so charged, I expected an electrical fire to break out at any moment. Landon grinned at my wide-eyed expression as he unscrewed the top, gulping some and dumping the rest over his head. "Let's give the people what they want." Rivulets of water mingled with the sweat on his naked torso as he ran toward the riser lifting his drum kit. A huff of relief shot out of my lungs as the crowd went wild.

Shane took a step toward the stage, but then backtracked, his hand wrapping around my neck, fingers threading into my hair. "I'm so fucking hard for you," he growled, pushing me up against an unused black speaker. This kiss wasn't soft or gentle. It was as hard and fierce as the lyrics he'd been belting out all night. Full of passion and rage and need, he stole my breath. My heart leapt into my throat as if it were lunging for Shane, too. Instinctively, my fingers threaded into his sweaty head, holding him to me, knowing there wasn't a single woman under this roof who didn't wish she were in my shoes.

Ending as suddenly as it began, Shane's amber eyes glinted gold as he pulled away and headed back to the stage. Meanwhile, I clung to the waist-high black speaker as if it were a lifeboat. I sure as hell needed one. Working for Shane, this was all supposed to be an act. A lucrative job to get me back into school and my father into a better environment. But there was nothing counterfeit about our chemistry.

Living with Shane Hawthorne was like standing in the path of an incoming storm, gathering force and speed. I was already swept up in his chaotic energy, and there was no escape in sight. Either I could bend and sway, let myself be pulled into Shane's whirlwind. Or I could stand my ground, dig in my heels—and hope I wouldn't snap in two.

"Enjoying the show?"

Travis's voice was an unwelcome distraction from watching Shane. "Are you here to check up on me?"

"Do I need to?" he shot back.

When I didn't answer, Travis tipped his chin toward Shane. "You keep him happy, I'll keep up my end. These six months will be over before you know it."

And there it was. I flinched, recoiling not just from the crude words that made me feel like a whore, but the reminder that my time with Shane was limited, and merely a means to an end.

I folded my arms over my chest. "I'll keep that in mind."

His response was forfeit to the thunderous applause coming from thousands of Nothing but Trouble fans as the band finished their final song and, saluting the audience, walked off the stage.

Shane greeted Travis with a slap on the shoulder, but he only had eyes for me. Grabbing my hand, he pulled me into the maze of wires and equipment backstage, glowing with pride and perspiration as we headed for his dressing room.

Nearly tripping as I struggled to keep up with Shane, I cursed Travis for altering my center of gravity. Just as I'd been getting comfortable with Shane and enjoying my place by his side, Travis had stolen my training wheels.

Chapter Twelve

Shane

W hat did Travis say to piss you off?"

Delaney's eyes widened. "You saw that?"

A laugh rumbled from my chest. "I don't miss much when I'm onstage." Technically, that wasn't true. The lights restricted my vision. But I'd kept Delaney in the corner of my eye all night, wanting to see the expressions on her beautiful face.

She bit the inside of her cheek, let go. "He reminded me to keep you happy…so he would help out my father."

Guilt slammed into me. Of course. The whole reason Delaney was here with me. "Oh," I grunted, turning my head to look out the window. We were in a car heading back to my house. Although the tour had officially kicked off tonight, there was no reason to sleep in a hotel just yet. Streetlights flashed by, their individual bulbs blurring into white streaks of light against a dark sky. "He's lucky to have you out here, fighting for him."

Delaney blanched, a bitter laugh gurgling from her throat. "Some fighter. He's been locked up for three years already." She clamped her mouth shut, lips pursed as if the caustic response left a harsh aftertaste.

I reached out, gathering a lock of her hair and twirling it around my finger. "How are you so sure he's innocent?"

Anger flared beyond her blue veil. "He's my father," she rasped.

I grimaced, my eyebrows bunching over the bridge of my nose. "One doesn't make the other true."

Delaney's mouth opened, but no words came out. Instead she turned away, resting her forehead against the car window, letting the cool glass soothe her heated skin. "I just know, okay?"

A pain lanced through my gut as Delaney defended her father with absolute certainty. How would it feel to have someone believe in me like that? I relaxed my grasp, watching the dark strands unspool, sliding down my wrist to curl at Delaney's shoulder. "I'll have Travis get the ball rolling on his transfer. He'll be moved by the end of the month."

She twisted back my way, expelling a grateful sigh and looking at me as if I'd parted the sea. "Thank you, Shane."

I opened my arms and Delaney fell into them, her hair like satin ribbons fluttering around my neck, both of us staring out the window at the moving ocean, its vastness amplified by the infinite expanse of sky above. Neither of us said anything for a while. "It must be hard to leave this to go on tour."

Resting my chin on the top of her head, I considered the view and realized that Delaney was right. She even made *fucking Malibu* feel like a place I could stay. "True. I used to like being on the road though. It's easy to dodge things you don't want to face when you're moving from city to city every other night."

She rubbed her cheek against my shirt, my heart thudding against my ribs as I patted the riotous plume of hair spilling over her shoulders. "You say that like you still do." Her voice was barely audible, even in the quiet car.

Hide, me? Never. "Nah. Just talking out of my ass."

Delaney pulled back, her eyes narrowing as they searched mine. "What are you hiding from, Shane?"

I swallowed the groan abrading my throat. "No one. A ghost."

She started to move away, but I wrapped my hand around her tiny waist and held her tight, realizing if I wanted to keep her close, I would have to answer her question. "I was in a car accident, too. A long time ago." The words skated, just barely, through my clenched teeth.

"What happened?" Delaney prodded gently.

"It's a long story. But I lost someone. My best friend; his name was Caleb."

"Is that why—"

"Yeah," I interrupted, knowing she was asking why I'd stopped that guy from getting in his truck.

"I'm sorry." Her whisper floated within the stagnant air of the limousine.

I tilted my head back against the headrest and closed my eyes, holding on to Delaney as the flashbacks came, blinding and fast. Red on white. Blood on snow. Crumpled, twisted metal. A scream, a thunderous crash. Then the oppressive silence of a snowy night, eventually pierced by sirens coming too late to do any good.

Delaney

"You tired?"

Standing in the foyer of Shane's beach house, the glare of headlights bouncing from wall to wall as the driver backed out of the driveway, I was anything but. "No. You?" Even without any of the details, Shane's revelation made me feel closer to him.

Shane shook his head, his face softer, more vulnerable somehow, after our conversation in the car. "Come on, I think a little sand in our toes is just what we need." He grabbed a bottle of wine and two glasses from the kitchen, and then the thick blanket lying across the back of his couch.

The wind was strong but warm as I followed him through the sliding glass door and down the deck stairs to the beach. "I thought you called the people who drink out of glasses on the beach assholes," I said, when I caught up with him.

A few feet from the water's edge, Shane was glancing up and down the stretch of shoreline. Was he checking for photographers? I wanted to ask, but there were too many other things on my mind. I laid out the blanket while he opened the wine.

"I said that?"

"Yeah, right after I stepped on the broken glass."

We sat, and Shane poured each glass three-quarters full, before making a well in the sand and putting the bottle into it.

"Guess I'm one of them," he responded, tempering his sarcasm with a wink that had me choking on my first sip.

After I got control of myself, he lifted his glass in a mock toast. "You survived your first Nothing but Trouble concert. Bravo."

I laughed. "Well, it was pretty tough to take. I wasn't sure I would make it."

"Not to worry. You came through with flying colors."

We both sipped, staring out at the water as our toes wriggled in the sand. "Aren't I supposed to be keeping you away from alcohol, not sharing a bottle with you?"

Shane's eyebrows lifted. "If I'd wanted to get drunk I would have grabbed a different kind of bottle, and I wouldn't be sharing it either."

A thought occurred to me, flying off my tongue. "Did you drink to feel closer to Caleb, or to forget him?" Immediately I wanted to chase after it with an eraser, rub away the intrusive collection of words as if I'd never said them.

There had been nights when missing my mom had felt like a bitter blade, cutting into me a little deeper with each breath. I tried to dull the pain with vodka once, but after two drinks I'd just fallen asleep on the couch and awoken with a massive headache in the middle of the night. Missing her more.

Facing the water, Shane said nothing, scanning the horizon as if he were searching for the fine line, far in the distance, where sea met sky.

"Crap, I'm sorry. That's really none of my business," I backpedaled, the blunt intimacy of my question staining my cheeks pink.

Shane didn't seem to mind. "No, it's fine. Don't apologize. It's been a long time and talking about him doesn't hurt the way it used to." As he spoke, Shane ran his fingers along the ridges of my spine, sending a tremor of awareness racing along my nerves. "Sometimes. But usually it was so I could forget. Forget about everything, actually. Alcohol, drugs—they create a void you don't have to fill. You can just float. It's almost peaceful, you know." His broad shoulders shrugged. "Until you wake up in your own vomit, not remembering where you are or how you got there. That part's not so fun."

Waves rolled in, filling the silence. "What made you stop?" I asked, my voice wavering.

"Life. Fate. I was fucking things up. Forgetting lyrics, sometimes showing up too far gone to get onstage at all. Most days I wasn't even thinking clearly enough to write. Our label was on the verge of dropping us." Shane shook his head at the memory, which obviously still haunted him. "I wanted out. So I bought enough drugs to OD, but I got caught in a bust. I was feeling pretty sorry for myself, too, until I learned the guy next to me was there because he'd left his kid alone so he could work a double shift to pay rent. The kid climbed out the window and had to be rescued by the fire department. Now he's in jail and his son's in foster care. Another was arrested for shoplifting to pay for his brother's chemo."

"I'd wasted years wondering: Why me? And that night I finally realized something. Why *not* me? Shit storms don't discriminate." Shane took his last sip and let the glass fall on its side in the sand. "I don't know what strings Travis pulled or even why he bothered. But somehow he got the charges dropped and I walked out of that cell. Nothing I do will ever bring Caleb back, but I realized that if I got my head out of my ass, I could have a career that allowed me to help people like the ones I met in jail. I didn't finish high school, but my voice gave me options. There are a lot of people out there who don't have any options at all."

I was quiet for a long time, absorbing Shane's words as I sipped slowly from my glass, the tart bite of the wine enhanced by the misty breeze. Was I supposed to meet his confession with my own, like calling a bet in a poker game?

I opened my mouth, but only to take a sharp inhale. No. I wasn't ready, and the risks were too high. Instead, I pushed aside my own memories, my own guilt, and focused completely on the man in front of me. I wanted to acknowledge his admission while adding a bit of levity to our heavy conversation. "When we first met, I pegged you as some kind of singing Ken doll."

Shane's bark of laughter was carried away by the wind. "I've been called a lot of things, but Barbie's boyfriend is a first."

I leaned into Shane's side, nudging him gently with my elbow. "I'm just saying there's more to you than I expected."

He looked down at me, a smile slanting across his face. "Same here."

Goose bumps pricked at my arms. "So, what do you do now? When you need to forget, to escape?"

Shane didn't bat an eye. "I fuck."

I gulped down a damp breath. "Oh." His blunt honesty sent my heartbeat lurching into overdrive, unexpected jealousy rushing through my veins at the thought of Shane with other women.

"Or write."

"Oh." Much better. "What do you write about?"

The slow twist of his lips sent me spinning. "Lately...you."

Me. "Do you write about all your fake girlfriends?"

Tension swelled as Shane waited a beat, then another. "No."

Why the hesitation? I chased my confusion with another sip of wine, another question. "Is that why you asked about my family? Because you think it would make a good song?" A thin ribbon of suspicion threaded through my words.

The waves rolled in, each one getting closer to our feet. Shane stretched his legs out, salt water foaming between his toes. "It might. But that's not why I asked."

I set my glass in the sand and turned to face him again, waiting to speak until he'd angled his head toward me again. "Then why did you?"

His voice softened, as if he were a pediatrician holding a needle behind his back. "We're going to be on the East Coast in about a month or so. You know, if you want to visit your father."

I could feel the blood drain from my face. Not even the smooth timbre of Shane's voice could dull the sting of my father's prison sentence. "I thought you said the road was a good place to hide."

"Hey." Shane placed a hand on my shoulder, his thumb sweeping along the line of my collarbone. "If you don't want to see him, it's your business."

A shiver wrestled through me. "It's not that I don't want to," I said, the lie quick on my tongue. "I just don't think it's a very good idea."

"How long has it been?"

Too long. I released a ragged sigh, trying to tamp down the panic I felt at Shane's suggestion. "A while."

He squinted at me, his voice brimming with concern. "What are *you* hiding from, Delaney?"

The truth. "It's just…I don't know if I can handle seeing him in there."

"Because you blame him for your mother's death?"

I choked on my last sip, sputtering as Shane rubbed my back. His incisive questions were chipping away at what remained of my conscience. "No, of course not," I finally wheezed. I knew exactly who was responsible for that, and it wasn't my father. "He doesn't want me to visit. He made me promise, just before they took him away." After what I'd done, keeping that promise was the very least my father deserved from me.

Shane

I recognized the fear and sadness tightening Delaney's expression, bleeding into her voice. Two emotions I'd been on intimate terms with for as long as I could remember. "And you can live with that? Not seeing him for years—maybe never?"

"I don't have a choice." Her eyes were as turbulent as the churning sea.

The wind picked up, blowing thick handfuls of hair across her face. "You always have a choice, Delaney."

A breathy sigh. "I'm not so sure about that."

We weren't talking about her parents anymore. I reached out, smoothing the wayward strands back, my touch lingering on the silky shell of her ear, the curve of her jaw. But in an instant, that soft vulnerability shuttered closed, her tight body bristling with anger as she stared off at a point in the distance. "Is this another photo op?"

I dropped my hand, pulled back. "What?"

She gestured to the wineglasses, the blanket. "Did you stage this? Just another publicity stunt, like the other night?"

Delaney must have spotted something, a flash or a flicker of movement. Feigning a calm I didn't feel, I scanned the beach where Delaney had been looking, but didn't see anything untoward. "It wasn't a stunt." Grabbing for the empty wineglasses, and the still half-full bottle, I hoisted myself to my feet and headed back to the house. Leaving Delaney to follow, or not.

I wasn't angry with her, not really. It was a fair question, one I should have addressed before Delaney felt the need to ask.

But…didn't she feel what I was feeling? Most of my life had been a revolving door of bullshit and betrayal. Delaney was the first person to make me think that maybe, just maybe, it had only been a phase. A trial to get through so I'd be worthy of what came after. Like a rainbow arching over the misty remnants of a storm, beauty rising from debris.

Except with just one sentence, Delaney had accused me of *being* the bullshit and betrayal in her life.

Rationally, we'd been together only a few days. The accusation shouldn't bother me. It shouldn't, but it did. It fucking did. And I didn't even try to hide it.

Delaney's muffled curse was only slightly louder than the surf, and by the time I opened the sliding glass door, she was right behind me. "I want to believe you, but…" Her voice trailed off, ending in a murmured, "I'm sorry."

"Forget it." I choked out the words, slamming the glasses and bottle onto the granite countertop. "All of it, actually."

Her brows knitted together as she gave the sandy blanket a quick shake and came inside. "What do you mean?"

I swallowed hard, resignation straightening my spine. "I'm going to tell Travis to pay you in full and rip up the contract. And I'll make sure your father is transferred. Go pack your suitcase and I'll take you to a hotel tonight."

Delaney's eyes were swimming with confusion, and I took some small comfort in knowing she wasn't immune to whatever crazy roller coaster we'd jumped on together. "I don't understand. What about the tour?"

"Fuck the tour," I gritted out. I would probably regret everything I was about to say, but a dam had burst and the words kept coming. "You were dealt a bad hand. I get that. But I'm not the dealer. I'm not out to hurt you. Every intimate moment between us isn't some phase in a PR campaign. You've thought the worst of me at every turn, and a week ago you would have been right." My gut twisted as I forced unfiltered honesty through my clenched jaw. "But seeing myself through your eyes, it's a pretty fucked-up picture."

I huffed a resigned sigh. "I don't want to be that guy, Delaney. Not anymore."

Chapter Thirteen

Delaney

I stared at Shane for a beat, not believing my ears. Not wanting to believe that Shane meant what he was saying. "So don't. Don't be that guy. Prove me wrong." *Fight for me.*

"Prove you wrong?" An incredulous expression twisted his features. "How can I when the truth is—I think you're fucking right? What if *that guy* is who I really am? I'm doing you a favor, Delaney."

I set my hand against the wall, needing to lean against something solid because it felt as if Shane were ripping the ground from beneath my feet. "I don't need any favors. What if all I need is—"

An ugly sound ripped from his throat. "Don't even say it. I was just using you, all right? Using you to pretend I'm someone I'm not. But the show's over."

"You don't mean that. I know you don't." The hurt clenching my heart made my voice quiver, like I was asking a question rather than stating a fact.

Shane only shook his head and turned away. I considered going after him, but I needed a moment, some time to pull myself together before I lost the only man I'd ever wanted. Time to figure out how to convince him that learning to trust each other was a process and that we needed to cut each other some slack. Sure it would take a bit of effort, but Shane Hawthorne was worth it.

And damn it, so was I.

I trudged upstairs, my heartbeat loud and sluggish as I struggled to breathe through the cage enclosing my lungs and absorb everything Shane had just said. He was right. I had thought the worst of him at every turn. *Singing Ken doll. Blackmailing asshole. Publicity (man)whore.* Why would he want to have me around?

The only problem was—I didn't want to leave.

Shane wasn't the man I thought he was. Maybe he wasn't even the man *he* thought he was.

And I wanted to scrape off the layers of paint and pretense and get to know the guy who'd offered to sing me a lullaby like he meant it. The guy who'd hit rock bottom, flamed out, and then rose from the ashes like a damned phoenix. The guy whose songs made me ache inside.

Opening the door to my bedroom, I stared out the window as if I could find answers in the tide. Why did I feel so lost? After only one week, Shane was giving me all the incentives he'd promised at the end of our six-month contract. I should pack my bag and get the hell out of his million-dollar beach house and back to my crappy little L.A. apartment where I belonged. But I didn't want to go.

Sure, it wasn't long ago that I'd crushed on Shane Hawthorne: the untouchable, unattainable rock star. But the guy I'd spent the past few days with—*Shane*—he was guarded and vulnerable, intuitive and volatile. The jury was still out on attainable. But touchable…hell to the yes. I liked *Shane*. A lot. So what if the circumstances we'd met under were a little unconventional? It didn't mean that our relationship had to be tainted. Did it?

Or had it already been tainted by my deception?

By the secrets I was still clutching to my chest like a shield. As if they could protect me. Hardly. They were a wall between us. One I didn't know how to knock down. At least, not until I trusted Shane completely. I wasn't there, not yet.

And if I left tonight, I never would be.

A breeze wafted in through the open window, carrying all my doubts and extinguishing the tiny flicker of hope within me. What relationship was I trying to save? The fake one created by Travis?

A groan rumbled past my quivering lips and I jerked my suitcase onto the bed, throwing in the few items I'd bothered to unpack and zipping it closed. Blinking away tears, I dragged it downstairs, the wheels battering each step, announcing my exodus with the restraint of a twenty-one-gun salute.

Shane was on the couch, quietly strumming his guitar, an open can of Sprite on the side table. He eyed my suitcase, regret etched into the planes of his famous face. "Ready to go?"

I'd packed while my mind fumbled for a way to salvage the mess I'd made. But I wasn't ready to leave, and I didn't want to go. Wiping at my wet eyes, I launched myself at Shane, straddling his strong thighs and wrapping my arms around his neck, threading my fingers into his hair and tugging. "No."

Shane remained still as a statue, barely breathing. As if I scared him. "Why not?"

A part of me cleaved open and the truth slipped out. "Because I want to stay."

There was movement behind those golden eyes, a softening. I plowed on, desperate to get through to him. "I want to stay with you, Shane. Because of you. Only you."

"You're a fool."

"No." I brought my hands to his face, my thumbs on the sweep of his cheekbones. "But if I let you throw me away, I will be. You said you needed me by your side, remember? Well, I need you, too."

Shane's hands waited a terrifyingly long time before coming around me. But they did, pulling me close. "You sure, Delaney?" His voice was a roughened husk, stoking the fire between us.

I'd never been more sure of anything in my life. "Yes, I'm sure." With barely an inch between our mouths, I could feel his desire burning as hot as mine, the proof of it throbbing against me. And I was done waiting. I wanted to feel him inside me now. "Shane." I planted two tiny kisses, one on each side of his lips, before whispering in his ear, "Make me yours."

He made a noise that was somewhere between a bark and a growl. And then his hands were gliding up my spine, tangling in my hair, his lips teasing mine. When Shane stood, I clung to him like a monkey. He carried me up the stairs and deposited me on the bed gently, reverently. I caught a glimpse of the emotions fighting for space on his handsome face, wanting to reach out my hand, gently trace each plane and angle. Absorb all the need and want and hunger through my fingertips. And I would have. But then my eyes locked on his, and the air left my lungs in a dizzying whoosh. What I saw was piercing, primal. Shane Hawthorne was no pretty-boy, Auto-Tuned boy-bander. He was flawed and fierce. And I wanted to submit to the lust pulsing between us, to be swallowed up in it.

I wanted to confess, too.

Not yet. Soon maybe. But not tonight.

Tonight I wanted to give myself over to reality and fantasy until I didn't know where one ended and the other began.

Tonight I wanted to chase the rapture Shane had promised with every kiss, every look, every touch.

I wanted to be *his*, and I wanted to make him *mine*.

Shane

I let my eyes linger on the sight of Delaney in the middle of my bed, a river of dark hair tumbling onto her shoulders, her lithe legs and soft curves barely denting the mattress, wide eyes shooting sparks at me. I wanted to pounce, to maul her, to swallow her whole. But it was her eyes that stopped me. If I saw another tear fall out of them, it might just kill me.

"Delaney, is this really what you want?" I grabbed at the hem of my shirt, whipping it up and off and into a corner of the room, resisting the urge to close the distance between us.

Delaney's response was to do the same, her breasts quivering in a barely there lace confection. She was sitting now, kneeling with her feet tucked beneath her perfect ass. My heartbeat tripped as she reached behind her back and unclasped the band of her bra, letting each silken strap fall down her arms while she held the cups to her skin.

"I do. But if you want *this*," she whispered, tossing a nervous grin my way just before casting her bra to the floor, "you're going to have to come a little closer."

Goddamn, Delaney was beautiful. My eyes soaked up every inch of perfection, stomach lurching as I let myself believe she was all mine. Lust buoyed the air between us, energized oxygen crackling along my spine. "I want," I growled, ripping at the buttons on my fly, shucking off my jeans and briefs in one smooth movement. Finally free, my dick bobbed, straining toward her.

Delaney's breath hiccupped. "Good."

I crossed the remaining steps to the bed, setting one knee on the mattress, then the other, sliding my way toward Delaney until I had a leg on either side of her thighs and her head was in my hands, piles of dark chestnut silk covering my forearms.

Her hands slipped between us, fingertips delicately tracing the ink tattooed into my skin. Her movements were slow and steady, and completely foreign. I was used to grasping and clinging. Women who wanted what I so freely offered—meaningless sex and bragging rights. Everything about Delaney's touch rang of intention and poise.

Steeling myself, I watched the play of emotions on Delaney's face as she sat rigidly upright, studying every inch of my chest. Bleeding crucifixes, weeping angels, vengeful demons. My torso and arms were a visual rejection of everything I'd learned from the fire-and-brimstone preacher I'd been forced to listen to every Sunday—and the man who'd dragged me there. Scattered between was a tombstone for Caleb, a monster chasing after two boys, and the Nothing but Trouble logo. Holding myself still, I sucked in a harsh breath as her gaze scraped along the surface of my skin, leaving a trail of need in its wake. "This is your story," she breathed. "Like a graphic memoir."

My hands lifted, fisting Delaney's hair with one, fingertips of the other grazing her collarbone. Her skin was so smooth. Flawless. No ink or scars to mar her pale flesh, just a heat that rose from her blood to burn my fingertips. I let go of her hair, cupping her breasts in my hands, thumbs sweeping across her peaked nipples, thrilling at her quick intake of breath, the way she leaned into my hands.

Delaney's palms slid up my chest, her head tilting back to look into my eyes. What I saw in them had me spinning. Falling. So hard, so fast I was dizzy. "You should know that no contract could ever make me do this," she said in a throaty whisper. Those little hands of hers continued up my shoulders, up my neck, finding purchase on either side of my face. "I *want* to stay."

It was exactly what I needed to hear. Not because I'd ever had a single qualm about fucking any of my fake girlfriends. But because I'd had a dozen qualms about doing anything to make Delaney doubt me. Doubt *us*. Tonight, right now, there was only one thing I knew for sure. Delaney and I, we were linked by something I didn't quite understand yet, but I already cherished.

I'd never had sex with someone who owned my heart. Did Delaney have mine? I didn't know, not yet. But she had more of me than I'd ever given anyone.

"Delaney." My voice quaked on her name. Unable to say anything else, I swooped down, finding her lips. Words were entirely inadequate to express the depth of what I was feeling right now.

Delaney

Shane swallowed my sigh of pleasure, his tongue running along the porcelain tracks of my teeth, teasing the corners of my mouth. Tasting. Savoring.

Lustful shivers charged down my spine as he kissed and licked his way down my neck. His hands were everywhere, coiled in my hair, wrapped around my waist, cupping my ass as his cock throbbed against my belly.

"Shane." I offered his name as a plea, clinging to his shoulders. *More. Now. Please.*

Quick as lightning, Shane had me flat on my back, palms skimming along my rib cage. He tugged at my white jeans and lace thong until they were just a discarded memory on his floor. Then he fell on me, recapturing my mouth, his knees nudging my thighs apart until he was cradled between them. My head spun with the intensity of my need. It was like a living, pulsing current inside my bloodstream, an undeniable craving for the man on top of me.

A few minutes ago Shane had stared at me as if I were not just in the center of his bed, but the center of his world.

And I fell a little more under his spell.

But then he paused, and my heart lurched in panic. I was afraid Shane would change his mind, walk out the door. "You still sure, sweetheart?"

Something about his face, the gorgeous combination of his tanned skin and piercing gaze, made me want to comfort him, tell him everything was going to be okay because I would make sure of it.

But it wasn't Shane's face or his body that made me want to give myself to him. It was the wounded soul inside of him, the one he kept hidden from the public. The one he'd shown me on the beach.

The connection between us was powerful, and it ran deeper now than it had the other night. Where our trajectory would lead, I had no idea. But in this moment, and for the first time in three years, I was exactly where I wanted to be. In Shane's arms.

Hope fluttered on tentative wings as I realized Shane wasn't hesitating because he had doubts of his own. Shane was holding back because he was worried about *my* doubts.

And I fell just a little further.

My head was cluttered, filled with turmoil. But not a single regret. "Yes. God, yes," I rasped, energy spiking as I roughed my fingers through his hair, pulling his face down to mine once more.

His eyes locked onto mine, fiery and fierce. "I didn't wanna give you up. It would have killed me." He covered my mouth with his own, and I could taste his smile.

It slipped beneath my skin, teasing and taunting. So delicious.

Moments later, a moan bubbled up from my throat as Shane tore his lips from mine, a moan that became a hiss as he toyed with my breasts. Licking, sucking, biting, soothing—Jesus, the man knew how to use his tongue. And he was moving south at a determined pace. My hips bucked upward, and Shane pulled at my knees, nibbling the tender skin inside my thighs, sending explosions of pleasure zinging everywhere. My body was an arcade game with a dozen balls shooting every which way. He wasn't just winning; he was setting the bar so high, the only one who would ever have any chance of breaking it would be him.

Bells, whistles, lights—Shane knew how to *play*.

I wanted to beg, to plead, but I wasn't capable of speech. Not when his hands were gliding down my legs, kneading my insteps, and then back up to the part of me that was on fire. Braving the flames, he slipped a finger inside of me. I arched up, choking on my own breath, my pulse pounding against my eardrums. I was a needy, naked, trembling mess of nerve endings and body parts, every single cell in my body wanting whatever Shane was willing to give. I wasn't a crazy stalker fan. I was worse. I was a beggar.

And I didn't care.

Because that tongue...*Fuuuck*. That tongue of his slipped inside my wet center, swirling around my throbbing bundle of nerves with just the right pressure, just the right speed. Just. The. Right. Everything.

My muscles clamped down on Shane's fingers, ground zero of the orgasm roaring through me. I twisted the sheet into my palms, needing to hold on to something, anything.

When the tremors finally subsided, Shane lifted his head, laying it along my thigh as he dragged his fingers out of me, tracing my own wetness on the skin of my belly. "Wow," I breathed, knowing I sounded awestruck. Knowing I *was* awestruck.

A low chuckle flew from Shane's mouth as he rose, centering himself above me. "Don't be too impressed by the opening act, Delaney. The headliner's just getting started." There was a grin lifting his lips, but his eyes were serious, roiling with an emotion I couldn't read.

Swallowing the knot in my throat, I wrapped my arms around his neck. "Your opening act might have just stolen the show."

His grunt was proud, defiant. "I've never shied away from a challenge, Delaney. Definitely not going to start tonight." Reaching between my legs, he guided the head of his cock until it nudged my opening, and I was suddenly grateful for the birth control clause I'd initially found so objectionable. I didn't want anything between us, not even the thinnest of latex barriers.

With one hand tangled in Shane's hair, I brought my other between us, holding it flat against his chest until I could feel his heart hammering against my palm. "Give it your best shot, Shane."

The look on his face would have brought me to my knees if I weren't already lying down. Like the North Star, Shane beamed with a light that was so bright, so full of promise, I would follow it anywhere. He pushed into me, slow and steady. When I thought he couldn't possibly go any further, there was still more of him to take. His eyes locked on mine as I squirmed in his grasp. "You okay?" His muscles rippled beneath my hands as he reined himself in, holding back out of concern for me.

I'd had sex only once in my life and it was years ago. Adjusting to him was…well, an adjustment. But I didn't care if he broke me in two. I wanted everything Shane Hawthorne had to give. I wrapped my legs around his back and jerked my hips upward in a quick, purposeful movement. The brief twinge was immediately smoothed by the look of pleasure that overtook Shane's face. "Now it is," I answered.

"You're fucking amazing," he muttered, pulling out gently and then sliding back in, filling a part of me I hadn't known was vacant. Over and over and over again. Each thrust adding fuel to the flames threatening to consume me and leave Shane holding a pile of ash.

I was mindless, breathless. "Don't stop, Shane," I begged. "Please—don't ever stop."

Chapter Fourteen

Shane

Heaven was for real, and it was in Delaney Fraser's arms. And in her pussy, which was so damn tight each stroke was a transcendent experience.

That moment, when I'd held back out of fear of hurting her, and she'd had none of it…I felt like I knew what the Grinch meant when his heart had grown three times in size.

I don't know how Delaney knew what I needed, except that she did.

And it made me want to blow her mind.

With Delaney's legs trembling against my hips, I pulled out, almost to the tip, and then drove back home, sheathing myself inside her with one thrust. Her hands were roving, nails scraping my skin as she pulled me into her. I gave myself over, following the rhythm of her breath, chasing after those little squeaks and moans she doled out like bread crumbs as she soared to the same faraway land I was aiming toward.

I would have changed positions, but basic missionary gave me the best view of Delaney's gorgeous face, and I wasn't willing to give her another orgasm without watching it break over her. I studied the soft line of her jaw, the arch of her cheekbones, the gentle ski-jump of her nose, the inky half-moon smudges of her lashes. And those full, pouty lips that had called to me since the moment I first laid eyes on her.

Her hot center clenched around my cock, my balls tightening as they slapped against her perfect ass. I was inside Delaney, and yet she was sliding deep beneath my skin, marking me in countless places and immeasurable ways.

She gasped my name, and it sounded like a strangled plea. I slowed down on the upstroke, dragging against her as I pushed in, sweetening each thrust with an extra dose of friction. I was close to the edge and so was she, and there was no way on earth I'd ever make the dive first. Every movement was meant to nudge Delaney in front of me, watch as she succumbed to rapture, as the lightness inside her, inside me, overtook us both.

"Look at me, Delaney," I panted, wanting her eyes on mine as passion turned her pupils into black dots in a deep blue ocean. I wanted to drown in Delaney's sweetness, master her body like any musical instrument I'd ever gotten my hands on.

Delaney's eyelids fluttered open as she focused on my face, and a moment later I felt her tremble from deep within, her spine arching, lips quivering as she cried out a final time. Radiant. Glowing. Mine.

I finally gave in to the tender smile tugging at Delaney's mouth. Burrowing into her neck, breathing in her scent, I found my release, collapsing onto her for a brief moment before rolling onto my back and gasping for air.

I turned my head to the side, needing some kind of confirmation that I wasn't the only one rocked by the experience. And damn if I didn't see a droplet snaking its way down Delaney's cheek.

What. The. Fuck.

Delaney

Shane reached out to cup my face, worry creasing his forehead. "Hey," he whispered, swiping his index finger across my skin and holding it up for me to see. "You're leaking again."

I dipped my head in embarrassment. "Happy tears."

Lifting my chin with that same finger, Shane locked his gaze on mine. "Happy tears? That's a thing?"

"I guess so, for me at least."

Relief smoothed his brow. "So, do you always cry after sex?"

Ummm…how to answer that? Did I really want Shane to know my experience before tonight could be summed up in less time than it took to microwave a bag of popcorn? I glanced around the room, as if an answer that didn't make me sound like the somewhat nerdy, nose-in-a-book girl would suddenly appear on a wall. The kind of girl I'd been before having hair and makeup people. Before I was "Shane Hawthorne's girlfriend." I chewed at the inside of my cheek, heat racing up my neck, breaking over my skin. "I—I don't know, exactly."

Shane rose onto his elbow, looking down on me with a mix of confusion and amusement. "You don't know?"

"Well, I've only—"

His eyes widened, and he choked on a breath. "Jesus Christ, were you a virgin?"

"No." I hurried to ease his fear. "I'm not. It's just…"

"It's just what?"

"There was only one other—"

"Guy?"

"Time." His prompt came out in the same moment as my answer, and I wish I had waited just one more second before finishing my sentence. Because I wouldn't have finished it. I would have let his answer stand.

Yes. One guy. I had a boyfriend. That I had sex with. Several times. Maybe even lots of times.

God, that sounded much better than the truth. A truth that Shane repeated, rolling it around in his mouth as if tasting it. "Time. One time. You only had sex once before? One time, before tonight?"

Embarrassment gave way to irritation. "Yes. One time. Is there some sort of rule that says the women you bring to your bed must be some kind of sex expert in order to get an invitation?"

A deep belly laugh shook the sheet slanting across Shane's rib cage. A sheet I was about to wrap around my entire body as I stalked out of the room. "What's so funny?"

Shane's laughter dried up as quickly as it began. "Delaney, you're fucking killing me." Definitely getting up, sheet and all. I pulled at it, tucking it more securely beneath my arms. "Why didn't you say something? I mauled you like a dog. No wonder you're crying." His hand rose to cup my jaw, thumb sweeping along my cheekbone, regret slashed across his face. "I'm a jackass for not realizing, for not taking things slow."

I stared into Shane's eyes as I leaned into him. So close I saw horror snag the whirl of gold, unfurling. "Shit—did I hurt you?"

"What? No." I shook my head. "Really, I mean it. Me getting all misty, it was because I've never felt that *good* before. Didn't even know it was possible." That last part slipped out before I considered how much of myself I wanted to give away. My body Shane could have. He'd just proven he knew how to take care of it better than I did. But the rest of me? He could do more damage than I'd be able to repair.

Especially since I had absolutely no idea what he thought of me. Was it even possible I could be more to Shane than just the next girl in line?

Shane dropped a kiss on my shoulder, making a fist of his hand and running his knuckles above the edge of the sheet cutting across my chest. Goose bumps raced across the nape of my neck as his fingers curled around the thin fabric and tugged it down. I let him expose inch after inch of my trembling body, so sated a minute ago but needy once more. "It's possible, Delaney. In so many different ways."

I wanted to swim in the waves of appreciation surging from Shane's eyes. "You're so fucking beautiful." His words were almost an afterthought, as if they sprang from his mouth not to compliment me, but just to voice the thought in his head. Something warm and tingly unspooled deep in the pit of my stomach, and I shivered as he feasted on the sight of me.

Where his eyes went, his fingertips followed, tracing intricate patterns on the surface of my skin and causing turmoil below it. "You know what this means, right?"

Not a clue. I fumbled for an answer, my thoughts tripping over themselves in their awkwardness. That we should have sex again? Sure, totally on board. Or that we shouldn't? Boo. "Tell me."

"It means we don't have to fake it. The whole, Shane

Hawthorne's new shiny toy. The contract you hated from the minute you read it. We don't need it anymore. We're real now."

An eager kind of hopefulness expanded in my lungs, like helium blown into a balloon, making me feel light and buoyant. A high-pitched laugh overflowed from my mouth. "Are you asking me to be your girlfriend?"

Shane gave a slight shake of his head, his mouth set into a sober line. "No."

His single-word answer was as effective as a sharp pin.

"I'm not asking. You're my girl. Period."

Shane

I was at the top of my career, but my personal life revolved around looking good in public.

Taking a chance on Delaney, on a real relationship…It could cost me everything.

But I didn't have a choice.

Fighting to hold on to something is a hell of a lot different from clawing your way to the top. I didn't know what I was missing until Delaney came into my life. Sex with her was just the beginning. A fucking fantastic beginning…but I wanted more. So much more. And I wanted her to want it, too.

My girl.

Brushing wayward strands of hair from her face, I touched my lips to the center of her forehead, the tip of her nose, lingering over her mouth. Giving, taking, tasting.

When I pulled away, her brow was smooth, her eyes clear. Her shy smile yanking at my heart. "I can be your girl. But…I gave up my job for this."

I followed her line of thinking. "I know. You packed up your entire life to come on the road with me. But even though my services are pretty damn phenomenal"—I gave an exaggerated roll of my hips, loving the laugh that tripped from Delaney's lips and grateful that she saw the humor in this ridiculous situation—"I'm not trying to skimp out on monetary compensation for your time."

Her full breasts pushed against my chest. "Real relationships are messy, Shane. And both of us have avoided them because, let's face it, our lives are messy enough. Having a contract, a defined set of expectations—maybe we need that."

What she said was true, yet I still shrugged my shoulders. This might be the dumbest thing I'd ever done, opening myself up, exposing what was underneath my rock-star veneer. But it might turn out to be the best. I roughed a hand through her sex-mussed mane. "Maybe I like things a little messy."

She eyed me cautiously, and I wondered if Delaney could hear the forced bravado in my voice. "So you want to throw away the rulebook you and Travis came up with? The one you've followed ever since he got you out of jail, the one that helped you turn your life around?"

I took a shaky breath, trying to see things from her side. If Delaney decided to get up and walk away, I wouldn't have blamed her one bit. I was all over the place. First I wanted to hire her. Then I wanted to fuck her. Then I didn't. Then I wanted to, and did. And now I wanted to blur all our carefully constructed lines. It was a lot to absorb, and I sounded like a flighty kid with one buck to spend at the candy store.

Blood pulsed, hot and heavy, within my veins. "I'm not that same broken guy anymore. Wounded maybe, but not broken. Not anymore."

Lowering my chin to rest atop her head, I felt pulled in two different directions. I cared for Delaney more than I ever thought possible, and yet letting go of the safety net I'd constructed was terrifying. A relationship without predefined expectations could lead to chaos. Growing up, I never knew who to trust, who was safe. But now *I* was the grown-up, and it was time for me to act like it.

I'd avoided this kind of uncertainty for the past decade. And yet here I was, throwing away everything that made me feel in control and begging Delaney to get on the ride with me.

No seat belt. No destination. No plan.

At Delaney's arched eyebrow, I relented. "Fine. If a few pieces of paper will keep you by my side for the next six months, I'm all for it. But as far as I'm concerned, it's in name only. Written assurance that you'll get everything you were promised, because I don't want you worrying about a job for the next six months. Maybe I'm being a selfish asshole, but I still need you by my side. And besides," I teased, "I think I've grown on you. Maybe you need me, too."

She shoved at my chest, a sideways smile pulling at her mouth. "Sure, you keep telling yourself that."

Fear and hope clogged my lungs as I rolled onto my back, pulling Delaney with me. "Not many sure things in life, at least not in mine."

She settled onto my shoulder, her hair sweeping across my neck like a mink stole. "From the outside, your life looks pretty perfect."

My voice softened, tinged with regret. "You make it feel that way. But not long ago it seemed pretty damn empty."

Delaney looked up at me, empathy etched into her face. "Do you have any family? Anyone who loves the real Shane Hawthorne, not the fantasy you project to the world?"

I grunted. How could I explain? Shane Hawthorne wasn't real, and the guy living in his skin wasn't someone she'd want to know. "I do, but I don't want to think about my family, not right now."

A seed had been planted though, and I felt the slow burn of anger coiling around my heart. My parents were both dead, but I did have a brother. Except he'd given up the right to be called *family* a long time ago. My mind started down the rutted path that only led to a dead end. No. There would be no walks down memory lane tonight.

The best way to prevent the pointless journey was lying in my arms. Closing my eyes, I let myself sink into Delaney's sweetness, absorb all the good I felt within her arms. I needed every last bit.

* * *

Sipping at a steaming cup of coffee from thirty thousand feet, I stared out the window at the rippling white blanket of clouds stretching as far as I could see. When I was a kid, I imagined heaven would be spent jumping around these clouds as if they were a playground, a guitar slung over my shoulder and an ice-cream cone in my hand.

I was nearly twenty by the time I boarded a plane for the first time, and it had been a shock to see just clouds and nothing else. No bearded man in a white robe. No angels, no happy cherubs. Just clouds and sunshine.

Emptiness.

Peace.

Right now I felt anything but peaceful.

Two hours ago, I had slipped out of bed while Delaney was

still asleep. Tired after a long night of very little sleep, she'd barely stirred when I dropped a quick kiss on her cheek, leaving a note on my pillow.

This trip was a spur-of-the-moment decision. One I never thought I would make.

What the hell was Delaney Fraser doing to me?

Oh, I knew why she made my pants feel two sizes too small. That was easy. More than any drug, Delaney was the highest high.

Standing just out of bounds, she tempted me. And last night, I hadn't stayed behind the line.

I'd crossed it.

And here I was, flying across the country, about to cross another one.

I would be landing in New York City in a few hours, one of my favorite places in the world. Madison Square Garden. Barclays Center. I loved the New York venues nearly as much as New York fans.

Gavin, my brother, lived in New York, too. He had moved right after graduating high school, never looked back. Now he was a criminal lawyer, one of the best in the country

The last time I saw Gavin was on my sixteenth birthday. The accident happened a few months afterward. A nurse at the hospital told me she'd gotten in touch with him, but he never showed, not that day and not by the time I left town a couple days later.

I didn't just leave.

I ran.

Pretending that I hadn't lost everything I cared about in the blink of an eye. Filling myself with drinks and drugs, fucking any girl with a pulse. Getting lost in music.

My life was different now. I was different now. My drinking was under control. I didn't do drugs. And while I still loved making music, these days I only felt lost in Delaney's eyes. I would do anything for her. Including reaching out to the one person from my past whose absence still felt like a gaping wound.

Travis would get Delaney's father moved to a better prison.

But I wanted to do more. I wanted to set him free.

And Gavin could make that happen.

Chapter Fifteen

Delaney

The next morning I studied my body in the mirror, expecting to see Shane's handprints covering the surface of my skin. Not because he'd hurt me, but because his touch had burned into me. All night, everywhere. My muscles were deliciously sore, and it seemed strange not to see evidence of our coupling, like stamps on a passport. I caught a few darkened smudges, but only in places where he'd squeezed me tightly. If Shane's skin weren't so tanned, I'm sure I would have marked him, too.

Not that he wasn't marked enough already. Shane's journey was etched on his skin, in vivid colors and deep, dark black. His tattoos were beautiful, and disquieting. They told a story he hadn't yet painted with words. I wanted to know every detail, but I'd been distracted by the electric current sparking at every

point of contact. So much heat, so much intensity. His fire fuel-
ing mine, and vice versa.

Last night Shane had looked at me with raw need, his desire
propped up by desolation, vulnerability shining from every
pore. As if he expected to be turned down. But why?

Shane Hawthorne was gorgeous and successful, an idol to so
many. And yet it was obvious he'd been hurt by those closest to
him, was still hurting.

I was falling for Shane, every minute with him another
chance to break my heart.

And yet with every fiber of my being, I wanted to *heal* his.

So I'd agreed to a contract in name only, weakening the rigid
set of rules Shane had imposed on his life. What would being
Shane's girlfriend, for real, feel like? I had no idea. And I wasn't
going to find out today, either.

This morning I'd woken up to a note on my pillow encourag-
ing me to spend the day relaxing, that he would be back tonight.
It was signed, *XO, me.*

I traced the letters with my fingernail now. *Kiss. Hug. Shane.*

What if last night had been too intense? If he regretted letting me stay, or deciding we were more than a convenient
arrangement?

What if he regretted *everything*?

Deep in the night, his voice thick with passion, Shane had
drawn me close, his cheek flattening my hair, breath hot on my
ear. "Do you know what you do to me?" he'd whispered.

No, I didn't. Although maybe it felt something like what he
was doing to me. Driving me half crazed with lust and fear.

Lust was self-explanatory. Shane was an international sex
symbol.

But my fear stemmed from wanting too much. Scared of

being slapped down by disappointment. Swept away by loss. Again.

Did I have any instinct for self-preservation at all? Obviously not.

Because all my instincts had jumped up and leapt on Shane.

Who was he exactly?

Every time I thought I had him figured out, he showed me another side, unveiled a new piece I hadn't even guessed at.

Shane was like a thousand-piece puzzle bought at a garage sale. The chances of all the pieces being in the box were slim to none, and even if I slowly and laboriously fit the jigsaw together, I had no idea if the pieces would eventually form the picture on the cover, something else entirely, or if they were just a bunch of mismatched segments I couldn't figure out no matter how hard I tried. And yet giving up was unthinkable.

Oddly enough, so much of what I had discovered, reminded me of...*me*.

I couldn't quite tell if that made me understand Shane more.

Or myself less.

I didn't come to L.A. to find myself, like I'd heard so many other people say. What did that mean—finding yourself? I knew who I was. Or at least I had, three years ago.

No. I came to L.A. to lose myself. To forget who I was, what I wanted, what I believed in.

In this crazy town I'd been just another waitress. It was the perfect job title. Because I'd been waiting for my life to begin again.

And then Piper recognized me, introduced me to Travis, and I met Shane Hawthorne.

Last night hadn't been about waiting.

It was about finding.

Not myself. Not even Shane. But finding something to believe in again.

And it felt good. Really good.

Shane

A baseball cap pulled low over my face, I lurked in the elegant lobby of an Upper East Side apartment building, bribing the doorman who'd been none too thrilled by the presence of a tattooed stranger in ripped jeans and a leather motorcycle jacket sprawled across his couch. The older man's uniform was perfectly pressed, shoes shined, gray hair buzzed close to his skull. Definitely not a Nothing but Trouble fan.

After nearly two hours, I finally spotted a face that was as familiar to me as my own, despite not having seen it in more than a decade. "Gavin." I called out my brother's name, the syllables skating through my clenched jaw.

He jerked to a stop on the polished marble floor and swiveled toward me, recognition spreading across his face.

Unfolding myself from the uncomfortable upholstery, I stood. "I probably should have called first."

"I didn't realize you had my number, Sean." His voice was flat, even.

I swallowed past the lump in my throat. No one had called me that in years. "It's pretty easy to find someone these days. If you make any effort at all."

Gavin ignored the not-so-subtle barb. "Do you want to come up?" He spoke slowly, keeping his hands at his sides, as if he was afraid any loud noise or sudden movement would scare me away.

I hesitated, then shook my head. "No."

"So…" Gavin drew the word out, looking at me expectantly. "What can I do for you?"

A hint of the recalcitrant younger brother I'd once been resurfaced, my attitude a mix of sheepish and surly. "What makes you think I'm here because I want something from you?"

He gestured to the bank of elevators, the reception desk. "If all you're after is a reunion, we don't need to have it in public."

My nerves were as shredded the tattered jeans I was wearing. *Just spit it out.* "I'd like to hire you."

Gavin blinked several times in rapid succession, as if he was trying to make sense of my explanation. "You could have called me for that. Or come to my office."

I shot a grin at my brother. "The press would have a field day. Shane Hawthorne hires top criminal defense attorney." A quick flare of pride streaked across Gavin's face. Good. He should be proud. Gavin had always been the smart one in our family. Years ago I'd put a Google Alert on his name, and my in-box was regularly cluttered with links to articles about cases he'd won, honors he'd been awarded. He'd done it all without running away, without lying about his real name. Gavin may have given up on me, but I had never stopped looking up to my older brother.

"Fair point. Okay, consider me hired. Why don't you come up to my apartment? We can discuss your case—"

"No. It's not for me. It's for a friend of mine. The father of a friend of mine. Will you still take the case?"

A deep furrow gathered between Gavin's brows. "You're not connected at all?"

Someone came through the revolving door, and a rush of cool air pushed my hair in front of my eyes. I swiped it away. "To the case, no. Just the girl."

Gavin lowered his briefcase, his eyes searching mine. "She's important to you?"

"Yes. Very." My answer was immediate, automatic.

I didn't breathe until he answered. "Okay. E-mail me the details and I'll make it my top priority." He handed me his business card.

The way Gavin said the words, with a confident sincerity, reaffirmed my decision to come here. "Thanks, Gav."

His expression softened at the nickname I tossed out so instinctively. "You think we can catch up one of these days? Been a long time."

"Sure. We can do that."

Silence rippled between us, churning with unsaid accusations and unmet expectations. My brother offered a skeptical nod. "How about now?"

Now? No. Too soon. "I have a show in L.A. tomorrow. I'm heading back to the airport now."

"Oh, all right." Gavin bent to pick up his briefcase, but not before I saw a disappointed crease slash across his forehead.

I took a step toward the door, thought better of it. "Actually, the jet's chartered, so I can stay for a while. You know, if you're free." Curling my hands into the pockets of my dark jeans, I rocked back on my heels, holding my breath.

Gavin's familiar smile warmed me from the inside. He waved his hand in the direction of the elevator. "After you."

A few minutes later, I collapsed into the nearest chair in Gavin's spacious living room and glanced around his apartment. "Nice place. You've come a long way, huh?"

He lifted a sardonic brow. "Not quite as far as you."

Winning this particular competition was cold comfort. Alone with my brother for the first time in years, I wasted no more time. "You left me." My voice was ragged with emotion and hurt.

Gavin winced, as if my accusation hit him like a sucker punch to the kidneys. "I had to. I couldn't stay there, not even for you. Not all of us are born with talent like yours, knowing it's only a matter of time before you hit it big. If I wanted to get anywhere in life, I needed to leave home."

I snorted. My success had been far from guaranteed. I could just as easily be singing on a corner for spare change as selling out stadiums. "So that's what you've been telling yourself all these years?"

Gavin reared back, incredulous. "Jesus Christ, Shane. You were almost a teenager by the time I took off. Dad was barely around by then, and even when he was, you knew as well as I did how to avoid him."

My jaw dropped. "You think I care about our piece-of-shit father? What gets me is that you knew about the accident. You were my next of kin; I gave the hospital your number before they released me. And you never showed."

"They said you were fine. And I came home the very next weekend."

I exploded. "Yeah, I was fine. Lucky fucking me! But did they tell you I killed someone that night? Did they tell you my best friend wasn't as lucky as I was?" I felt sick. "Caleb died, Gav. He fucking died—and you didn't even come home. Where the hell were you?"

Gavin swallowed. "I was in law school, working three jobs to pay my tuition. I could barely afford my rent, let alone a plane ticket home and a weekend off. And no, they didn't tell me. They said you had been in an accident but you were fine. You weren't actually admitted to a room, so I couldn't call. I didn't find out what had happened until I came back a few days later, but by then you had already taken off."

I turned wary eyes on Gavin. "You went to Caleb's house?"

He nodded. "His parents weren't helpful."

"Can you blame them? It's my fault we were out that night, my fault we got in an accident. But I'm here and their son is buried six feet under." My voice cracked. I was still struggling to accept Caleb's death, and to live with the guilt. It wasn't easy.

He dipped his head, pulling out old memories. "I drove around to every one of your friends that weekend. Your bandmates, your teachers, the music store you practically lived at. I even scraped up enough money to hire a private investigator after I got back to New York, not that it did any good."

A rueful echo of a smile tugged at the corners of my mouth. "Hitchhiking across the country doesn't leave much of a paper trail."

"I had the guy looking for you for years. Of course, he wasn't looking for Shane Hawthorne." Gavin waited a beat, glancing at me expectantly, but I remained silent. "Five years ago, I was in San Francisco for a bachelor party. We all went out to a club one night and there you were, headlining. Not that I recognized you at first. Gone was the scrawny kid with a buzz cut. You'd grown nearly half a foot, gained at least fifty pounds. I couldn't believe it. My little brother was up onstage, belting out songs like you'd been doing it all your life, chicks screaming your name. I was so damn proud of you."

My gut twisted. There was a time when I would have given anything to hear those words come from Gavin's mouth. But that time was long gone. "Proud, huh? So proud you didn't even try to see me after the show?"

"Are you kidding me?" Gavin howled, an outraged boar insulted by a glancing hunter's arrow. "I gave the bouncer five hundred bucks to let me backstage, and I walked in on some chick blowing you in your dressing room. You took one look at me and said, 'This ain't part of the show, brother. Get the fuck out and don't come back.'"

Shaking my head, I tried to dredge up some semblance of memory. I'd been drinking so much in those days it was a wonder I could stand up, let alone remember any of my lyrics. "You thought I recognized you because I called you 'brother'?"

"Of course! Didn't you?"

A harsh laugh erupted from my throat. "I don't remember much from those days, but believe me, I wouldn't have recognized jolly old St. Nick if he'd gotten on his knees and taken the girl's place."

Gavin looked on, confused. "Why not?"

"Gav, back then I was so hopped up on drugs, booze, girls…It sounds like you walked in on me when I was high on all three. I can't say for sure, but I doubt I recognized you then and I sure as hell don't remember it now."

Slumping into his chair, Gavin completely deflated. "You left home, never made any effort to let me know where you ended up, or even if you were still alive. When I finally found you, heard straight from your mouth you didn't want me around…" Gavin's words faded as the truth pressed in on him. "I'm sorry. I should have known. I'm so sorry."

I lurched forward, clutching at my brother's shoulders. "No, I'm sorry. You were always my hero, dude. I was sixteen at the time of the accident and you were what, twenty-three? We were kids. I shouldn't have expected you to know what was going on, to just appear out of thin air and rescue me from a disaster I'd created all my own."

Gavin's face twisted, long fingers wrapping around his knees. "Yeah, well. I'm no hero. Not then and not now. But if I could do it all over again, I would have been there for you. Been there for everything."

I swallowed a lump that had been building for more than a decade. "Thanks, Gav."

* * *

I spent most of the flight home fighting the urge to drink the entire bottle of Jack Daniel's I knew was on board. Seeing my brother had stirred up a hornet's nest of emotions, and it felt like my brain was on fire. But I needed to feel them, work through each one. Otherwise, I was primed to spend the next ten years much like I'd spent the last—surrounded by people and yet entirely alone. Lonely.

I didn't want to be lonely anymore. Maybe I didn't have to be.

I arrived back in Malibu sober, shucking off my clothes as I trudged upstairs. It was late, and Delaney was asleep in my bed. Naked, I slipped between the sheets and pulled her to my chest, her flimsy teddy offering scant barrier between us. She moaned softly, and I kissed her ear. I thought about doing more, but my mind was too restless to focus on anything, even sex with Delaney.

Seeing my brother had brought back a tidal wave of memories, not all of them good. Seven years older than me, Gavin had always been the golden child. Smart, athletic, good-natured. If there was anyone who could prevent our father's apoplectic rages, it was Gavin. I'd always felt like an afterthought. An "oops" baby, delivered too late to two people who never should have had children in the first place. Our mother was timid, beaten down by years of abuse from her husband and relieved to pass the burden of caring for her younger son onto her firstborn. Growing up, I followed Gavin everywhere, and Gavin knew better than to complain. If he left me alone, even as a toddler, I would either be neglected by our mother or kicked around by our father.

Unconsciously, I made a sound low in my throat. Part growl, part moan. Delaney rolled over, blinking sleepily. "You're back."

"Sorry. Go back to sleep."

The lights were off, but various electronic devices throughout the room glowed softly enough that Delaney could see my face. "What's wrong?" she asked immediately. "What happened?"

I considered brushing her off, or lying. Did I really want to talk about my family?

I didn't, but I didn't want to lie either. I was so tired of lying. "I went to see my brother. In New York."

Delaney drew her hand up, propping it beneath her temple. "I didn't know you had a brother."

"I haven't seen him in more than ten years."

She sucked in a quick breath. "Oh."

I brushed the hair back from her forehead, but it slipped through my fingers like strands of silk. "You asked about my family the other day. You sure you want to hear it? It's not exactly Stepford."

Her face was open, receptive. "If you're ready to talk about them, I'm ready to listen."

A soft grunt left me. "I don't even know where to begin."

She gave me the push I needed. "Was it good to see your brother again, after all these years?"

"Yeah. Great, actually. Except for realizing that those years were just wasted. It didn't need to be that way, and I'm mad at myself for assuming the worst of him. Of all the people in the world I should have known I could count on, it was Gavin." I sighed, shaking my head against the pillow. "I was stupid."

"When was the last time you saw him?" Delaney prodded cautiously.

"He managed to get back for my sixteenth birthday. Our mom had died two years earlier. Cancer. Gavin was in law school then. He was only on partial scholarship and there wasn't ever enough money, so it was a big deal that he came back."

"Were you close to them? Your parents, I mean," she qualified.

A pained cackle rattled up from my chest. "No. Close would not be how I'd describe my relationship with my parents. Hell, I spent most of my youth trying to hide from my father's fists." I looked down at Delaney's sweet face, now cradled between my shoulder and arm. "You really sure you want to hear this? It's not pretty."

She nodded. "I'm not the delicate flower you've made me out to be, Shane."

Smiling, I leaned down to kiss the tip of her nose, then gave in to the tempting pull of her full, pink lips. Lingered there for a minute. "Okay, here you go, the full saga. Shane Hawthorne isn't my real name. The Shane part was a fluke. I was nervous about people finding out about the accident, so at an open-mic night, when I said my name was Sean and the guy with the clipboard wrote down Shane, I didn't correct him. By the time I got to a level where I needed a last name too, I spit out the name of my high school guidance counselor."

She barely blinked at my deception. "So your real name is Sean…?"

"Sutter," I filled in.

Delaney tried it out on her tongue, "Sean Sutter." She smiled. "Cute."

I grunted. "It makes me sound like a weatherman."

"Don't knock it. Al Roker's made quite a career out of telling people what's going on right outside their own door."

Another kiss. Delaney was nearly irresistible. I would have been content to forget the family history, but she nudged me in the ribs. "Come on, story time."

More like a nightmare. "My father was a long-distance trucker, so he was gone a lot, and when he was around, Gav and I knew better than to come home much. But we tried, mostly so that he would have someone else to beat on besides our mom. And every time he left, we begged her to pack a bag and take us somewhere, anywhere he couldn't find us. But she wouldn't. Except once."

In the darkness, I squinted at the flashbacks of memory. "Gavin was older, and I guess he was nervous about going off to college and leaving us alone, so he borrowed a car from one of his friends and drove us across state lines to some shelter. None of us had been to a doctor in years—no insurance—and the shelter offered free medical care. When it was my mom's turn to get checked out, they found it. I don't even know what kind of cancer it was, except that it was already in a few places by then. There wasn't anything to be done, or at least that's what they told us. And anyway, my mom wasn't a fighter. So we drove home. We were back before my dad returned from his road trip." I cleared my throat. "The bastard didn't even know we'd finally convinced her to leave him."

After a few moments, Delaney gently nudged me. "So you took care of her while she was sick?"

"Of course, but she didn't last long. Just a few months. And believe it or not, my dad got what was coming to him, too. He got into a fight at a truck stop about a year after her passing. It must have been pretty bad, because he wound up in the hospital. And wouldn't you know, he came down with some kind of bacterial infection. They started cutting him off bit by bit. Ironic that the first to go was his right hand, the one he used to punch us with. For a while they thought they could save him. He was there for months. I would get these hopeful calls from his nurses at the hospital, saying my father missed me and that it would mean the world to him if I could visit." Every syllable dripped with disgust. "I never did. Figured the only reason I would want to see him would be to shut off his life support. But he died anyway, all on his own. Karma, I guess."

Through the open windows, the tide was a steady drumbeat. "What happened then? Who took care of you? You were only fifteen."

"My parents' medical bills couldn't be passed on to us, but they took every cent that was left, which was next to nothing anyway. Caleb was the lead singer of our band. We practiced in his garage, and I practically lived at his house. His parents were kind people. I think they'd always wanted to have a house full of kids, but they only were able to have the one. They took me in, gave me a bedroom and an allowance for chores, even paid for me to take guitar lessons." My voice cracked. "The Branfords were great, just really great people." A wave of guilt crashed over me, so powerful I had to fight to take a breath. "And I paid them back by killing their only child."

Chapter Sixteen

Delaney

My gasp was loud in the quiet room. Is that how Shane thought of himself—as a murderer? No wonder there was such a strong connection between us. Needing to know more, I prodded. "Tell me about the accident."

Shane sighed, his breathing labored. "One afternoon, we got a call to play in a bar that was pretty well known for discovering new talent, or at least we thought so. It was an hour away and we'd only been asked because another band had canceled due to a storm moving in. I begged Caleb's parents to let us borrow their car so we could drive up for the gig."

Shane's voice turned hard. "Of course, it didn't occur to me that no one would actually show up to hear us play in the middle of a blizzard. It wasn't snowing when we left, but by the time we got there it was coming down hard. There were only two people in the audience that night, and one of them was the owner of the bar. But we played well, and he booked us for another gig the next month."

"Feeling like studs, we'd asked the bartender for beer. Knowing we were underage, he laughed us off. But whether he slipped us a few under the table, or one of the guys took them while he wasn't looking, we had four cans by the time we pulled out of the parking lot." Regrets rolled from Shane's big shoulders, making the air in the room feel heavy and cloying. "The other guys drank theirs while I was driving. I didn't touch mine. I swear. Was planning to save it, kind of like how businesses frame their first dollar, you know."

I reached out a hand and set it flat on Shane's chest, so I could feel the reassuring thud of his heartbeat. He covered my hand with his own for a moment, then pulled it up to his mouth to press a kiss against my palm.

"It feels almost like a bad dream now. I was driving pretty slow, and visibility was shit. We were just a few miles from home, my beer untouched in my cup holder. The guys were razzing me, wanting it." As the story unfurled, Shane's voice changed, growing increasingly quiet and thin with strain. "I went to smack whoever's hand was reaching from the backseat—I only took my eyes off the road for a second. But it was enough. I skidded on black ice, and we plowed into a tree. It wasn't even a big tree, but the impact was smack in the middle of the passenger door, where Caleb was sitting."

"So fucking stupid." Shane wiped at his eyes, fingers coming away wet. "His parents had given him a red hat for Christmas. His blood was the same color as the hat, so at first I didn't understand how badly he was hurt. Caleb just looked like he was sleeping." He shuddered, recalling the scene. "But he wouldn't wake up."

Shifting closer to thread my legs through his, I slid my hand from Shane's chest to his back, wrapping him up in a tangle of limbs and heat, waiting patiently for him to start talking again, even if it was in a faraway tone that was so filled with pain it hurt to listen. Seconds went by, then minutes. Shane gathered me even closer, the swoosh of his heartbeat beneath my ear merging with the pulse of the ocean. A shaky breath rattled from his lungs. "I got off without a scratch, if you can believe it. The guys in the back had a few minor injuries—a broken ankle, stitches." Shane coughed, his voice still thick with sorrow. "But Caleb was gone before the ambulance arrived."

My stomach churned at the similarities to my life. Sorrow and sadness radiated from him, throbbing between us. Shane's grief felt so familiar to me. I knew it as intimately as he did. It was like the tide. It might recede, but it always came back. Constant. Relentless.

"I passed the Breathalyzer, but there were whispers in town, and a bad energy that went beyond mourning. They blamed me for his death, kept pointing out the beer cans found in the car, saying the Breathalyzer was broken or incorrectly administered. Building a case to send me to jail. The cops, the Branfords, the whole town. Or at least that's how it felt to me. I didn't even stick around for the funeral—was told I wouldn't be welcome. I didn't blame them. I was the driver. The accident was my fault. Caleb's death was my fault. So I grabbed my guitar and took off."

His words, all of them, piled on top of my chest. I couldn't get a deep breath. "That's just too much for one person, let alone a sixteen-year-old kid, to deal with." I rose on my elbow, my breasts pushing against Shane's chest as I stared down into his eyes. "How did you survive it, Shane?" *Tell me. Teach me. Because I'm still struggling.*

His hand lifted to fit against my cheek, thumb sweeping across my lower lip. "Surviving is the easy part. All it takes is not dying, and that was just dumb luck."

I shivered. "What's the hard part?"

"Letting go of the anger. Not spending every waking moment anesthetizing myself against everything. Living, really living."

The air between us was electric. Somehow we'd moved beyond the accident. That's the way grief worked. You could only wallow in it for so long before needing to laugh or dance or scream. "What else?" I asked, needing Shane to acknowledge this connection between us, too.

He did, his face pinched with tension. "This, what's happening between us. Caring about you. Letting you in. I don't want to, Delaney. When you go, I'm going to be lost. Again."

I blinked against the turbulence raging in his eyes. "I'm not going anywhere, Shane." *At least, not tonight.*

Shane's brow twisted with doubt. "You sure? Now you know the truth, my truth. I'm not the guy you thought I was."

I sucked in a quick breath, needing oxygen. Shane was trusting me with his secrets and I still couldn't give him mine. "No. You're not. You're so much better." He'd stopped a drunk driver before I'd gathered the nerve to call 911. He'd gone to see his brother, but I was still hiding from my father. Shane was brave and I wasn't.

His hoarse cackle split the thick air. "Why?"

For a fleeting moment, I was tempted to tell him everything. My truth. My pain. My lies.

I opened my mouth, a confession at the tip of my tongue. Until I looked into Shane's eyes and pushed it back down. It churned in my stomach, back where it belonged.

Unlike the last time I'd been tempted to tell Shane the truth, I wasn't holding back because I didn't trust him.

But this was Shane's moment. He'd been brave enough to share his ugly truths with me. Unloading my own would only diminish the weight of his.

For a man who lived in the spotlight, Shane kept so much of himself shrouded in darkness. Tonight he'd lifted a candle—just for me.

I wanted to honor that.

Or maybe I was just scrounging for an excuse to linger in the darkness myself.

Because if he knew what I'd done, would he ever look at me the same way?

Sliding my palms along Shane's strong jaw, I cupped his face in my hands, wishing I could erase the skepticism staring back at me. "Because you're real. And tonight you're honest." I dropped a kiss on his pursed lips. A kiss he didn't quite return. My heart skipped, and I leaned back. "Let's live, Shane. Just us, just tonight. Come alive with me."

The gold sparks in his eyes lit up. His hand curved around my skull, threading through my hair. "Anyone ever tell you you're fucking irresistible?"

"No," I groaned as Shane held me a breath away from his lips. "Just me?"

My chest heaved at the solemn rasp of his voice. "Yes. Just you, Shane. Only you."

A sensual smile tugged at his full lips, the sight more beautiful to me than even the sunrise. "That's right," Shane whispered. "My girl."

Shane

Once the high of performing began to fade, it was tempting to keep it going with whatever inducements were on hand. Booze, pharmaceuticals, girls. They were all part of life on the road, and because of them, there were more than a few tours I barely remembered.

Sex, drugs, and rock 'n' roll.

After I opened up to Delaney, the next few shows passed in a blur, and not because I was shit-faced the whole time. If I wasn't at sound check, onstage, or sleeping, every minute was spent devouring Delaney. By the time I walked offstage and into her arms, I had no interest in anyone else, so I generally avoided the post-show parties that broke out after our performances, but tonight was Landon's birthday.

Reluctantly, I unwound myself from Delaney's arms, pulled away from her sweet, sweet lips. "Come on, gotta go toast the birthday boy."

Catching sight of my face in the mirrored glass hanging above her head, I was startled by the expression on my face. Out of necessity, I'd perfected the kind of rock-star, pseudo-angry gaze I used during magazine shoots and the flattered but not necessarily interested look I used with fans. But at the moment I wore neither of those. I looked...*happy*.

I turned away, scrubbing a palm over my face. Must have been a trick of the light.

Still sweaty from the show, I took a quick shower before heading to the reception room with Delaney, where a post-show/birthday party was already in full swing.

As soon as we stepped into the room, I knew it was a mistake.

The acrid notes of cocaine floated on air already heady with exhilaration and laughter. Girls wearing more lipstick than clothing were sucking back champagne, guys fisting bottles of beer or tumblers brimming with Jack Daniel's finest. My favorite. Landon and the guys were easy to spot. They were in the middle of the room, surrounded by an eager, boisterous throng.

Three chicks were hanging off Landon, their stance possessive and imperious, winners of the groupie gauntlet claiming their prize. I snagged a flute for Delaney and a beer bottle for me, fighting Jack's pull. Maybe I could have handled a few sips, but I knew it would make turning down a line of coke that much harder. One would lead to another, and half a dozen after that. Eventually some oxy to even things out.

Knowing all three were within reach, I felt a tingle at the back of my neck. My throat was dry, my palms itching. "To the ugliest fucker to ever get behind a set of drums," I said, clinking my beer with an array of bottles and glasses. "For your birthday I'm getting you a bigger set, to hide that mug from our fans before they stop coming to our shows."

Landon's head tilted back, laughter booming out of him. "I'll show you a bigger set, jackass." An eager blonde hooked her fingers around the band of his jeans, Landon doing nothing to stop her.

I pulled Delaney against me, knowing the only *set* she'd lay eyes on tonight was mine. "Yeah, yeah. You do that. I'm sure no one here would take a dick pic or anything."

Flashing his trademark wink, Landon tilted the neck of his beer bottle at me. "Don't you worry there, brother. I'll send one to your girl personally. Make sure she's not missing out on anything."

If I didn't love him, I would have ripped the jugular out of his neck. "You do that, Landy, and I'll make sure you choke on it." We had shared girls in the past, and he'd made his interest in Delaney perfectly clear.

I didn't blame Landon for his interest, but Delaney was off-limits.

My eyes slid back to her, watching as her lips closed around the delicate glass and she took a small sip. "Let's get out of here," I growled.

Delaney was all mine.

* * *

A car was waiting for us, not far from a small horde of fans clustered behind a few ropes. I heard their screams of "I love you, Shane! You rock my world, Shane!" through the walls as we walked along the underground tunnels leading to the exit. Disgust curled my lip. These girls, screaming things they thought I wanted to hear, pledging an emotion that should mean something, they didn't *know* me. They listened to my songs without hearing them, looked at me without actually seeing me.

They swallowed every single lie I fed them.

And it was all part of the show. The facade I'd erected in place of a life. Trading my sneer for a smile, I ambled over to the ropes, signing autographs, taking selfies, giving just enough of myself to make them think I might love them back.

By the time I got into the car with Delaney, she was staring dubiously through the window at the squealing pack of girls we were leaving behind. "I'm beginning to understand why you hire your girlfriends."

I still had that strange post-show energy buzzing inside my

veins, and my hands crept up Delaney's skirt. I needed to work it off. "Oh yeah?" I pulled her into my lap, settling her legs on either side of mine, reaching around to cup her perfectly sculpted ass.

"We've been on tour for a few weeks, and so far the only women I've seen are the groupies, who look at you as if you're their next meal or fans whose heads practically explode if you look their way." She sucked in a breath, wide-eyed and guileless. "I had no idea."

My heart lurched. When Delaney looked at me, she really saw me. Me and my crazy, fucked-up life. "Now you've got a front-row seat."

Delaney traced my lips with her fingertips. "Yeah. I do."

Her touch sent a shudder rippling through me. I edged aside the strip of lace in my way, dragged my fingers through her wet center. "I've been missing this all day." It was the truth. Sound check had run long, and then I'd called Travis to tell him about the shift in my relationship with Delaney. Even though Delaney and I had agreed to a contract in name only, I wasn't sure I wanted even that.

Maybe she still needed to believe that a set of rules defined our interaction, but I didn't. Not anymore. I wanted Travis to tear up our contract. Wanted to know that the hold I had on her was body, mind, and soul. That it ran too deep to be contained by a sheet of paper.

He'd kept me on the phone for an hour. *Are you out of your fucking mind? What do you really know about Delaney? You sure she's not playing you?*

Travis was more than just my attorney. He'd gotten me out of jail, gotten me sober, believed in me when he shouldn't have. I could understand his frustration, and I let him vent it. His biggest concern, that I would fall back into abusing drugs and alcohol, was a moot point. I was entirely confident that Delaney had my best interest at heart. Beyond that, I wasn't willing to let anything dull the buzz I got just from being around her. In the end, he promised to shred the employment contract Delaney had signed, although of course she would still be paid the money she was promised.

Maybe I didn't know everything about Delaney Fraser, but I knew enough. Enough to take a chance on her. On us.

I was ready to let go of the edge and dive deep.

Bliss descended on Delaney as she broke apart in my arms, gripping my shoulders and groaning my name. And in that moment, I knew with one hundred percent certainty, only one thing mattered. *Us.*

Delaney

The phone rang before five. The one on the nightstand, not either of our cell phones.

Shane pulled the covers over our heads, then wrapped his arms around me more tightly. "It'll stop," he mumbled, his voice thick with sleep.

But it didn't. Four rings, seven rings, ten. The air around my head was vibrating, not from the phone, but from Shane's wrath. Finally, he bolted upright so violently, I expected him to grab the phone and hurl it across the room. I'd learned that touring was filled with early mornings, and this was one of the few we were able to sleep in. "Someone better be dead," he growled.

Tension coiled around his muscles, flexing and contracting as he held the phone to his ear. I waited, each passing second making it less likely we'd be going back to sleep anytime soon.

After he hung up, Shane sank back into the mattress as if a heavy mantle had been dropped onto his shoulders. I rested a steadying hand on his thigh. "What is it?"

He huffed, indignant. "That was Travis."

I didn't pick up on the warning in his tone. "Let's not talk about Travis right now," I whispered, sliding my palm up his chest, the last of my sleepy fog swept away by the ripple of muscles beneath the surface of Shane's skin.

Catching my hand, Shane pressed it over his heart. "No, don't." Horror radiated from his expression as he turned to me, his pulse racing against my palm. "We have to talk."

I blinked, brows knitting over the bridge of my nose. Talk? Since when did Shane, or any red-blooded male, turn down sex to *talk*? Fear spiraled through me, sending tingles down my limbs.

"Delaney." He drew my name out, so sorrowful. An apology.

My stomach knotted, turning over on itself. I lifted wide, questioning eyes to Shane, tears already starting to gather. "What happened?" Vulnerability bled from my words. I could hear it, hated it. Hated waiting to be told bad news, as if I hadn't heard enough of it in my lifetime. Like I would somehow collapse under the weight of whatever Shane was holding back from me. *I can take it, whatever it is. Just tell me, damn it.*

"Fuck. I'm so sorry." Blazing eyes swept over my face, fierce shards of remorse scraping my skin.

"What happened?" I repeated, feeling the kind of adrenaline rush I got from a Red Bull. But this wasn't caffeine, just a double dose of anxiety. "Tell me, Shane." *What happened?* I wanted to shake the answer out of him.

"Travis was…" The Adam's apple in Shane's throat bobbed as he swallowed heavily. "He was reviewing your contract last night, and he thinks someone from his cleaning crew picked it up and sold it." His jaw clenched, biting out the last two words. "It's out."

The blood drained from my head. "What do you mean, it's out? Where did it go?"

Shane stared down at my face, looking at me as if these were our last few seconds together. Dread pricked the base of my skull, skittering down my spine. I grabbed my phone from my purse, pulling up the Internet browser. There, on the front page of my news feed, was the blaring headline GIRLFRIEND FOR HIRE: SHANE HAWTHORNE PAYS TO PLAY.

A small shriek flew out of my mouth, too fast for my hand to hold it back. I pressed my fingers against my lips anyway, as if I could contain the panic spiraling inside my stomach like a tornado, swallowing me within its angry funnel.

I was breathing, my heart pounding. Very much alive.

Reading my obituary.

The whole reason I'd signed that damn contract was to make a new life for myself. Go back to school, become someone my parents would be proud of.

Lately I'd been thinking about changing my major from economics to prelaw. Since my father refused to hire an attorney on his own behalf, maybe I could help his case. Eventually, a law degree would allow me to help others, too.

Where did it go? Shane didn't have to answer my question, because I already knew the answer.

Viral. This filthy, grossly exaggerated story that added prostitution to my résumé had gone viral.

How many law firms welcomed former prostitutes into their ranks? No need for a pesky trial. I'd been convicted by a tabloid that would probably show up on the first page in any Google search of my name. Had my future career been cut short before it even began?

A wave of loathing crashed into me. So many lies, I couldn't escape them.

My father would see it. Read it.

Would he believe it, too?

Chapter Seventeen

Shane

Unfuckingbelievable.

Actually, no. This was my life. I tried to do something good, something right... and just wound up making things worse.

Needing to see Delaney's face, I swept aside the curtain of hair that had fallen over her cheek. "Travis is working on it. He'll fix it." My voice was a tortured growl, spewing an empty promise.

Delaney looked up from her phone. "They're calling me a prostitute," she whispered, horror leaching from her words, slashing at my eardrums like razor blades. Even worse was the misery and embarrassment vandalizing her beautiful features. The past few years hadn't been easy for Delaney, but she'd never been through the meat grinder of public persecution. Until today. Until this.

Until me.

"You should go see your father."

"I know." Her answer was a hesitant whisper.

I waited a minute. "Does that mean you're going to go, or that you know you should but haven't made up your mind yet?"

She lifted sheepish eyes to mine. "I don't know. It would mean leaving you."

A sigh shuddered through me. "Don't do that, Delaney."

She broke our gaze, tucking her head into my shoulder, laying a hand flat across my chest. "Do what?"

I reached for it, planting a kiss at the center of her palm. "Don't hide behind me. You're braver than that."

She dipped her head, but not before I saw the fading glory of crushed hope staining her gaze. "I guess I'd just always envisioned striding into the prison like some kind of filial Joan of Arc, keys to my father's cell in one hand and a pardon in the other." She lifted her head, tears brimming. "What do I say to him? Hey, Dad, just driving by to apologize for this little story you may have read—the one calling me a whore. Hope your new digs are worth it."

Guilt slammed into me, churning and twisting in my gut like a virus. "I know. It sucks. But you still have to do it."

She choked out a sob. "What a fucking mess, huh?"

My entire life was a fucking mess.

I pulled Delaney into me, holding her tight. She shook, and I absorbed every tremor, wrapping my arms around her waist like an iron band. Tight. Secure. Unbreakable.

"I'll go with you, if you want me to." I'd go to the seventh circle of hell if she asked. Had spent years there already. Might be time for a return trip.

Delaney's head rocked against my neck. "No. You're right.

I do have to see him. But if you come with me…" Her voice trailed off.

"I know. It will be a damn circus. Like always." I spat out the words as if they were venom. Didn't make them any less true.

Dark hair swished back and forth along my collarbone. "It's not your fault you have fans everywhere."

I practically choked on the excuse Delaney was spoon-feeding me, her light tone only making it worse. Had this damn story taught her nothing?

Everything was my fault.

I swallowed, hard. I was used to all kinds of things being said about me in the press. Some of it was the truth. Most of it was lies.

My skin had hardened over the years. And when it came to downloads and ticket sales, I'd learned that it didn't really matter what was said about me. If people were talking, it worked in my favor. Even so, I paid Travis and a PR team a hell of a lot of money to spin bad press into good.

I glanced at the phone, hoping, for Delaney's sake, they could handle this. Knowing they couldn't. This story was too salacious, too juicy. A bag of catnip to a den of lions.

My chest squeezed tight. Not for me. I could take it. But Delaney…she was about to get mauled. And there wasn't much I could do about it.

"I'm so sorry. For all of this." I meant it with every ounce of my soul. The black cloud that followed me, I'd dragged Delaney under it, too.

She stared at me in stunned silence, absorbing the blow that had come out of nowhere. Disillusionment twisted her lips as she offered a somber nod. "Okay," she choked out.

I didn't know what was worse—causing Delaney any

pain…or that she'd so easily accepted it as a by-product of life with me.

Now she knew exactly how much bullshit would be thrown her way if she continued to stand at my side. When was she going to realize what I knew already? What I'd known for more than a decade.

That I wasn't worth it. Nothing but Trouble. That wasn't just the name of my band. It was my fucking motto.

The voice that had warned me to leave Delaney alone before I ruined her, I should have listened to it.

I studied Delaney's tortured expression, feeling like I'd just slain an angel. My angel. Ruined.

Reaching for her phone, I put it facedown on the bed and swept Delaney into my chest. Maybe I should walk away now. Tell Travis to deny everything and chalk it up to a breakup gone bad. If we weren't together, the story might shrivel up and die on its own. Without us, there would be no fuel.

The only problem was—Delaney was *my* fuel. Just the sight of her face filled me with hope, with joy. Lit me up in a way no one ever had before. How could I walk away from her?

I couldn't. I wouldn't. Because I was a selfish bastard. Nothing but fucking trouble.

Why did she have to be real? Since the moment I laid eyes on Delaney Fraser, I hadn't been able to walk away from her. And now she was paying the price for my greed.

Smoothing the hair away from her temples, I fisted my hand and stroked her cheekbone with my knuckles. "You gonna stay?" My voice was a husky plea, but still. I had to ask.

A strangled laugh shuddered through her. "Why? Are you trying to get rid of me?"

Not a chance. A wave of need stole my breath as I kissed the crown of Delaney's head, then buried my face in her mess of thick dark hair, willing myself to inhale. "Never," I groaned, my mind tumbling out of control. Lust and greed. Fuck. I wanted to consume her. Devour her.

I trailed my fingers along her bare spine, feeling her heartbeat picking up in time with mine. Our breath quickened as the air in the room changed, shimmering with unspent energy. I hardened against the thigh she'd draped casually over my hip. "Delaney…?" I rasped. A question.

"Shane." An answer.

I pulled her on top of me, her whole body stretching out against mine. Nerve endings fired, shooting off bright bursts of pleasure at every point of contact. My hands roamed lower, cupping the lush globes of her ass, rocking her against me. "You shouldn't stay. We both know that."

Delaney lifted her head, eyes as tortured and confused as mine. "Maybe. But you don't want me to go, do you?"

I wish I were a stronger man. Wish I could have lied as easily to her as I did to everyone else. But I couldn't. "No. I don't want that."

A flicker of a smile lifted the corner of Delaney's pout, the other side following as her thighs opened, knees sliding over my legs to rest on the mattress. "Good. Because I'm staying." Mischief made a tentative dance across her face and I stared, caught up in it. Was I really lucky enough to make this girl mine?

My girl.

It seemed wrong. Impossible.

And yet here she was.

Staying.

Delaney

Maybe I should have left. Tossed off the covers and run out of the room, out of Shane's life. My fight-or-flight instinct had definitely kicked in, bleeding from every pore. Except that the flight part of the equation wasn't very strong. I wanted to *fight*. Fight hard. For me, for Shane, for the us we had just barely become. But who was my enemy? Travis? The janitor who stole my ridiculous contract? Whoever paid him for it? The slime that had written the TMZ post?

The only one in the room with me was Shane.

A nervous kind of willfulness gathered, gaining strength. I finally had something, someone, to fight for. The only question was, would he fight with me?

I spread my hands flat on Shane's chest, my fingers tracing the swirls of ink that marked his skin, skating along the ridges and plains of his abs. My heartbeat took off in a full-on sprint, desire cutting the sting of the scandal making its way across the Internet. "You hired me, Shane."

He swallowed, cupping my cheek and running his thumb along my jaw. "Yeah."

"There's money in my bank account that came from you."

A nod. "Yeah."

"You paid me." My stomach clenched with need. "And according to TMZ, now you get to play with me." I tilted my face back, daring Shane to disagree.

"Is that what you want?" His voice was gravelly and low, dark brows setting off eyes the color of melted caramel.

"Yes. That's exactly what I want. Now." My answer was sure and unambiguous. I needed Shane to know that I trusted him to deal with our fucked-up reality beyond these walls. But right now I needed him to deal with me.

Shane got the message, loud and clear. I could see it burning inside his eyes and in the tight set of his jaw. One hand curved around my neck, my pulse racing beneath his palm. The other skated along my spine, leaving a trail of fire in its wake. His mouth came down on mine, his kiss leaving me senseless.

Just when I thought my life couldn't get any crazier, along came Shane Hawthorne. That contract was a grenade—I knew it the minute Travis had dropped it on the conference room table in his Beverly Hills office. That it exploded shouldn't have surprised me at all. But it had. Anger and lust heating my blood, I wrapped my arms around Shane, digging my nails into his skin. Leaving marks.

Shane's breath hissed over his teeth, his muscles tensing and flexing beneath my hands. "That's how you want to play this, huh?" he growled.

A shiver rolled down my back. "Shut up and fuck me." There was nothing I could do about some minimum-wage janitor selling my story to the highest bidder, but this burning knot of fury sitting in my gut—Shane had better wring it out of me.

I was flat on my back in an instant, Shane's eyes blazing into mine as he held my wrists captive above my head. "You sure you know what you're asking for?"

"No." I met his gaze, begging Shane to prove there was a reason my life had been upended. "But you're going to give it to me."

His head dropped to my breast, mouth closing tight around my nipple, teeth biting down. I squealed, arching into him. His tongue flicked at my throbbing peak, and I dragged my nails along his back. Shane released his prize and my cry of frustration sounded in the quiet room. "Oh, it is *on*." His tone was low, guttural.

I struggled. His grip was tight, and I couldn't escape. Not that I wanted to. But everything inside me was tense, held together by nerves stretched to the point of snapping. I needed Shane to fight me, take me, soothe me.

His thumb ran along my rib cage, the roughened callus scraping my skin. "You wanna get some of that anger out, Delaney? That what you want?"

Sweat broke out on my skin, my legs kicking at the sheet wrapped around them. "Yes," I bit out, trying to pull my arms away and having no success whatsoever. It was maddening, infuriating. And it felt so damn good. I turned my head, sinking my teeth into his bicep.

Taken by surprise, Shane released my wrists, and I pushed against his chest, wriggling out of his grip. I nearly made it off the bed, but he caught me by my hair, fisting it inside his grip as his other hand wrapped around my waist like an iron band. "Ah," I grunted, just before Shane pulled me back against him so hard I lost my breath.

"I gotcha."

Oh, Shane Hawthorne definitely had me. His fingers slid along my scalp, gripping my neck and pushing me into the mattress as his knee pressed between my thighs. His body dwarfed mine, his weight on my back, each breath a struggle. Every sense sharpened as he dragged his chin, rough with stubble, along my spine. Dizzying desire unfurled in my belly, and I moaned, spreading my knees outward along the smooth cotton sheets.

"How far do you want to take this?" Shane's voice was a low rumble as his fingers slid along the crease of my ass, lingering over my puckered hole before dragging through my wetness.

How far? *Far*, I wanted to scream. *Take me far, far away, Shane.* But my answer was still trapped inside my head when his palm made contact with my ass. I jerked up, the sting sharp and swift, soothed away in the next instant by the swirl of his tongue on my heated skin, his kiss a tender counterpoint. "Shane," I moaned, pushing back against him. I wanted, *needed* him to take me. Fill me. I could feel his shaft, hard and insistent along my hip. Another slap, another kiss. Jesus.

Realizing I wasn't going to make him chase me, Shane released my wrists and scooped me up onto my knees. "Fuck, I love your ass," he murmured, squeezing it as he positioned himself behind me. My breath caught in my throat as his shaft nudged between the same place his fingers had teased earlier before pausing at the entrance of my slit. Shane chuckled. "Don't worry, Delaney. Eventually, but not tonight." And with that, he buried himself to the hilt in one smooth, powerful thrust, all the breath leaving my lungs in a delicious *whoosh*.

Nothing was gentle about our coupling. Shane fucked me hard and deep, and I loved every minute. There was a darkness inside him, inside me, that needed this. Maybe not all the time, but for tonight, I wanted to straddle the line between good and bad, right and wrong, typical and taboo.

Shifting his stance, he bent over me, his hands on either side of mine, his mouth close to my ear. "You want this, Delaney." It was a question and a statement. It was the truth.

"God, yes," I rasped, jerking back against him, meeting every one of his thrusts. I closed my eyes and all I could see were stars, blinding against the blackness. My walls tightened around his invasion, the spark he'd ignited inside of me taking root. The fire spread, growing hotter, more volatile. Until I could hear the roaring blaze in my ears.

"Take it, baby. Take everything." The turmoil reigning outside wasn't as strong as the passion enveloping us right here, bringing us closer together. We were caught up in it, caught up in each other. Shane was, too. I could feel it in the harshness of his breath, the jagged edge to his voice. The just barely contained ferocity of his assault. But it was controlled. I was controlled.

Shane Hawthorne *owned* me.

Chapter Eighteen

Delaney

My father's prison was two hours from the New Jersey arena Nothing but Trouble was headlining tonight, and a world away from the luxurious hotel where I'd spent the night in Shane's arms. It smelled like a hospital, with underlying notes that were much more pungent and sinister. A stern guard warned that I would be allowed to hug my father only twice, once at the beginning and once at the end of our visit. He shuffled into the room, looking so much smaller and more fragile than the man who had carried me high on his shoulders at every parade, and when my arms encircled his torso, I could feel the hardness of his ribs beneath the rough fabric of his prison-issued shirt.

"Daddy," I cried, reverting back to a name I hadn't used since I was a child.

"You promised me," he said gruffly.

"I know. I'm sorry. But I can't…I can't forget about you. About why you're in here and I'm out there."

My father dipped his head, running both hands over his thinning hair, kneading at the muscles of his neck. His voice was thick with strain. "That's the way it has to be, Delaney. You know that."

That's what he'd told me seconds after impact. Before we heard the sirens. Before we knew my mother was gone. When the police came, he told them he'd been behind the wheel.

A lie that had led to so many others, I was drowning beneath the weight of them all.

"You're the reason for my transfer." His eyes probed mine. "Upstate to here. Maximum to minimum."

I nodded. "It's the least I could do. You shouldn't even be here at all." Tears slid down my cheeks, words wavering.

"It's better. Thank you," he conceded. "But, Delaney, stop worrying about me."

How can I? "Have you seen the news?"

"About you and the musician?"

That answered my question. "What they're saying about me, it's not true. I would never…you know, *be* with someone because he was paying me. I needed to come here today, to tell you that in person."

He gave me a long, sober look. "How many weeks did you go without an allowance because you didn't feel like cleaning your room?" A wisp of a smile curled his lip. "You've always been interested in numbers, but you're the least motivated by money than anyone I've ever met." He cleared his throat. "Are you happy?"

Happy? I recoiled. How could I be happy? But then I realized that after three years of brutal darkness, when even getting out of bed felt like a superhuman challenge, being with Shane made me happy. "I am. Sometimes."

"Because of the singer?"

"Shane. Yes."

"Good. You deserve to be happy, Delaney. Just make sure you follow your own dreams, too. Your mother wanted to be an artist, you know."

I cocked my head to the side. "Really? She never said anything."

He gave a rueful grimace. "School loans, a mortgage, a husband, a baby she adored. She thought spending time and money on herself was frivolous." His words took on an urgency. "Get out of here, Delaney. Forget about me."

I was shaking. "Forget about you?" I cried in a choked whisper. "You're my father. I can't. I can't do it, Daddy."

"You have to, Delaney. Let me do my time knowing you're out there, living your life. Please."

I pressed the heels of my hands into my eyes, memories from that awful night running through my mind like a film reel.

Three years ago I had been home from school, going out to dinner with my parents before meeting up with a few friends. The restaurant was near the train station, so my father walked there after work. I'd been running late, my nose in a book. By the time my mother and I arrived, my father had finished his usual martini. I offered to drive home, and my parents proceeded to share a bottle of wine with dinner.

We were at a light when I picked up my phone and began texting my friends that I would be there in half an hour. The next thing I knew, there was a screeching sound and the car was spinning.

Texting while driving was illegal, and even though my father knew he would probably be over the legal limit, he hauled me out of the car before anyone realized which one of us had been behind the wheel.

Before we saw my mother's lifeless body, slumped in the backseat.

Shame flattened my words. "How can I live my life when it feels like I've stolen yours?" *And Mom's.* I left that second thought unspoken though. It was too much.

His eyes, darker than mine, flashed. "Because if I have to see you in here, it would kill me, Delaney. Don't do that to me." My father's voice was adamant, his thin frame bristling with anger.

So I gave in, nodding weakly. "Okay, Daddy." Feeling like the worst daughter in the world.

He sucked in a breath and rose. On trembling legs, I stood, stepped into his embrace. Too soon, there was a buzz, a clang. He broke away, spine stiff.

Two sets of heavy footsteps dead-ended at the metal door, one guard to take my father back into the bowels of the prison and the other to lead me back to freedom.

Freedom I didn't deserve.

* * *

By the time I arrived at the hotel, the clanking of heavy metal gates still echoing inside my ears, Shane had already left for the arena. Desperate to erase the smell of prison that had seeped into my pores, I took a scalding-hot shower, liberally applying every scented product in the bathroom to my skin and scalp. Earlier, I wasn't sure I would make it to tonight's Nothing but Trouble concert, but now every cell in my body was crying out for Shane.

Piper was back in L.A., and with no hair and makeup people to fuss over me, I reached for a formfitting tank dress that was made of silk jersey the same color as my skin and overlaid with a delicate pale-gray fabric. From afar, I would appear naked beneath bits of carefully placed lace. I straightened my hair, somehow managed to create a smoky eye without looking like a raccoon, then stepped into a pair of strappy high heels.

It didn't take long to arrive at the concert venue, and the driver had obviously called ahead, because a roadie was waiting to escort me to Shane's dressing room. My heels tapped along the concrete floor of the labyrinth of underground tunnels, an all-access badge swaying between my breasts.

Before meeting Shane, I had always tried to fade into the woodwork, but those days were over. Tonight I was not immune to the looks from people I passed in the hallway, desire from the men and jealousy from the women. Their stares only enhanced the buzzing in my veins, adding to the sense of unreality tinting the strange world I now inhabited.

The bodyguard stationed outside Shane's dressing room opened the door and stepped aside. Shane's eyes met mine before falling away to take in my dress, widening slightly in appreciation. "Everyone, clear out."

There was the usual ribbing as Shane's guests left the room. Before the door had even shut behind them, Shane closed the gap between us and took me in his arms. "How did it go today?"

"Fine." I pressed my cheek against his shoulder. "My head is spinning. I need you to make me forget everything for a bit. Can you do that?"

Shane reached for my chin, tipping it upward with his thumb, fingertips sliding along the curve of my neck. On a sigh, my lips opened and I leaned into him, fitting my body against his, inviting his tongue to slide deeper into my mouth. He sucked on my bottom lip and I groaned, my need for him as strong and insistent as my own heartbeat. Craving friction of any kind, I twisted my waist to rub against Shane's shirt, hating the layers that separated us.

I was a hot mess, skin prickling with desire and desperate to feel him inside of me. Shane's hand slid along my cheekbone to cradle my skull, the other following the arch of my spine. Moving lower. Cupping my ass and pulling me in closer, the outline of his cock digging into my belly.

"Shane," I whimpered.

Like it was an invitation, he pushed me up against the wall, reaching for the inside of my knee and pulling it over his hip. "That's right, baby. The only name you need to know is mine. Gonna make you call it out all night long." My dress hiked up, bunching at my waist as I clung to Shane's shoulders. I was lost. So lost.

His kisses grew harder. Giving, taking, pushing, pulling. I kissed him back like my life depended on it. But I was greedy. I wanted more.

And Shane knew. He knew. He ran his palm along the side of my dress, to my naked thigh and lower still. I swung my other leg up, crossing my ankles behind his back. Shane's fingertip ran along my thong, pressing the lace into my crease, finding my clit. "This what you want?"

"Yes," I panted, arching my hips into his hand. *Fuck, yes.*

Pinning my body to the wall with his weight, Shane pulled back just enough to look at me. Eyes like a tumbler of brandy sitting beside a flickering candle. So many shades of brown and gold. "You miss me?"

I sucked in a quick breath, nails digging into his neck as I fought to form the only word I was capable of. "Yes." It came out like a hiss.

Shane pressed harder, deeper, his lips curving into a smirk at my ragged groans. Pleasure spiked, swirling inside me, the pressure building. I closed my eyes, tightening my legs around his hips. A shudder rippled along my spine, leaving me breathless. Breathless but so completely alive. Heart pounding, limbs tingling, blood set to boil. Oh my God.

Shane brought me back to life. With his body and his words. With the way he looked at me, the way he talked to me. The way he fucked me.

I was spinning.

Falling.

Flying.

Floating in a place lit by fireworks and shooting stars.

Shane held me tighter as shudders racked though me.

Kissed me gently as I came back down to earth.

As if on cue, there was a sharp rap at the door and Lynne poked her head into the room, recoiling like a scared turtle when she caught sight of us. "You're on in two, Shane. Everyone else is already on their way."

With a savage breath Shane broke our kiss, his hands gripping my shoulders as he pulled away. "In a minute," he growled.

I unwound my legs, standing shakily on my own feet. "You have to go." My words were flat.

Shane pressed his palm against my neck, his thumb and fingers squeezing just enough to make my head pound. "You're not coming?" he asked.

"I am." I hesitated, tugging my dress down. "I will. I just—"

Shane kissed me again and took a step back. "Take all the time you need." And then he was gone, leaving only the searing imprint of his touch on my skin.

Shane

Two days after Delaney met with her father, she and I sat down for an interview to be aired, teaser by teaser, all of next week, culminating in an hour-long, primetime special. Travis was a firm believer in "no publicity is bad publicity," and even though I didn't really agree with him, I knew that the sooner I addressed the scandal head-on, the sooner it would be in my rearview mirror.

By eight, the hotel suite was a mess of people, lights, and wires. Piper had taken Delaney into one of the bedrooms to get her "camera ready." As far as I was concerned, Delaney was perfect as is, her face bare, hair a dark river of untamed waves. I loved that her lips were still puffy from my kisses, the delicate skin of her neck sporting a pinkened bite mark. She looked like what she was, a gorgeous girl who had been well and thoroughly fucked. For hours. By me.

Except now I was in the other bedroom, too many people touching me, talking to me. Travis and a headphone-wearing, clipboard-clutching production assistant were the loudest. Over the past few weeks Delaney had proved to me that she understood me. I'd laid out all of my demons and secrets, and she had faced them head-on, daring me to use them as an excuse to run away. Escape. And then my already fucked-up life had thrown another curveball. That stupid, goddamn contract.

The first night Delaney came to my beach house, I'd kissed her, wanting to do more. Until she'd said something I'd been trying to disprove ever since. *Don't make me your whore.* Well, now the whole world thought that's exactly what she was. My whore.

She wasn't.

Delaney Fraser was my everything.

Possessiveness pounded through my veins, along with a boil-
ing rage. Definitely not the right mind-set to take into an interview. I should be aloof, impersonal. But how could I? They were
talking about my girl. They were hurting my girl. And I wanted
to fucking kill them.

This was probably how Delaney felt after she'd pulled up the
story on her phone. And we used it. Funneled all that rage into
a blistering sexual marathon that left us completely spent. That
was what I needed now. I needed to fuck. Not give a fucking interview.

The PA finally left, getting nothing from me but a series of
grunts and hostile stares. He was wiry and anxious, and I wanted
to rip him limb from limb.

"Listen," Travis was saying, "I know you're pissed. I get it. This
bullshit happened on my watch, and I'm pissed, too. But we
have a chance to come out on top of this, Shane. You need to
step up. Not just for you, but for Nothing but Trouble. The guys
are depending on you. Delaney's depending on you."

Finally, the mountain of words he'd been piling on me started
to make sense. I sucked in a deep breath, uncurled my hands
from the arms of my chair, and offered a stiff nod.

"Good. This isn't some slimy reporter from *In Touch Weekly*.
This is NBC. This is Mike Lewis. This is their A-team. Guaranteed they've done their homework. Both you and Delaney have
skeletons in your closets. And we have to assume they've found
most, if not all, of them."

My eyes blazed. "What are you trying to say?"

"Shane, this is no puff piece. And that's not a bad thing. Let
everything come out at once, not in dribs and drabs. A little
from *People* here, another piece from TMZ, something else up-

loaded to Radar Online. That's not going to do us any good. We need a major network to shine a spotlight so bright, there won't be any shadows left."

I couldn't even imagine a life with no shadows. The second I walked off the stage, I dove for my shadow like a mole into a dark tunnel. God knew, it was big enough. "You think they know—" I couldn't even say it.

"About the accidents? Delaney's, definitely. And yours, probably. We legally changed your name to Shane Hawthorne, but there's still a paper trail if you dig deep enough."

"Fuck." Sean Sutter died the same night Caleb had. And today he would rise from the grave and be broadcast into every home in America. I'd been just a sixteen-year-old kid when I left. By the time Shane Hawthorne strutted across the stage at the VMA's for the first time, I was in my twenties, a shiny new product of the big-name studio putting out my albums. I'd grown another few inches, added fifty pounds of muscle to my gawky teenage frame. The only one who'd recognized me had been Gavin, and I'd been too wasted know.

Now I was nearing thirty, with everything to lose.

And if I lost Delaney, nothing else would matter.

Chapter Nineteen

Delaney

Piper had barely taken a breath for the past hour, talking non-stop to me and to the people working on my appearance. Quite a feat, since it had taken six outfit changes to decide on a simple white sheath dress, the back held together by safety pins to accommodate a mic pack, and two hours in a chair for hair and makeup.

Rolling my fingers into my palms to keep from scratching at my cheek—apparently television required a different level of cosmetic application than magazines and websites, because the makeup on my face had to be an inch deep—I went over my notes from an intensive one-on-one media training workshop with Shane's publicist.

No looking up when I thought about a question.

No fidgeting, no "ummms," no "likes."

Answer only the question being asked, keep answers short and sweet.

Send lots of loving looks Shane's way, but keep touching to a minimum.

I also had a list of potential interview questions and had practiced my answers until I could give them in my sleep.

A hand on her hip, Piper offered more unsolicited advice. "Stop worrying, Delaney. Just stick to the script and you'll be fine."

What script? I would have lifted my eyebrows, but the heavy coating of makeup made it difficult. I didn't have a script. I had one page of notes. I had answers to questions that *might* be asked. Definitely not the same thing as a script.

A production assistant poked his head in the door. "We're ready for you."

Piper beamed. She'd been assigned to work with me because of our high school connection. I was her first real assignment, and was minutes away from being interviewed for national TV. We'd come a long way from Bronxville.

There was a last flurry from everyone around me, lots of primping and fixing and *zhuzing*. And then, as if they'd coordinated it, everyone backed away, and I stood up on heels that were absolutely gorgeous, but incredibly painful.

Shane's door opened at the same time as mine, and immediately my nerves felt just a little less frantic. "You look beautiful," he said, before leaning close to my ear and adding, "Although your blissed-out, post-sex look is still my favorite."

A trembling knot of desire unfurled deep in my stomach. "Blissed-out, huh?" What a perfect description of how Shane made me feel. Dizzyingly infatuated.

He reached for my hand as we headed into the main part of the suite. The windows had been covered in favor of huge artificial lights, and several cameras were already in position. Off to the side, Mike Lewis was consulting with several of his colleagues, shuffling through color-coded index cards and scribbling notes in the margins. Either I was about to meet the genial morning show host I'd enjoyed waking up to for years, or the best-dressed executioner in America.

Greetings and handshakes were exchanged all around. Mike Lewis was thinner and slightly fussier than he seemed on camera, but very engaging and personable. Maybe this wouldn't be so bad.

The PA called for silence, red lights on the cameras flashing. Lewis launched into his welcoming spiel as if we hadn't already met and chatted for a few minutes.

Ten questions in, the one at the heart of the interview finally came. "Shane, recently a document has come to light indicating that your relationship with Delaney is professional, rather than romantic. That you pay for her company." Mike took off his glasses, leaning forward as he held them up in the air, a move I'd seen many times before, always before a question that hit below the belt. "You're the lead singer for Nothing but Trouble, arguably the most popular band in the country. You've been named *People* magazine's Sexiest Man of the Year not once, but twice. Tell me, why does Shane Hawthorne have to pay for sex?"

There it was. The moment I'd been dreading. I'd just been called a whore on national television.

Shane

Delaney stiffened at my side, and I knew if I turned to see the hurt and embarrassment smoldering in her eyes, I would lose my mind. My temper. Probably Delaney, too.

Guilt pricked at my soul, knotting in my gut and spreading to every organ like an invasive cancer, corrupting all the good feelings Delaney had stirred up. Somehow I managed to rein in the fury swirling through my veins, even as the light kit shined on me with an accusatory glare. "I have never paid for sex, Mike. Not with Delaney, not with anyone."

"Are you saying you've had similar contracts with previous girlfriends, or with women you presented in public as your girl-friends?"

"No. I'm not here to discuss prior relationships, and I'm not going to."

Pursing his lips, Lewis paused as he considered his next question. "Fair enough. Let's get back to Delaney, then. Why a contract? Why not just date her?"

I should have taken a moment to gather myself, but instead I let loose with an answer that wasn't at all what I'd intended. "That contract was meant to remove an element of unpredictability from my already unpredictable life. But as it turned out, life is pretty unpredictable, too. Delaney Fraser is the best thing that's ever happened to me, and if getting her to come on tour took a ridiculous contract, so be it. I'm not sorry, and I'd do it all over again."

Lewis slumped back in his chair, clearly surprised by my answer. But I wasn't finished. "What I do regret, though, is your suggestion that Delaney is a prostitute. She is not, and the only reason I agreed to sit down with you today is to put that slander-ous accusation to rest."

Lewis shifted his focus to Delaney. "How do you feel about what Shane just said?"

I slipped my hand over hers, dragging my gaze to her perfect profile. "I—I'm not going to apologize for my relationship with

Shane either," she said softly, but with conviction. Delaney turned her face to me, a tremulous smile tugging at her lips.

She saw *me*. And she *stayed*.

For a second, everything else faded. The lights, the cameras, the people crowding into the room, the scandal itself. For a moment it was just the two of us, and if lightning struck, I would have died a happy man.

Until Lewis shot an arrow straight into my euphoric bubble. "Let's talk about something you two have in common. Both of you lost people close to you because of car accidents, correct?"

"You know we have." It felt like I had rocks in my throat, or maybe hot coals.

"Do you want to tell me about it?"

I cocked an eyebrow. Fuck no, I didn't want to tell him about it. But I did, reciting the same details I'd shared with Delaney.

"Were you on drugs?"

"No."

"Drinking alcohol?"

Remorse climbed up from deep in my belly, coating my throat, its foul taste lingering in my mouth. "No. I was driving in a blizzard, and I skidded. It was an accident. A tragic one."

"Then how do you explain the beer cans that were found in your vehicle after the crash?"

"My friends each had a beer on our way home."

"Just to be clear, all of you were underage, correct?" He didn't wait for an answer before continuing. "So somehow you obtained alcohol, which your friends drank…and you didn't?" His skepticism was blatant, and clearly intended to taint the viewer's perception.

"You don't have to believe me. I took a Breathalyzer at the scene. The results were negative."

"But those results were later called into question, correct? And you left before the police concluded their investigation, didn't you?"

I gave a tight nod. "Yes." The word was short, clipped. I could get into more detail, but I knew it wouldn't do any good.

He lifted a brow. "Why?"

My jaw clenched, hands fisting at my sides. This interview had become an interrogation. "There was nothing to keep me there anymore."

"You didn't even attend the funeral of—" he consulted a note card he'd slipped into the crease of the chair "—Caleb Branford. He was your best friend, wasn't he?" Lewis was testing, pushing, pressing. Trying to find a way in.

And he was succeeding. I cleared my throat, pulled at my collar. The lights were bright, hot. Intense. "I've mourned Caleb's death every day since then."

"I'm told that the police wanted to question you further, but they couldn't find you. Do you know why?"

"Sounds like someone's been telling you an awful lot about me," I shot back defensively, immediately clamping my lips shut and willing myself to breathe normally. I was one question away from coming off like an arrogant celebrity who got where he was by taking the place of his best friend. By killing his best friend. I couldn't see Travis from where I was sitting, but he was probably hunched over in a corner, breathing into a paper bag.

Lewis crossed his legs and put his glasses back on. "It might have something to do with not knowing to look for Shane Hawthorne."

I hoisted one shoulder. "Makes sense."

"Because Shane Hawthorne isn't your real name, is it?"

My chest tightened, knowing exactly where Mike was headed. I glared at him. "No."

"Sean Sutter was the boy involved in an accident that killed his friend and injured two more. Sean Sutter walked away with barely a scratch."

I nodded, each word hitting with the force of a sledgehammer.

But Mike wasn't finished. "And then Sean Sutter headed west, became someone else entirely. Someone named Shane Hawthorne."

Delaney

I could feel Shane's cocky swagger bleeding out of him, replaced by the shamefaced kid he'd once been. Lurching forward, a defensive retort burst from my mouth. "And just what would you have done, Mike? Imagine you were a sixteen-year-old kid who'd been kicked around by your father your whole life, watched your mother die of cancer, and your only brother was unreachable in New York. Imagine losing control, of a car, of your life. Imagine everyone blaming you for the death of a friend you would have given your own life to save. Shane didn't run away because he was guilty. He left because of the guilt." *I know exactly how heavy a burden he carried.* "I don't blame Shane for that, and no one else should either."

Mike blinked, a pleased expression settling on his face. We were giving him one sound bite after another. "So, you've told Delaney about your past?" he asked Shane.

He squeezed my hand, threading his fingers through mine. "I've told Delaney everything."

"Has she done the same?" Skepticism edged his tone.

Shane shrugged, but the rigid set of his jaw was lined with strain. "You would have to ask her."

Mike's eyes slid to mine. "Why don't we talk about that?"

The mama bear I'd been just a minute ago lumbered back into the forest. "You mean my father," I said, my voice rising several octaves.

"Yes. Your father was convicted of vehicular manslaughter in the death of your mother. A conviction that came with a fifteen-year sentence, earning him a place in one of New York's toughest prisons. And yet, just a few weeks after signing a contract to become Shane Hawthorne's girlfriend, your father was moved to a minimum-security facility. What would you like to say to the people questioning your commitment to Shane? People who believe your relationship is nothing more than a sham in return for cash and favors."

I took a moment to consider Mike's accusatory question, knowing exactly how I *should* answer it. Instead, the truth came out. "Honestly? Nothing. I don't think my relationship with Shane is anyone's business but ours."

He drudged up a chuckle. "Fair point. But I have to ask, would you deny it?"

"Yes, I would. My mother's death and my father's subsequent arrest and conviction devastated our family, and I won't discuss his incarceration. I'm here today because of my genuine feelings for Shane, not for any other reason."

"Do you believe the alcohol your father consumed that night was a factor in the accident?"

My palms were sweating, and I slid them beneath my thighs. The plain truth was that no, his drinks didn't cause the accident. But my back was against a wall. Too much was at stake to speak the truth now. "That's not for me to say."

Mike leaned back in his chair, clearly considering how much he wanted to push this topic. But Shane was the one his viewers were interested in. I was nobody, and my father even less interesting. His chin tilted toward Shane, gesturing with his glasses. "Shane, Delaney mentioned earlier that your father 'kicked you around,' I believe was how she put it. What did she mean by that?"

My heart pounding in my ears, I mentally chastised myself for saying too much earlier. The NBC team hadn't unearthed details about the abuse Shane had suffered at the hands of his father, and I'd just hand-fed it to Mike. Damn it.

Shane rolled his shoulders, trying to relieve some of the tension I could sense curling around his muscles. "I'd rather not speak ill of the dead, Mike."

"Are you saying you don't have anything good to say about your father?"

"I repeat, I'd rather not speak ill of the dead." His voice was hard, flinty.

Mike Lewis's expression changed, processing Shane's non-answer and giving a slight nod. "Tell me more about Caleb Branford. He was the lead singer of your band, correct? You were the guitarist. You didn't take center stage until after his death. Why is that?"

I shifted on the couch so I could look directly at Shane, gave his hand a squeeze. For a moment we were back at the karaoke bar, and I could see the flash of pain streaking across his face when I asked if he did anything else besides sing.

"I don't really know. Writing songs was how I coped with Caleb's death. I could have given them to someone else to sing, but that didn't feel right. Eventually, I was singing more and playing guitar less."

Mike's eyes flicked to someone over our shoulder, and he gave a slight nod. "I think it's fitting to conclude this interview with a statement we received from the Clark County District Attorney's Office." He reached for another note card and put his glasses back on. "We are reviewing the circumstances surrounding Caleb Branford's tragic death. If we believe Shane Hawthorne is criminally liable for Caleb Branford's death, we will prosecute to the fullest extent of the law."

Chapter Twenty

Shane

Ratings for the NBC interview were through the roof. Travis was in his element, fielding all kinds of offers that I wanted absolutely nothing to do with. The tour was going well, and so was my relationship with Delaney. I wanted to focus on the future, stop living in the past.

A part of me still felt unsettled, though, like the clear horizon was only giving me a false sense of security. Trouble had a habit of finding me, following me wherever I went. I couldn't see it yet. But I knew it was there. Lurking.

Two weeks later, we were back in New York City. Same hotel, same suite. Manhattan had a different, more frenetic energy than any other place on earth, and it had taken three encores to satisfy our ravenous fans. After the concert, Delaney and I rode the elevator with Landon and the two strays he'd decided to take home for the night, enduring thirty-three floors of increasingly vulgar requests for us to join them.

I didn't need to look at Delaney's face to give him an answer, I could feel her reluctance in the way she pressed closer to me and squeezed my hand tighter with each floor.

Not. Interested.

I shut the door without a backward glance, ignoring the knocking that started just after I pressed Delaney against the nearest wall, running my palms over her rib cage, sighing at the fullness of her breasts. Except it didn't stop.

Landon was starting to remind me of the way I'd once been—at my worst. I knew he was fighting his own share of demons, and Travis was considering shoving him in a detox center once the tour was over, but right now I wasn't feeling much empathy. I slammed my hand against the plaster. "Jesus Christ, Landon. You ever hear the expression 'no means no'?"

I flung open the door, pissed off as a swatted wasp.

It wasn't Landon.

Every last bit of oxygen catapulted straight out of my lungs. Two police officers looked at me expectantly.

I glanced back at Delaney, standing with her hand over her mouth, all color drained from her face. I reached out for her, pulled her into my chest. Whatever news they had come to deliver, we would handle together.

"Sean Sutter." It wasn't a question. The officers announced my name like it was a death sentence.

Maybe today it was. "Yes."

"You are being arrested on charges stemming from the death of Caleb Branford. Please place your hands behind your back." There was a flash of metal as I unwound my arm from Delaney's waist, wincing as one of the officers snapped cuffs around me.

Panic sent adrenaline racing through my veins, my breath coming in quick, short pants. I was an animal, caught.

"Do you have any weapons on your person?" The words sounded slow and distorted, almost as if we were underwater.

"No," I bit out, fighting the urge to run, to struggle. He frisked me anyway. No leniency for rock stars.

Delaney retreated to the nearest wall, swallowing frantically. I focused on her, on her gorgeous, terrified face. Guilt skittered along my nerve endings, rubbing them raw. What had I brought her into? She didn't need this, didn't need me dragging her down. "Baby, this was bound to happen," I said anyway. "Just call Travis. And Gavin. They'll take care of—"

"You have the right to remain silent and refuse to answer questions. Anything you do say may be used against you in a court of law. You have the right to…" The torrent of words became background noise, an ominous soundtrack to the final act of a movie that had been paused in my mind for more than a decade.

I'd always known this day would come to pass.

I ran. I hid in plain sight. I lied.

But none of that mattered. Those tactics—they had only delayed the inevitable.

Caleb was dead because of me. It was time for me to pay. And in that moment, I wished I had stayed to take whatever penalty I deserved. Back then I had nothing to lose, not really. But now? I had Delaney. A relationship with my brother. A successful career.

I had everything I'd ever wanted.

And none of that mattered, because I didn't deserve any of it. If not for Caleb's death I would probably have been content to play guitar on nights and weekends, maybe as a house band doing covers at a local bar. I'd never intended to get behind the microphone. Never believed I had the talent to headline major world tours, to rock out in front of fifty thousand screaming fans.

Not until Caleb's death did I decide to live out my dreams, or die trying. I bled my grief onto the page, writing song after song. Channeling his spirit, I sang into the mic. I lived for the moments I could sweat out my sorrow beneath the spotlights, sing away my rage, my regrets. I hadn't gone to his funeral, but I'd honored Caleb's memory with every performance.

"Everything is going to be okay, Delaney. I promise." Where did I get off, promising things there was a damn good chance I wouldn't be able to deliver on? Even so, Delaney's small nod made me feel better.

The cops nudged me forward, one on either side. Pushing off the wall, Delaney followed us into the corridor. "Where are you taking him?" she asked.

They named a precinct, although I knew it was only a matter of time before I would be extradited home. Despite calling me "Sean," these guys only knew me as Shane. I was just another celebrity who had taken a few too many liberties with the law. But the cops back home, maybe even the same ones who had been at the scene of the accident, they'd been waiting for years to get their hands on me. And I couldn't blame them.

We walked outside, and it was obvious someone had leaked the news of my arrest to the press even before the cuffs were locked around my wrists. The street was filled with police cruisers, their lights flashing angrily at me, reporters and cameramen hurtling out of network news vans like invading beetles.

"Shane, why did you run from your crime?"

"Have you been hiding your identity for years?"

"Did you kill your friend?"

I refused to bow my head, looking straight ahead as I was pushed into the back of a police car, driven away by two cops who didn't seem unhappy about the possibility of making it onto the nightly news. All that was missing from their cheerful banter was a request for a selfie.

We drove a few blocks, pulled up to the curb. They opened my door, hauling me out by my elbows. More lights, more cameras, more combative reporters. I was escorted through the churning, deafening sea into a police station. Fluorescent lights bounced off gray linoleum floors that must have been white before being trampled on by thousands of criminals. And now by me.

I expected to be fingerprinted, photographed, searched. Instead I was escorted into a small, dingy room lined with what I assumed were two-way mirrors. My handcuffs were removed, and two men in cheap suits, not the uniformed officers who had brought me here, entered the room.

"Should we call you 'Mr. Sutton' or 'Mr. Hawthorne'?"

Call me Fucked. Royally Fucked. I hoisted up a shoulder. "Shane's fine."

They exchanged a glance, one I didn't bother trying to interpret. "We're from Clark County. New York officers executed the warrant, and we're just waiting for your extradition papers to be approved before bringing you back home."

I don't have a home.

"Will you be contesting the extradition…Shane?"

I leaned back in the rickety chair, crossing my arms and pretending I wasn't jumping out of my skin. "You'll have to ask my lawyer."

Offering dual grunts, they sat down across from me, one of

them opening a folder and poising his pen over the enclosed notepad. "So, why don't we get started. Tell us about the night of—"

I interrupted. "You really think I'm going to tell you about *anything* without my lawyer present?"

He shrugged, not fazed at all. "Why not? You talked to Mike Lewis about it."

These guys reminded me of my father. Bullies who latched on to their target with malicious glee. I glared at them through narrowed eyes, fury churning inside my gut. And a sickening sense that I'd brought this all on myself.

Another shot of adrenaline flurried in my belly. I lifted my chin. "Lawyer."

The one with the pen unclicked it, put it back in his pocket. Closing his folder with a snap, he turned to his partner. "How long have you been waiting to get your hands on the asshole who forced good people to bury their only child before he was even old enough to shave?"

"A hell of a long time."

Dread welled in my throat, so thick I could have choked on it. Somehow I forced it down, swallowing hard, staring harder. If this was the only contest I could win, I sure as hell wasn't backing down.

There was a metallic squeal as he pushed his chair away from the table, immediately echoed as the other man did the same. His thick chuckle rebounded off the cement walls. "Yeah, me too. A hell of a long time."

And that's exactly how long it felt until Gavin showed up. A hell of a long time.

Delaney

Fear lanced through me as I watched the officers escort Shane away. I was breathless, dizzy with terror. The scene was all too familiar. My father had been led away from me in handcuffs, too. Except in his case, I could have said something to make it stop. Could have. And didn't. Tonight, though, my hands were just as tied as Shane's.

They turned the corner and I began chanting, forcing words out of my mouth in a relentless, meaningless pattern as I scrambled back into the room, eyes darting around for my phone. "Oh my God, oh my God…" Where the fuck was it? I dug inside my purse, scanned every flat surface, ripped the covers off the bed. "Shit, shit, shit." I didn't know Travis's number by heart. Or Gavin's. I needed to find my phone.

The pillows on every chair and couch came next, toppling over a lamp in the process. Where *was* it? Diving onto the floor, I army-crawled around the suite, looking under everything. Ohmygod, ohmygod. Shit, shit, shit.

Shane, Shane, Shane.

Not knowing where else to look, I stared around the trashed room until the edges of my vision blurred. Helpless. I felt so fucking helpless. A sob tore through me and I sat up, wrapping my arms around my stomach and rocking back and forth. Pain battered my sides as all my fears clogged my mind, turning the room dark and heavy. My mother dead. My father in jail. Shane hauled away in handcuffs. Everyone I loved, they had all been taken from me. Why had I thought Shane would be any different? After what I'd done, and maybe even worse—what I hadn't done—what made me think I deserved to find love?

My relationship with Shane had begun as a fraud, every phony aspect clearly spelled out in black and white. But then it had changed, become something different. Feelings that couldn't be contained on a contract page sprang up between us.

But it didn't matter, because everything we built together was sitting on a fragile foundation of lies. His past. My past.

We were liars.

Maybe we deserved each other. Maybe Shane would understand why I had lied to him, because of a promise I'd made to someone else. Why I was still lying. To him, to everyone.

Maybe. So many maybes.

As if heaven sent, I heard a ringing and raced into the bedroom. *There.* My black iPhone cover had blended in with my suitcase. I snatched it up, frantically swiping the screen without glancing at the caller ID. "Travis?" I asked breathlessly.

"No. This is Gavin, Shane's br—"

My heart splintered. "Gavin! They've taken Shane," I screeched, falling apart.

"Delaney, calm down. That's why I'm calling. One of my contacts in the NYPD tipped me off about his arrest." His tone was calm, purely professional even though we were talking about his brother.

I focused on Gavin's voice like it was my lifeline. "They've *arrested* him for Caleb's murder."

"I'm heading to the precinct now. I'll call you when I know more."

"Wait," I rasped, hating myself for taking even a second more of his time when he should be going to Shane, but needing direction. "What can I do?"

He didn't hesitate. "A long time ago, Shane needed me and I didn't realize how much. I let him down then, and I won't do it again. Stay strong, Delaney. But most important, if you care for him at all, just stay."

Gavin's words resonating in my ears, I took a few calming breaths. I couldn't afford to break down, not when Shane was in trouble. Gavin would fight tooth and nail for him, I knew, but I wanted to be there, too. I wanted to stay. Not because Gavin told me to, but because there was no place I would rather be.

Of course, that was the problem. I didn't deserve to be by Shane's side, unless it was sharing his cell.

Maybe that was why I couldn't catch my breath. I'd spent the past three years insulating myself from my mistakes, my secrets. My lies. But, like Shane, I was living on borrowed time.

I hiked my shoulders up to my neck as a knock sounded at the door. Was it another police officer? Was I being brought in for questioning? My knowledge of police procedure didn't extend much beyond Olivia Benson's dialogue on *SVU*. "Delaney, it's me. Piper. Open up."

A wave of relief crashed over me as I jumped up and jerked at the knob. "Shane's been arrested."

"Sshh." Looking as immaculate as always in crisp, dark jeans and a white silk tank, Piper stepped into the suite, her eyes wide as she took in the wreckage. "Christ. Did the police do this?"

I scanned the room, seeing it from her perspective. "I couldn't find my phone," I offered lamely as I bent to replace the couch pillows on the naked frame.

Piper righted a fallen lamp and straightened its shade. "Travis is already on his way. He's furious he wasn't notified about this."

"Gavin's heading there, too." I sat down heavily on the couch, raking my hands through my snarled hair. "Why now? All these years later?"

Replacing the cushions of the chair, Piper took a seat across from me. "From what I gather, Shane's from a small town. He was the kid from the wrong side of the tracks, and the boy who died was the only son of one of their most prominent families. No one's gotten over it, and now that they know Sean Sutter is really Shane Hawthorne, it's a big deal. They're going to try to make an example out of him. Besides that, it's going to put their town on the map. Reporters from all over the world are going to descend on them, renting rooms in their hotel, eating at their restaurants. This trial is going to be one hell of a cash cow. Even if they can't make the case, they're looking for their fifteen minutes of fame."

What the hell was wrong with our legal system? First my father, now Shane. Was Lady Justice not just blind, but deaf and dumb, too? Or maybe Shane and I were so busy shielding ourselves from the truth, we'd become convinced—wrongly—that it didn't exist.

I swiveled back to Piper. "Who is *they*? Caleb's parents, the police? Or do even small towns have PR departments?"

She lobbed a remorseful smile my way. "That's exactly what we need to find out."

I sagged into the cushions, feeling overwhelmed. So much was at stake.

Piper hopped up and retrieved a pack of peanut M&M's from the minibar. "Eat these before you pass out. I called hair and makeup. They'll be here in a few minutes. I'm going to pick out something gorgeous, but conservative, for you to wear. We're going down to the station, and everyone is going to see you there. Not sure how long it will take, but it's important for you to be by Shane's side through all of this. Now, more than ever, your relationship needs to appear genuine."

I bit down on the candy, its chocolate coating tasting like dirt in my mouth. "Our relationship *is* genuine. I love him, Piper." The admission slipped through my teeth effortlessly, and I knew it was true. *I love Shane.*

She patted my knee, a pleased smile smeared across her glossed lips. "That's perfect. Exactly how you should act."

I wasn't acting.

"Piper, have you ever been in love?"

Longing streaked across her face, so quick I wasn't sure I'd read it right. She started to turn away, but I caught her wrist. Piper looked at me, frowning, then down at my fingers.

I let go, mumbling an apology.

She didn't move though, as I'd expected her to. "Once."

"Someone from home?" I prodded.

As the seconds ticked by, I began to think she wouldn't answer. That I'd pushed my luck. But, again, Piper surprised me. "No. I met him here, my first year at UCLA."

She disappeared into the bedroom then, and I heard her rustling through my clothes. When she emerged holding an outfit, I swallowed the gritty remnants of the last M&M. "What happened?"

She sighed. "Nothing. The guy turned out to be a complete jerk." Squaring her shoulders. Piper extended the hanger in my direction, clearly signaling that our brief conversation was over.

I changed quickly, then endured another session with hair and makeup. The thrill of being fussed over had definitely worn off.

By the time I walked out of the hotel at two in the morning, I looked like a mannequin and felt just as animated. My brain was sluggish, my movements stiff and slow. "Look sad and take your time getting into the car. Let them get plenty of photos," Piper whispered before pushing me out the door.

Her advice was redundant. I *was* sad, and putting one foot

in front of the other required herculean effort. But I did it, and repeated the process in reverse at the police station. "Where is he?" I asked Piper once we were inside, the closed door immediately reducing the shouts of the reporters to a muted rumbling.

"I'm not exactly sure. You probably won't get to see Shane tonight, unless they release him."

I sat down on one of the folding chairs lining the wall, a confused frown denting my forehead. "Then why am I here?"

"If you didn't come, the story would shift to you abandoning Shane, either because you think he's guilty or because you lied about your feelings for each other. We have to stay on message. You love Shane and you support him, one hundred percent." Her eyes bored into me as if she doubted my commitment.

I nodded weakly. Right now I was doubting just about everything.

Everything except my feelings for Shane.

For the next hour, the door opened and closed several times, people came and went. Drunks, dealers, prostitutes, well dressed, barely dressed, loud, silent. Piper barely looked up from her phone, giving me play-by-play updates from Travis, news alerts from social media, and online tabloids.

The door swung open again as a female police officer escorted a wraith of a woman into the station, the officer's face a puckered show of distaste at her charge's filth and pungent stench. "Got another one for the drunk tank," she called to the man sitting at the front desk.

I crossed my leg just as the woman jerked her arm out of the officer's grasp. "Not drunk, damn you! Had one drink; jess out for a walk." She knocked into my foot, sending my shoe flying across the hall. Losing her balance, she pitched forward on the dingy floor.

I sprang forward. "I'm so sorry. Are you okay?"

"Miss, you'll have to—"

"Take her," the disheveled woman slurred angrily, making no attempt to get up. She pointed at me, looking back at the officer. "She deserves to be here, not me!"

A river of terror slid down my spine as I grabbed my shoe and backed away. The officer threw me a pitying glance, hauling the woman to her feet. "Let's go."

Piper took one look at my overflowing eyes and jumped up, dragging me into the ladies' room. "Here." She shoved a stack of paper towels into my hands. "Do you know that woman?"

Unable to speak, I shook my head and wiped at my tears. "No." But apparently she knew me better than anyone. Looked at me and saw the guilt all over my face.

Piper grabbed my earlobes, squeezing them fiercely.

"Ow," I screeched, pulling away. "What are you doing?"

A wry smile slanted across her face. "Just a trick I learned. No one likes to ugly cry in public. You good now?"

A couple of years ago I never would have dreamed "Perfect Piper" had anything to cry about.

I blinked, realizing my tears had dried up. "No. But I'm not crying anymore."

"Well, that's enough for me." She spilled the contents of her purse on the counter, makeup rolling everywhere. Picking up a travel-sized pouch of makeup-remover towelettes, she began wiping at the mess of mascara streaking my skin.

"That guy…Was it hard seeing him on campus after you broke up?"

Her hand stilled. "He wasn't a student. And we didn't break up. He basically took off, dumped me without a word."

"He dumped *you*?" I asked, incredulous.

She crumpled the towelette and threw it at the wastebin attached to the wall. "Yes. Not my fondest memory, so…" Her voice trailed off as she uncapped an eyeliner.

I took the hint. "Got it. Didn't mean to pry."

"Musicians are trouble. Some are worth it, some aren't."

Musician? I wanted to ask more, and not just because it was a relief to focus on something besides my fear for Shane. But it was obvious Piper didn't feel the same. She rarely came to Nothing but Trouble concerts, and I'd never seen her talk to any of the guys in the band except for a few brief exchanges with Shane. The man must have left one hell of an impression if he'd permanently turned her off all musicians, even rock stars at the top of their game.

Piper finished with my liner and picked up a tube of mascara. "All right. Once you're fixed up, we're going back out there to sit down. And as soon as Travis is done talking to Shane, he'll fill us in."

I gnawed at my lower lip, rocked by a fresh wave of anxiety. "You know, by the pool at Travis's house, I asked what he did for a living."

Piper dotted concealer beneath my eyes. "Oh yeah? What did he say?"

"He said he solved problems."

She let out a soft laugh. "Well, he's got his work cut out for him tonight."

Shane

"You okay?" Travis bounced into the room as if he'd been drop-kicked from the corridor.

"Just great. My favorite way to spend the night." I glanced at the clock on the wall. "How did you get here so fast?" If Travis had come from Los Angeles, he would still be in the air.

"Believe it or not, high school reunion. I drove down from Westchester as soon as I heard." He looked around, as if finally noticing I was alone. "Where's Gavin?"

"He just left to get copies of the extradition agreement. He'll be back in a few minutes."

Travis nodded. "Good. Okay, listen. I can't practice law in Clark County, but Gavin can. He's going to fight this charge with every resource at his disposal. Meanwhile, I made a few calls on the drive in. Both sides have agreed that we'll fly back private rather than commercial, given the circus that's going to follow you wherever you go. Make no mistake. They're not shying away from publicity, but they're not going to push for chaos at a major New York City airport."

I expelled a deep breath, splaying my hands out on the metal table. "It's finally happening, huh?"

Travis regarded me soberly, offering a curt nod. "Hopefully not for long. You and I both know this is bullshit. They're not looking to try Sean Sutter. They just want to tie Shane Hawthorne to their bumblefuck town."

My chest squeezed, and I pressed my lips together to keep back the tortured howl rattling in my lungs. Caleb's death wasn't bullshit, but I knew what Travis meant. "How's Delaney?"

"I have Piper with her now, making sure she's on the same page. The NBC interview made the two of you look like some kind of rock 'n' roll fairy tale, and we're going to ride that horse-drawn carriage away from the courthouse and all the way to the bank."

"Travis." My tongue felt heavy in my mouth. "Leave her out

of it. I don't want to use Delaney like that. She's been through enough. I don't want her sucked into my mess."

Travis leaned back in the tiny chair. "What are you talking about? How will it look if she doesn't stand by you? You can barely spend more than a few days at a time at your beach house. You want to spend the rest of your life in a six-by-eight cell?"

Bile rose, bitter and harsh, stinging the back of my throat. "If she wants out, let her go." Maybe she would finally make the smart choice and leave me.

Chapter Twenty-One

Shane

"You shouldn't be here," I gritted out, fighting the urge to gather Delaney's lush body in my arms and breathe her sweet scent in deep. My hands rolled into fists as I stalked off to the shower, jaw clenched tight enough to crush diamonds. Travis had rented the nicest house in town, and after I'd spent the night in county lockup, Gavin had managed to get me assigned to home confinement. I couldn't say anything else, couldn't even look at her until I'd washed the stench of prison from my skin.

I should have locked the door.

"Why? Why don't you want me here?"

I twisted the shower knob, set the water to hot as I balled up my shirt and threw it angrily in the corner. And then I turned, saw the hurt and confusion streaking across Delaney's face. "So you can witness another shit storm firsthand?" I asked.

Her attention fell to the side, shoulders slumping as if considering defeat. But no, she straightened almost immediately, posture stiff. Not backing down, ready to fight. "As opposed to watching it play out in the media?"

My hand stilled over the top button of my jeans. "You need to forget about me." Her flinch sent a lancing pain into my gut, and I forced myself to lower my zipper and kick my jeans away. "You should go." *Stay. Please stay.*

Delaney's eyes were fierce as she leaned against the cabinet, her hands wrapping around the edge of the stone top. "Why don't you want me here?" she repeated.

I hesitated, exhaling a breath weighted down by frustration. Oh, I wanted Delaney. I wanted her here. I wanted her on top of me, under me. I wanted her mouth on mine, her arms around my neck as I slid into her sweet center. I wanted to taste her, hold her, lick her, fuck her.

Maybe even love her.

My cock twitched, and I stepped into the shower before she could see exactly how much I wanted her. "I might spend the rest of my life here. Get out now." Besides, what the hell did I know about love? Even the idea was laughable. Shane Hawthorne, lovesick fool? Fool, yes. Sick, yes. But love? Hell-to-the-no.

I closed my eyes, letting the water drill into my scalp. I didn't hear the door open or close, but I assumed she took my advice and left. The loneliness was suffocating.

Until the curtain was wrenched aside and Delaney, naked and so fucking gorgeous she took my breath away, stepped beneath the spray. "You're not getting rid of me that easily. Are we real or not?"

I swallowed, trying to muster up the strength to lie. Just say no, let her walk away.

As if she could read my thoughts, Delaney spread her hands out flat on my chest, my heart racing beneath her palm. "Don't you dare lie to me, Shane. You'll hate yourself for it." Those whorls of aquamarine locked onto me, a captivating chaos I couldn't look away from.

She was right. I would. I already did. "Delaney." My voice broke as I stared at her helplessly. She was finding every one of my fault lines with an accuracy I couldn't comprehend, making them deeper, wider.

"What fairy-tale castle do you think you're sending me back to, Shane? You think you're the only one with baggage?" Delaney's voice trembled as she slid her hands up my neck, cradling my face between her palms. "Don't shut me out. Don't send me away. Let me stand with you."

I held on to the last shards of my control, barely breathing. "Do you really know what you're getting into? There's no way of knowing how this is all going to play out. I can't make you any promises." Delaney's thumbs swept along my cheekbones as I kept my hands rigidly at my sides. There was a roaring in my ears that had nothing to do with the shower. If I touched her, I wouldn't be able to let go. Right now I only wanted to make love to her, to sink my body so deeply into hers that we became one.

She inched closer, her nipples already tempting pebbles. "I know exactly what I'm getting into, Shane. I'm a big girl, and I can make my own choices. And today, right now, I choose you. I don't need empty promises. In this moment, all I need is you. And I think you need me, too."

My resolve crumbled beneath the intensity of Delaney's stare, my chest squeezing tight. "That's enough for you? Living day to day, moment to moment. Not knowing what's coming next?"

In a voice laced with optimism, she answered. "When it's all we have, yes. Let's not throw it away just because you don't think it's enough."

Delaney's words battered at the logic that told me to end things with her until my life was figured out. Her eyes were wide open, and she wanted to *stay*. A frisson of hope sputtered to life, warmth racing up my spine, melting my resolve. Why was I fighting her so hard?

Delaney

With a forcefulness that took my breath away, Shane pulled me into his embrace, his lips crashing down on mine. The water sluiced over both of us, and I clung to him as if I were drowning.

"Delaney," he groaned, tearing his mouth away from mine to stare down at me. A crooked smile tugged at his lips. "I don't want to need you. But God help me, I do."

Shane's words sent an electric thrill racing along my nerves. "I'm here now," I whispered, wrapping my arms around his neck, my fingertips threading into his wet hair. "And just what are you going to do with me?"

"Everything," he growled into the shell of my ear, guiding me against the marble wall. Starting at the tender spot where jaw met earlobe, he kissed his way down my neck, his tongue swirling against the wet flesh until he reached my collarbone. A shiver rolled through me. "I'm going to fuck you in this shower until the water runs cold."

I gasped, pressing against his legs, angling my hips to feel his shaft pulse against my belly. But it wasn't enough. I reached down, wanting to wrap my fingers around him.

"Don't." Shane caught my wrists, gathering both of them

above my head and holding them there as he took the soap in his other hand and glided it along my body, leaving a thin white film in his wake. He slid the white bar across my abdomen and down my sides, circling around my breasts. Then he moved lower, slipping along my hipbones and inner thighs. Practically boneless, I was lost in a whirl of sensation.

"You are so damn beautiful," he said in an unfamiliar voice, husky with reverence. I wanted to say something, even just a simple "thank you," but I couldn't speak.

His golden eyes flashed with heat, shooting sparks at me, igniting a dozen different fires that blazed beneath the surface of my skin. Spinning me around to face the wall, Shane pressed my hands flat against the tiles as he massaged my back with the soap, caressing between my shoulder blades until I was drooping in pleasure. I gladly rested my forehead against the smooth marble, pushing back against him as he followed the curve of my ass, wanting more from Shane than soap.

Finally, he dropped the soap to the floor, threading long fingers into my hair, bunching it into a knot at the top of my head and licking at the rivulets of water sluicing down my neck. I sucked in a deep breath, fogging up tiles on my exhale.

"Shane," I moaned.

Shane released my hair, gripping my shoulders as it fell like a wet curtain against his wrists. "I need you, Delaney," he murmured, turning me to face him. I tilted my chin upward, Shane's breath minty as he tugged at my lower lip, sliding his tongue along the sensitive skin.

I whimpered into his mouth, feeling something shift between us, leaving an opening I hoped would last longer than the heat of the water. Shane let go, his hands intertwining at the back of my neck. I gazed at him through the misty air wafting around us.

It was as if we were in a cloud, suspended between heaven and earth, indifferent to the past or the future.

"You have me," I said, finding my voice.

Shane drew in a shaky breath, understanding dawning in his eyes. I fitted myself against him, and this time he didn't pull away. My soap-lathered skin slid against his, his shaft insistently pressing into my belly.

Covering my mound with his palm, Shane's finger made its way inside my cleft, rubbing slowly, precisely. There wasn't enough oxygen in the thick air, and I sagged against the wall, grasping hold of Shane's broad shoulders for support.

"Please," I begged, dizzy with want.

The look he offered was so open and sweet I felt flayed, my heart raw. If he hadn't been holding me up, I would have easily lost my balance. Aching with need, I kissed Shane with all the pent-up hopefulness that had been accumulating inside of me since we first met.

"Please Shane, now."

A grin broke across Shane's face as he lifted me upward, settling my thighs around his hips. Impatient, I clung to him, encircling my ankles and pulling him tightly against me.

Resting his forehead against mine, Shane reached between us to align his engorged shaft with my entrance. I was hot, hotter than the water still flowing over us. He pushed into me with a low growl, sucking the tender skin of my shoulder as he held me against the wall.

Bare, wet skin.

Thick steam.

Hot water.

God, this man.

Shane released his grip on me, gravity sheathing him completely. I squealed, biting down on his neck as I clung tight. "You feel so fucking good," he said, his voice rough as he glanced down to the place our bodies met. A piece of him at home inside of me.

"I know, baby."

"No. You don't." His shook his head. "Nothing's ever felt this good. No one." There was a tremor in his voice that shook me to the bone. "Just you, Delaney. Just you."

I wanted to respond, to reassure, but I was incapable of forming complete sentences. Shane began moving again, pulling out until I was ready to cry from the loss. Pushing back in slowly. Shane's deliberate movements, the words coming out of his mouth...too much. Excruciating. I rocked my hips forward, energy rippling through me. "I want...I want..." Tears stung my eyes, my body shaking.

"Can't believe you're here. Can't believe you fucking stayed," he muttered against my neck as he finally gave up the last of his control, holding nothing back as he slammed me against the wall.

Breath punched from my lungs as he filled me, thrusting deep and fast. Tiny spikes of pleasure chased a path to my center, forming a thick knot that churned and grew. This was what I wanted. No—what I needed. To be filled by Shane. Not just my body. My heart was full to bursting. Maybe it wouldn't last much beyond the length of our shower, but for now I knew Shane was with me, really with *me*—and not just because I was the right size and shape to fill a void in his life. He wanted me, and he was proving it with every delicious kiss and passionate thrust. Every whispered admission.

We moved in unison, both of us rocketing toward our ultimate goal: paradise.

That knot compressed, growing tighter, denser. Heavy as lead.

Until it exploded, taking me up, taking me away. I closed my eyes and there was no darkness. Only light.

I came to earth as Shane shuddered and jerked inside me. I nuzzled against his straining neck. We clung to each other, chests heaving as we gulped down the steam-thick air.

The water finally running cold.

Shane

The rental house was fairly large and new enough. Selfishly, I was glad Delaney had chosen to stay.

Selfish, selfish, selfish.

Even so, the walls were closing in on me. But I couldn't leave, not unless I'd rather spend the next few months awaiting trial in a jail cell.

Our tour had been canceled. Our label was having a fit. The guys were bored and pissy, stirring up trouble of their own back in L.A. I couldn't even record with them because—even if I were allowed out of the damned house—there wasn't a single recording studio in Clark County.

My fans were my biggest defenders. There was an online petition, hundreds of Facebook groups and Twitter accounts popping up. They all wanted to #SaveShaneHawthorne.

As if anyone could do that.

The prosecution was pushing for another deposition. Mike Lewis's people were pushing for another interview. *People, US Weekly*, TMZ, Radar Online, *National Enquirer* were all here, their reporters crawling all over town. I couldn't turn on the TV or scroll through my phone without seeing someone claiming to be my best friend or former girlfriend. Some I recognized. Most

I didn't. Some of what they said was true: I was a loner, ditched school whenever I could, cared only about one thing—making music. Everything else could have come out of a script for a teen drama on the CW.

But at the heart of it all, the truth was staring me in the face.

Caleb was dead.

Because of me.

Call it an accident. Call it a crime. His death was the only fact that mattered.

The dining room of the rental house was filled with too many people, tension as dense and obvious as the smog back in L.A. Travis and Gavin, of course, plus the legal team they'd assembled on my behalf. My publicist had brought two assistants. Piper was in the corner, her face rapt with attention, fingers tapping on the keyboard of her laptop as she took notes. Everyone was plotting and planning and strategizing.

Getting nowhere fast.

I stalked out of the room, disgust oozing from every pore, my boots thudding up the stairs. "Hey." I poked my head into the bedroom.

Delaney was reading a book with a half-naked guy on the cover. I arched an eyebrow. She'd come apart in my arms barely an hour ago. "Am I not enough for you? You need a book boyfriend?"

A soft laugh floated my way as she set it aside. I fucking needed to bottle that sound. "You're the only boyfriend I need," Delaney said, the look on her face one she reserved solely for me. I fucking loved that, too.

I hurled myself onto the mattress beside her, the book bouncing to the floor. She didn't seem to notice, curling up against me and resting her head on my chest. "What's wrong?"

I would have given anything to shield Delaney from all this, but I couldn't. There was just so damn much shit. "You mean, besides everything?" I asked, releasing a pent-up breath that sent dark strands of Delaney's hair skittering across my chest.

"That really narrows it down for me," she murmured, her palm sliding over me to curl around my shoulder, her thumb sweeping along my neck, lingering over my pounding pulse.

It was getting late, darkness seeping in through the open windows. Only one lamp was lit, on Delaney's side of the bed. We lay in silence for a while, voices from the dining room drifting upstairs, although I couldn't discern individual words. "It's frustrating being stuck here, waiting for Gavin to figure out the legal end of things. For Travis to do his fucking job."

Delaney's head lifted, her brows pushing together over the question marks shining from her eyes. "I understand your brother's role in all this. But what do you mean about Travis? Isn't he in a holding pattern until all this is resolved?"

"Exactly. He's supposed to resolve it. All of it," I shot back.

"But…" Her words dragged. "How can he—"

"Because that's what Travis does. He makes my problems disappear."

Delaney jerked back, a flash of distaste streaking across her features.

"What?" I asked, instantly on the defensive.

"What?"

"That look."

Her face pinched, eyes sliding away from me. "What look?"

I caught Delaney's jaw between my fingers, waiting until she was looking my way again. "Like the opinion you're holding back tastes like dirt. You might as well spit it out, because it's threatening to burst through your lips."

She pulled away and rolled to the side, studying her fingernails as if the answer were written in nail polish. "Is that really what you want?"

I seethed. "For this to all be over so I can get out of this house and back onstage? Yeah, that's what I want."

"No. I just mean…" Delaney wavered, drawing her lower lip between her teeth as she decided how much to say. Finally, she let go, exhaling a frustrated sigh that reverberated through me. "Do you really want a buffer between you and every unpleasant aspect of your life?"

My shoulders bunched together at the nape of my neck. "Travis is my agent."

Delaney shook her head, her still-damp hair undulating in dark waves down her arm. "No, he's not." Her tone was firm. "He's your fixer."

Every fiber of my being rebelled against the truth behind Delaney's certainty. And yet I couldn't deny it. I grabbed at the bottom of a curl, pulling it straight and letting go, watching it spring right back. Reached for another one.

She took my hand, holding it between her own. "Shane, I think you need to talk to them."

I shuddered. "I've been down there for the past hour. They're too busy listening to the sound of their own voices to bother listening to me."

"No. Not them."

I shifted, rolling onto my side and propping my head on my palm. "You don't mean…"

Delaney nodded, dragging her fingertips over my ink. The barbed wire. The screaming gargoyles. The little boy. She lifted her sad gaze to mine. "Yeah," she said. "I do."

I ran my tongue over my front teeth, absorbing the impact

of her words, each one burning my skin like acid. "They won't want to talk to me." Wind gusted through the branches of the tall maples surrounding the house, rustling their leaves.

"I bet that's exactly what they want," she said softly. "You were the last person to see their son alive."

I could barely stay still under her patient gaze. "Because I'm the guy who killed him."

Delaney didn't flinch. Her hand slid up my chest, fingers threading into my hair. "Stop saying that. It was an accident. They're still grieving, and they should know you are, too. That you didn't forget about him."

She found the *C* etched over my heart, planting a kiss on the bleeding letter. "Talk to them. Explain about the drinking. Let them know that you've never forgotten about their Caleb."

"What if they don't want to see me?"

"What if they do?"

Reluctance bristled along my skin like velvet rubbed the wrong way. I sucked in a deep breath, blowing it out through pursed lips. "Maybe I'll give it a try."

Shadows danced on the walls as the sun slid lower on the horizon. "So, if you—" Delaney cut off.

"If I what?" I prompted.

"Well…Not that it's going to happen, but if you were—" She stopped, restarted. "If things here don't go your way, would you let me visit you?"

"You mean, in prison?" I asked, not really needing clarification as much as a second to gather my thoughts. Every cell in my body was screaming in protest. "No. I wouldn't want you to visit," I admitted, shaking my head.

"Why not?" she demanded, her body tense.

I lifted a hand to her face, running my knuckles along the

plane of her jaw. Studying the perfectly symmetrical set of her features, her flawless skin. Delaney Fraser was the Gerber baby, all grown up. I had to make her understand, even if it hurt her feelings. How could I survive being locked up if she could come see me but I couldn't touch her? Couldn't run my fingers through her hair, smother her with kisses, make love to her. How could I watch Delaney walk away from me, iron bars holding me back, and not go crazy? "If I go to jail, you have to forget about me. Your father is your blood. I'm not. If I go to prison, promise me you'll forget about me. About us."

Her voice was a husk of itself. "I could never forget you, Shane," she breathed. "Ever."

Chapter Twenty-Two

Shane

My request for a face-to-face meeting with Caleb's parents didn't go over well. Not with Travis, or Gavin, or the team they had assembled on my behalf.

And I didn't care.

If the Branfords didn't want to talk to me, I could respect that. But in my heart, I knew Delaney was right. I had to try.

So I called the DA's office myself and asked them to extend the offer. Just the three of us, in a room. No cameras, no attorneys. Just them and me, and a thousand regrets between us.

Travis looked like he was going to have a heart attack when I told him what I'd done, and even worse when I said they had accepted. Gavin just looked resigned. I was escorted to the meeting by a uniformed cop. Travis insisted on going with us, even if he wouldn't be in the room. Gavin hung back, poring over my case file.

I was nervous. Not because I didn't know what to say. All I had was the truth. A truth that had weighed on me so heavily for so many years. I was nervous because I would be face-to-face with the pain I'd etched into the Branfords' faces...I didn't know if I'd ever recover from that.

My boots thumped along the paved walkway to the prosecutor's office. We were meeting in a nondescript conference room without two-way mirrors or intercom systems like there had been at the jail. The Branfords were waiting for me, both of them standing against the far wall, putting as much space between us as possible. Travis opened his mouth as if to voice once more his reluctance to leave me alone. I quelled it with one look, closing the door in his face with a decisive *click*. When I turned back, the Branfords hadn't moved.

I let out a shaky sigh, eyes darting around the room before settling back on their faces. It had been thirteen years since the accident. Mr. Branford had always been tall and athletic, and he still was. He studied me warily, as if he wasn't quite sure this was a good idea. Mrs. Branford was heavier than I remembered, with a pinched look to her full face. Her expression was resolute; she wanted to hear what I had to say.

My gait less than steady, I walked to the nearest chair and sat down, hoping they would do the same. "Thank you for agreeing to see me." They each gave a small nod and I continued. "I'm not here to defend my actions, any of them. Not the accident, or leaving town. I wanted to see you, to offer you answers to all the questions I was too scared to give back then. And to apologize. Caleb was my best friend. My only friend. I loved him like a brother—"

A low whimper escaped from Mrs. Branford, and her husband helped her into a chair. He sat down beside her, one hand on her back, their graying heads close together as he whispered softly, soothingly. Their heartbreak filled the room, rolling from their bent shoulders, crashing into me.

Pain splintered my chest, prying it wide open and letting loose all the emotions and memories I'd kept trapped inside. I didn't know whether to keep talking, but I did anyway. Words poured out of my throat until it was raw and scratchy. I talked about how it had felt to perform that night and the beer we'd thought we *earned* for playing our first real show. I told the truth about the accident, and why I left when I did. I talked about the scholarships I funded anonymously for kids with dyslexia, like Caleb had, and the wake-up call I'd had in jail that motivated me to give a significant portion of my earnings to causes Caleb would have supported. But mostly I talked to them about Caleb himself. The stories he told me about them, funny things he said, the hopes and dreams I knew he'd only shared with me. How he gave me the confidence to get on a stage when I could barely handle playing to a few friends in their garage.

As the words poured out of me, a strange thing happened. Caleb came alive again. It was almost as if he were sitting in the room, in a corner just out of view. I could hear his voice in my ears, so clearly. I could see his face, that wide grin of his splitting it in two. The atmosphere changed, became lighter. Like it always did when Caleb was around.

Caleb wasn't like me. His whole life, he'd known only love. Family dinners, bedtime stories, cheers from the sidelines at every game. He was confident and kind. Not just to me, but to everyone. I was the misfit. Caleb was the kid everyone liked.

One hour became two, and the Branfords didn't utter a single word. When finally there wasn't anything left to say, when every memory had been taken out, dusted off and given life, I scrubbed a palm over my face, readying myself for a verbal assault.

But none came. I looked back and forth between their faces, searching for something to tell me whether to stay or go. Their tears had dried, and I'd caught a few smiles while I talked, even one or two soggy laughs. I wiped my hands on my jeans, feeling almost reluctant to leave. Not just because of the Branfords, but because in this room I'd felt a sliver of forgiveness. From Caleb.

I stood up, feeling completely gutted, but lighter than I'd felt since the accident.

I was halfway to the door when I heard Mr. Branford clear his throat. "Caleb looked up to you. He always said you would be famous one day. I guess he was right."

I didn't know what to say to that, but I turned, meeting his sad stare head-on. A deep sigh rattled from his lungs. "Thank you for coming here, for sharing your memories of our son, and for the good you've done these past years. Caleb would be proud."

Recalling my initial reluctance to reach out to the Branfords, I nearly choked on the shame rising in my throat. My head tipped forward in a dejected nod. I didn't deserve their leniency, not when I should have made this effort years ago.

But no matter what happened with my case, I resolved to spend the rest of my life proving him right.

* * *

"Let's sit down. I want you to tell us everything." Travis's bullying tone grated on my nerves as we got back to the house. The last thing I wanted to do was share anything about my conversation with the Branfords, let alone everything. But Gavin was there, too, and even Delaney was waiting in the dining room. Of all the people gathered in the room, she mattered the most. I walked to her, pulling her to my chest and leaning over to kiss her head, breathing in the citrus notes of her shampoo.

"You were right," I whispered to her. "I needed to do that. For them, and for me."

"Piper," Travis suddenly boomed, pointing at her. "Turn up the TV!"

We all swiveled to the flat-screen that had been set up on the buffet. Anxiety squeezed my chest as the local news cut to a shot of the Branfords in front of the brick office building where I had just met with them. They were no match for the horde of reporters pressing in on them as they walked to the parking lot. *The police were so busy they couldn't have bothered to escort Caleb's parents to their car?* Anger sizzled along the back of my neck as Piper pointed the remote control, increasing the volume to deafening levels.

"What were you doing at the courthouse?"

"Do you want Shane Hawthorne to spend the rest of his life in jail?"

"Have you spoken with Shane?"

"Do you blame Shane for the death of your son?"

The Branfords flinched with each question, reporters dogging their steps. Caleb's father stopped as he fished in his pocket for his keys. He unlocked the car, opening his wife's door and helping her in before rounding the hood. Before opening his own door, he paused. "No. We don't blame Sean for the accident. We weren't sure what to think after he left, when he disappeared all those years ago. But after speaking with him just now, and after praying and searching our hearts for what Caleb would want, we'd like the district attorney to drop the charges." His head hung low, voice thick with exhaustion and grief. "Now, please, leave us alone."

They didn't, though, shouting out more questions as Mr. Branford opened the car door and slid behind the wheel. The cameraman must have edged in closer, because I could see inside the car as the Branfords turned to each other, resignation etched into their weathered skin.

I choked on a breath. They shouldn't have to defend me. Not that I wasn't grateful. Knowing the Branfords no longer blamed me for the accident…it was like a huge weight that had been digging into my shoulders for years suddenly eased.

The screen cut to a news desk, a talking head dissecting my case with a cheerful smile on her face. "Come on." I tugged at Delaney's hand, my stomach churning. "I can't watch this."

Travis was rooted to the floor next to me, the light from the chandelier reflecting off his scalp. Completely oblivious. "Jesus Christ, you are fucking brilliant!" He slapped my back, eyes still trained on the TV. "My guess, we'll be out of here by the end of the week."

With my fingers rolled into fists at my sides to keep from throttling him, I trudged up the stairs, Travis's excitement making my stomach turn. Talking to the Branfords hadn't been about getting off.

It had been about getting real.

Delaney's hand was comfortingly warm in mine as I opened the door to our temporary bedroom, although I was anything but comforted.

She closed the door softly behind us, a hopeful smile fluttering onto her face. "I'm proud of you."

Pain shot through me. There was nothing about me to be

proud of. She lifted her hand to slide around my neck, and I winced. "Don't."

Delaney stilled, her eyes searching mine. Thinking. And then she lifted onto her toes and planted a feather-soft kiss on my lips.

I was rooted in place by the rush of guilt filling me like a broken faucet. There was no turning it off and no wrench in sight. "Delaney," I groaned, sucking in a breath as her sweetness rocketed through my lungs.

Delaney pulled back, looking at me as if she saw someone who actually mattered, someone worthy of her love. "I'm here, Shane. I'm right here."

She was wearing a casual pink and white dress, and a pair of wedges with straps that wound halfway up her toned calves. She should have had a backpack slung over her shoulder with nothing more to worry about than whether or not the others in her study group were pulling their weight.

I threaded my fingers possessively through the crown of raven strands framing Delaney's softly rounded face, blue overtaking green until her eyes were the same color as the sapphire at her throat. The stone I'd put there.

Encircling Delaney's neck, I felt for the beat of her pulse beneath my fingers. It was racing.

Our bodies fit together like a preschool puzzle, shapes sliding into each other with ease, not needing to interlock. Not yet. The top of Delaney's head fit perfectly beneath my chin, and I kissed the fine line where her pale scalp shone through, reaching for the metal tab of her zipper. Its low whine split the air as I traced her spine, the pads of my fingers skimming the surface of her skin.

I shuddered as a wave of desire coursed through me. My hunger for Delaney was more than lust. It was need—in its purest form.

And I was scared to *need* her.

I groaned her name. "The first time I saw you, it took everything I had not to kiss you. And when I heard you singing my song, it took everything I had not to run away from you."

"And now," she prompted, her voice breathless and enticing. "What do you want to do with me now?"

"Baby, I've already given you every piece of me." I dropped my forehead to hers, cupping her gorgeous face within my palms, feeling as if I'd been stripped bare. "You have it all."

Delaney wound her legs around my hips, pulling me in tight, tighter. "I'll take good care of you. I promise."

I let myself sink into her sweetness, drown in the comfort and compassion she gave so freely. Silently swearing that I'd never let her go.

Delaney

A storm was brewing. The night sky hung low, weighted down by bloated purple clouds that had blocked the sun for most of the afternoon, stubbornly refusing to release their liquid burden. In the distance I could hear a low rumble of thunder, energy crackling through the air and sending the hair on the back of my neck shooting straight up.

Shane and I had spent hours talking after coming upstairs. Someone must have ordered pizza, because the smell of grease and garlic came wafting beneath the closed door. Neither of us was hungry though. He told me about his conversation with the Branfords. Or rather, what he'd told them. What it had been like, seeing their faces after so many years, and how the energy in the room changed once he began talking about Caleb.

With a monitoring device on his ankle and the threat of a prison sentence hanging over his head, Shane held me tightly as we listened to the drone of multiple, overlapping conversations from downstairs. Waiting. Wondering if the Branfords' statement to the press meant anything at all.

I had questions of my own, too. Ones I didn't dare voice.

Who was I to tell Shane to come clean to *anyone* when I was still keeping secrets from *everyone*? How could I absolve him of his guilt while I was still carrying my own?

Would Shane wind up in jail when the person who really deserved to be behind bars—me—wasn't even allowed to visit?

Part of me wished I'd never met Shane. That I could go back being to the girl who had bundled up a riot of volatile emotions into a fat, misshapen lump and then pushed it so far, so deep, it sat like a rock in the pit of her stomach.

I couldn't though. That girl was gone.

I was someone different now.

Shane had turned my life upside down, and the bundle had come loose. Unfurled completely. And now I couldn't figure out how to wrap them all up again. Fear. Guilt. Grief. Shame. Emotions that were too big, too unruly. Trampling all over my conscience with wild abandon, not caring about the mess they left in their wake.

Shane's breath fanned my ear, becoming deep and regular even as his hand remained wrapped around my waist with possessive pressure. He didn't have to worry. I wasn't going anywhere. Not yet, anyway. My hands fisted the edge of the sheet, drawing it into my chest as I breathed deep. The scent of pinecones and ivory soap and something uniquely Shane—as bracing and clean as the sea—tickled my nose.

Too bad I couldn't stay wrapped in Shane's arms forever.

Because the truth wasn't going away. It was out there, as restless and angry as the lightning I felt in my bones but couldn't yet see.

They say energy never dies; it just changes form, becomes something else. Believing that had given me some comfort over the past few years. My mom was gone, yes. But I could feel her all around me. She was in the first sip of a glass of good wine, the first bite of chocolate cake. I saw her in sunrises and sunsets, felt her in the warm caress of a breeze across my face on a clear, sunny day. I battled my grief on a daily basis by looking for her in everything good that came my way.

But it was getting harder and harder. I couldn't just *take in* good. I needed to *do* good, too.

Taking care of Shane, loving him from the sidelines, wasn't enough. My soul sagged with the weight of the promise I'd made my father.

Stay silent.

Let me do the talking.

Follow my lead.

Staying silent wasn't easy when the truth was eating me up inside.

Staying silent was too big a burden. And yet if I let it go, if I told the truth, if I accepted responsibility for what I'd done… I was scared my father would never forgive me. Scared those little glimpses of my mother would disappear.

And Shane… What would he think of me if he knew I committed the same sin he had? Would he hate me as much as he hated himself? Would he think of me the same way he did Sean Sutter, the misfit he'd spent more than a decade trying to erase?

If our situations were reversed, would I really want Shane to visit me in prison? Posing for selfies with guards, signing autographs for inmates.

Could I burden him with the weight of my sins?

I'd had my chance. So many chances, actually, to tell him the truth. And I had run away from every single one of them.

My mind was tripping over itself, trying to come up with a one-size-fits-all solution. And getting nowhere.

Meanwhile, the storm outside moved closer, rumbles of thunder growling ominously as the wind whipped leaves and small pebbles against the glass windows. My heart picked up its pace, and I pressed Shane's palm to my chest, hoping his steady pressure would calm its skittish beat. Lightning flashed, turning everything in the room bright, a white light the sun could never replicate. I shivered.

BOOM.

The storm arrived, rain pelting the roof directly above our heads. I listened to the howl of the wind, the swell of the rain, feeling something inside me ease. I didn't have to make any decisions tonight. What was done was done, and it would take a lifetime to chip away at my regret. I needn't lift the blade tonight, though my time was coming. Even if Shane was absolved of wrongdoing, I couldn't stay sheltered in his arms forever.

For tonight I would live through this storm. And tomorrow, or the next day, or a day not too long after that, I would face another, one of my own making.

And I would survive that one, too.

Chapter Twenty-Three

Shane

Two days after my meeting with the Branfords, and their ensuing statement to the press, the prosecutor announced he was dropping all charges against me for lack of evidence. It also helped that Gavin had sent the crime scene photographs to an expert. Blown up to ten times their original size, it was possible to see that one of the four cans scattered on the floor mats was unopened. A fact the accompanying report had made no mention of.

I would never forget about Caleb, or go a day without missing him. He was up there somewhere, watching over me. And I wanted to make him proud.

Caleb wouldn't want me to live without really living.

Nothing but Trouble was going back on the road. With all the press coverage surrounding the TMZ story, the NBC interview, my arrest and then release, our tour was extended by two months to accommodate the dates we'd had to cancel. More dates were added, too.

But those were just details. What was really different…and strange, very strange, was not having secrets anymore. The press knew everything. *Everything.*

They had dug up every last detail of my childhood. Things I thought I'd kept hidden were being recounted by people I barely remembered. My father's drunken fits. The abuse my mother had suffered at his hands. The accident. My given name. That I didn't get behind a microphone until after Caleb's death. My battles with addiction.

It seemed all those secrets I'd been ashamed of had never been secrets at all.

Some of the press coverage wasn't true, though. Dozens of women I'd never even met were popping up in the press, claiming I had paid them for "a girlfriend experience."

My fans didn't seem to care about any of it. If anything, the added attention spawned a new level of interest. I had to disable notifications on my iPhone because it wouldn't stop lighting up with tweets, messages, and Google Alerts, finally throwing the damn thing out because some hacker figured out how to track my moves and was posting my location online.

Nothing but Trouble's sales had gone through the roof. I was deluged with offers to write a book, star in a movie about my life, film a reality series or docudrama while on tour. I couldn't turn on a radio without hearing my songs, browse the Internet without seeing my face, or open a magazine without seeing my name. The more of me there was, the more my fans wanted.

Landon and the guys teased me about it, but they made no complaints about the increased royalties.

Travis was completely in his element and loving every minute. Fielding offers left and right and, mostly, staying out of my hair.

Gavin came to as many shows as he could, and we spoke or texted often.

I was grateful for my freedom. And for Delaney.

Everything else was just background noise.

Except for one thing. Delaney's father was still in jail. She was putting on a brave face, but I knew it was killing her. And even though my legal squabbles had nothing to with her father, whenever I put myself in her shoes, guilt curved around my rib cage and squeezed tight.

I reached for my new phone and called my brother, our rekindled relationship another good thing to come out of my relationship with Delaney. "Hey."

"Let me guess. You're calling to remind me to take my vitamins?"

When we were kids, Gavin would steal bottles of Flintstones chewables and made sure I took one every morning. "Did you?"

"Of course. You?"

"I will, right after you give me an update on Fraser's case."

He grunted, obviously preferring a more concrete answer. "I wish I could say that the wheels of justice are moving slowly, but that's not all."

I braced myself for a long, boring explanation I would only understand about half of. "Tell me."

"It's almost like he *wanted* to go to jail."

"What do you mean? No one wants to go to jail."

"Exactly. But I can't explain it any more clearly. I've met with him. Twice. He doesn't want this appeal. Is adamantly against it. Doesn't want me talking to Delaney, reviewing the evidence against him, or petitioning the court. I'm at loose ends."

A frown pinched at my forehead. "I don't get it."

"Me neither. But I have to tell you, I don't think it's because he's guilty."

"Then why?"

"I think he's hiding something. Or protecting someone. I just don't know what, or who. But I'm going to find out."

My mind flashed to Delaney and the way she'd looked beneath me just this morning. Sweet and beautiful. Trusting. "Thanks, Gavin. Delaney's been by my side through everything lately, and I know it's been hard for her to think about her own father behind bars."

"That girl of yours is a keeper, Shane."

"Don't I know it."

Delaney

All Nothing but Trouble concerts were exciting, but tonight, the first show since Shane's arrest, was completely insane. Pulling up to the venue, walking through the crowded underground tunnels, navigating the riotous scene backstage—we might as well have been climbing a mountain as a storm rolled in, darkening the sky above our heads. All around us, barely harnessed energy crackled through the air, just waiting to explode. Shane and the guys breathed it in, letting it fill their lugs, quicken their steps, shine through their bright eyes and potent smiles.

Shane stayed quiet though, saving his voice even as he squeezed my hand, keeping me close. Landon tapped out a frenzied drumbeat on his thigh, his bare chest exposed by yet another unbuttoned shirt. Jett's and Dax's fingers were restless, running up and down the fret board of instruments they weren't holding yet.

For the past few weeks, I'd been terrified that my greatest fear would be realized. That Shane would wind up behind bars. Just like my father. Seeing Shane now, completely in his element, without the prosecutor's noose hanging over his head, felt like a gift.

Even so, my heart squeezed. I had promised my father I'd stay quiet, but I just didn't know if I could do it anymore.

I couldn't forget about my father and leave him to rot. I had pushed Shane to face his problems head-on—why couldn't I do the same?

Roadies hefted equipment, deftly navigating a sea of twisting cords littering the ground without incident, setting them down according to a map they seemed to hold in their minds. Yelling to be heard above the opening act, they cursed at one another with an easy camaraderie that belied their coarse language.

Shane led me to a back corner, somewhat removed from the chaos. "You okay?" Worry radiated from his eyes as he hunched over me, his shoulders shielding me from view.

As much as his fans had rallied around him, they hated me with equal vigor. They called me a gold digger, a whore, a slut. #DumpHerPickMe was trending, and T-shirts with my face and that hashtag were worn by every other girl in the venue. I wasn't sure I disagreed with them. Shane had conquered all his demons. He didn't have any more secrets, and even Caleb's parents had absolved him of blame.

Meanwhile, I hadn't been honest with Shane about my role in the accident that had ripped my life to shreds. Hadn't let him see the darkness that was slowly eclipsing all the light I'd been so determined to shine his way. And my father was still sitting in jail. So, what the hell was I doing here? Was this my future, standing in the wings, watching Shane onstage, owning his talent, owning his truth? I didn't need a stage, didn't want the glare of the lights on me. But I needed something of my own. Needed to be someone besides Shane Hawthorne's girlfriend or Colin Fraser's daughter.

But I shoved all that as deep as I could, hopefully deep enough that Shane couldn't see it. I would deal with it…later. "I'm great. Happy to see you back where you belong."

His eyes softened, tenderness shining from each amber iris. "I wouldn't be here if it weren't for you."

I shook my head, palms pressing on his chest. I'd never get tired of touching this man. "That's not true."

"It is. You told me to talk to the Branfords, to stop hiding behind mouthpieces I pay to do my talking for me. Because of you I reached out to Gavin. I have my brother back." Shane's arms wrapped around me, pulling me close. "I owe you everything, Delaney."

Owe? I didn't want him to owe me a damn thing. I wanted him to *love* me. I ran my hands up Shane's shirt, entwining them around his strong neck. "You don't, really."

"I do, baby." He breathed into my hair, kissing the top of my head and tracing the curve of my spine with his thumbs. My skin thrilled at his touch, every nerve ending feverish with desire. "And I want you by my side, always."

My brain was lagging behind, not quite as willing to go along with the lust burning through me. Questions piled on top of questions. *Why? Is that all you want from me? Another set of adoring eyes? What about love? If I love you enough, will you ever love me back?*

But this wasn't the time or the place. We were surrounded by people and noise and chaos. Just as I was figuring out what to say, there was a shout from Landon. "Dude, you can play with your toy later. We're on!"

Toy. With my head turned in his shoulder, Shane didn't see me flinch. And when he leaned in closer, his lips tickling my earlobe, to say, "Can't wait to play later," he probably thought I shivered with anticipation. But no. It was unease that vibrated along my spine. I didn't want to be Shane's "toy." Or his "whore" or any of the other smears that had been tossed my way. As he ran onstage, my stomach twisted into knots.

Loving him.

Hating myself.

Because my parents, both of them, had raised me to be more than a man's accessory. Even if that man was Shane Hawthorne.

I wanted to do something with my life, something useful.

Shane's jail cell epiphany had given him a focus, channeling his efforts into building his career so he could use his name and money to help those without the gift of his talent.

Academia was calling to me. *My* life was calling. There was so much I wanted to learn, and I craved the validation that came with earning a degree. It was a stepping-stone to figuring out what I truly wanted to do with my life. And I wanted to find a way to forgive myself. Wanted to finally help my father. I just hoped Shane would choose to be a part of all of it.

But first I had to figure out a way to come clean. Not just to Shane, but to the people who had put my father in jail for a crime he didn't commit. Because otherwise, my secret was a bomb that would undoubtedly go off at the most inopportune time, destroying everything I was building with Shane. I needed to control the inevitable explosion.

And to do it, I would have to distance myself from Shane. Protect him from the backlash.

Maybe then he could forgive my deceit.

More than fifty thousand screaming fans were packed into

MetLife Stadium tonight. And every one of them would probably say they were in love with Shane Hawthorne. As he came
into view, there was a roar that nearly lifted me off my feet.

And Shane, he looked…happy. Beyond happy. Exultant.

This was where he belonged. Center stage, belting out lyrics
that resonated with everyone listening, adored by thousands.
He needed their love, their recognition. Without it, he wouldn't
be *Shane Hawthorne.*

Did he need me? Did he love me? Right now, at this moment, I had my doubts.

I owe you.

Those words scraped at my soul, leaving a stinging, jagged
gash in their wake. I crossed my arms around my waist, holding
myself tight. I wanted to remember this moment always. The
sheer beauty that was Shane, using his God-given talent to elec-
trify an entire arena, and loving every minute.

I wanted to remember the hurt, too, because this might be
the last time I had the chance. I could never truly be a part of
this life, not if *this* was all there was.

My mother had wanted to be an artist but had never pursued
her dreams. Had she secretly resented my father for it? Had he
felt guilty for letting her give up her passion?

Resentment. Guilt. Such ugly emotions. If I didn't take action
now, they were bound to come between me and Shane eventually.

I breathed deep, tasting the acrid smoke of the pyrotechnic
effects on my tongue like dregs at the bottom of a coffee cup.
I wanted to memorize everything—the flash of lights illumi-
nating pockets of the crowd, the dancing, screaming fans that
looked like algae churning in rough seas. The way the pulse of
the music reverberated through the soles of my shoes. And always—Shane.

Tonight I was wearing open-toed silver stilettos and a shimmery, pale shift that barely reached midthigh. It was dressier than I normally wore, but Piper had insisted that tonight's victory concert was special and I should look the part. Her phrase resonated with me now, because that's just how I felt. Like I was playing a part.

I'd known exactly what I was getting into when I'd signed on to be Shane's girlfriend. Well... maybe not exactly. I didn't know I would fall so deeply in love with him, or that not knowing if he felt the same was like a malignant cancer stalking its way through my bones. I wasn't acting anymore. This was real to me. I wasn't an actress. I was a lovesick fool.

I loved Shane, absolutely. But I couldn't be his fool.

What did he feel for me? Gratitude? Lust? Was that all?

Happiness and misery were like twin tides, pulling at me from opposite directions.

Shane came running offstage after his set, stopping just short of pulling me against his sweaty chest. "If I hug you now I'll ruin your dress," he said, frowning.

"I don't care." I leaned forward, every pore straining for contact with him.

His hands curled around my shoulders, keeping me at a distance. "No, baby. Not tonight."

Confusion twisted my brows. "Why not?"

A roadie appeared at Shane's side, holding a towel and a fresh shirt. Shane took off his sweat-soaked tee and rubbed himself off as I watched, traitorous heat throbbing between my thighs. He caught the naked want in my expression, grinning lewdly. "Trust me." Putting on his fresh shirt, Shane gulped from a bottle of water, glancing around to see if the guys were ready to get back on.

Landon met his eyes. "You sure you're up for this?"

A grin streaked across Shane's face. "Just get your drumsticks ready, Landy."

"Don't you worry. I'm pulling them out of my ass just for you, Shaney-baby," Landon teased. There was a jagged edge to their banter tonight.

Shane turned to face me as Landon strutted back onstage, performing a drum solo before Jett and Dax took their places, each of them reveling in their individual performances before coming together as a group for Shane's entrance. "You're going to stay right here. Don't move, okay?"

I would have laughed, but there was a seriousness to his instruction that quelled the impulse. "I'll be right here. I promise."

He gave a tight smile, squeezing my shoulders. And then he was off, the crowd welcoming him like the second coming of Christ.

This time he launched into a song I'd never heard before. And I knew instantly it had been written after our night on the beach together. The night I'd been convinced he was dead and had run to him out of fear. Fear that had morphed into something much different the second my hand touched his skin.

That night that had ended with me alone in the bedroom he'd assigned me, a Band-Aid on my foot and a certainty somewhere deep inside my gut that it wouldn't be the last time I'd be hurting because of Shane.

Until tonight, I'd lulled myself into believing that if I loved Shane enough he would love me back.

He wanted me, sure.

Thought he needed me.

Thought he *owed* me.

But did he *love* me?

The song ended, and I wiped at the tears streaming down my face with the back of my hand, knowing I was probably ruining the makeup that had been so expertly applied less than two hours ago. Not caring.

Could that four-letter word be strong enough to withstand the bombshell I was about to drop?

Shane turned his back to the crowd, looking at me as he lifted the microphone to his lips. "And now I want to introduce you to the person who's responsible for me being here tonight. We started off in a very unconventional way, as I'm sure you all know." Most of the crowd was with him, laughing on cue, although there were a few "dump her pick me" shouts scattered among them.

"I started my career after the death of my best friend, Caleb Branford. He's the one who should be with us tonight, holding this microphone." There were no more shouts. Fifty thousand people were silent, mesmerized by Shane's remarks. "But he can't be here. Someone else is, though. Someone who taught me to face the truth head-on. To stop hiding behind lies, hiding behind people lying for me."

The enormous LED screen behind the stage came to life, with a new hashtag in bold, bright letters. #SayYesToShane.

The crowd began chanting it. "Say yes to Shane. Say yes to Shane. Say yes to Shane." It rippled through the arena like a hurricane gathering speed. I sucked in a quick breath, my lungs scorched from the overheated air.

Landon started a low, almost ominous beat on his drums, and Shane looked at me again. "Come out here, Delaney."

There were catcalls and whistles and applause. And a few *boo*s.

My heart plummeted. I knew what was about to happen. What was happening. Everyone in the audience did, too.

My eyes were as round as saucers, but my feet wouldn't move. Until they did.

In the wrong direction.

Chapter Twenty-Four

Shane

Dread seeped into my pores as I turned away from the audience to seek out Delaney's face. Something was wrong. Really wrong. I took a few steps toward her, thinking maybe the lights were distorting my view. But no. I froze, the emotions radiating from her face tearing through me like shrapnel. "Delaney?" I breathed, forgetting about the microphone in my hands until her name reverberated in my earpiece.

Delaney's eyes were wide as she shook her head. One hand flew to her mouth, flattening a palm against her lips as if holding back a scream.

I blinked, and she was gone.

Gone.

Before I could ask her to marry me.

Tearing my eyes from the empty space Delaney had occupied

just seconds earlier, I shot a confused glance toward Landon. The LED screen went dark, hashtag fading. The disappointed crowd was already restless, and if I took off after Delaney like I wanted to, there was no telling what would happen. Landon launched into the opening riff of one of our most popular songs, the one we usually closed with. Good. I could sing it and then get the fuck offstage. My mind raced as the familiar lyrics skated smoothly through my lips, clutching the microphone so tightly my knuckles glowed white.

Maybe Delaney would be back in my dressing room. Maybe asking her to be my wife in front of fifty thousand fans wasn't the kind of proposal she wanted. Maybe, maybe, maybe.

Small hopes that were as faint and thready as the sulfur tail of a match. After it's been extinguished.

Fear squeezed my chest, so tight I had to cut a few notes short.

Maybe I should let her go.

But why? Surely that black cloud hovering over my head was moving on, or at least had run out of rain. Everything I'd been so ashamed of was out in the open, and life still went on. Delaney knew me. Had seen the very worst parts of me, up close in all my scarred, ugly glory. And she hadn't run.

No. Delaney had planted her feet in front of me, wrapped her arms around me. And stayed.

Why was Delaney running? And why now? When it looked like we might have a future—a real one—together.

Somehow I managed to get through the song, then choked out a half-assed joke about going to find my stage-frightened girlfriend. I knew she wouldn't be in my dressing room before I flung open the door, but even so, the sight of the empty room hit me like a kick to the head. The door slammed into the opposite wall and bounced back toward me, but by the time it clicked closed I was halfway down the corridor, confusion and betrayal stewing in my gut.

"Shane, wait!"

My heart leapt at the female voice, the unmistakable *tap-tap*ping of heels on cement. But they didn't belong to Delaney. "Where is she?" I asked Piper, my hands clenching and un-clenching at my sides.

"She took a car back to the hotel. I have the driver on the line. Do you want me to have him pull over?"

I thought for a minute. I didn't want Delaney to feel trapped, or spied on. "No. Let him take her back to the hotel. Just tell him to drive very, very slowly." No way was I going to let her go. Not without a fight.

Piper spoke into the phone at her ear and hurried to keep pace with me as I raced toward the exit door. "There's a car waiting, right?"

"Yes. We always keep a few on standby." Although Piper had been assigned by Travis to keep tabs on Delaney and ensure she was always camera ready, she rarely came to our concerts. Tonight's show was special though.

It was supposed to be special.

I nodded but didn't say anything more until I pushed through the door and jumped into the car. There were nearly a hundred fans held back beyond ropes. They must not have had tickets, because anyone who had been in the arena couldn't have gotten out here this fast. Normally I would have signed a few au-tographs and posed for selfies, but not tonight. I plastered a fake smile on my face, lifted my hand in a wave, and slid into the car before they could tell me how much they loved me. I wanted to hear those words, was desperate for them. But only if they came from Delaney's mouth.

There was an empty part of my soul that was lined with bitterness and self-hatred. The part I'd tried to fill with booze and drugs and meaningless sex. And when that hadn't worked, I'd filled it with fake relationships I could control, women I pretended were with me because I was worthy of love. But they weren't with *me*. They were with Shane Hawthorne, rock star. They wanted money and fame and exposure. But Delaney had never given a damn about any of those things. She saw *me*. She wanted *me*. She'd stayed with *me* when anyone else would have run for the hills.

If nothing else, I needed to know why she was leaving me now. When I finally believed we might have a real chance.

Piper scooted in beside me, and I stifled the brief flare of annoyance. My misery and frustration filled the car enough without another body sharing the space. But she'd been useful so far, and there was a chance I would need her again. Until she huffed out a sigh reeking with judgment. "Did you say something to Delaney? I mean, I made sure she was perfectly made-up and dressed once Travis told me what you were planning to do tonight. She seemed fine earlier, and she looked gorgeous. I don't understand."

I turned pained eyes on Piper. "Of course I said something to her. I told Delaney how much she meant to me and how grateful I was to her for supporting me through the bullshit Greek tragedy that is my life." I ran anguished hands through my hair, tugging at the ends. "You tell me, Piper…Where did I go wrong?"

Piper's mouth pursed, almost as if she was holding something back. "That's something you're going to have to figure out, Shane." She hesitated, pressing her lips together.

My patience was in shreds and I didn't offer any. "Spit it out."

Hoisting one shoulder upward, Piper dipped her head toward it. "Maybe it's what you *didn't* say that made her leave."

I pushed my fingers beneath my thighs before I could wrap them around Piper's neck and squeeze the life out of her. What the hell was she talking about? How could Delaney be upset about something I didn't say? But before I could prod further, we pulled up to the entrance of the hotel. Without waiting for the driver to open my door, I flung it aside myself and bounded out.

As I strode through the lobby, heads swiveled and called my name. I ignored them, aiming straight for the elevators, but there was nothing I could do about the gaggle of girls that came rushing up and followed me into the elevator car. For twenty-two flights I signed autographs and stared into cell phone cameras, not even attempting a smile, fake or otherwise. As I put the room card into the lock, I had to shake off a particularly aggressive pair intent on a threesome. "Not tonight," I hissed, closing the door and bolting it shut.

I knew instantly Delaney was there, could smell the delicious scent that wafted off her skin like pollen suspended on a summer's breeze. My boots slapped the polished marble floor, announcing my presence well before I made it to the carpeted bedroom. Delaney's black suitcase was open on the bed, clothes haphazardly tossed in its general direction. She stood a few feet away, clutching her toiletry bag to her chest like a security blanket.

The look in her eyes slammed into me with such force I rocked back on my heels. They were a cerulean riot of confusion and pain. "Hey." The word scraped through my throat, sounding harsher than I intended. I lifted my hands and wrapped my fingers around the molding edging the doorframe, squeezing tight. "What's going on?"

A ripple of warning skidded along my spine as I waited for her answer. One beat passed, then two. Delaney pressed her lips together, her tongue fluttering between the crease, then disappearing. "Don't, Shane," she murmured, eyes shimmering. "Please, just don't."

Delaney

The mechanical sweep of the lock against the door made my heart skip a beat. A tiny sound and yet it reverberated through my bones like a sonic boom.

It was too much to hope that I could have gotten away before Shane came looking for me. He must have left the arena as soon as possible without provoking a revolt by fifty thousand angry fans, because I'd been in the suite only a few minutes.

I shouldn't have fallen for him. Should have followed the rules of that stupid, stupid contract and left my heart out of the mix. But I had broken the rules and fallen in love. Hard.

Not with the Shane Hawthorne I'd crushed on since I was a teenager, but the man behind the facade, stuck somewhere between Shane and Sean. And now my heart felt like it had been torn in two, stomped on by those rugged boots he wore everywhere.

Shane's bulk filled the doorframe. Energy radiated from every brawny inch, exuding confusion and anger. His wounded eyes cut me deep. I looked from his head to his boots, knowing I'd touched and kissed every inch of the man standing before me. And that in a few minutes I'd go back to seeing Shane only in magazines and on album covers.

Hands straining to reach for him, I instead hugged my cosmetics bag tight to my chest, my heart thudding against a rib cage that felt as if it had shrunk overnight. Could I even put my emotions into words?

There was a good chance I would be the one in jail in the not too distant future. I certainly deserved to be. Would Shane ever be able to trust me once I admitted what I'd done...and that I'd been lying about it to everyone? Even him. Especially him.

Shane had invited me into his life to keep chaos at bay, and I'd brought only upheaval.

I was everything he didn't want in his life. And now that he'd finally found peace?

I loved him too much to destroy it.

"Don't what, Delaney?" Shane stood just inside the doorway, hurt smeared all over his gorgeous face. "Don't sing your praises to an entire arena full of fans?"

"No, that... That was really sweet." My tongue tripped over the words. "Thank you." Walking away from Shane was ripping a hole in me so jagged it would never heal without leaving an ugly reminder of what I'd lost.

"Then what? Don't ask—"

I threw the toiletry bag into my suitcase, shoving the smattering of clothes in after it and furiously tugging at the zipper. "Exactly. Don't ask me anything."

"Wow. So that's how you're going to play this?" Each syllable dripped with barely restrained fury.

I wasn't playing. That was the problem. This wasn't a game of charades for me. Every emotion I'd shown to the cameras was real. Wrenching the suitcase off the mattress, it landed with a *thunk* on the carpet and promptly tipped over. I stared at it, wishing I could just throw myself beside it. "I guess I am," I said quietly, avoiding Shane's angry stare.

Shane made a sound, an almost primal growl, slamming his fist into the wall with a violence that made me jump.

"Don't," I cried, cringing at the streaks of red on the white wall, the sight of Shane's bloody knuckles sending me running toward him. "Jesus Christ, stop it."

The moment I took a step toward him, I knew it was a mistake. That I should have stayed where I was. Because the closer I got to Shane, the more of his energy wrapped around me, stampeding over the last shreds of my willpower. And when I touched him…

A spark lit into me, feeding on the oxygen in my blood, bursting into flames I didn't know how to extinguish.

I was his.

In surrender, I lifted my chin, and Shane's mouth settled over mine. Like an airtight seal, our kiss held back the words I was too scared to let escape. Because once I did, there would be no going back. I didn't know what Shane would say, what he would do. If he would hate me for what I'd done. If he would leave me.

Which was why I'd left him first.

But he'd come after me. And just like that, with one touch, neither of us was going anywhere.

Shane's tongue teased me slowly. Excruciatingly slowly. Gathering the ends of my hair in his hands, Shane bunched it inside his fists, tugging my head back farther, tiny prickles alighting on my scalp. Not enough to hurt, just enough to send those same tingles everywhere. I yielded gratefully, curling my fingers around his neck, squeezing, urging. But no. Shane was setting the pace. A soft cry bubbled up from the back of my throat as I gave in. He licked at the corners of my mouth, nibbled at my lips. My eyes closed, escaping into the dizzying whirls of lust as I reached for the edge of Shane's shirt, dragging it over his head.

Needing it off. He did the same to my dress, flinging the designer creation across the room. A vent was at my back, blowing a cool, air-conditioned breeze along my spine, prickling my skin.

Shane cupped one pebbled breast in his good hand, his mouth closing over the other one. Licking, sucking, flicking his tongue over the needy peak as I arched into him. My mouth fell open, head tipping back, hair swishing against my shoulders as I made noises that sounded like a cornered animal. I was captured. Trapped in a gilded cage. A minute ago I'd been ready to fly away. But now I was in Shane's arms, being worked over by that mouth of his that brought me to the edge of heaven and then pushed me beyond it. So. Many. Times.

My body came alive beneath his hands, his mouth. It had been like this since the first moment I'd set eyes on him. Maybe before that. Maybe all those magazine covers had predisposed me to fall apart in his arms. And every time our bodies met in this ancient, primal dance, the tide that swept me away seemed to grow more powerful. This thing between us, whatever it was, grew bigger, more overwhelming.

Because I was overwhelmed. Heat raced within my veins, leaving me gasping for breath.

Shane pulled away, pinning me with his stare. There was a nakedness to his need that mirrored my own. I could see it in his eyes, taste it on his lips. Moaning, I ran greedy fingers over the inked skin covering his rippling muscles. God, everything about this man was beautiful. His face, his body, his skin, his tattoos. His spirit.

When had I given him my heart? Could I trace back the exact moment it left my body and became his? The question flitted at the edge of my mind, scurrying away as Shane lifted me, setting me down on the center of the mattress as he stepped back to shuck off his jeans. Standing there for a moment in his full naked glory. And he was *glorious*. I shivered as I took in every last inch of him.

"Delaney." My name was a groan, as if he knew anything else would put an end to what we were doing. There were so many words littering the air between us. Questions and answers that sizzled like grease on a hot skillet, popping and hissing. If we got too close, we'd be burned. By mutual consent, we focused on the one thing that required no words.

Lust.

Right now it was the only honest thing I had to offer.

I was wearing a nude lace thong, and he dragged it over my legs as if he were opening a present. He moved over me, knees indenting the mattress on either side of my thighs. Sliding long fingers beneath my head, Shane cradled my skull in his hands, kissing me until the room spun.

The tension and chaos that had seeped into my pores tonight, over the past couple of months, throughout the past three years—all of it fought for space in my body, leaving my skin as thin and tight as a cheap party balloon. I reveled in the weight of him against my chest, lending me his strength, keeping me centered as our heartbeats knocked along together. Shane. Me. Us.

This was what I wanted. Did anything else matter? If the truth would take him from me, did I really need to say a damn thing?

But I did. I did. I did.

Even lying beneath him, I could feel it eating away at me like acid. I would tell him. Just not now. Not yet. I needed *this*. It might be all I had, ever again.

I sighed as Shane guided himself into me, sinking deep. Deep, so deep. Filling that empty part of me that was a black void of guilt and grief.

Our hips rocked together, hands entwining above my head. Sweetness rushed through me, like drizzles of honey, as our mouths roamed, feasting on each other. Lips, necks, ears, collarbones. Our tongues lashed every bit of skin we could reach. Both of us so hungry.

My ankles hooked around Shane, drawing him even closer. Our panting breaths filled the air around us. Fast, shallow gasps. We sounded like sprinters, the end of the race in sight.

My eyes drifted closed, lost in an inner maelstrom of sensation.

"Delaney," Shane barked. "Look at me."

I didn't want to. I didn't want to see Shane's face. See what I was doing to him. A reflection of what he was doing to me. Our coupling was too intense to look closely. Too raw. Too desperate.

And it might be our last.

With a roar, Shane slammed into me. Except he didn't pull back out. "Don't shut me out, Delaney. I won't have it." It was more than a request.

I whimpered, giving in to Shane's command. The sight of his bare chest, every muscle vibrating with the strain of holding himself in check, was enough to make me weep in awe. But it was his amber gaze that burned into me, penetrating through the top layer of my skin and leaving me defenseless. There was no armor strong enough to protect me from this man. His shameless charm, his stunning body. My sexy bad-boy rock star. My sweet Good Samaritan.

Head and heart of a lion, soul of a wounded boy.

Shane Hawthorne, I'm yours.

"I've got you," he said, easing out of me with a tender look in his eyes, as if he'd read my mind. Pushing back slowly. Setting a new rhythm.

Shane released my hands, dragging his fingertips along my neck, my breasts, continuing lower until his calloused fingertips dug into my waist, holding on. His pace picked up, thrusts becoming frenzied. I met every one of them with equal force. We crashed into each other, pleasure darkening my vision until I was grasping at his shoulders, dizzy and out of control.

Everything in my body condensed, drawing tight, tight, tight. "Shane," I screeched, nails digging into his back as I burst apart, splintering into tiny, glittering shards.

Shane growled into my neck, biting as he thrust one last time, and gathered my boneless body into his. "That settles it, Delaney. We're getting married."

Chapter Twenty-Five

Delaney

*N*o. *No, no, no.*

My limbs, which had been so languid mere seconds earlier, tensed up, and I flinched at Shane's casual pronouncement. I shoved at his shoulders. "Get off me."

Was that a proposal? Two sentences. Neither one a question.

Every little girl dreamed of this moment, including me. Especially me.

That settles it. We're getting married.

Not one of my daydreams had ever ended that way.

Maybe I shouldn't be surprised. My life hadn't exactly gone according to plan so far.

The only world I'd ever known had been completely obliterated in the blink of an eye. Happily married parents, top schools, no worries beyond finding a boyfriend or a summer internship.

All it took was a quick text to distract me for a minute, to take my foot off the brake just long enough for the car to drift a few feet into an intersection, setting off a chain of events that killed my mother and stole my father's freedom.

From that moment on, guilt had eclipsed my carefree life, leaving just an inky darkness that seemed as if it would never end.

And then I'd met Shane Hawthorne.

He rolled off me, his amber eyes studying my face from beneath furrowed brows.

Shane didn't know that the most recent chapter of my life had been written with a poisoned pen. He'd kissed me until I was senseless, and in the next breath offered me a future I'd thought was out of reach forever. And as if that wasn't enough, he'd faced his own checkered past, found redemption in the truth.

There would be no redemption for me. I was the one behind the wheel that day. Once I told the truth, my father would be free.

And I wouldn't.

If only I hadn't promised to keep my mouth shut. Promised my father he would never visit his daughter in jail.

That pledge had tied my hands more effectively than a set of handcuffs.

I couldn't keep it anymore.

"That wasn't the response I was hoping for," he said, his scowl deepening.

Hope was a dangerous thing. It could only carry you so high before gravity pulled you back down to earth. The higher you flew, the harder you fell. Being with Shane these last few months had been a wild, crazy, exciting ride—especially after the past three years wallowing in guilt and grief. Somehow I'd discovered a frantic, feverish hunger that only Shane had ever spawned in me and that only he could satisfy. Shane had brought joy into my life again, and I'd let his wounds eclipse mine. Living life in his arms, looking at it through his eyes...I'd nearly forgotten that no matter how *real* my feelings, I was still hiding behind them.

Deep inside though, I was holding out hope that once I told him the truth, he would stay by my side. That he would fight for me, for *us*, as I'd done. Even if it meant walking back into a courthouse and holding my hand while I faced whatever was coming my way.

But Shane couldn't do any of that until I told him the truth.

This time, the choice would be his.

Would he stay?

"Frankly, that wasn't the proposal I'd dreamed of either." My softly spoken rebuke coated the back of my throat with burnt ash, incinerating any lingering desire pumping through my veins. "But that's not why I can't marry you."

Shane's jaw clenched as he rolled off the bed, grabbing for his clothes, which littered the carpet. Worn jeans were left unzipped as he pulled his shirt over his head and settled his mussed hair with those elegant fingers that had worked such magic on me just a few minutes ago. "Why the fuck not?"

Somehow I managed a tremulous smile, reaching for the lowest-hanging fruit first. Delaying the inevitable. "For starters, you can't replace an employment contract with a marriage pact. It's like you're trying to frame our relationship with an arbitrary set of rules and expectations. We don't need that."

Shane sighed. "What do you want from me, Delaney?"

My tongue swept across suddenly dry lips. "I want you to

know that I've been with you because it's where I wanted to be. Maybe not from day one, but definitely from day two. I stayed because I couldn't bear to leave. Because I fell in love with you, Shane. You don't *owe* me anything." *Only your heart.*

"I—"

"Wait." I put my hand up, drawing the sheet around my chest as if it could protect me, and took a shaky breath. It was time to stop beating around the damn bush. No matter what Shane had or hadn't said, right now the only thing that mattered was what *I* hadn't said. Shane's secrets were all out in the open, his legal battle in the rearview mirror. But mine was just beginning. Because after I spoke my truth, I was going to have to face the consequences, the condemnation. Including Shane's. I couldn't hide anymore. "There's something else. Something you don't know."

That I'd done the very same thing he still hated himself for. I had been behind the wheel of an accident. I'd walked away. My mother hadn't.

I was the murderer.

"I can't marry you—can't even *be* with you—until I'm not betraying you with every other word out of my mouth. I've wanted to tell you the truth so many times, for so long. I'm ready to take responsibility for my lies, face the consequences of my actions. But first I need to be honest with you."

Caramel eyes held mine, and I drank up this moment, these last precious seconds before Shane would know what I'd kept hidden for so long. The horrible, awful truth that was killing me a little more every day. "I was the driver. It was me. I picked up my phone, just for a second, on our way home. I caused the accident. Not my father. Me."

My heart sank as those eyes hardened into amber, tightening around the truth. Going dark. *No. Don't walk away. Don't let me go*. But even as my soul cried out, I knew it was no use. Standing right in front of me, Shane was already gone.

"You were the driver," he repeated, the words cold and harsh.

I flinched as if he'd banged down a gavel. "Yes." The word was little more than a puff of air.

I watched as hardness spread to Shane's face, the muscles in his cheek twitching until they turned into granite. Fury rolled off his skin, leaching into the air between us. He stood up slowly, tugging at his zipper as he stepped into his boots.

"Say something, please," I begged, a sense of urgency winding through my misery. Was he really going to leave without saying another word? Was he really going to *leave*?

"What's there to say?" he shot back.

"I don't know. But something. Anything."

Shane leveled a hard look at me. "You're a liar. You've lied to me day after day, even after I was honest with you. And you were going to leave, just walk away from me—from *us*—without ever admitting your deception?" His eyes burned with fury. "You were right, you know. That first night we met."

"What—" My throat closed, and I swallowed. Started again. "What do you mean?" I asked, fear rising in my gut like a summer squall, heavy and drenching. I knew what he was going to say before he said it, and I wanted to cover my ears and drown him out. But I didn't, my hands wrapping around my chest instead, preparing for the inevitable blow.

Shane delivered, repeating the same words I'd spoken to him in Travis's backyard. "You're no one I want to know." His voice was practically emotionless, and it dragged along my flesh like a serrated blade.

Months ago, I'd used them in a desperate bid at self-preservation.

But right now, Shane sure looked like he meant every word.

The tears I'd been trying to hold back overflowed, falling unchecked down my cheeks as he walked away. I pitched forward, Shane's parting jab eating me up inside. I had told him my deepest, darkest secret. I'd opened up, let him see me. All of me. Deep down I thought he would fight for me. For us.

Shane's delicious swagger was just a blur as he covered the distance to the door, his quick pace further proof he couldn't wait to get away from me.

I was no better than any of the groupies stalking Shane across the globe. I'd allowed myself to fall, so hard and so far…for what?

Shane had been honest about his needs and expectations at the outset—and then he'd thrown them all out the window when we became *real*.

But Shane didn't want real. He wanted flawless.

Shane

The hurt written across Delaney face was the perfect counterpoint to the shock I felt at her admission.

No wonder we fit together so well. We had the same wounds, the same cracks in our soul. We'd both been responsible for the death of someone we loved.

We'd both stolen lives.

Delaney's mother was dead. She was living free while her father wasn't.

My best friend was dead. I'd taken center stage because Caleb couldn't.

Stolen fucking lives.

Would I have to watch my gorgeous girl go through what I just had? Tried in the court of public opinion. The possibility—no, probability—of jail time.

Could I stand to see Delaney caged behind iron bars? *Jesus.* The thought was a cattle prod dragged along my spine. Agony.

I loved her too damn much to lose her.

All this time I'd worried about dragging her beneath my dark cloud. Didn't want to ruin her.

Now I knew better.

Delaney *was* the cloud.

Caleb's death had nearly killed me. But Delaney gone…that would ruin me.

How could she do this? How had I gotten so wrapped around her damned finger that the thought of being without her set my soul on fire?

I'd let my guard down. I'd trusted Delaney with every piece of me, even the ones I despised. And she'd lied to me in return.

All I wanted to do was move past what I'd done, and now I would be reminded of it every time I looked into Delaney's eyes. Because she'd done the same thing.

She killed. She ran. She lied.

Delaney shouldered crushing guilt and self-hatred every goddamn day. Just like I did.

The girl I'd put on a pedestal didn't belong on one. She should have been standing with me toe-to-toe. Trusting me with her deepest secrets, as I'd trusted her with mine.

After all this time looking up at her, could I look down? Could I get past Delaney's flaws? Could I reconcile who I thought she was—who I fell for—with this new reality?

Not tonight. Maybe not ever.

Even though my love for Delaney Fraser flowed through my

veins with every caged beat of my heart, it was chased with the bone-deep knowledge that I didn't know her at all.

We were on a goddamn merry-go-round of secrets and lies. Bliss and betrayal. Fuck-ups and forgiveness.

Delaney had forgiven me my sins without question. But I was drowning in hers. Maybe that made me a selfish bastard.

But I wanted off.

Trudging down the hall, I felt like a thousand-pound bag of dog shit on a hot summer day. Dirty. So fucking dirty.

Disappointment and disgust brewed in my gut, polluting my lungs, hurting my chest. I should have known. Should have known from the first moment at Travis's house when Delaney looked at me.

Delaney *knew* me. And I'd let her in. Told her everything. And she didn't run away. She had stayed.

I'd been so fucking stupid.

Yeah, Delaney knew me all right. Because she *was* me.

But I didn't know her at all.

She was living in a web of lies. Lies she was still spinning. How could I be with someone who mirrored the worst choice I'd ever made?

"Two wrongs don't make a right" was one of my mother's favorite sayings.

In the elevator, I scoffed. Then why the fuck had the past few months with Delaney felt so *right*?

She had made me *feel* again. Crave the future I saw in those gorgeous whorls of blue and green, her eyes shining like a beacon within that angelic face.

I pulled up short just as I set foot outside, and it wasn't because of the flash of a dozen cell phone cameras documenting my departure.

I fucking loved her. I *loved* Delaney Fraser.

And she loved me.

Fuck.

Dizziness assaulted my mind, the feeling that Delaney was just another penalty for what I'd done swirling right along with it. I pressed a hand to my stomach, feeling gutted.

Slipping back into the car parked just a few feet away from the hotel's entrance, I swiped a hand over my mouth as if I could erase the bitterness filling it. Piper was still in the backseat, thumbs and eyes glued to her iPhone.

I dropped into the cool leather seat, feeling shredded by Delaney's betrayal. Piper glanced up, a sleek eyebrow arching as she set her phone aside. "I take it congratulations aren't in order?"

A sour laugh gurgled from my throat, and I glanced out of the window, my eyes immediately going to the highest story. Even now, all I wanted to do was go back to Delaney, take her in my arms and devour her until I'd forgotten everything she'd just said. She had told me to live in my truth, to face everything and everyone I'd once run from. What a crock of shit.

Now I was running from her.

I turned away from the window, glaring at Piper. "There any whiskey in this car?"

Delaney

I didn't leave the room. I couldn't. Instead, I spent the rest of the night with my face burrowed beneath covers that still smelled of Shane. Taking deep, longing breaths. Desperately hoping he would come back. Knowing he wouldn't.

It wasn't until the sun began to creep above the horizon,

turning the hulking silhouettes of the buildings surrounding the hotel into oversized, pockmarked gray tombstones, that sleep finally came. I fell into its embrace, grateful for a respite from the pain splitting me in two. But even then, I couldn't quite escape. It throbbed in the emptiness of my lungs, and I kept sputtering awake, trying to catch a breath.

As I lay there panting, scared to go back to sleep, scared to fully wake up, I heard a noise that sounded like the click of a key-card reader. I bolted upright. "Shane," I called out, my tone blatantly hopeful.

Only silence answered back.

Leaving the empty bed to investigate, I saw an innocuous envelope pushing crookedly beneath the door. My full name was clearly printed across the middle, the return address still obscured. I peered through the keyhole in the hopes of catching a glimpse of the delivery person, but I saw no one. Whoever had pushed it beneath the door was gone.

Dread unspooling in my stomach, I tugged at its edge, the words in the upper-left corner sliding into view. TRAVIS TAGGERT & ASSOCIATES.

A soft whimper escaped my lips as I extracted the crisply folded stationery through the unsealed back flap. As I unfolded the letter, pulse racing, blood buzzing in my ears, a cashier's check fell out, fluttering slowly to the carpet before landing, faceup, at my bare feet. Containing more zeroes than I'd ever imagined on a check with my name on it.

I remained standing, still and quiet, as I read the short paragraph.

The enclosed check contains all monies owed to Delaney Fraser, including a performance bonus. The nondisclosure agreement remains in effect. No further contact with the Client is necessary. Thank you for your service.

It was unsigned.

Pain assaulted my senses, the attacking shards so razor-sharp I looked down, expecting my skin to be in ribbons. *Performance bonus? Thank you for your service?*

I shuddered, staring at the words on the crisp linen page until they blurred, then crushing the paper into a ball and throwing it across the room. It should have made a sound as loud as a meteor hitting the earth. It should have exploded like a grenade, shattering the windows and turning the suite into a fiery, gaping hole.

It did neither of those things.

The wrinkled parchment ball didn't travel very far, and it landed softly. Harmlessly. With absolutely no correlation to the damage it had done to my heart.

Tears came, and they were not nearly as quiet. Racking sobs burst from my spasming rib cage, scraping my throat and shattering the silence. I pulled my knees into my chest, rocking back and forth as hot tears streaked down my face. They tasted bitter rather than salty, and I rubbed at them with a sleeve of my terry-cloth robe.

In an angry haze, I fought an urge to tear up the check. The words in the accompanying note might have been venomous, but I'd sure as hell earned the obscene amount staring at me. Not on my back, but with my heart.

Surely Shane had taken the vital organ with him. I felt so empty, completely hollow. And yet I was still breathing, still crying.

Whoever said "the truth shall set you free" had never been dumped by the love of their life because of it.

I thought I would feel better after being honest with Shane, even if he decided to walk away. Especially since a part of me had wanted him to walk away, wanted to keep him out of my contamination zone.

But I'd thought wrong. Big-time.

Shane's absence had left a black hole in the space my heart had been, and I was being pulled into the void.

Foolishly, I'd hoped that he could have looked past that awful link between us. That he could forgive me. But I should have known better.

My eyes were red and puffy as I stumbled into the bathroom and turned on the shower. I couldn't stay here anymore. Not with the smell of Shane still clinging to the pillows. Maid service couldn't remove the knowledge that Shane and I had once lain together on that bed, finding rapture in each other's arms.

I'd wiped it all away with a few words. Words that had been clogging my throat for three years. A truth that had pushed between us like an electrified fence, miles of barbed wire heaped on top.

In a frenzy, I emptied tiny bottles of shampoo and conditioner into my hair and lathered my body with the contents of another bottle. The scents clashed with each other, the combination jarring. Lemon and jasmine and vanilla. I nearly gagged.

Without a stylist, or hair and makeup people fussing over me, I stumbled out of the hotel in still-damp hair, wearing my oldest, most ragged pair of jeans and a stained T-shirt that I'd meant to throw out ages ago. I didn't have many clothes from my old life, and I couldn't stomach wearing something Shane had paid for. Ridiculous, I knew, since the check in my purse basically proved that he'd paid for *me*.

Chapter Twenty-Six

Delaney

An Uber took me to a cemetery in my hometown, just an hour away. Since my mother's death, there had been a constant ache within my chest, a heaviness that wouldn't allow my lungs to expand fully. I had been slowly suffocating, weighed down by a truth I couldn't speak.

And then I'd met Shane. Suddenly I could breathe again. I could feel again. I could cry again.

But today was different. I wasn't crying just because of Shane. My tears were for everything I'd kept bottled up for so long.

My mother's death.

My father's insistence on taking the blame.

The lives that had been shattered because, for a split second, my phone was more important than the world beyond my windshield.

I cried for the college coed who'd foolishly thought she had her future all mapped out.

I cried for Shane. For the little boy he once was, and the man he'd become.

I cried for the connection we shared. The couple we'd been for just a little while. Two people with one heart, who had found themselves in each other. Or so I'd thought. And I cried for myself. Because my heart, whatever part of it remained, didn't feel like it would ever be whole again.

I fisted my hands at my sides, nails leaving half-moon imprints in my palms. No. No—I wouldn't do that again. I was done letting someone else dictate what I would say. Where I should go. What I should think. How I should feel.

Who I would love.

One day my heart would be whole again. One day I would love again.

Someone who loved me back just as fiercely. Someone who would fight for me, who would fight alongside me.

The sun broke through a narrow gap in the clouds, slanting across my face, drying my tears. The headstone at my back warmed, the heat spreading along my skin, radiating through my chest. I pulled away, facing the stone, which was now reflecting the sunshine, glowing almost white. I looked around, expecting the neighboring markers to look the same. But no, I was surrounded by a sea of gray. I swallowed, tracing my mother's name with my fingertips. Feeling her presence.

The sun slipped back behind the clouds, the headstone fading back into gray. But for just a moment, the inscription brightened, one last pulse of warmth lighting up the epitaph I'd been too devastated to notice.

Love Has No Ending.

I pressed my palms against the slab, felt the warmth draining from it even as I was filled with certainly that mother was still be there for me, no matter what. I spread out on the soft green grass, watching the clouds floating by. "Thanks, Mom," I said softly.

The first moment I realized I loved Shane, a part of me had relaxed, loosening with relief. I had thought I'd crossed some kind of invisible finish line.

But what I hadn't known then, not even a clue, was that I'd only been standing on the starting block. The real race, my race, was just beginning.

I'm not sure how much time passed. Ten minutes. An hour. Two. It didn't matter. I knew what I needed to do. I'd known it for a while now. I was tired of lying. Tired of hiding. Tired of pretending to be someone I wasn't.

Three years ago, I did a bad thing. A very bad thing. And I was still stuck in that moment. Caught. I'd never be able to move forward until I faced it squarely. Admitted it, not just to Shane, but to those who had been too eager to accept my father's explanation. After a few drinks, he'd gotten behind the wheel with his wife and daughter in the car. One lived, the other didn't. And he was serving a fifteen-year sentence for the choice he made.

Except that he hadn't been behind the wheel.

I was at fault, not him.

Whether Shane was by my side or not, I had to make things right.

Shane

Reluctantly, I opened one very bloodshot eye. Regretted it immediately.

My cell was ringing, loudly enough it was obviously nearby, but all I could see was the empty bottle of Jack Daniel's lying on its side. Empty.

Daylight streamed into the room, no doubt because I'd forgotten to close the shades last night. The past days were a blur. What city was I in? I couldn't remember. Reaching out for a pillow to cover my throbbing head, my fingers touched something hard.

The damned phone.

Against my better judgment—Who was I kidding? I'd thrown out anything resembling good judgment the second I'd walked away from Delaney—I answered it.

"Colin Fraser is being released tomorrow." Gavin's delivery was matter-of-fact.

"Great," I croaked, trying to inject a note of enthusiasm into my hoarse voice. Had I been smoking, too? What other vices had I indulged in? I glanced down at my pants. Still on, zipper up. It was a relief. I wasn't the slightest bit interested in kissing anyone other than Delaney, touching anyone but her. Although after a bottle of grain alcohol, what I did or thought was anyone's guess.

"Did you hear me? I said Colin Fraser is being released. Tomorrow."

Through a thick fog, the meaning behind his words finally made it through to my brain. "What? How the hell did that happen?"

"If you had taken my calls at any point during the past day, I would have told you that Delaney came to me with the truth of what really happened the night of the accident."

Delaney was the driver.

"You got her a deal?"

"Actually, no. I told her you had requested I look into her father's case. And since I was working with her father, I couldn't take her case."

"What the fuck, Gav? You didn't help her?"

My brother snorted. "Unlike you, I didn't leave her high and dry. I said I would get her a lawyer, a good one. I just needed a day."

Still flinching from his barb, all the more painful because of its accuracy, I rolled onto my back and released a deep breath. "And?"

"And nothing. The girl walked right out of my office and into the Bronxville police station."

"What?" I bolted upright, my brain banging painfully against my skull. "Where is she now? Did they arrest her?"

"No. The cops told her to come back with her lawyer."

Thank God. "Then did you go with her?"

"Yes. Right after I sent a notice to the court terminating my relationship with Colin Fraser."

"So, what happens now? Is she okay?"

"There was a bit of legal wrangling, but in the end, the cops didn't want to have dirt on their faces. Turns out there was a red-light camera that caught the whole thing. They never checked it because Fraser confessed. Delaney has agreed to plead down to a misdemeanor. She'll do community service, but no jail time."

No jail time. I wouldn't have to see my girl behind bars.

I considered Gavin's news. Did it make a difference?

"Shane? You still there?"

A long breath shuddered out of me. "Yeah, I'm here."

"She's going to be there, waiting for him. Tomorrow morning."

I grunted as a vision of Delaney, naked and beautiful, her

lush body wrapped in a nearly translucent white sheet, flashed against the back of my eyelids.

"I looked at your tour schedule. You don't have a show tonight."

"You're a master of subtlety, Gav."

"Fine. Fuck subtlety. What happened between you two?"

I barked out a laugh, the sound reverberating painfully within my throbbing head. "You wouldn't believe me if I told you."

"Try me."

"I asked her to marry me."

The silence on the other end of the phone was blissful. I closed my eyes, suspecting that of all the explanations Gavin could have imagined, a marriage proposal was possibly last on his list. "What happened after that?" he finally prompted.

I pressed my lips together. What would be the point? I'd screwed up my life a long time ago, and there was no use pretending otherwise. Delaney had fucked up, too. Big-time. But she was making amends, putting things right. Took me thirteen years to do what she was doing.

My hands fisted at my sides as my heart rattled around in my chest, all flimsy and cracking. I hated myself for being weak. For feeling. For loving. For hating.

I wanted to go back in time and do everything differently. *Everything.*

Because I would make the right choices, the smart choices. I wouldn't destroy families. I wouldn't hurt people.

I'd fall in love, and stay there.

"Shane." My brother's voice pulled me out of my roiling thoughts.

"Yeah. I'm here. But I gotta go."

"Jesus Christ, Shane. That's the best you can do—you gotta go?" I winced at his tone, but didn't hang up. "You know what? You're right. You do have to go. Get the fuck up, get in the shower, and go to Delaney."

"You know what she's done, Gavin. Same thing I've done. And she lied to me about it. You think we can be together? We can't." I reached for the empty bottle and threw it across the room. It didn't even have the courtesy to break into a million jagged pieces, merely thudding against the wall and rolling, none the worse for wear, across the carpet. "Leave it alone, Gavin. Delaney deserves a chance to start fresh. Not sure I know how to do that—and if she does, I can't be the one to get in her way."

"You think the Branfords hate you as much as you hate yourself? They're grieving, man, but do you have any idea what they've been doing all these years?" I could feel Gavin's disgust through the airwaves. "Did you even ask?"

My forehead pinched, and I rubbed at it, wanting to hang up the phone but somehow unable to pull it away from my ear.

Gavin scoffed. "They've taken in half a dozen foster kids since the accident. They've *loved* their way through the grief. That's how they survived, Shane. By choosing love over hate. And that's why they met with you, why they forgave you. Because they stopped hating you a long time ago." His voice quieted. "It's about time you did, too."

"I can't." My voice broke, the words shredding my throat.

"Damn it, we lost so many years because you couldn't unlock the door of a prison you built your goddamn self. And then Delaney came around and, for whatever reason, she brought us together again. I thought you were lost to me forever, but you weren't."

"Gav—"

"No. Listen to me. Not everyone is lucky enough to get a second chance. Remember Mom? By the time we finally got her to leave Dad, it was too late. Do you want to wait until it's too late, too?" Gavin paused, a disgruntled sigh echoing in my ear. "This is your second chance, Shane. Take it."

My stomach roiled, and not just from the whiskey polluting my gut. Who said I deserved a second chance?

"Gav—"

"Don't. Don't try to explain why you're throwing away the best thing that's ever happened to you. Yeah, you fucked up. Yeah, so did she. But you've both owned up to your mistakes, and now you have the rest of your lives to make up for them. Do it together, damn it. Choose happy."

"Happy?" I wiped a hand over the back of my mouth, so much bitterness. Could I ever be *happy*?

"Yeah, happy. You think Caleb's not up there somewhere, rockin' out to your songs? I'll bet he's your biggest fan. If the situation were reversed, you don't think you'd be pulling for him? Come on, Shane. You know you would be."

A flicker of memory streaked across my mind. Caleb and me, the first time we found a place willing to let us take over the stage. How he'd kept handing the mic to me, wanting my voice to make it through the speakers, too. An echo of the song lit up inside my ears. A cover of "Don't Stop Believin'." Maybe, just maybe, I didn't have to live in a lonely world anymore. "Not sure she'll take me back," I muttered, doubt heavy on my tongue.

"Since when have you taken no for an answer? Go to her. Fight for her. Soon. Because if you think you can show up at her door in ten years and she'll welcome you with open arms, you're not just sad. You're stupid. News flash—any guy without shit-for-brains is going to scoop her up, buy her a house with a white picket fence, and give her two kids and a goddamn golden retriever. What will you have, Shane? A microphone? A few Grammy Awards and magazine covers?" Gavin's voice softened. "You have those already, brother. Now go get the girl, too."

Chapter Twenty-Seven

Shane

I always knew Gavin was the smart one in the family. The only problem—I didn't even know how to do what he was telling me to do. Where the fuck did I even start?

My life had ended the same day as Caleb's. His death had defined me. Governed every single choice I'd made since the day he was buried. And now…I was just supposed to let that go? How?

I'd run away from home, become another person. Spent thirteen years convincing everyone I was Shane Hawthorne, Rock Star. Rich. Talented. Untouchable. Unknowable. But now I was unmasked. Everyone knew who I really was. What I'd done.

How could Delaney want me? Love me?

It was so much easier to pretend she was unlovable instead. Because she'd lied to me about who she really was. What she'd done.

I'd been pretending for the past forty-eight hours…when I hadn't been drowning myself in whiskey.

But the truth was pressing against my sides, squeezing my chest, burning in my veins.

Delaney wasn't unlovable. Because I loved her. Still.

And if I could forgive Delaney her sins, if I could love her—logic told me I could forgive myself.

Pain rippled through my veins, every cell in my body recoiling in disgust. I didn't want to forgive myself.

That was it. The real reason I'd walked away from Delaney.

I didn't want to forgive myself.

Drowning in guilt and regret and hatred was as easy as putting a bottle to my lips and drinking until I didn't feel anything at all.

I'd been drowning for so long. Much easier to stay beneath the waves, shoved along by the tide, than swim to shore and get burned by the sun.

Delaney Fucking Fraser.

She'd ruined me all right. Ruined me for anyone else.

Damn that girl—*my girl*—for making me love her. Because I did.

Even more than I hated myself.

She'd been so brave, marching into the police station all by herself, taking ownership of her sins. So much braver than me, hiding behind the facade I'd built until it came crumbling down. Would have hidden behind Travis and my brother and the throng of lawyers and PR people they had amassed on my behalf, too. But Delaney had seen through them. She'd seen me. And without ever meeting Caleb's parents, she'd known what they needed, too.

Delaney was younger than me, had been coddled by her parents for most of her life. She should have been as perceptive as a poodle. But those whirling dervish eyes of hers saw everything.

I was the one who had been blind.

Deaf and dumb, too.

Delaney had confided in me. Had asked me to see her. To believe in her. To *stay*.

And what had I done? I'd run. Because I was a coward. And a fool. I'd taken the easy way out, running away from Delaney because she wasn't the girl I'd thought she was.

But the truth is, I know everything about Delaney Fraser I need to know. She likes cold white wine and salty ocean air. Malibu sunsets and Hello Kitty T-shirts. Shower sex and sleeping in.

I also know that she's the kindest, sweetest, most selfless person I've ever met, and her smile lights up my world.

But the second I found out she'd been going through the same pain I had, possibly even worse, instead of being a comfort to her, like she'd been to me, I'd run.

With a jerk, I wrenched myself from the twisted sheets and headed for the shower. It was time for me to man up and get my girl back, convince her that we could overcome our pasts together.

Time for me to become the man she deserved.

Delaney

A blur of pink kissed the horizon, just the barest brush of it smeared across an endless lilac sky. If it were possible, the stunning sunrise made the hulking, gray prison look even drearier by comparison. Parked outside the electrified gates, I shivered in my rental car as I waited for my father to be escorted beyond the barbed-wire fence. It might be a while. I was early by nearly an hour.

It felt strange to me that I wasn't taking my father's place in prison, that my punishment was so minor. I should have owned up to the truth three years ago, but I was grateful that the police's mishandling of the accident meant that my father and I would both be free. Free to move forward as a family, to mourn and heal from our loss together.

A lump had lodged itself in the base of my throat, a younger sibling to the one that sat in my stomach, lead leaching out and turning my blood toxic. I hadn't told my father before I confessed. I couldn't, because I knew he would talk me out of it.

No. Actually, that's not true. There wouldn't have been any talking. He would've demanded I keep my mouth shut and that would have been that. Why should he expect any different, after all? That's the way I'd grown up. That's what my mother had taught me.

Father knows best. Just like the fifties TV show Shane compared my home life to during our first dinner together.

Shane.

Damn him.

He'd only wanted the fake, innocent version of me. But I was done pretending. I had an opinion and a voice and I'd finally found the nerve to use them.

As I waited I glanced through the pages of a magazine, but I couldn't even focus on the photos. Until I saw one of Shane. And me. It was from the last night we spent together, taken backstage. Our fingers were entwined, bodies leaning into each other as we looked off at something beyond camera range. I ran my finger across the paper, tracing his strong jaw, his broad smile. I was smiling, too. Both of us. Real smiles. Because, no matter what Shane thought, we'd been real. And in that captured moment, happy.

Shane.

My heart tripped, too wounded to keep a steady rhythm.

Missing him so damn much.

I drew in a shaky breath and pushed it out slowly.

I heard the car before I saw it, pulling up the winding drive to park behind me. I didn't expect to recognize the face behind the wheel as I peeked through the crooked rearview mirror. But as our eyes locked, a blast of heat started at my toes and worked its way throughout my body. Beneath my lightweight coat, it could have been Texas in July.

Only one man had ever sent my body into overdrive with a simple, searing glance. *Shane.*

I opened the door and scrambled out of my car, desperate for the cool afternoon air. "What are you doing here?"

Thumbs tucked in his pockets, Shane ambled slowly toward me until he stood so close that the back of my jeans were pressed against the car door. Another step and the tips of his scuffed boots were toe-to-toe with my ballet flats.

"You're still wearing it," Shane said softly, reaching up to trace my collarbone, feverish skin and cool metal skimming his fingertip.

I swallowed against the tightness in my throat, nibbling on my lower lip as I stared into Shane's fathomless amber eyes. My hands balled into fists at my sides, fighting the nearly overwhelming urge to tuck my head beneath his chin and breathe deep the scent that I'd missed so intensely. "I'm sorry. I meant to return it." I swept my hair to the side, inclining my head toward his torso. The faintest whiff of the sea tickled my nose, almost as if he'd swum in the ocean just that morning. Shane was so close it hurt not to touch him. "You can take it off. It's yours."

Shane sighed, catching a handful of my wind-blown strands and wrapping them around his fingers. With his other hand he cupped my face, thumb sweeping against my jaw as his fingertips assessed the racing pulse at my neck. "Are you?"

I rocked back on my heels, feeling almost dizzy from his proximity. "Am I…yours?"

"Tell me you're mine, Delaney."

My breath caught as his voice raced across my skin, leaving goose bumps in its wake. "I—I don't know," I stuttered, completely torn. I wanted to stay. I wanted to run. What I'd been through the past two days…I couldn't do that again. I wouldn't.

Hurting so badly I couldn't breathe. But the hurt was just plaster sand; add enough tears and it solidified. My body felt like a fragile sculpture. Empty in the middle, cracking and flaking all over the place.

I couldn't—wouldn't—let Shane put me through that again.

I'd never survive it a second time.

"Please." Shane's anguished eyes burned with hunger. "The past few days without you have been hell. I've hated myself for what I've done for so long, it became the only thing I knew was true. Everything else was fake."

Shane's hand ran up my back, palms cupping my shoulders, squeezing. "And then I met you. And you saw me. Really saw me. We were real."

His touch warmed me, healing what he'd destroyed. I couldn't pull away. "After meeting with Caleb's parents and the DA acknowledging that the accident wasn't my fault, I thought all the guilt would slide off my shoulders like it had never been there at all. But I'm learning that it's not that simple. I'm always going to feel responsible, to live with regrets.

"When you told me the truth about your accident, a part of

me hated you for it. For lying to me. For knowing exactly how it felt to do what I'd done. For loving me anyway." A laugh trembled from him. "I jumped on an excuse to run away, because that's what I'm good at. But I know you, Delaney Fraser, and I've loved you since the moment you flew across the sand like an Olympic sprinter the very first night we spent together. I'm sorry I didn't tell you that sooner. I don't need a contract or a wedding. I just need you."

Incredulous, I stared at him. "Since then? You didn't even spend the night with me, remember? You put me in my room and walked out the door."

"Yeah. But I wanted to stay with you." His amber eyes softened until I was caught inside the whorls of gold. "Tell me you'll be mine. Tell me we'll figure out how to heal together. How to get back to *us* again."

Shane's words washed over me like a rainbow, so beautiful and pure. For a moment I said nothing, merely closing my eyes as I leaned into him, luxuriating in every single point of contact between us. Could Shane really mean what he said? A shaky breath vibrated against my ribs as he wrapped his arms around my back, pulling me closer.

Tears overflowed my lashes, spilling heat and salt down my cheeks. A gust of cool wind dried the tracks before I could wipe them away.

It would be so easy to say yes.

Yes. Yes, yes, yes.

The three-letter word was doing cartwheels in my mind. I could hear it in the swoosh of the breeze, the squawk of the birds.

Yes. The answer Shane wanted was at the tip of my tongue, threatening to burst through lips desperate for his kiss. There was no denying that I loved this man with a fierceness that made me doubt my own sanity. Still, I hesitated. If I capitulated to my own impulses, what was I really agreeing to?

"Shane, I—" I struggled to put my feelings into words. They were so tenuous I didn't know if I could. Sweeping my tongue over trembling lips, I reached for one last bit of strength. Prayed it would be enough. "I was wrong not to trust you. Wrong to keep the truth from you. And I am so sorry, Shane. I am. But if we have a chance of making it through this together, we have to learn to forgive. Each other and ourselves. And we have to trust each other, even when it's easier to hide, to lie, to run." My words scraped at my throat, burning me. But they had to be said, as much for me as for him.

Shane shifted, hands moving up my spine, fingers threading into my scalp as he leaned toward my lips. He stopped an inch away to whisper, "I know. You're right." Pain dented his forehead, etching itself into tiny lines at his temples, bleeding from his eyes. "I love you, Delaney. So fucking much. Too much to lose you."

My soul was spinning, buoyant with hope as I curled my hands into fists on Shane's chest, balling his shirt into my palms. Holding on.

"I'm sorry it took me so long to figure out I was trapped in the past. To realize you're my future. I'm sorry I hurt you, turned my back when you needed me. It's something I'll always regret. I didn't deserve your heart, not then. And I don't even know if I deserve it now. But, Delaney, I'm going to spend every day of the rest of my life becoming a man who deserves you. And one day, I swear to God, one day I'll get there. I promise."

Shane's words hung in the air between us, as luminous and incandescent as Christmas lights. My body shook with want.

I wanted to believe him. I wanted to trust him. I wanted to spend every day for the rest of my life in his arms.

Loving him.

Being loved by him.

"And I promise to always be honest with you. In your arms, you've taken me places I've never been, made me feel things I've never imagined." I smiled up at him. "We'll figure this out together, as equals. I can't just be Shane Hawthorne's girlfriend. I want to go back to school, get my degree."

"Done."

"It means I won't be waiting for you at the end of every set."

He pressed a kiss to my temple as the wind whipped up, blowing silken strands against my face. An exquisite caress. "How many years until you graduate?"

"One and a half. More if I decide to go to grad school."

"I'll manage."

"I might not want to go to UCLA."

He expelled a placating breath. "Delaney, I spend most nights in hotel rooms. The only home I know is wherever you are. New York, L.A. . . . Alaska. I don't care."

"Okay, then."

Confusion creased his brow. "Okay?"

"I'm yours, Shane." I put a finger against lips that had broken into a blinding grin. "But don't ever throw me away again. I can't take it."

He drew my finger into his mouth, the heat from his tongue sending a surge of electricity crackling between my thighs. I trembled as he moved to my wrist, licking the tiny patchwork of veins pulsing beneath my skin before laying my palm flat against his cheek and staring down at me. Drinking me in. "I'm never going to let you go. I mean it. Never again, Delaney. I support all your dreams. I'm not a singing Ken doll, and I don't need a Barbie by my side. I want *real*. I want you."

I swallowed the lump in my throat. "I love you, Shane. All of you. Even the little boy inside of you that will always be Sean Sutter."

"And I love you, too, Delaney Fraser." He cracked a teasing smile. "But if you want to come up with another identity, just so we're even, I'd love her, too."

I shook my head, returning his grin. "Nope. I think one of me is enough for you to handle."

The wind picked up, rustling over the dry road. Shane let out a *whoop* of joy, and I shrieked as he picked me up and twirled me around before leaning me gently against the car door and burying his face in my hair, his breath hot on my ear. "My girl," he whispered, the words filled with reverence. "And one day, when you're ready, when you want it as much as I do, I'll give you a proposal you can't refuse."

Loosening his grip just enough, I slid down against the length of Shane's frame. The charge between us electrified the air. My palms cupped his strong jaw and I tilted my face upward, eyes fluttering closed as the fullness of Shane's lips met my own. Our kiss was filled with love, with promise. Tender and needy. Sweetly sinful.

We broke apart like skittish teenagers as the gates to the prison creaked open, moving slowly outward. I laughed at Shane's flustered expression. "You ready to meet my dad?"

"Yes." His answer was firm, decisive.

Our hands intertwined as we faced the gate.

In that moment, a butterfly flew overhead, dipping low enough that I could see the vibrant colors of its wings. Amber edged with black. The gold even more vibrant for the darkness.

Author's Note

Rock King deals with substance abuse. Shane Hawthorne may have conquered his addiction with the help of hired girlfriends, but in real life, the struggle is likely much more difficult and can feel completely overwhelming.

There are resources out there to help. Alcoholics Anonymous, Narcotics Anonymous, and Sex Addicts Anonymous, like I mention in the book. You can also speak to a parent, a trusted friend, or a religious counselor. There are rehab centers, both residential and outpatient. Guidance counselors and school psychologists. Support groups and online communities.

Even when it feels as if the entire world is conspiring against you, please take that leap of faith to try again.

You are not alone, and your life matters.

All my love,
Tara

Don't miss Landon and Piper's story in *Rock Legend*, coming in summer 2018!

Chapter One

Piper

I would have missed the call, but I'd just flung my purse into my car, the contents spilling out onto the passenger-side floor mat like a burst piñata. Despite the tears clouding my vision, it was impossible to miss the flashing letters—DELANEY FRASER—vibrating from within a sea of tampons, makeup tubes, and spare change.

Unable to check the impulse, I reached for it, taking a second to wipe at my wet eyes before swiping my thumb across the screen. "Hi, Delaney."

I sounded like a frog had crawled into my throat. If I was lucky, Delaney would be too polite to mention it.

"Piper, are you sick?"

Of course I wasn't lucky. I'd never been before. Why should today be any different?

But despite the cocoon of self-pity I wanted to wrap myself in, I couldn't miss the genuine concern bleeding from Delaney's voice.

Not that I deserved it.

Delaney and I had known each other since nursery school back in Bronxville, the insulated suburb of New York City where we'd both grown up. From throwing sand in her face rather than sharing my pail and shovel, to snubbing her in favor of the mean girls clique in high school, I'd done nothing to deserve Delaney's concern, or her friendship.

The truth was, Delaney's *niceness* had always scared me. I had secrets to keep, even back then. Especially back then. I couldn't afford to let my guard down for a minute. And being friends with a girl like Delaney, someone who cared about more than just the labels sewn inside her clothes, or her boyfriend of the month, terrified me.

Crazily enough, Delaney Fraser was now a close friend. My only friend, actually. As a public relations assistant for one of the hottest talent managers in Hollywood, I had yet to master work-life balance, but since Delaney was clear across the country finishing up her degree at NYU, my overscheduled calendar wasn't an issue.

Forcing a huge, fake smile on my face even though she couldn't see me, I automatically shifted into my default mode: Fake-It-Till-You-Make-It. Maybe that was why I'd been so drawn to Tinseltown. Here, whether you had your SAG card or not, everyone was an actor. "Nope. I feel great. How are you?"

There was a pause. "Piper, you don't sound great."

Delaney was no one's fool, and she'd picked up on the truth. But I wasn't ready to talk about what had happened just before she called. "Of course I am," I insisted, even though it was obvious I was one step away from falling apart. "And I'm going to be late for work, so…"

"Wait."

My finger hovered over the END CALL button on my screen. As much as I wanted to, I couldn't hang up on Delaney.

"I was calling to tell you that I just booked a flight to LAX. I want to surprise Shane at his show tomorrow."

The knot in my stomach drew tighter, the warm, stuffy air inside the car choking me. If Delaney was coming to Nothing but Trouble's show tomorrow, that meant I would need to book a car service from the airport to the venue, get her an all-access backstage pass, possibly transportation back to the airport, hotel—no, she would be staying with Shane, of course…

Details. My mind latched on to the expanding to-do list in my mind, anything to avoid thinking about what I'd just seen and a certain member of the band I'd have to avoid tomorrow. "What time are you getting in? Do you have an outfit to wear? I'll arrange for hair and makeup—"

"Piper." She cut me off with a laugh. "You don't have to fuss over me anymore."

That wasn't exactly true. Since Shane Hawthorne and his multiplatinum band, Nothing but Trouble, were my boss's biggest clients, part of my job involved fussing over Delaney. Initially their relationship had been a press stunt, and my assignment had been to acclimate Delaney to her new role as "Shane Hawthorne's girlfriend."

"And how exactly would I explain leaving you to fend off the paparazzi that stake out LAX like a pack of hungry wolves?" Although Delaney wasn't a celebrity herself, after the media circus surrounding Shane had gotten ahold of her, her face was nearly as recognizable, and profitable, as her rock star boyfriend's. "Believe me, fussing over you is a hell of a lot easier than trying to placate my boss."

"I don't know how you put up with that man," she conceded.

Right now I was pretty sure all men were the scum of the earth, but as far as bosses went, Travis Taggert wasn't bad. And it was because of him that Delaney and I had reconnected.

Faced with the unenviable task of informing an A-list actor that the director of his current film had hired a body double for his sex scenes because his ass wasn't as finely sculpted as it had been a decade ago, we'd decided to strategize over drinks.

Delaney had been our waitress.

Neither of us had realized it at the time, but Travis had taken one look at her and had known she would be perfect for Shane.

As always, Travis's instincts had been spot-on. Once Shane and Delaney became an item, I was assigned to her. At the time, it had been a huge promotion, but because of our prior relationship, Travis had wanted me on board.

Her involvement with Shane wasn't a press stunt anymore, and the second Delaney moved to New York, I'd asked to be taken off the Nothing but Trouble account.

Rock stars were not my thing.

"He's my boss, so it kind of comes with the territory. When are you getting in?" Just because I wasn't assigned to Nothing but Trouble didn't mean I wasn't expected to pitch in where Delaney was concerned. We spent the next few minutes going over her travel itinerary, and after we hung up I jotted down notes in the planner I kept with me at all times.

I'd almost forgotten why I was still sitting in the parking space right outside my building when I jumped at the knock on my window.

Adam was standing there, looking regretful and apologetic, and irritatingly pulled together. Had he taken the time to shower after I'd walked in on him?

I didn't bother rolling down the window. I had nothing to say to my boyfriend.

Ex-boyfriend, as of twenty minutes ago.

Starting the ignition with shaking hands, I backed out of my parking spot, not caring if I ran over Adam's toes. Not caring if I ran over any part of Adam's anatomy, although there was one in particular I would have preferred.

Delaney might have found her Prince Charming, but so far I was more of a frog magnet.

Landon

I should buy stock in Trojans.

The random thought skittered across my brain as I flushed the condom down the toilet, my gut twisting as I watched it shudder and swirl before finally disappearing. I know flushing them is bad for the plumbing, or the environment, or maybe both, but when they're filled with my sperm—you don't go leaving that shit around.

Over the years I'd dealt with more "baby daddy" scandals than I wanted to think about. None of them had turned out to be valid, and I intended to keep it that way.

Forever.

Not only was I the drummer of Nothing but Trouble, the most successful band of the past decade, according to the tweet that just vibrated through my phone, but I was also…wait for it—

The Most Fuckable Rock Star on the Planet.

Apparently, I was a fucking legend.

Was I surprised? Fuck, no.

It was a reputation I earned behind my drum kit *and* behind closed doors. In the dark corners of dingy bars and in full view of anyone with eyes. I was nothing if not generous with my skills. Spreading the wealth and all that.

But when it came to my sperm, I knew better than to leave it unattended.

Ridiculous, really. I mean, chicks weren't exactly lining up to bring me home to meet Mom and Dad. And I would have hardly fit in at a PTA meeting—not with my tattoo sleeves and penchant for illegal substances washed down with one-hundred-proof liquor.

Turning on the tap, I splashed water on my face, roughing my hands through my hair. I didn't bother checking out my reflection in the mirror. I knew what I looked like, saw myself reflected in the hungry eyes of people wanting a piece of me every damn day.

I was desperate for a shower, but that would have to wait. I needed to rouse the girls in my bed and get them out first. Otherwise they were bound to wake up while I was scrubbing their scent from my skin and strip the hotel suite of everything I'd touched. Clothes, sheets, dirty glasses still sticky with the residue of whatever liquor I poured down my throat last night—given the opportunity, they'd all be up on eBay before I reached for a towel.

I was living the dream.

Except that when I wasn't onstage or in a recording studio, pounding away at my drum kit, it felt more like a nightmare.

There, my chaotic thoughts suddenly made sense. I could

spot patterns. Arrangements of energy to be identified and interpreted, set to a unique rhythm.

From the relentless noise inside my mind, I made music.

But when I didn't have a pair of drumsticks in my hand, I spent most of my time doing another kind of banging.

Hence, the two girls in my bed.

Because otherwise I'd be banging my head against the wall.

Maybe I should have checked into the hotel alone last night. Today, of all days, I wasn't fit company for anyone.

One day out of three hundred and sixty-five. A day spent trying to forget about what I'd done, the lives I'd destroyed.

Lost in an oblivion where yesterday never happened and tomorrow didn't exist.

Unfortunately, I had a show tonight.

It's my own damn fault. If I'd paid more attention when Shane had thrown out potential dates for a concert benefitting the foundation he'd started in the name of a childhood friend, I could have vetoed this one.

Except, as usual, I'd been breezing through life, not sweating the details. Agreeing to everything. Caring about nothing.

But since tonight's show was important to Shane, it was important to me.

Which was why I'd checked into the hotel near the arena last night. Wouldn't be the first time I drank the day away in a hotel room. Played a perfect set even when I couldn't walk a straight line.

But I couldn't play if the guys couldn't find me.

Time to get rid of the girls I had brought with me. "All right." I rapped on the headboard, "Time to get up. I've got sound check."

The one with dark hair stirred slightly. Not enough. We'd just finished round three—no way she could be sleeping so soundly already.

I reached down to nudge her shoulder, and she countered by rolling over and trying to pull me back into bed. Normally I'd have let her. Hell, on any other morning, I'd have still been between them.

See? This day brings out the worst in me.

Instead I wrapped my hands around her shoulders and tugged her upright. The sheet fell away from her body, exposing a pair of large breasts I'd loved last night but that looked more like a pointy flotation device this morning.

I backed away, striding to the windows and yanking at the drapes. Sunlight flooded into the room, eliciting a pair of irate groans.

The bottle blonde sat up. "C'mon, Landon, what's your rush?" Her attempt at a seductive pout was hindered by the streaks of makeup crisscrossing her cheeks.

"Sorry, ladies." I spread my hands out, gritting my teeth as I forced a niceness I didn't feel. "Gotta give the fans a good show tonight."

"How about we give you a good show right now?" The brunette rose onto her knees, turning to her friend, one hand plowing through the blonde's sex-mussed mane, the other cupping her breast. She lowered her mouth, giving a lick as she glanced my way. "You know you want to."

An all-too-familiar blend of lust and loathing curdled within my gut, and I rubbed a palm over my face to keep my expression neutral. Watching two gorgeous women going at it, knowing I could join in the party at any moment, was tempting, despite it being a frequent opportunity. But not today.

Somehow I managed to lure them out of bed and into their

clothes, although not without calling our show coordinator to come to the room and hand deliver two tickets and backstage passes for tonight. Lynne didn't even bat an eye. She was used to it.

Once I was finally alone, I sagged back against the door, thumping my head against it once, twice, three times.

Growing up, no one would have laid odds that I'd become famous. Infamous, maybe. Notorious, probably.

But successful? Never.

Not that I could blame them. I sure hadn't believed it myself.

I didn't come into my own, if that ridiculous expression made any sense, until I arrived in Los Angeles and connected with Shane Hawthorne. We'd both had a lot to prove, although I didn't realize that he needed to succeed as badly as I did until recently.

At the time, we'd just been finding our footing, connecting with other musicians, playing in shitty venues for nothing but beer and, at the end of our set, blow jobs from groupies who would happily take care of our *equipment*.

There had been one person who believed in me though.

At least, until I'd fucked her over, too.

A blonde-haired, blue-eyed, sharp-tongued temptress—who should have been too smart to fall for me—studying her ass off at UCLA, that beautiful face of hers always buried in a book, focused on her goals, her résumé, her fucking five-year plan. I should have left her alone and walked away, contented myself with women who told me exactly what I wanted to hear. Preferably garbled moans around my cock. But I was stupid, too. Too stupid to stay away.

I made it my mission to woo her—pursuing her as fiercely as my music career. Giving her my heart with one breath and promising the moon with the next.

Until the day I had to make a choice.

My girl or my career.

I chose music. Fame and fortune. Hollywood Hills and chemically induced thrills.

Of course, I'd spent every day since then trying to convince myself I didn't regret it.

Want to know the difference between a legend and a fairy tale?

Only one of them ends happily ever after.

About the Author

TARA LEIGH attended Washington University in St. Louis and Columbia Business School in New York, and worked on Wall Street and Main Street before "retiring" to become a wife and mother. When the people in her head became just as real as the people in her life, she decided to put their stories on paper. Tara currently lives in Fairfield County, Connecticut, with her husband, children, and fur-baby, Pixie. She is represented by Jessica Alvarez of BookEnds.

Learn more at:

www.taraleighbooks.com
Twitter @TaraLeighBooks
Facebook.com/TaraLeighAuthor
And if you'd like to keep in touch: https://goo.gl/394ppn

You Might Also Like...

Looking for more great digital reads? We've got you covered!
Now Available from Forever Yours

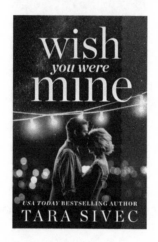

FROM THE *USA TODAY* BESTSELLING AUTHOR OF *THE STORY OF US* AND *FISHER'S LIGHT* COMES A NEW, STAND-ALONE NOVEL—A HEART-WRENCHING STORY ABOUT FIRST LOVES AND SECOND CHANCES THAT WILL MAKE YOU FALL IN LOVE ALL OVER AGAIN...

Five years. I would've stayed away longer if I hadn't received the letter. Not a day has gone by that I haven't thought about her, haven't missed her smile, haven't wished that things were different.

The last time I saw my two best friends, I vowed to not stand in the way of their happiness, even if that meant I couldn't be a part of their lives. Cameron James and her emerald-green eyes were too much of a temptation and I couldn't stay and watch them together. Cameron deserved better than me. She deserved him.

But now that I am back, things are different. I'm not going to stand by and watch the woman I've always loved slip away again. I'm done living my life with regrets and I'm ready to tell her the truth. And I'll do whatever it takes to show her that I always wished she was mine.

RULES ARE MEANT TO BE BROKEN.

Carmen Dane was a self-assured Domme who *always* maintained control…until she submitted to sinfully sexy Master Thomas Regala. She gave him her trust and vulnerability, and he betrayed her. She's avoided him for months, but now he knows the truth and refuses to let her hide. Her all-consuming hunger for Thomas has only grown stronger during their time apart. But Carmen will never submit to him—or anyone—ever again.

Thomas isn't about to give up that easily. Carmen is his Mistress *and* his submissive. He'll do almost anything for a second chance—even if it means giving up some of his power for her pleasure. Now they've embarked on a game of desire and dark, greedy need that breaks *both* their rules. But can Thomas ever wholly submit to Carmen when he wants to *claim* her as his own?

IN NASHVILLE THE MUSIC IS LOUDER, THE DREAMS ARE BIGGER, AND LOVE CAN BRING A COWBOY TO HIS KNEES.

Ethan Walker is Nashville royalty. Born to the King and Queen of Country Music, he's spent his life trying to escape the spotlight of his parents' fame, even walking away from his own promising singing career. He's the kind of cowboy who prefers flannel to flashbulbs, hay fields to hit records, and the solitude of his horse farm to the nightlife along Music Row. The last thing he wants is attention, especially when it comes from country's latest star...

Chelsea Harris's meteoric rise up the charts and string of celebrity boyfriends mean that wherever she goes, the paparazzi follow. A duet with Nashville's favorite son is exactly what her new charity album needs, but when she approaches Ethan, he turns her down flat. To win the camera-shy cowboy over, Chelsea will have to approach him on his terms. Trouble is, the more time she spends on his farm, the more Ethan wants to keep her there.

CPSIA information can be obtained
at www.ICGtesting.com
Printed in the USA
BVHW03s0348220218
508835BV00001B/1/P